What people are saying about …

FEAR HAS A NAME

"It takes a lot for a suspense novel to impress me, but this one definitely did. Anyone who likes my books will love *Fear Has a Name*. The plot is skillfully woven, and the story has a spiritual depth that will resonate with readers. Creston Mapes is an author to watch in the suspense genre."

Terri Blackstock, author of *Intervention*, *Vicious Cycle*, and *Predator*

"*Fear Has a Name* is a fast-paced page-turner that offers not only a great story, but an intriguing view into evil and its place in our society."

Kristin Billerbeck, author of *The Scent of Rain*

"Sometimes you want a comfort read—sometimes you don't. Mapes has crafted an edgy tale that will grab you from the start and then send you reeling. With a heart-pounding pace, he takes us to some disturbing places but safely delivers us home. Great job, Creston!"

Melody Carlson, author of *Deceived* and *Shattered* and *Damaged* (Secrets series)

"I love novels where I look for any spare moment to keep reading. *Fear Has a Name* is one of them. Maybe because the tension never lets up. Maybe because Mapes left out all the boring parts. Maybe because of a plot that kept me on edge from the first words till the very end. Well done."

James L. Rubart, best-selling author of *Rooms*,
Book of Days, *The Chair*, and *Soul's Gate*

"*Fear Has a Name* is an exceptional treat, a story of unrelenting tension that dares to stare evil in the face. Mapes has a gift. He reveals wickedness and vice yet sprinkles it with something rare that kept me riveted: the hope of redemption."

Harry Kraus, MD, best-selling author of *The Six-Liter Club*

"Creston Mapes is one of my favorite authors. *Fear Has a Name* mesmerized me from the first page. Multiple plot twists and terrific characters kept me glued to the page. I loved it and highly recommend it!"

Colleen Coble, author of the Rock
Harbor series and the Lonestar series

"Captivating from breathless start to throat-clenching finish, *Fear Has a Name* possesses everything a great thriller should, and more. A *must-read* for fans of Terri Blackstock and Brandilyn Collins."

Tamera Alexander, *USA Today* bestselling author
of *To Whisper Her Name* and *A Lasting Impression*

"A stunning portrayal of redemption and mercy, *Fear Has a Name* kept me on the edge of my seat. Interwoven with themes of forgiveness, hope, and courage, Creston Mapes's latest masterpiece is a story readers will not want to miss. The dedication and determination of Jack Crittendon in protecting his wife and being a man of God proved powerful and compelling. This story will leave Mapes's fans clamoring for more by this master of gritty storytelling! Bravo!! Creston Mapes once again ripped my breath away!"

Ronie Kendig, award-winning author
of the Discarded Heroes series

"Creston Mapes does a superb job of instilling real suspense and even fear in this novel, making it un-put-downable. I especially appreciated the way Mapes takes the suspense to a much more thought-provoking level as he handles well the questions we Christians ask ourselves in the midst of the pain, suffering, and evil things that intrude upon our lives. An incredible read!"

Elizabeth Musser, author of the Secrets of the Cross
Trilogy: *Two Crosses, Two Testaments, Two Destinies*

"*Fear Has a Name* is a powerful, up-all-night story that grabs you from the first page and doesn't let go until the incredible end. Creston Mapes has spun a tale so real and rich it could have been pulled from today's headlines. Dynamic characters, pulse-pounding scenes, and the grace of God abound in this remarkable novel. Highly recommended!"

Mark Mynheir, former homicide detective
and author of *The Corruptible*

"*Fear Has a Name* gripped me from page 1 and didn't let go until I closed the cover for the last time. There were moments when it left me breathless. Creston Mapes's signature blend of heart-pounding suspense, angst, and deep spiritual questions made for a robust, riveting, thought-provoking read!"

Kathy Herman, author of the Sophie Trace
Trilogy and Secrets of Roux River Bayou series

"Why endure a story of raw terror that will keep you awake at night, turning pages when you should be sleeping? 'Perhaps …,' as author Creston Mapes concludes, 'to show a man mercy. To show a man Christ on the cross.' And in that showing, Mapes examines all of the 'why' questions we ask God in our more mundane but no less disturbing faith struggles."

Dave Jackson, author of *Lucy Come Home,*
the Harry Bentley novels, and more

"*Fear Has a Name* is another page-turning, heart-touching must-read from Creston Mapes. The brilliant intersection of two story lines packed a powerful punch, and I'm not sure I've ever felt for a villain so deeply. Another surefire winner in the vein of *Nobody.*"

Deborah Raney, author of *The Face of the
Earth* and the Hanover Falls novels

"Jaw-dropping suspense. This book should carry a warning: **Don't read if you're in the house alone.**"

Nikki Arana, author of *The Next Target*

"Mapes is at the head of a new breed of Christian authors, those who write gripping and gritty stories that ring loudly with gospel truths.

Fans of Mike Dellosso, Shawn Grady, and Brandilyn Collins will love this powerful thriller. Mapes draws the strands of his plot ever tighter, leaving us short of breath and anxious for answers. And the final answers are not only satisfying but eternal."

Eric Wilson, *New York Times* best-selling author

"Nail-bitingly great: Creston Mapes does it again with a pulse-quickening plot, memorable characters, and suspense that satisfies fully."

Tom Morrisey, Christy-nominated
novelist and author of *In High Places*

"Embezzlement. False accusation. Blackmail. Abduction. A wolf hidden in sheep's clothing. Creston Mapes takes readers on a psychological roller coaster that feeds on our deepest fears."

Mark Gilroy, author of *Cuts Like a Knife*

"In *Fear Has a Name*, Creston Mapes proves once again that he is a master of building deep characters and sending them on a twisting, breakneck journey of terror and triumph. His vivid and concise storytelling pulls you in, and by the time you realize you can't breathe from all the suspense, it's too late: you're riding this baby to the end. A truly captivating work of ratcheting thrills and surprising grace. You will not be able to put it down—or get it out of your head once you finally do."

Robert Liparulo, author of *The 13th Tribe*,
The Judgment Stone, and *Comes a Horseman*

FEAR
HAS A
NAME

Other Novels by Creston Mapes

Dark Star: Confessions of a Rock Idol

Full Tilt

Nobody

FEAR
HAS A
NAME

THE CRITTENDON FILES

CRESTON MAPES

David C Cook®

transforming lives together

FEAR HAS A NAME
Published by David C Cook
4050 Lee Vance View
Colorado Springs, CO 80918 U.S.A.

David C Cook Distribution Canada
55 Woodslee Avenue, Paris, Ontario, Canada N3L 3E5

David C Cook U.K., Kingsway Communications
Eastbourne, East Sussex BN23 6NT, England

The graphic circle C logo is a registered trademark of David C Cook.

The website addresses recommended throughout this book are offered as a
resource to you. These websites are not intended in any way to be or imply an
endorsement on the part of David C Cook, nor do we vouch for their content.

This story is a work of fiction. Characters and events are the product of the author's
imagination. Any resemblance to any person, living or dead, is coincidental.

Epigraph Proverbs 16:4 quotation taken from the New American Standard Bible®,
Copyright © 1960, 1995 by The Lockman Foundation. Used by permission.
(www.Lockman.org.); Galatians 6:9 in chapter 10 is taken from the King James
Version of the Bible. (Public Domain.); 2 Corinthians 12:10 in chapter 11 and
John 14:27 in chapter 30 are taken from the Holy Bible, New International
Version®, NIV®. Copyright © 1973, 1984 by Biblica, Inc.™ Used by permission
of Zondervan. All rights reserved worldwide. www.zondervan.com.

LCCN 2013934366
ISBN 978-0-7814-0816-5
eISBN 978-1-4347-0605-8

© 2013 Creston Mapes, Inc.
Published in association with Natasha Kern Literary Agency,
PO Box 1069, White Salmon, WA 98672.

The Team: Don Pape, LB Norton, Nick Lee, Jack
Campbell, Caitlyn Carlson, Karen Athen
Cover Design: Amy Konyndyk
Cover Photo: iStockPhoto

Printed in the United States of America
First Edition 2013

1 2 3 4 5 6 7 8 9 10

032913

Dedicated to
Natasha Kern and Don Pape
For the second wind …

ACKNOWLEDGMENTS

When writing a novel, I jot down the names of the people/
organizations who helped with research, insights, and moti-
vation. For this book, my deepest thanks go out to:

Natasha Kern, Don Pape

LB Norton

Ingrid, Amy, Caitlyn, Jack, Karen, and the awesome team at Cook

Patty, Abigail, Hannah, Esther, and Creston

Joseph Cheeley III

Mark Mynheir, James Scott Bell, Jerry B. Jenkins

Terri Blackstock, Colleen Coble, Harry Kraus

Donna Lampkin, Randy Powell, Bob Lutz, Tommy Woodsmall

Julie Garmon, Belinda Peterson, Amy Wallace

Missy Tippins, ACFW/Word, ChiLibris

John Njoroge, Scott Bull

Ian Hunter, Stephanie Powell, Wayne Scott

Jesse Garcia and Building 429

Ginny Owens

Steve "Boxcar" Vibert

Buck and Frank

Jason Chatraw

Mark and Janet Sweeney, Julee Schwarzburg

Ivy Creek Church, 12Stone, CCG, and North Metro Church

My readers

"It's a very long story, but the short version is this: I realized that I could no longer reconcile the claims of faith with the facts of life....
I could no longer explain how there can be a good and all-powerful God actively involved with this world, given the state of things. For many people who inhabit this planet, life is a cesspool of misery and suffering. I came to a point where I simply could not believe that there is a good and kindly disposed Ruler who is in charge of it."

Bart D. Ehrman

"The LORD has made everything for its own purpose,
even the wicked for the day of evil."

Proverbs 16:4

I

The husky man lurking outside the front door of Pamela Crittendon's house carried a black leather satchel, like a doctor's bag.

Hiding behind a column between the foyer and dining room, Pamela could see the stranger through one of the narrow vertical windows situated on each side of the door.

His face was hardened and pasty, with tiny eyes and a thatch of curly red hair. He wore all black, from his T-shirt and leather vest to his jeans and cowboy boots. And he stood uncomfortably close to the door.

The doorbell rang a third time.

Pamela's head buzzed.

Backlit by the midafternoon sunlight, the man turned toward the street. Covering half his face with a blocky, gloved hand, he shifted his huge frame from one foot to the other. Then he turned and rapped hard at the glass, knocking the wind out of Pamela.

"Who's at the door, Mommy?" Seven-year-old Rebecca appeared at the top of the stairs wearing pink plastic high heels, a red sequined dress, and a purple boa. Bumping into her from behind was her five-year-old sister, Faye, who wore a long white dress, a furry brown stole, and turquoise gloves that went up to her armpits.

"I'm not sure," Pamela said, her voice constricted. "Go back to the media room and play. Hurry, go on."

Taking a deep breath, she fought her way through a force field of fear to within three feet of the door and made herself yell deeply, sharply, "Who is it?" She searched the man through the glass.

He clamped the doorknob. "Open!"

The hardware made a sickening racket.

"Get out of here!" Her stomach turned. "I'm calling the police!" She rushed for the phone in the kitchen.

Boom!

Pamela halted, turned toward the noise at the door, and gawked in horror as the stranger bent over and drove his shoulder—the size of a medicine ball—into the door, splintering the wood frame.

BOOM!

"Mo-omm-my?" Rebecca cried from the top of the steps. She was clutching Peep, her favorite doll. "Who's banging at the door?"

"Get down here, *now*. Both of you!" But as soon as the words left her mouth, Pamela realized she couldn't wait. She shot up the stairs, swept up both girls, and plunged back down.

Each frantic step felt like an adrenaline-laced nightmare.

As they passed within four feet of the front door, the glass shattered.

"Ahhh!" Pamela shrieked, dashing away from the eerie closeness of the intruder, hoping the girls wouldn't see the man, but their little eyes were huge. Rebecca let loose a terror-ridden scream. Faye was frozen. Pamela kept going, like a soldier bolting through a minefield, with both girls locked in her arms, one thought in her brain: *get out.*

She heard the man reaching in, groping for the bolt lock.

This cannot be happening.

Dropping the girls to their feet, she flipped the lock to the back door and shoved it open.

She heard glass crunching beneath the man's boots.

"Wait!" he called.

Pamela grabbed the girls' little hands and rocketed through the door onto the screened porch.

She could feel him coming, maybe fifteen feet behind.

She kicked the screened door open.

They hit fresh air.

And grass.

Run.

Faster than you ever have.

Pamela flew toward the neighbors' house, ripping at the girls' hands, feeling as if their little legs had left the ground, as if they were the dollies now.

Across the flat green lawn they dashed, the girls whimpering and squealing with each panicked stride.

Without knocking, Pamela tried the handle, found it unlocked, and burst into the Sweeneys' house with the girls—slamming the door and dead-bolting it behind her.

Tommy Sweeney shot out of his office then stopped when he saw them. "Pamela? What on earth is going on?"

"A man broke in … while we were there …" It was difficult to breathe. Her heart hurt. Her brain banged against her skull. Her neck and shoulders felt torn from the weight of the girls. "He may be coming … check, Tommy. He was right behind us." She stroked the girls' hair with trembling hands and drew them tight against her body.

Tommy darted toward the kitchen window, reaching for the phone on his belt clip. "I see him out back. He's turning around … He's going back in."

Pamela could only nod, relieved that at least someone else had seen him.

"It's okay. You're safe now." Tommy punched at the screen of his cell phone and looked out the window. "Tell me what happened."

"He rang the doorbell a bunch, then pounded. I told him to go away, that I was calling the police—"

"Did you?"

She shook her head. "No time. He broke the glass at the front door and came in."

When he'd shattered the glass, found the bolt lock, and entered, there must have been only ten feet between them. Ten feet and how many seconds? Three? Maybe four? If she'd delayed only that long in getting the girls, the monster would have had them. And done what? To her? *To them?*

"Jesus took care of us," she whispered and nestled the girls close.

Tommy was still peering out the window, focused on her backyard.

"Do you see him?" Pamela asked.

"No. He's still inside." He held up an index finger and spoke into the phone. "Yes, ma'am, we've had a break-in next door to the address I'm calling from … I will in a minute, but you should know the intruder is still on the property … *hurry.*"

2

"You still working on that water-rate-hike piece?" Cecil Barton, editor of the *Trenton City Dispatch*, approached Jack Crittendon's computer with his thin arms crossed and a crisp white piece of paper sticking out of one hand.

"Yep." Jack looked at his watch, certain Cecil was about to toss another ball into the mix he was already juggling. That's how the extra assignments always came from Cecil, on a folded white piece of paper, just like the one tucked in his jittery hand. "And the mayor's homeland security address, and the follow-up on the bereaved parents feature, and the editorial Hernandez assigned me this morn—"

"Forget the editorial. I'll have Sheets do it. She's light right now and chomping at the bit to do another." Cecil unfolded his arms and, sure enough, thrust the piece of paper toward Jack. "This is hot."

Everything was *hot* to Cecil. He yanked at his thinning fray of brown hair. His narrow eyes appeared to be forced wide open by his taut nerves. The up-and-down motion of his protruding Adam's apple was difficult to ignore.

"Someone emailed it to me a few minutes ago," Cecil said, "from the online magazine of the Methodist Church."

Jack snatched the piece of paper.

"He's a local pastor," Cecil said. "I want you to cover it. You're the perfect fit. We'll be the first to have it." Cecil lived to scoop the popular local radio station WDUC 550 AM.

Great. It was 3:48 p.m. and Jack knew whatever it was, Cecil would want it for the next day's issue, which would mean Jack would have to stay late to make deadline. Rebecca and Faye would probably be asleep by the time he got home. He hated missing time with them on the evenings he had to work late.

Cecil's heels bounced left-right-left-right-left as he waited, arms crossed.

Jack wheeled his chair away from his computer, stretched, sighed, sank back, and read the copy his editor had handed him.

FAITH LINE

The Official Web Magazine of the Methodist Church

Ohio Pastor Missing

Dr. Richard Billings, clerk of the Central Ohio Methodist Church Office, wrote to inform us of the following: Pastor Evan McDaniel of Five Forks Methodist Church in Trenton City, Ohio, disappeared Friday, taking with him a significant quantity of medication and leaving behind communication indicating his intention to take his own life. This is all that is known at this time. His body has not been found, but coworkers believe he was genuinely determined to follow through on his expressed intentions. The church and the family—Wendy McDaniel and her three boys—are

finding the grace and mercy of God through the ongo-
ing ministry of associate pastor Dr. Andrew Satterfield,
the elders, deacons, and others. Please keep the family
and church in your prayers.

Now *that* was intriguing. Jack and Pam had attended a marriage retreat at Five Forks Methodist that spring. He distinctly remembered McDaniel, a soft-spoken, balding man, middle-aged, in good shape. He and his wife, Wendy, led one of Jack and Pam's favorite sessions that weekend on rekindling the fire that brought couples together in the first place.

Jack would never have taken McDaniel for a suicide candidate. However, after working as a newspaper reporter for more than twelve years, he knew full well that things—and people—were not always what they appeared.

"Well?" Cecil snapped. "Sound like something you can sink your chops into?"

Jack raised an eyebrow. "Interesting."

"Darn right it is." Cecil smirked and loosened the too-big knot in his tie. "I knew you'd be all over it. I mean, considering how religious you are."

Religious. After working closely with the frazzled editor five years, Jack had hoped he'd come across in a more alluring way to Cecil than simply "religious." Apparently not.

"How 'bout you give me two or three hundred words for tomorrow's front page?" Cecil pressed. "That'll get the ball rolling, make sure we get the scoop. Then it's yours daily after that. Whaddaya say?"

"What about the water-rate-hike piece?"

"Still need that for tomorrow; the other stuff can wait."

Jack got a bit of a rush thinking about immersing himself in such a mysterious and timely piece. Who knew, maybe he could even help Evan McDaniel or at least be there to support his family through a heart-wrenching time.

"Tell me you can handle it." Though an exceptional journalist, Cecil wasn't the best manager. He had an annoying habit of piling too much work on his star reporters—often at the last minute. Under Cecil's economy of scale, the most thorough and efficient writers worked harder and longer than the others, but got paid basically the same.

The new story would, however, get Jack out of covering a school board meeting or two, and probably at least one group photo down at the local VFW hall.

"Okay, I'll do it." Jack wheeled back to his computer with a new zeal and dropped the piece of paper onto a sea of other notes. "I'll have the first story to you by the time I leave."

Cecil turned to go. "Fine, and listen." He stopped. "If you can get more out of it tonight, even four or five hundred words, we'll find room for it."

Right.

Too often Jack had stayed late to write more in-depth stories, only to have them sliced and diced by the editors at the copy desk—the remnant of the story getting buried on page 12 next to the obits.

"I'll do what I can," Jack said, determined to finish the rate-hike piece, do his two hundred on the missing pastor, and get home.

Cecil forged off, bouncing down the five steps, past the city desk, and on toward the double doors of his cluttered office.

Maybe Pam would let the girls stay up late. They always thought that was better than ice cream. He would come into the lamplit house after dark, and the girls would race in and tackle him, screaming, "Daddy, Daddy, Daddy!"

While he and Pam chatted quietly, either standing at the kitchen island or sitting on the couch in the family room or back porch, the girls would dart about the downstairs, dancing in their little flowing pink nightgowns and nibbling crushed ice from their plastic Disney cups. Eventually Jack would gather them up in his arms on the carpeted floor of the family room and tickle them until their freckled cheeks turned pink and they cried breathlessly for him to "Stop, Daddy, *stop!*" He felt a smile lift his tired face, and his heart calmed at the thought of all that was good in his world.

Pam would be interested in the McDaniel story. She had spent time with Wendy during one of the breaks at the marriage retreat and had liked her very much.

Jack turned to reread the water-rate-hike copy that glowed back at him from the computer screen on his desk in the bustling newsroom.

His phone rang.

"Jack Crittendon."

"Jack, Tommy from next door."

"Hey, neighbor." Jack was quickly reminded how fortunate Tommy was to work out of his house as a regional sales rep for a large food distributor. "What's new in the 'hood?"

"Well ... I'm with Pamela and the girls at your house." There was a catch in Tommy's voice.

Jack sat up on the edge of his chair and peered out at the glowing computer screens, reporters, and editors dotting the newsroom. "Is everything okay?"

"The thing is, there was a break-in, Jack, here at your house, a little while ago ..."

Jack was suddenly standing.

"Is Pam okay?" He swallowed hard, snatched his keys, and started walking hurriedly toward the rear exit, ignoring the blur of faces and several gestures from colleagues. "What about the girls?"

"No one was hurt. Pamela and the girls are right here with me. They're perfectly fine. The police are here—"

Police ...

"Who did it, Tommy? How'd they get in?"

"Guy came in through the front door. Broke the glass, turned the dead bolt."

"The girls were home?"

"Yeah, but Pamela was awesome, Jack. She grabbed them and got out of there fast. Out the back door. She came straight to our house. Barged right in!"

A blistering streak of rage fired through Jack's mind like a missile.

"Did he have a gun?"

"Pamela didn't see any weapon. He had a big black leather bag with him."

Jack seethed as he flew down the back steps of the old three-story newspaper building, imagining the intruder—the slime bucket—on *his* property, in *his* house, with *his* girls! "Did they catch him?"

"Not yet." Tommy exhaled loudly. "He was in your house for ten or fifteen minutes—"

"And the cops didn't get there by then?"

"No. It took forever. I yelled to him from across our yards when he was heading for his car, but he was gone like a bat out of hell."

"Did you get a good look at the guy?"

"Kind of. White guy, maybe in his thirties, really big. Driving an old brown Toyota. The cops are after him now. They'll get him."

"I'm on my way," Jack huffed. "Did you get the plates?"

"No, but it was an Ohio tag. Couldn't make out the county."

"Was the guy on drugs or what?"

"We don't know, Jack. But your wife was smart. She couldn't have played it better."

"You're sure they're okay. They're right there with you?"

"That's right, man. They're here with me—and the police. Everything's cool. Pamela asked me to call you. She's holding the girls, still talking to the officers."

Jack's body bogged down as he approached his car. He felt like he'd hit a patch of molasses. The pavement zoomed into focus, as did his brown leather shoes. A wave of heat rolled over his face and chest. He opened the door and dropped into the driver's seat, but it all seemed like slow motion.

How dare he? How dare this stranger break down my door and enter my home, with my wife there ... and my two innocent little girls!

He felt violated. He wanted to *hurt* the creep.

"Did he destroy anything? Take anything? I mean, what did he *do*? What did he want?" Jack buckled his seat belt and started the car.

"The house looks almost untouched," Tommy said. "He cleaned out Pam's jewelry box. But your laptop is here, your camera is here. They're still checking. They've got two people in here dusting for prints."

There was commotion at Tommy's end of the phone. Jack heard Pam say she would call him in a few minutes, when the police were finished with her.

Jack shook his head. It didn't make sense. The guy could have gotten a good chunk of change for things like the laptop and camera. He thanked Tommy and hung up.

As he roared out of the *Dispatch* parking lot, he realized the only thing that mattered was that Pam and the girls were safe.

His work reminded Jack daily of the dark, evil world they had to raise their girls in. Some people, he believed, were possessed by demons. It had been true when the Bible was written, and Jack believed it was true now.

But Pam and his girls had been protected. And this wasn't the only time. God had an uncanny way of showing up, often right in the middle of the trials life dealt.

He breathed a sigh of thanks and asked for help to keep his cool. Then he checked his cell to make sure the ringer was on. He couldn't wait to hear Pam's voice.

Please, let them be calm, let them feel safe …

He thought of Pam's paranoid mother, Margaret, and how she would absolutely flip out if she heard about the break-in. Pam fought hard against such fears, which she grew up watching and learning from her mother.

Blanket Pam in peace …

As he merged onto the Ohio freeway and jetted toward home in the light pre-rush-hour traffic, Jack struggled to decipher what could possibly be of such value, such urgency, and such *risk* to break into someone's home in daylight—with people inside.

The guy had to have been high.

Pam could have been raped … the girls kidnapped or murdered.

Jack pushed harder on the gas.

Faster.

My girls need me.

3

Pamela had gotten virtually no sleep the night of what the Trenton City police were now calling the Crittendon "home invasion." Until yesterday, that term had been something Pamela had only skimmed in the *Dispatch* or heard in the background of the TV news. It was something that happened to *other* people, in *bad* parts of town—not in Merriman Woods, one of the nicest suburbs of Trenton City, Ohio; and never to *her* family.

Never say never.

It happened.

She was curled up on the screened porch glider with Jack's Bible and a cup of hot tea. The girls were upstairs getting dressed for what was going to be another hot day. The humidity was already thick and heavy. The grass was blanketed in dew. A rabbit sat between two azaleas in a row Jack had planted along the boundary of their property the fall before. Birds chirped and picked at the feeders that hung from the eaves. Her daisies and blue hydrangeas had perked up thanks to the night's dark relief from the heat, but would droop again by afternoon. She pictured the girls in their bare feet, swinging on the extra-tall swing set that Tommy had helped Jack build, and that the girls practically lived on in nice weather.

That's about all Pamela could do: look around. She tried to concentrate on the psalms opened before her, but all she could think about was the magnitude of the previous day's events and what *could* have happened—especially to the girls. Or what they could have witnessed …

She examined the screened door she had kicked open the day before and relived the adrenaline-packed moments.

"Thank you for getting us out," she whispered as she watched the sun's yellow brilliance rising over the trees beyond the property next door.

Pamela and Tommy had worked into the evening with an artist from the police department to provide a thorough description of the intruder. The artist created a fairly good black-and-white rendering of the man to distribute to the Trenton City police force.

Jack installed an extra heavy-duty dead-bolt lock that night, which worked with a key instead of a lever. He also paid a guy double to come out late and fix the broken glass next to the front door.

Even so, Pamela had spent most of the night not daring to close her eyes. Listening for the girls. Her neck and shoulders tense. Straining to hear sounds of the large, scary man she hoped, and literally prayed, would never return.

Faye cried out once in a sweat at about two thirty. Both Pamela and Jack hurried into her room. Jack covered her forehead with a cool, damp washcloth while Pamela knelt at her bedside.

"I had a dream I saw the bad man at Target."

"The man who broke in?" Pamela asked.

Faye nodded and squeezed Pamela's hands. "He was in my dream. I know it was him. He had on black clothes and he looked mean. He was following us."

Jack shot Pamela a glance in the darkness. She knew what he was thinking, that he wished Faye had never seen the intruder. It would be more difficult to forget the experience.

"Well, you don't have to worry about anything, sweetie pie." Jack turned the cloth over to the cool side. "Because Daddy is here to protect you. You know Daddy is big and strong, right? Daddy would punch the lights out of anyone who came near our house." Jack jabbed the blackness with his fists—"*Bam, bam, bam*"—making all three of them giggle. "And guess who's even bigger and stronger than Daddy, who's watching over all of us?"

"Jesus."

"That's right, sunshine. The maker of all the huge mountains and big oceans and bright stars and moon is here to protect us. His angels are all around us. He is *so* mighty. And he loves us so much."

Jack may not have realized it, but his words soothed Pamela as well. They not only reassured her about God's protection, but they also reminded her of Jack's past. His tough streak. His ability to fight. It was a dark side that had been dormant for many years, but she'd seen a hint of it in his eyes that afternoon, when they hugged for the first time following the break-in.

"Speaking of the moon and stars"—Pamela stroked Faye's stringy blonde hair—"how about a lullaby?" Her voice filled the quiet room, and even to Pamela it felt like a healing balm. "Baby's boat's a silver moon, sailing in the sky ..." she sang, and Faye quickly drifted back to sleep.

Jack had stayed home that morning for an early breakfast with Pamela and the girls before heading to work. Something about a new day made the break-in a little easier to talk about. As they rehashed what had happened, both girls admitted they'd caught a glimpse of the intruder when Pamela rushed them down the steps.

"They're gonna be fine." Jack squeezed Pamela's hands as they stood at his car in the garage. "We're all going to be just fine."

"Why did this happen?" Pamela looked into his blue eyes. Jack's once-blond hair was getting darker, more a dirty blond now. His features were clean and simple; the bones in his forehead, cheeks, and jaw gave him a lean, rugged look. He was easy to look at and quick with a cool, bright smile. His shoulders were round and his arms firm.

He shook his head. "I don't have an answer."

"But we're okay."

"Yes." He let go of her hands, put his arms around her, and pulled her close. "We're okay."

"And the police are going to catch him ..."

He nodded. "He would never come back here, Pamela. He was probably so wasted, he couldn't find our house again if he tried."

"Do you think it's okay to go to the pool?"

"Absolutely. There'll be neighbors there. Lifeguard. It'll be good for the girls. Get your minds off it."

"I still can't believe he came in here when he could see the Accord in the garage. How did he know there wasn't a man in here ... with a gun?"

"That's what I'm saying," Jack said. "He had to have been high or drunk. He probably needed money for drugs. He'll sell your jewelry and get his fix. It's over, baby." He cradled her head in his hands and gently brought it to rest against his hard chest. "It's all over. And it's all the more reason for us to be thankful."

"But what if he wasn't on drugs?" She pulled back and looked up at Jack. "What if he scoped out the house and knew you were gone?"

"The cops said this type of thing is almost always drug related—"

"I don't know." She shook her head. "He didn't look drugged up to me. He looked like he was on a mission, like he knew exactly what he was doing."

"All right, listen." Jack took her hands in his and squeezed. "Let's give this to God, the whole thing, right now. Let's just leave it in his lap and turn around and go our way. He's big enough, right?"

She nodded and fought back the tears as they prayed, as Jack talked to God in a way only he could. While she was dumping her fears on God, she sensed in Jack's words that he was leaving something else with God too: that anger of his that once reigned so strong. And she felt relief; it fell over them gently, like a cool rain.

She shook an index finger at him as he backed out of the garage and rolled down the passenger window. "You let me know if the police call you. I want to know when they get him."

"You do the same." Jack saluted, blew her a kiss, and started out the driveway. "Use plenty of sunscreen on the girls!"

Pamela waved at his car as it rolled out of sight. Then she closed her eyes. *Thank you for such a good husband.* A gentle wind kicked up, stroking her face and blowing her hair. God was there. She didn't understand why the trouble had arisen. She didn't understand much of anything at that moment, except that he was there.

She shut the garage door. As she walked through the family room toward the kitchen to fix a cup of tea, something on the mantle caught her eye.

What had happened to their wedding photo?

She approached it, feeling more sick to her stomach with each tentative step.

Pamela and Jack were in the middle of the picture, surrounded by the people in their wedding party: three men to the right, three women to the left.

As she drew closer to the mantle, Pamela's hands began to tremble. Her breathing quickened. She scanned the room, the whole downstairs, the doors, the windows …

In a flash, she grabbed the photo and dashed through the family room, up the steps two at a time. Turning Faye's doorknob, she opened the door, stuck her head in, and caught a glimpse of Faye just as she was leaning into the closet.

She hurried down the hall to Rebecca's room and eased the door open. The room was dark.

"Rebecca?"

No answer.

Pamela's heart thundered as she entered the bathroom. No one there.

"Rebecca?" She yelled it this time.

"Yes?" Rebecca called.

"Oh …" Pamela's whole body went limp as she continued down the hallway, following Rebecca's voice. "Hey, honey. I just wondered where you were."

"I'm in the media room."

Thank God.

Still clutching the framed photograph, Pamela walked halfway down the hall and stopped in front of the three carpeted steps leading up to the media room.

Lying on the couch in her nightgown, her long, silky brown hair draped over her face, Rebecca was reading a library book.

Pamela held the photo against her side. "Hey, you're not dressed yet?"

"Not yet." Rebecca didn't look up.

Normally Pamela would have made Rebecca look up when she was speaking to someone, but this was no time for manners training. Pamela started toward the steps.

"What are you doing, Mommy?"

"Just running around, tidying up." She leaned back around the corner so Rebecca wouldn't see the photograph.

"What have you got?" She nodded toward the picture Pamela held behind her back.

"Just a picture I was looking at."

"Can I see?" Rebecca stuck her hand toward her mom.

"Maybe in a minute, sweetie. Mommy's got to get back downstairs, and you girls need to get dressed and on with your morning chores, okay?"

"'Kay."

Knowing Rebecca would go right back to her book, Pamela walked quickly down the hall past Faye's room and down the steps. She entered Jack's study, opened one of the blinds, and looked down at the photograph in her shaking hands.

From the waist up, Jack had been sliced out of the photograph.

It had been done quickly, with a knife, by the man whom Pamela was growing sickeningly afraid was much more than a robber.

4

Jack hit more traffic than usual because he'd stayed to eat breakfast with the girls, but it had been well worth it. Faye and Rebecca didn't seem the least bit fazed by the break-in and were more jazzed up about going to the pool and trying out the new goggles Pam had found for them at Target.

Pam had accidentally burned his bagel, then snapped uncharacteristically at Faye for spilling a glass of chocolate milk. He'd done his best to reassure her of what he truly believed was a one-time break-in by a drugged-out freak. As he drove, Jack reminded himself to call Pam sometime that morning to make sure she was okay. He also planned to follow up with the officer in charge of the case, Dennis DeVry.

In his office the night before, Jack phoned their insurance agent, who asked them to gather receipts and/or photographs of the items that were missing, so proper reimbursement could be made. Pam volunteered to do it that day.

Traffic or no traffic, Jack's was a simple and enjoyable drive compared to his rush-hour commute when he and Pam had lived in Atlanta. He was glad to be back in central Ohio, near where he'd grown up. From their house in Merriman Woods he scooted along shady, tree-lined streets and dozens of old traditional two-story homes with large front porches and American flags. Kids often bumped their bikes along the uneven sidewalks that fronted the small green yards.

There wasn't a whole lot of criminal activity in the area, but having done his share of police beats for the *Dispatch*, Jack knew there was crime everywhere these days. Since the break-in he had contemplated getting a security system for the house, something Pam could arm even while she and the girls were inside.

After their starter home in Atlanta and their first house in Ohio, in a different section of Trenton City, Jack and Pam agreed they'd found a lifelong home at 1422 Callanwolde Boulevard. They loved the neighborhood schools and the fact that the Cook County Public Library and the new Cook County Hospital were within a few blocks. They could walk or bike to Campolo's Pizzeria for dinner, to the Donut Hole on Saturdays for breakfast treats, and to Gebralter's Grocery to pick up anything they needed.

Jack smiled as he drove by the stone entrance to Crogan Park where he and Pam often took the girls for picnics. They would play Frisbee, ride bikes, hike the paved trails, and wade barefoot through the cool, clean water that funneled down from the Trenton City aqueduct and ran like a creek across the concrete riverbanks.

Dodging potholes on the Ohio interstate and passing the sprawling fiberglass manufacturing plant that kept half of Trenton City employed, Jack exited at Tenth Street and made his way past the library and Tiffany's sandwich shop. He made a quick right on James Avenue past their church, Grace Bible Fellowship, then shot down a back alley by his all-time favorite restaurant, the Golden Wok.

After turning down various narrow alleyways that ran behind tall city buildings, Jack wheeled the VW into his usual parking spot at the rear of the *Dispatch*. As he made his way inside, he smiled and lifted the plastic photo ID that hung around his neck to grumpy Debbie who sat on a stool behind the glass at the back door.

"Good morning, Debbie."

As always, the middle-aged blonde with amazingly thick glasses and equally thick black eyebrows managed a half smile. "Hav-a-gudday," she droned, blinking her big, tired eyelids.

Jack hustled up the steps to the somewhat-sedate newsroom on the third floor. Things didn't get cranking until mid- to late afternoon when the evening deadline approached. Right now, most of the reporters and photographers were out on their beats, following leads and gathering news and photos.

Throwing his leather satchel over the back of his chair, he grabbed the day's edition of the *Dispatch* from his desk and headed for the coffeemaker. He scanned the front page for the piece on the missing pastor, thinking Cecil surely would have found someone else to write the first story.

There it was, lower-right quarter, in a blue box with a head-and-shoulders photo of Pastor McDaniel.

Trenton City Pastor Missing
By Derrick Whittaker

Evan McDaniel, 39, senior pastor of Five Forks Methodist Church in Trenton City was reported missing late Friday by Dr. Richard Billings, clerk of the Central Ohio Methodist Church Office. McDaniel, the husband of Wendy and father of Nathaniel, 14, Zachary, 11, and Silas, 7, has been the pastor of FFMC for three years.

According to *Faith Line*, the official web magazine of the Methodist Church, McDaniel took with him "a significant quantity of medication" and left behind communication "indicating his intention to take his own life." Associate Pastor Dr. Andrew Satterfield is serving as interim pastor in McDaniel's absence.

Anyone with information regarding Pastor McDaniel's whereabouts is urged to call the Trenton City Police Department: (740) 844-1000.

Whoa.

Heavy insinuation …

Although reporter Derrick Whittaker was one of Jack's closest friends at the paper, his stories sometimes lacked instinct and foresight. Jack headed for Derrick's work area, excited to take over the McDaniel story.

Derrick, who was on the phone, cupped the receiver with one hand and pointed to it with the other. "McDaniel's wife," he whispered. "She's ticked!" Derrick was African-American, about thirty, and wore an inch-thick Afro and retro black glasses.

Jack lifted two innocent hands. *What do you expect when you write a front-page story speculating that her husband is suicidal?* He pretended to drink from an invisible cup, thumbed toward the break room, and took off for his coffee.

Cecil spotted him from a mile away and made a beeline toward him. Jack kept going, straight for the Bunn, determined to get himself a large black coffee before anything else could happen.

"Crittendon," Cecil said, "you see Whittaker's piece on the pastor?"

Jack finished pouring, sipped his coffee, and nodded. "I was surprised he mentioned suicide this early."

"What do you mean?" Cecil said. "We attributed it—to the Methodist news source."

"I know," Jack said. "I would have talked to the wife first. Did he?"

"He tried. He couldn't reach her."

"I didn't think so." Jack turned toward Derrick's desk. "But she's apparently reached *him* now."

"Oh, for the love of peace." Cecil shook his bony fists. At least he didn't have any new white pieces of paper with him. "It's your story now. Take it and run with it. Get with the family, go to the church, you know the drill."

"I'm on it." Jack started toward his desk.

"And I needed that water-rate-hike piece *yesterday*," Cecil called.

Jack stopped and looked back. Cecil was running his long, thin brown hair between his thumb and index finger.

"I'm almost done with it," Jack said.

Derrick met up with Jack and walked with him at a good clip to Jack's desk.

"Man, that pastor's wife is heated," Derrick said. "She's saying her husband's never been suicidal. Couldn't believe we ran it in the story."

"Dude, I would have talked to her before mentioning suicide."

"I tried! Repeatedly. I couldn't get her."

"Then you shouldn't have mentioned suicide. He was *missing*—that would have been enough to start with."

"That's how I wrote it! Barton made me put it in there, about the possible suicide."

"You're kidding me." Jack looked up to give Cecil the evil eye, but he was nowhere to be seen.

"I feel bad," Derrick said. "I mean, she was crying by the time we hung up."

"You have her number?"

Derrick ripped the top sheet from his pad and stuffed it in Jack's palm. "I told her you'd call and get her whole side of it. She's absolutely positive he's not suicidal."

"Where does she think he is then?"

Derrick bounced his shoulders. "She has no clue. Said he's had some personal issues but insists he'd never leave her and their boys."

"I thought there was a suicide note or something?"

"There's something. A note that turned up at the church maybe? She's gonna explain it all to you. And she's ready to talk now; she wasn't yesterday."

"Good." Jack looked at the number. "Where do they live?"

"Cool Springs. Close to the church he pastors. You gonna get right on it?"

"Yeah."

"'Cause I feel like a complete jerk."

"It's not your fault. That was Barton's call."

"I pretty much told her you'd make it right."

"Okay. I'll call her in a minute."

"Tell me about yesterday," Derrick said. "What happened, dude? Is Pam okay, and the girls?"

Jack's cell rang. He rolled his eyes. "They're okay. Pam was pretty shaken up. The guy broke right in while they were all home. They got out the back door, to the neighbor's."

Jack glanced at his phone. It was Pamela calling. "I gotta take this."

Derrick patted his shoulder. "All right. We'll catch up later. Maybe lunch?"

"Maybe."

"*Not* Golden Wok."

Jack laughed and answered his phone.

"How is the lovely Pamela Anne Crittendon this morning? I was just going to check in with you—"

"This was more than a robbery, Jack," Pam blurted. "He cut you out of one of our wedding pictures, one of the framed ones on the mantel—"

"Wait a minute, honey, slow down—"

"That's not all. The locket you gave Rebecca is *gone*. The one with the picture of you two, that you gave her at the father-daughter thing."

"She probably misplaced it, honey. Now just calm down."

"Jack, please come home. This is creeping me out. Please. There was more to this than a robbery. Something's wrong. We need to get the police back here."

"Okay, listen." He squeezed the back of his neck and made himself stay cool. "The guy is probably mentally disturbed. He—"

"He knew *exactly* what he was doing. I'm *not* freaking out. I'm just thinking about the girls."

Jack dropped into his chair, elbows to his knees.

"Okay … listen, you look for anything else missing, or disturbed." Of course he and Pam had done that the previous day, but apparently they hadn't looked closely enough. "I've got to take care of a few things here." He was sorting through his options as he tried to soothe her. "I'll be home as soon as I can."

"Thank you."

"I'll get with the lead cop, DeVry, and let him know what's going on. Call me if anything else is missing, okay?"

He heard nothing.

"Okay, Pamela?"

Jack heard her fumbling with the phone.

"Oh my Lord, Jack …"

"What?" He shot to his feet. "What's wrong?"

"Rebecca … Faye!" Pam was not talking to him anymore but was yelling into the house. "Come to Mommy, *now*!"

"Pam! What is it?" His stomach bottomed, and he felt for his car keys. "What's going on?"

There was only silence and a slight bumping of the phone.

"Talk to me!"

"It's the brown car." Her voice came back, trembling. "He's here …"

5

"He sat out there in his car for ten minutes." Pamela felt flushed as she talked to Jack and Officer Dennis DeVry at the kitchen table. "Right in front of the house. Not trying to be inconspicuous at all. I can't believe you guys couldn't get here any faster—especially after this just happened."

Pam couldn't stop her hands from shaking, and her palms were damp.

"I'm sorry, Mrs. Crittendon," said DeVry. "We got here as fast as we could." The officer was not a handsome man, with his wide, pockmarked face and yellowish teeth, but his broad chest and thick arms suggested a physical strength that Pamela found reassuring. "You're sure it was the same guy?"

"Positive. I could see him in the car."

"Could you tell what he was doing?" DeVry examined the framed photo from which Jack had been cut out.

Pamela moved to the edge of her chair. "He was looking at the house. I was sure he was going to get out of that car and come right up to the front door again."

Jack reached over and covered one of her hands.

"You weren't able to get a license number?" DeVry said.

"I called Tommy, the neighbor you met yesterday, to see if he could go out and get the plates, but he wasn't home. I wasn't going out there."

"And he eventually just left?" DeVry set the photo upright on the kitchen table.

She nodded and sniffed back the emotion. "Very slowly, looking at the house the whole way." She covered her quivering mouth with a wadded tissue. "I'm sorry. Excuse me a minute."

Pamela rose and hurried through the family room to the downstairs bath. Shutting the door and turning on the exhaust fan, she patted her eyes with a clean tissue, blew her nose, and stared at herself in the mirror.

Her mascara was running, and the skin beneath her brown eyes was dark and swollen. She ran a wet finger below one eye, then the other, and patted dry with a towel. She ran her fingers through her hair and applied lipstick. That would have to do.

She leaned all her weight through her hands onto the marble counter, sighed, and closed her eyes.

Jack's words from the garage the day before came back. *Leave it all in God's lap ...*

Lord, help me. I'm scared. I can't deal with this.

She looked into the mirror again. Her bottom jaw jutted forward. Tension had carved its signature in the crevice between her eyes and the sides of her nose and mouth. *Relax, Pam.* But she couldn't work up the tranquillity she had been seeking ever since the break-in.

She sucked in her cheeks, took a deep breath, and headed back out.

"Girls?" she called upstairs, where she could hear Rebecca's and Faye's giggles and the sound of a DVD they were watching. "You okay?"

"Yes, Mommy," Rebecca called.

"Yes," Faye echoed.

"Pam," Jack said as Pamela made her way back to the kitchen, "Officer DeVry is going to arrange for extra patrol."

"And I'll come by myself when I'm on duty, Mrs. Crittendon." DeVry stood and handed a white business card to each of them. "This has my cell. I want you to call me the instant you see that car again. Let's hope you don't."

"What about checking that picture for prints?" Pamela pointed to the framed photo on the kitchen table.

"Well …" DeVry hesitated. "You and your neighbor both saw the perpetrator at different times with gloves on, and we found no prints anywhere. I'm 99 percent sure there aren't any prints on that picture except ours."

"Why would he take Rebecca's locket?" Pamela said. "I just don't get it."

"Are you sure your daughter might not have misplaced the locket?" DeVry asked. "I know my kids are always—"

"No." Pamela shook her head. "It's her absolute favorite. Jack gave it to her at a father-daughter banquet, and she had a special place for it in her jewelry box. She's extremely organized for her age, and she says it was in there."

Jack retrieved the scarred photograph from the kitchen table. "Could you possibly have someone dust this anyway?" He handed it to DeVry. "Just to make sure."

DeVry took the photo from Jack and put it under his arm. "Sure. If anything turns up, I'll let you know."

Pamela blinked with a nod of gratitude toward Jack.

"Thank you." Jack placed a hand on the officer's shoulder.

"Is there anything more you can do, or we can do?" Pamela asked.

"I'm afraid not." DeVry rested a hand on the big black gun in his holster. "I realize finding this picture makes this whole thing even scarier for you and your family. But as I told your husband, we really will get by here every time we possibly can. Try not to lose too much sleep over it. People like this rarely hit the same house twice."

"Then why did he come back and sit out there?"

Office DeVry pursed his lips. "You folks need to be all eyes and ears, just as you were today. This might be some sort of stalker or someone with mental issues. Be careful. Keep the doors locked. Don't hesitate to call us."

Maybe there was something else the man saw in the house that he decided he wanted, Pamela thought—like her ... or one of the girls.

∞◦∞

The late morning sun flooded the white and yellow kitchen. Officer DeVry was back out on the hot streets of Trenton City, and Rebecca and Faye had just finished lunch and were playing with their felt-board dollies at the dining-room table. Jack took the carafe from the coffeemaker and poured the leftover coffee, now cold, into a tall glass. He set the empty carafe at the sink where Pamela was working, went to the freezer, and dumped a handful of ice into the glass and set it on the counter to chill.

Pamela finished rinsing the sink, hit the disposal for a few seconds, and dried her hands on a daisy-print towel as she approached him.

"I want us to get a gun," she said.

Jack's face fell.

"How else will we defend ourselves if he comes back?"

Jack's mouth sealed and his eyes narrowed.

"We can't count on a patrol car coming by here once every few days," she said.

He still didn't speak.

"If you'd have been here, you'd be thinking the same thing. It was so … brazen! This is *our* home. We need to defend it. It's against the law for a stranger to break his way in here."

Jack took a sip of the iced coffee.

"I want to learn to shoot," she continued. "We can go to Amiel's range, on the square."

The slightest smile curled at the corner of his lips.

"I mean it, Jack! This is *not* funny. We've got to think of the girls. I'm not going to be put in that situation again. We were completely helpless."

He set the glass down, folded his arms, and leaned back against the white tile counter. "First of all, I don't think it's funny. I'm sorry. I started to smile because when you get an idea, you are like a heat-seeking missile."

"Jack, I'm being serious."

"Okay." He lifted his open hands in front of his chest. "First of all, where would we keep it?"

"I don't know. In our closet, up high, with the safety on."

"If he broke in again, you wouldn't have time to go upstairs to get it."

"Then we'd keep it down here. That's a better idea anyway. We'd put it up in a cupboard." She motioned to one with her head. "The girls would never know."

Jack exhaled. "You know, they say if you're going to own a gun, you not only better know how to use it, you better be *ready* to use it *first* when you take it in your hand."

"I'd use it first," she practically spit. "Believe me, if that monster set one foot on our property again and I had a gun, I would *put—him—down*."

"I know, I know … I hear you, baby. But they say if an intruder, someone all pumped up on adrenaline and possibly drugs, sees his victim with a gun, someone in *that* house is more likely to die than in a house where there is no gun. I *am* thinking about Rebecca and Faye. I just don't want to add more danger."

"I don't know about the statistics, Jack, I really don't. All I know is what happened to us—and it should never be allowed to happen to anyone. We were violated! We were lucky to get out. What if I'd been upstairs and the girls were down? What if the girls had been napping? What if I'd been doing laundry? I've thought this through a million times."

She'd hit a nerve. She could see it in his facial muscles, the flare of his nostrils, the way his teeth clenched ever so briefly.

"I know." He nodded. "I have too." He lifted his arms toward her. "Come here."

"No!" She stomped a foot, then thought of the girls and lowered her voice. "I'm not going to let you sweet-talk me out of this. We are getting a gun. Period. I'll pay for it out of my own money."

"Okay, listen, honey. If we're really going to consider it, we need to ask ourselves if it's safe for us. What about when the girls get older and have friends over?"

"We can get rid of it when this passes."

She couldn't believe Jack wasn't right on the bandwagon with her.

"Your dad had a gun," Pamela said. "Mine has one."

"Does that make it safe?"

"Safe? Let's talk about safe! There'll be nothing left to *keep* safe if he comes back and hurts us!"

That too struck home. For a flash, Pamela felt like the devil's advocate for riling up the old Jack. But that's what she was trying to do. She steamed to the window near the kitchen table and stared out blankly, the stress blurring the outdoor landscape into a foggy mix of bright greens and yellows.

"He came back, Jack." Her voice quieted. "You said he'd never remember where we lived." She turned to face him. "He was *here*, this morning, and you weren't! I am here alone with the girls much of the day. I need protection. *Period.*"

The way he looked at her with his mouth locked shut, it was as if he was forcing himself not to speak, not to say something he would regret.

Pamela waited, resolute.

"Look," he finally said, "his coming back today raises the stakes, I admit it. I just think that before we buy a gun and learn to use it—which we can certainly do—we need to ask ourselves if that's the best choice, the wisest choice. Is it what God wants? If it is, great; we'll do it."

Pamela's head dropped into her hands. She didn't want to talk about what God wanted. Not now. She knew what she *needed*, and that was all there was to it. Her mind and body and spirit felt utterly spent, and the day was only half over.

"I'm not trying to belittle you," Jack said. "I understand you felt helpless. We just need to make sure we both agree completely before we decide to keep a weapon in this house that can take someone's life …"

6

As Jack sat on the flowery couch in the McDaniels' dark, cool living room while Wendy McDaniel went to the kitchen to get him some water, he found it difficult to believe anything could be as wrong as it was within this household, because everything seemed so right.

A smooth blacktop driveway sloped down, then led up to the small white ranch house perched on a hill about seventy-five yards off Iradale Drive. It was a quiet residential street in Cool Springs, just outside Trenton City. The home was surrounded by towering trees that swayed and rustled in the breeze, blocked out the hot Ohio sun, and smothered the acre-or-so lot in pleasant shade.

Jack looked around, guessing the house was forty or fifty years old. It had hardwood floors and thick, soft rugs. The interior wood trim was dark gray, and the walls were done in rich sage green and cocoa brown, giving it an early-American look. Rustic abstracts of doors and windows hung in just the right spots on the walls, and pretty colored glass bottles of all sizes sat along each window.

"I feel bad about getting so upset with the other reporter on the phone," Wendy said. She handed Jack a bottled water. "But I was absolutely shocked that his story talked about suicide. To see it on the front page …"

"I completely understand." Jack opened the bottle. "If it had been up to me … well, listen, let's just start from scratch. Can we do that?"

"Yes." She sat near him on the edge of a leather recliner. She had short, spiky brown hair and was slight and youthful looking in jean shorts and Crocs. "I'm ready."

"First of all," Jack said, "you saw the blurb from *Faith Line*?"

Wendy nodded. "I got it in a blanket email, like everyone else. That was the first I'd heard anything public about suicide. I couldn't believe they put it in there. When I called, they told me they hoped it would lend urgency and generate some leads to help find Evan, but again—to make public mention of it, before we even know what's happened?"

"When did you last see Evan?"

"Friday morning." She spoke confidently. "He left for work just like always."

"Did everything seem okay?"

"Normal. Everything was normal. He got up early, as usual, although he didn't go on his morning run; he hasn't been doing that lately. So I didn't think anything of it that he missed that day. Some mornings he's just not in the mood. But he had breakfast with Silas, our youngest, then showered and left for the church. I was up too. Our other boys, Nathaniel and Zachary, were still asleep. Everything seemed okay."

"And did he make it to the church?"

"Yes. One of the secretaries, Barbara Cooley, saw him. He was in his office for about an hour, then left. Friday is his day to do hospital and home visits. I've asked the assistant pastor if he can tell me who Evan may have been planning to visit."

"The assistant pastor." Jack looked for the name in his notes. "Dr. Andrew Satterfield?"

"That's right." Wendy bit the inside of her lip, and her eyes shifted to her lap, where her fingers were interlocked.

"I do plan on talking to him." Jack wrote a note to himself along the top-left edge of his pad, where he jotted things he needed to follow up on. "But as far as we know," he said, "Barbara Cooley was the last person to see Evan?"

"We think so."

"All right, let's see." He reviewed some quotes he'd written on his pad from the church news story. "Can we talk about this? Where it says Evan took with him 'a significant quantity of medication'?"

Wendy's shoulders arched back. She took in a deep breath and let it out. "On and off over the years, Evan has struggled with depression. He's taken antidepressant medications. He told me recently that it had been several weeks since he'd had any."

"And how was he doing without them? What state of mind was he in?"

Wendy peered out the sliding glass doors for a moment, then leveled her eyes on Jack. "He hasn't been sleeping well at night, so he's been dragging during the day," she said. "He thought he had the flu—a bit of an upset stomach. I thought that was why he hadn't been exercising lately."

"Anything else out of the ordinary?"

"He's been a bit down," Wendy said. "There are a lot of challenges with his work."

"I can imagine."

"A lot of pressure," she said. "Anyway, a few of the leaders at the church knew about the medicine. I guess he kept some in the restroom in his office. There was also some Valium in there. Apparently, since it's not there anymore, they reported it missing."

Jack took notes, then looked back at her. "Okay, I guess that leads us to the next obvious thing." He was careful to read the words he'd written from the church's news story. "The online story says Evan 'left behind communication indicating his intention to take his own life.'" He left off the part about Evan's body not yet being found, thinking it would be insensitive and morbid to mention. "'Coworkers believe he was genuinely determined to follow through on his expressed intentions ...'"

The corners of Wendy's pretty mouth turned down, and she pressed her trembling fingers hard against her forehead.

"I'm sorry, Mrs. McDaniel," Jack said. "Can I get you a Kleenex?"

She stood. "I'll get it. Excuse me. I'm sorry." She left the room.

Jack felt empty. What an odd case. The people at the church seemed so sure Evan was out to take his own life, yet his wife seemed so sure otherwise. Or perhaps she was simply in denial—it would be understandable.

"Okay, I'm going to pull it together." Wendy reentered the room holding a small box of tissues. "Thank you for your patience. I told myself I wasn't going to do that."

She sat back down in the same chair and folded her tan legs beneath her. "There was a note on Evan's keyboard, on his desk at the church, in an envelope. It was supposedly written by him, but it was typed. I couldn't find it on his computer. I don't think he wrote it."

"A suicide note?"

"Yes ... supposedly." She shook her head and wiped her nose. "Evan just wouldn't do this. He wouldn't leave his boys; he wouldn't leave me. Besides, the note doesn't even sound like him. I just ... I'm so confused."

"Can you tell me what it said?"

She crossed the room to a desk built into the kitchen wall, came back, and handed Jack a white folded sheet of paper. "I asked for a copy."

He unfolded it and read the plain type.

To those I leave behind,

I am sorry to have failed you. God knows I tried to be a good husband, father, and pastor. My goal has always been to live a life of service to you, my beloved Wendy and boys, and to you, my church family. However, after much struggle and spiritual warfare, I have come to believe certain people are not meant for this world. There have been glimpses of light, but overall the depression has simply overwhelmed me. Everyone will be better off with me gone. I will be at peace now, I pray (if God forgives me for this), and you will be free to move on and make a better future for yourselves.

With love, forever,
Evan (Daddy)

Jack looked at Wendy. "He didn't sign it?"

"I don't think he wrote it, Mr. Crittendon. And whoever did, didn't want to try to forge his handwriting, because we would have known it wasn't his."

She was really grasping.

"If Evan didn't write this, who do you think did?"

Her face melted slowly into a quiet daze, and she stared slightly off to Jack's left.

He turned to see what she was looking at. It was a framed painting of a small white cottage, an old wooden dock, some seagulls, and a vast body of blue-green water. The artist had left plenty of white space amid the choppy water, making it look real yet abstract at the same time.

"That's Evan's favorite place on earth."

Jack looked back at Wendy, whose glazed brown eyes were still fixed on the painting.

"Where is that?"

"Englewood, Florida. Gulf Coast. Between Sarasota and Fort Myers. Best seashells anywhere. And tons of sharks' teeth."

"Do you go there often?"

"Every spring since before the boys were born; sometimes more often." She continued to stare. "It's changed some. The beach has eroded a lot, but Evan and the boys still boogieboard in the surf most of the day. I read and walk. We never want to come home."

"Has Evan gone off the antidepressants before?" Jack asked. He knew that quitting some of those things cold turkey could send users into a deeper state of despair than before they started taking them.

"Yes, like I said, he's been on and off."

"Was he weaned off the meds under a doctor's supervision, or did he just quit taking them, do you know?"

"I know what you're getting at, Mr. Crittendon," Wendy said. "And I'm not sure of the answer. I think he may have just quit all at once." She squinted, as if trying to open the lid of a jar that was stuck shut. "Look, if you're implying Evan had antidepressant withdrawal symptoms, the answer is yes. His doctor cautioned him about it. He's been restless. He's even had a few of those electric shock feelings, like tremors. But I know my husband, and I know he would not quit on us."

Jack reached for one of the tissues and handed it to her.

She took it, nodded thanks, and wiped her eyes.

It sounded to Jack as if Evan had some kind of chronic biochemical imbalance—something he couldn't just will or wish away.

"Mr. Crittendon, Evan is a very difficult person to read, even by me. He's very emotional. But I believe with everything in me that he would not do this—not in a million years." Wendy shook her head and peered back up at the Florida painting. "He would not leave us."

"So what do you think happened?" Jack said. "Do you have suspicions?"

"Suspicions?"

"Does he have any enemies?"

Her eyes got wide. "Enemies? I wouldn't go that far. Disgruntled church people? Every pastor has those. Tension at work? Sure, but nothing I can think of that would cause someone to want to harm him."

"When you say disgruntled church people, are there one or two who stand out? I mean, who are angry at Evan?"

"You know …" She pursed her lips and made her head sway back and forth as if she had a kink in her neck. "You might talk to Andrew Satterfield about that."

"I take it he and Evan work closely—"

"On second thought …" She paused. "Write down this name: Hank Garbenger." She spelled the last name. "He cheated on his wife, and Evan ended up disciplining him in front of the church. It's a biblical procedure most churches don't adhere to anymore. There's a long story about how it all unfolded, but we don't need to get into that."

"Okay." Jack combed the scribbling on his pad and made a note to follow up on Hank Garbenger. "You mentioned tension at work. Is that worth getting into?"

Wendy looked at the shady scene beyond the sliding glass doors and scratched her forehead. "Just for background, I guess." She locked her fingers together again, turned to Jack, and sighed. "The associate pastor, Satterfield, has never liked Evan." She rubbed her face. "Oh, I shouldn't say that. Forgive me. I'm not sure of his feelings. But the thing is, he's made it clear he thinks Evan is unfit to pastor because he suffers from depression and has a need for medication."

"Really?"

"He's brought it up in meetings with the elders and deacons. He's made it very clear he believes Evan should step down as pastor or be asked to step down by the leadership, at least until he can 'overcome his deficiencies'—I think that's how he once put it."

"Wow. That's pretty harsh, coming from someone under your husband."

"Yeah, well, Satterfield has a very fundamentalist background. He views depression as a weakness instead of an illness."

Jack nodded.

"The unfortunate thing is, he's convinced some of the elders and deacons to believe the same thing."

The longer Jack sat with Wendy, the more intriguing the story became.

A door slammed in another room, followed by what sounded like Spain's running of the bulls.

Suddenly the kitchen was raided by three tan, sweaty, panting, pink-faced boys of all sizes. Ignoring their mom and the stranger sitting nearby, they methodically went to work. The littlest dropped to his knees, opened the cupboard, and filled his small arms with three huge plastic cups, each featuring the Ohio State University logo. Perched on a stool, the middle one yanked a huge ice tray from the freezer, hoisted it to the counter, and banged it down. The oldest one, who must have been approaching six feet in height, pulled an enormous pitcher of lemonade from the fridge and stood at the counter, poised to pour.

Wendy cleared her throat loudly enough for her sons to take notice. All three looked into the living room at the same time.

"Hi, Mom," said the little one.

"Hello there, boys." Wendy stood, rubbing her hands together. "We have company. Would you come in here and say hello for a minute?"

Each of them wore long shorts and tennis shoes with no socks. The oldest didn't have a shirt on, and Jack could see the waist of his blue-and-red-checked boxers. The youngest and oldest had their mother's eyes, while the middle one resembled their father, who Jack remembered from the marriage seminar and photo that ran in the *Dispatch*.

"This is Mr. Jack Crittendon." Wendy put her hand out toward Jack, who stood up. "He's a reporter for the *Dispatch*, and he's going to be doing some stories on Daddy and our family. Mr. Crittendon, this is Silas." She rubbed the blond hair of the youngest boy. "He's seven."

"Hi." Silas gritted his teeth, gave Jack a viselike grip, craned his little neck sideways, and stared up at Jack for a response.

"What do you say to Mr. Crittendon?" Wendy prompted.

"Nice to meet you." Silas shrugged.

"Next is Zachary." Wendy squeezed her middle son's shoulder. "He's eleven."

"How do you do?" Zachary's handshake was equally … painful.

"And last but not least," Wendy said, "this is Nathaniel, our fourteen-year-old."

"Good to meet you." His voice was surprisingly deep, and he shook Jack's hand with not quite so much thought about breaking every bone in it. "You can call me Nate."

"It's good to meet you guys. Wow." Jack looked at Wendy. "They have powerful grips!"

Silas hooted and slapped his leg on his way out of the room, and the other two laughed as they followed him back to the kitchen.

"What great manners," Jack commented.

Wendy nodded and rested her hands on her waist. "They're good boys. Their dad has had a lot to do with that."

Jack's phone vibrated, but he ignored it. He'd be out of there in a second.

He whispered to Wendy, "We're going to do all we can to help you find Evan."

Wendy crossed her arms and rubbed her biceps, as if she was chilly. "Thank you so much."

His phone vibrated again. Without looking at it, he hit the power button twice, sending the caller to voice mail.

"If anything else develops, or you need publicity," Jack said, "please don't hesitate to call me. I'll do everything I can. You have my number, right?"

"Thank you." She nodded. "Yes, I do. And I will be calling."

"Excellent." Jack made for the door.

"Will you be able to clear it up," Wendy said softly from behind. "About the suicide?"

Jack got to the door and turned to face her. She was indeed tiny. "What I plan to do is interview some people at the church and get with the police; then I'll write a detailed piece—"

"Is there any way I could see it before it gets printed?"

He frowned and shook his head. "No. Sorry. I can't do that. But it's going to have all the facts, including your side of the story. You know, much of what you've told me here today."

Wendy nodded like a scared child trusting her father when he says everything will be okay.

"You know what?" Jack said. "I should have a copy of that letter. Would that be okay with you?"

"You're not going to run it in the paper."

"Oh no. I just mean for me to have, you know, as the investigation continues."

"I don't have a copy machine."

"I could take a quick photo." Jack reached for his phone. "Can we do that?"

While Wendy smoothed out the "suicide letter" on the kitchen table, Jack glanced at a text message that awaited him.

Call me now!

Sent from Pam's cell phone.

He snapped a quick photo of Evan's letter and headed for the door. Surely Pam would call him if it were an emergency.

"Mr. Crittendon ... there's one more thing I need to tell you."

He opened the door.

"I should have told you earlier, but it just looks so bad."

"What is it?" Jack tried not to sound too hurried.

"We own a handgun, for protection."

"Uh-huh."

Ironic that would come up.

"Well ... it's gone."

Jack squinted. "Just since Evan's disappearance?" He needed to make this short.

"I think so. But I'm not positive."

"Was the gun loaded?"

She shook her head. "No, but he kept two of those metal bullet holder things in a separate place, and they're gone."

"The magazines? Okay." He let it sink in, then shook his head, trying to keep everything clear. "I assume you told the police."

She shook her head quickly. "I couldn't. It looked so—incriminating."

Jack's cell phone vibrated again; it was ringing now.

He put a hand on it. "That's a call I've got to take. It's my wife. We had a break-in at our house, and she's still shaken up."

"Oh my gosh, how terrible. I remember your wife," Wendy said. "Go ahead and take it, by all means."

"I'll grab it as I leave." He stepped outside.

Jack squeezed the vibrating phone in his hand, feeling dizzy from the pressure of both worlds colliding in his head. He nodded reassuringly but lifted a commanding finger toward Wendy's chest. "Call the lead investigator, *now*. Tell about the gun. They need to know *everything*. I'll be in touch."

He bounded down the steps and toward his car, sliding the answer button on his phone at the same time.

"Sorry, honey. What's going on?"

"My Bible's gone, Jack." Pam's tone was one of controlled chaos. "I couldn't find it this morning. I thought I just misplaced it, but it's not here!" Her voice trembled. "I searched the whole house."

Jack opened the door and dropped into the driver's seat, wondering if that nutcase really took Pam's Bible, or if she was having one of those paranoid fits for which her mother was famous. "Babe, it'll probably turn up—"

"No. It won't. It's gone! Do you hear me? I know. Jack, this thing is freaking me out. Why is he doing this to us? I just have the weirdest feeling, like he's stalking *me*."

7

"Come on, girlfriend," Rebecca said to Faye in her best mommy voice, "we need to get our babies home before another rainstorm comes. There's a big tornado on the way … a *hurricane*!"

"Okay, gewfriend," Faye called. "Hurry … help our babies!"

Even in her anxious state, Pamela chuckled as the girls raced their dollies in pink strollers up and down the wet sidewalk in front of the house, their big purses knocking against the backs of their skinny legs.

A late afternoon downpour had come up suddenly, drenching the already green grass and leaving clouds of steam rolling up from the blistering streets. In the distance the sky was menacing, the color of a deep bruise, but over where Pamela stood, the sun had returned, almost white, it was so bright. The humidity was stifling.

Wearing bright yellow slip-on gardening shoes, Pamela meandered through the wet grass in the front yard, looking for any clue the intruder may have accidentally left behind the day before. She was trying to wear the girls out before bed and waste time until Jack got home from the McDaniels' house.

She scanned the glistening street and nearby intersection for the infamous brown car, then double-checked the girls, who had ventured into the garage and were gabbing like two housewives next to their dad's tool bench.

Her neck and shoulders ached from tension. *Stop it*, she scolded herself, realizing she'd brought on the nagging pain by stressing too much about this whole break-in thing. Half the reason she was outside now was to overcome her fear and try to convince herself that everything was okay, that the man wasn't nearby and was not coming back.

Mustn't let the girls know I'm frightened. Not like Mom …

Pamela's mother, Margaret, lived in utter fear. She worried in excess, about *everything*, and had as far back as Pamela could recall. It was even worse now. All day she was double-checking the door and window locks. She kept all the blinds closed, so they had to have lights on all the time. And when Pamela's father, Benjamin, was away, she would pace, peering out the windows and nipping at the peppermint schnapps she kept hidden away in the broom closet until he had safely returned home.

What is she so afraid of? Pamela wondered for the thousandth time. *Physical harm? Life without Dad? Loss of possessions? Death?*

Margaret and Benjamin had brought Pamela up attending the big stone church that smelled like mothballs on Monticello Boulevard in Cleveland Heights each week. But as she grew up, became a teen, went on to college, Pamela realized that her parents didn't bear much good fruit from the ritual. On the contrary, her dark household was often filled with strife, gossip, and bitterness. The ritual of church had not delivered the goods, and for a long time Pamela had resented church and the God who supposedly dwelled there.

Meeting Jack had changed that. He had waltzed into her life like a vision, with a jovial countenance and graceful stability unmatched by any man she'd ever known. She not only wanted him, she wanted what he had—an uncanny, unabashed faith in God that seemed to serve as some magical, hidden reservoir of everything that was happy and good. The only chink in Jack's armor during their first months of dating had appeared one breezy summer night.

They'd attended a Cleveland Indians game and were leaving early because the contest was a blowout. As they headed to Jack's car in the vast parking lot, not far from the Lake Erie shoreline, they heard a woman screaming. Walking quickly toward the shouts, they saw a brawny, bearded man in a cowboy hat, obviously drunk, twisting his girlfriend's arm and shoving her toward his pickup truck, yelling obscenities. With the agility of a leopard, Jack locked Pamela in his car, zigzagged between vehicles, and zeroed in on the helpless woman, who had dropped to her knees in an attempt to keep from being forced into the truck.

As far as Pamela could tell from her vantage point several cars away, there was no talk, no arguing, not a word exchanged. Beneath the neon white parking lot lights she witnessed a barrage of swirling kicks, flying elbows, and compact punches that sent the drunk man's hat flipping into the air and his hairy head snapping back, back, back, until he literally left the ground with one last clobber.

Jack got in the car and drove without speaking. When Pamela pressed him, all he said was, "I don't like to see weaker people get bullied."

Eventually he told her that he'd learned to fight growing up near Columbus, hanging with an oddball group of characters who stayed out too late in the wrong parts of town. Beyond that, he insisted he and Pamela not speak of his temper anymore; he was embarrassed by his behavior and promised that would be the last time she would ever see him do such a thing.

And he'd been as good as his word. It had been years since she had seen him so much as look at another person with any kind of malice or vengeance—until, of course, the strange man broke into their home.

I just need to focus on God, like Jack does. Do something for someone else instead of focusing on myself.

She heard a car in the distance but decided to turn her back on it and head toward the house.

Enough of this fear. I'm a child of the King.

The sound of the car rolling slowly down the street grew louder, closer, and slower. She ignored the urge to look.

I have a Protector. A High Tower ...

"Hey, girls." Pamela felt the relief from the afternoon sun the instant she set foot in the garage. "Daddy will be home soon. Let's go in and start dinner, okay?"

"What're we having?" asked Faye.

"I thought we'd do some chicken nuggets and green beans. And we have a great big watermelon too. How does that sound?"

While the girls began bubbling about nuggets and watermelon, Pamela recognized the distinct sound of a car bumping over the entry to their driveway. She spun around.

A black Trenton City police car rolled in.

Her legs got rubbery, and a wave of the unknown seemed to lift her head two feet above the rest of her body.

Did they catch the guy?

The police car came to a halt, still running hard, fan in overdrive, air conditioner dripping steadily onto the white concrete. Although the windows were dark and sealed shut, she could make out two officers in front.

Maybe he's in the backseat and they want me to identify him? Would they do that?

The car shut off and the front doors opened, almost at the same time. Two officers in dark uniforms unfolded from the car. The driver was a thin older man, sunburned, wearing black sunglasses. His partner looked like a kid, medium build, light complexion, mustache, same dark sunglasses, but he took his off as he approached Pamela.

"Good afternoon," he said. "Mrs. Crittendon?"

"Yes?" She automatically put an arm around each of the girls. "Is this about the break-in?"

The officers looked at each other momentarily, then back at her.

"Is your husband Jack Crittendon?" the older officer asked in a deep voice.

"Yes … is everything okay?" She clutched the girls tighter. "He's not hurt, is he?"

"No, ma'am," the younger one said.

"Oh, thank goodness." Her head whirled.

"Is he home?" the younger one continued.

"No. He's on his way. What's this about?"

The young officer looked at Rebecca, then Faye, then back to Pamela. "If we could have some privacy, Mrs. Crittendon, that would probably be good."

Privacy? What for?

None of it was making sense.

"Girls"—she knelt to their level—"why don't you go in and set the table for Mommy, okay? And when you're done—"

"Daddy!" Rebecca yelled and lurched toward the street.

Jack's green Jetta jerked to a halt at the curb. He was out in an instant. "What's wrong? You okay?" He ran up the driveway, looking at them, then trying to see into the police car. "Did he come back?"

"Daddy!" Faye ran to him, and he scooped her up. Rebecca attached herself to his leg.

"It's okay, honey." Pamela got to him quickly as well and rubbed his arms. "We're fine, everything's fine. He hasn't been back. These officers just pulled in before you got here."

He closed his eyes, dropped his head, and exhaled. Then he looked up at the older officer. "What's going on? Did they catch the guy?"

Again the officers glanced at each other.

"You're Jack Crittendon?" the older one asked.

"Yeah." He nodded and squeezed Pamela's arm. "You've met Pamela, my wife? We had the break-in yesterday."

"We don't know about a break-in," said the older officer, still wearing the black sunglasses. "We're here on other business. I'm Officer Potanski, and this is Officer Nielson."

"Mrs. Crittendon," said Officer Nielson, "you may want to have the girls set that table now."

All Pamela could do for a frozen moment was stare at him, knowing her mouth was hanging open but unable to close it or move.

What else has that maniac done?

"We'll be inside in a few minutes, ladies." Jack ushered the girls into the house. "Set the table and play. See you in a little bit."

Jack shut the door behind them and returned to Pamela and the officers.

"What's going on?" he said.

"Mr. and Mrs. Crittendon, we received a tip from an anonymous caller." Officer Potanski tucked his thumbs in his black belt. "Mr. Crittendon has been accused of dealing in child pornography. Buying. Selling. Possibly trafficking."

The officer's mouth was still moving but his voice went to mute.

Pamela's eyes closed as if slamming a gate.

Crazy black scribbling and angry scratching filled the tablet of her mind.

Her head buzzed with static … *loud* static she turned *up, up, up* so as not to hear any more.

8

They took Jack's laptop, and they took Jack.

Thankfully, they had let him drive his own car to the station. Pam did not want to explain to their neighbors why they saw Jack hauled off in handcuffs by the police.

Hours later, an ashen Pam showed up at Trenton City police headquarters downtown and settled into the chair next to him in a cramped, dingy yellow room with badly stained gold carpet and the overpowering smell of salami.

"Girls are fine," she whispered, out of breath. "Darlene's with them at the house. She'll put them down. Tommy will come over if we're here long. Everything's fine."

Jack nodded as she wrapped her cold hands around his wrist. She was trembling and pale, her lips almost purple. He couldn't imagine what she must be thinking.

"All righty." The older officer, Potanski, reentered the room, holding something wrapped in wax paper that looked as if it had been kicked around the floor of a subway at rush hour.

He was followed by Officer Nielson, who jabbed the record button on a desktop recorder and slumped into a seat next to Jack and Pam.

"At initial glance," Potanski said, "we've got ourselves a *ton* of pornographic images of minors on your laptop, Mr. Crittendon."

For about the third time since meeting the two officers, Jack thought he might throw up.

"And that's just what Officer Nielson and I found," Potanski said. "Our experts will be able to find things no one can hide."

The tips of Pam's fingers seemed to bare claws and dig into Jack's arm. His tongue and throat felt as though they were coated with acid.

"The informant who phoned us told us where to look for the images on your hard drive." Potanski bit a large hunk of what turned out to be a salami sandwich, a dab of bright yellow mustard remaining at the corner of his mouth. "This individual—"

"Where?" Jack objected.

Pam squeezed his arm, urging him to stay cool.

He lowered his voice. "Where were they on the computer?"

"Most of them were within files labeled Family Outing," Nielson said.

"How would the informant know that?" Jack said. "If he knows a person downloads child porn, that's one thing, but to know *which folders* the porn is stored in? He'd have to be sitting at the person's computer to know that. And that's what happened! I'm telling you, the guy who broke in did this—"

"The informant told us"—Potanski raised his voice to drown Jack out—"that you mentioned—*with a laugh*—that you *always* store your kiddy pictures in folders marked in some way or other with the word *family*."

"He's sick!" Jack said. "This guy is framing me for some reason."

And I will destroy that slug if I ever get my hands on him.

"The photos are disturbing." Potanski pushed the last of the sandwich into his mouth with his thumb and middle finger. "Hard-core would be putting it mildly." He wadded the wax paper, dropped it in the trash, and moved around a small metal desk. Flipping the chair around, he sat in it backward. The leathery skin around his eyes, where the sunglasses had been, was almost white compared with the rest of his narrow face, which was the color of very rare steak.

He examined Pam, then Jack, with sad-looking watery blue eyes. "Based on the bits and pieces we've heard from you, Mr. Crittendon, I think I know how you're going to answer this, but tell us, for the record—did you have anything *at all* to do with these pornographic images on your laptop?"

Jack's mouth was a sealed slit. His cheeks burned with indignation. He shook his head. "No, sir. Absolutely nothing."

"You have suggested that the images were planted on your computer," Nielson said. "Can you explain that, briefly?"

"Yes." Jack gave one definitive nod, lowering his head all the way to his chest. He sat up on the edge of his chair. "Our house was broken into yesterday by a man my wife saw, who had a large bag with him when he entered. He not only took valuables and personal items, but now we're thinking he may have left some things behind that he brought with him in the bag. I believe he got on my laptop when he was in the house and dumped the pornography onto it from some sort of mini storage device."

"And you say Officer DeVry is overseeing the invasion of your home?"

"Dennis DeVry, that's right. His artist created a sketch of the intruder."

"We got that this morning," Nielson said to Potanski.

"Much of the place was dusted for prints," Jack said. "The man wore gloves; we're not sure if he ever took them off. I'm thinking he may have had to in order to use the touchpad on the laptop."

"Our people will dust it," Nielson said. "And our computer guys will go over it with a fine-tooth comb."

"Now the question is whether to arrest and hold you until our people find out more about where the porn came from, when, how … all the rest of it." Potanski's eyes took Jack apart, one layer at a time, and Jack just prayed the man was a good judge of character. "They'll find out everything and then some, I promise you."

"And I promise you, I'm innocent." Jack met Potanski's glare with his own.

Someone's cell phone rang. Nielson's. He answered simply by stating his last name. "Hold on." He handed the phone to Potanski. "Officer DeVry."

Good. Jack squeezed Pam's hand, then remembered that DeVry wasn't up-to-date on the missing Bible.

"Oh." Jack held up a hand. "Can I say one thing to him?" He reached for the phone. "It's about something more my wife discovered about the break-in … please."

Potanski swung his head lazily toward Nielson, closed his eyes, and stuck the phone out to Jack, who told the officer about the missing Bible. When he was finished, Jack handed the cell back to Potanski, who put it to his ear, said, "I shall return" and left the room.

It was quiet and close in that little room.

Nielson stopped the recorder with the jab of a button.

Jack felt an initial pang of guilt for not being with Rebecca and Faye, but when he remembered they were with Darlene and Tommy, he was relieved—the girls wouldn't even think of Mommy and Daddy while they had the fun neighbors over. Tommy and Darlene had never been able to have children, and they were close to Rebecca and Faye. Darlene would give them whatever they wanted, and Tommy would let them stay up way too late. The girls would be in heaven.

"Officer Potanski will get more of the scoop about the home invasion from Officer DeVry," Nielson said, "and we'll take it from there."

Jack debated how to phrase what he was thinking. It was a question. But it was also a plea. "You won't arrest me, will you?"

Nielson's almost gray eyes widened for an instant and he leaned forward, resting his elbows on his knees and joining his fingers in the steeple position in front of his mouth. "Don't know yet. You have no record—that's a big plus. You seem like an honest family man. You have little girls of your own. We're not *obligated* to arrest you, if that's what you're wondering."

Every part of Jack's body went limp. Pam covered his hand in hers and nodded at him, almost in tears.

"I'm not promising anything," Nielson said. "Officer Potanski's ultimately in charge. We'll see what he learns from DeVry. All I'm saying is, if something doesn't feel right to us about arresting you, if we just don't buy the charges, if we believe there's a good chance the porn was planted—we can make the decision to let you go and continue the investigation. We confiscate the evidence now, which in this case is your laptop. And we keep watching, we observe, we see what our computer experts say."

Jack dropped back in his chair for the first time all evening, locking his hands behind his head. He closed his eyes. *This is happening for a reason. I know it is. Help me, Lord. Find favor on me. Protect us …*

"I'm going to call Darlene," Pam whispered to Jack as she stood. "Check on the girls."

"Okay." He leaned his head back so he could see her standing above him. "Tell them I love 'em."

She squeezed his shoulders then quietly moved toward the door.

"Oops." Officer Potanski barged in just then, handed the cell phone to Nielson, and made his way back to his chair. "Okay, Officer DeVry filled me in on all the details, the items stolen from your home, all that."

Pam scooted back to her seat. Jack sat to attention. She clasped one of his hands.

"Did he tell you about our daughter's missing locket," Jack said, "and how he cut me out of one of our wedding pictures?"

"All that." Potanski waved, put a fist to his mouth, stiffened, and belched silently. "This is when our police sense really needs to kick in." He looked at Nielson, then Jack. "I'm confident these charges merit further investigation, so I'm not going to make an arrest at this time—that is, if you agree to be completely cooperative with us."

Jack let out a lungful of air and nodded heartily. Pam leaned into him, wrapping her arms around his waist and squeezing.

"Keep in mind, we have the goods on you," Potanski continued. "We can pick you up anytime—tomorrow, next week, next month. Our case will still be good because of the evidence we have, so we have no worries there. What I'm saying is, I'm willing to listen to you, be sensitive to your circumstances, and give you the benefit of the doubt—but when I call, you better pick up the phone. In fact, every time I call you'd better kill yourself to get to the phone. And if you ever lie to me, I will hammer you."

It was past ten o'clock by the time Jack walked Pam to her red Accord on the third floor of the dimly lit city parking garage and saw her off. He waited forever for the ancient elevator, took it down to the main floor, and found the Jetta by beeping its alarm from the remote.

He and Pam had agreed not to try to follow each other, because it was only about a fifteen-minute drive home and Jack needed to concentrate on a call he had to make to his editor. As he zipped down Washington Street toward the interstate, he saw a fissure of lightning off to the left, followed by a loud rumble of thunder. The humidity must've been close to a hundred percent. Raindrops began tapping his windshield.

"Where have you been?" Cecil Barton's jarring voice forced Jack's hand to his left ear.

He turned the volume down on the Bluetooth speaker attached to the visor above his head.

"Derrick had to finish the water-rate-hike piece, and I'm going crazy here wondering what's going on with the missing pastor story. Is your voice mail working? I've left messages. What the heck is happening with you, Crittendon?"

Jack explained about the evening's long meeting with the police, the accusations, and the break-in.

"For the love of peace, why didn't you tell me about all this?" Cecil said.

"I thought you knew about the break-in."

"No one told me! Derrick said you had some kind of minor emergency. I thought one of the girls skinned a knee for Pete's sake—a home invasion? With Pam and the children there? You should have come to me."

"You had your game face on."

"We could have had the sketch of that low-life in today's edition. You get it to me, pronto. We'll get it in ASAP."

"I thought we only did that for murder cases."

"And low-life slugs who invade the homes of my reporters!"

For once Jack didn't have a comeback for Cecil. Goose bumps rose on his arms and gave his entire frame a chill. It was one of the few times his editor had shown any sort of personal interest or commitment, and it felt good.

Jack filled Cecil in on his interview with Wendy McDaniel and informed him of his plans to go to Five Forks Methodist Church the following day to talk to as many people as possible. He planned to have an in-depth story for Cecil by that evening's deadline.

The rain came harder. Jack signed off with Cecil and flipped the wipers to high, slowing well below the speed limit on Highway 16. He chastised himself for not having replaced Pam's wipers; the last time he rode with her in the rain they streaked like crazy. He contemplated calling her to tell her about Cecil volunteering to run the police sketch of their intruder but didn't want to take her concentration off the road.

They would nail this guy, he was confident, and then it would all be nothing more than a weird memory. He just prayed it would happen sooner rather than later. At least he and Pam had each other. They'd be together tonight, with the girls, all under one roof. Not so for Wendy McDaniel and her boys. They didn't have a daddy at home tonight. In spite of Wendy's reservations about suicide, the evidence was difficult to deny—missing meds, gun and ammo, farewell note.

Wendy might be a widow right now and not even know it.

And those boys—no father …

His cell rang, and Pam's photo came up. While creeping along in the pelting rain, dodging lake-size puddles, Jack hit *answer* on the phone, and Pam's voice came over the Bluetooth speaker above his head.

"I'm going to beat you," she said.

"Where are you?" He gripped the wheel tight. "I just passed Sergeant Road."

"Sergeant?" She paused. "I didn't take 16. I'm going White Pond."

"White Pond? Shoot, I just assumed you'd take the highway. Is it raining where you are?"

"Not bad yet, but I need new wipers."

"I know. That's my bad. I've been meaning to do it."

"We've been a little busy …"

"It's a gusher here," Jack said. "Sounds like you took the right route."

"I told you, you should have followed me. Whoa!"

"What?"

"Some idiot just passed me."

"On that road? Was it a double-yellow line?"

"No, but it's no place to pass," Pam said. "Everybody's in a big hurry."

"Hey, Cecil's gonna run the police sketch on the front page."

"You're kidding me. You asked him?"

"No! He volunteered it. He actually sounded concerned."

"Come on," Pam said. "What are you doing? This is ridiculous—"

"What?" Jack said.

"The guy who passed me is riding his brakes all of a sudden."

"He's probably looking for a street."

"There aren't any streets out here."

"Where are you?"

"Almost to the bridge, by the river."

"Just be patient."

"He's starting and stopping, right in the middle of the road."

"Keep your distance. Your tires aren't that great."

He reminded himself to do new wipers *and* tires, all at once.

"If you get home first," Pam said, "hurry up and relieve Darlene and Tommy. They've been there forever. Tell them we owe them dinner."

"Knowing them, the girls are probably up partying."

"You have *got* to be kidding me. He's stopped!" she yelled. "We're right in the middle of the bridge and this guy is stopping his car."

Jack could picture the bridge's enormous rusty metal girders and rivets the size of baseballs. He'd done several stories on it, because the

Lincolntown River tended to swell and flood near the bridge. Big local issue.

"There is no way. I think he put it in park," Pam said. "What the …"

"Is there something in front of his car? Maybe he can't get across."

"The other lane's clear, he could go around. Oh wow, it's raining hard now. You almost home? I just wanna make sure everything's okay with the girls."

"I'll be there in a few," Jack said. "No worries. Rain's letting up a little here. What's going on with that guy?"

Jack could hear the rain ticking the roof of Pam's car.

"Pam?"

Nothing.

"Pam?"

He turned up the volume.

"Pam? Answer me!"

"Oh my gosh, Jack!" she screamed. *"It's him!"*

Something jolted the inside of Jack's chest, like a gong being struck by a sledgehammer. His insides went hollow and waves of electricity vibrated down his arms and out his empty fingertips.

"How do you know?" he barked. "What's he doing?"

"It's his car. Oh dear God, Jack … *he's getting out!*"

9

"Are you sure?" Jack's words were clipped, fierce.

One glance at the husky body as it emerged from the brown car ... the black clothes ... the boots ...

"Yes!" Headlights glared in her rearview mirror. "I'm blocked in!"

Lock doors, lock doors ...

She let the phone slip away and felt her armrest for the door-lock button.

The stranger hunched over in the driving rain and did a hop-skip-jog directly toward her.

His trot was more agile than she would have expected, with one blocky white hand above his small eyes.

She looked down for the lock button on the armrest, but the interior was black. Her fingers traced the small panel of buttons.

Jack's tinny voice chirped from somewhere on the floor.

Every organ in her pounded.

He was almost there.

Her mind seared white and she hit a button.

The window behind her buzzed down.

No!

Cold rain blew in.

Her fingertips danced over the buttons, and she hit another.

The passenger window dropped five inches.

"Pamela." He was there. Bulky. Immovable. Reaching for her door handle.

Saying her name?

Cold air and rain swept in as he pulled open her door. He smelled like an ashtray.

"I've never forgotten you, Pammy Wagner ..."

Her maiden name?

She pinched her door handle with ten adrenaline-laced fingertips and slammed the door shut.

His head cocked back with a laugh.

She jammed another button.

All four locks clicked.

The smirk on his face disappeared.

Window behind you ... get it up.

His mammoth body shifted like a cat.

He reached for her!

His hand was rough, cold, wet. It slimed her cheek and pinched the back of her neck. She jerked forward, but he caught her hair, and she screamed.

Jack's voice echoed in rage from the phone on the floor.

She jammed the button for the back window with her left hand and smashed the horn with the other. And kept smashing.

His tiny eyes swelled at the continuous blare, and his small mouth curved sour. Her hair went free as his hand banged its way out. The window sealed shut.

Thank God for the horn.

People will come …

He turned toward the cars behind her.

Did they understand she was in trouble? Would they call the police?

Headlights rose up and doused him in a flood of white neon. His dirty red hair was matted and twisted against his wide forehead. Rain dripped from his hooked nose. "I don't want to hurt you," he yelled.

The headlights rolled off him.

No, don't leave!

Horns honked behind her.

The freak bent over, and his enormous shoulders and ghastly face filled her window again. Inches from her. Dripping. Sweating. Every pore oozing evil.

"I want to take care of you … and Rebecca and Faye."

How dare you!

Something deep within her blazed, and she reeled around.

She wanted to hurt him—this bizarre, disgusting *thing* that had used names he should not know, names he had no right to utter.

Rain sheered in from the still-open passenger window.

The man retreated toward his car, turning to say one last thing, pointing at her, orange eyebrow arched, his mouth moving as it would in a civilized discussion, as if she was supposed to understand. *A threat?*

It didn't matter. She'd had enough.

Methodically, she reached for the gear shift, slick from the rain, pinched the button, and clicked it to the illuminated R.

The car behind her was trying to go around, but she cut it off by backing into its path.

She could barely breathe. Her insides pumped liked pistons in a roaring engine.

The stranger was almost to the door of his car.

Pamela quickened her movements, jamming the shifter to the D, getting the car rolling.

Her headlights hit him, and he looked at her, frozen for an instant. His tiny eyes flared. He moved fast for his door handle.

She gunned it. Her car seemed to rise from the wet pavement, heated, lurching for the fiendish man.

He slipped into the brown car just in time, his door banging open, then shut again. She just missed him, then slammed the brake to the floor, sliding and bending to a stop ten feet past his car.

She sat still, blocking the left lane, fingers stapled to the steering wheel, hands vibrating. A booming echo pulsating in her ears.

He could have shot forward in the right lane, slipped past her, and taken off—but his car did not move.

His car was to the right, behind her, purring like a black cat with shiny eyes, kneading its paws, wiggling its hips, poised to pounce.

She couldn't go forward because he'd just follow her. Why hadn't she gotten his plates when she was behind him?

Stupid, stupid ...

She had to reach the phone. Get Jack. Call the police.

The bridge was blocked. Other cars were still there. Jack would be there soon. Surely someone had called the police.

His car inched closer.

Pamela's heart coiled like a tension-riddled steel spring. She slammed her left palm on the horn and kept it there.

If she didn't move her car, he was going to plow it into the steel rails of the bridge. But if she was going to drive, she had to get hold of the phone …

She jabbed the button for the overhead light, spotted the phone on the floor, bent, stretched, and snatched it.

His car was so close to hers she couldn't even see its headlights.

"Jack?" She put the phone to her ear.

The connection was gone.

The rain had slowed. Just as she was about to lift her foot from the brake and drive forward over the bridge, the man reappeared at the front of her car, lit up by headlights like a villain on stage.

Something flashed in his hand.

Knife.

He bent at her front-right fender and his elbow began flailing, as if he was beating someone …

Had someone approached to help, and he was pounding the tar out of him?

She didn't want to move the car because she thought someone was up there, close to the front fender.

But, no …

The car rocked, then a hiss …

Just as the villain stood, winded, and stuck his mammoth chest out with a proud smirk, she realized he had punctured her tire.

He pointed the blade directly at her, with his fist above it, like a fencer preparing to spear his victim. His wet head moved back and forth in the rain. He shouted, "Pamela, you were the only one!"

Go!

Her brain sent the message to drive—*Run him down! Get away while he's out of his car!*—but her body bogged down. She examined the phone in her hand, but everything in her was crisscrossing and misfiring, and she just sat, immobilized, like an overmedicated blob.

His eyes moved from her and settled on something to her right.

She followed them to her still-open passenger window. *"No!"*

His arm was in. He patted savagely for the unlock button. "I'm not going to hurt you," he yelled.

Pamela lifted both knees, swiveled on her rear, and bashed his arm with every muscle she could recruit. Drawing her legs back quickly, like machine parts, so he couldn't grab her, she did it again … *bam* … and again. Like a shovel smashing a rotten log.

One after another, the kicks landed.

Don't slow down … he'll grab you …

Suddenly—like a shark inexplicably turning and swimming away from its prey—the arm slinked out of the window.

Everything slammed eerily still.

Blue lights danced off the bridge like the reflection of water by a pool at night and filled the interior of the car.

Police.

Pamela had kicked her way onto her back. Drenched in sweat, she forced herself to breathe, grabbed the steering wheel, and pulled herself up.

His car hurled backward, did a one-eighty, and spun to a stop facing the opposite direction.

She made out three letters on the Ohio license plate: CVJ.

But with a slight skid and a squeal, the car's tires found road, gripped, and sent the stranger sailing into the night, past two Trenton City police cars just arriving at the bridge.

10

A day and a half had passed since Pam's run-in with the stalker at the bridge. She'd barely eaten since, and she looked it. She and Jack had been chilled to the bone to realize the man knew Pam's name, and the girls', which made the crimes eerily personal.

Police were running the letters Pam had remembered from the guy's plates, and the report about Jack's laptop was still forthcoming. Cecil had not only kept good on his promise to run the sketch of the intruder in the *Dispatch*, he offered to let Jack work from home temporarily.

Jack went to say good-bye to Pam before heading out for his appointment with Pastor Satterfield and found her alone in the study, curled up with one of her old Bibles. Her face was gaunt, her eyes glassy; she sniffed and clutched a fistful of tissues.

"You okay?"

She turned to him with tired eyes. "Just need this time."

"The girls are watching cartoons, you're fine."

He crept in and sat on the ottoman next to her. He covered her hand with his, and they talked quietly. It crossed his mind to pray with her, but he dismissed the thought. He wasn't feeling very spiritual. Besides, Pam was being spiritual enough for both of them.

Jack hadn't seen her without a Bible since the night at the bridge. She had been jotting down scripture on the back of his old business cards and glancing at them while busy in the kitchen or playing with the girls. And though she hadn't said anything, he quickly figured out she was fasting. The incident had numbed her. Her movements were slow and contemplative. She listened intently and spoke less, not depressed or sedate, but reflective.

"I'll be back here as soon as I can, okay?" he said.

"We're fine—really."

They agreed to say nothing about the man to Pam's parents. If her mother knew what was going on, they would most assuredly need to get her a rubber room at the nearest asylum.

As he waited to interview Dr. Andrew Satterfield in his frigid office at Five Forks Methodist Church, Jack shivered and shifted uncomfortably in his chair.

Satterfield's office looked and smelled as if it had just received several thick coats of Sherwin-Williams' brightest white paint. A wide window overlooking dense green woods made it even brighter. The long, shiny reddish wood desk in front of Jack held only a small calendar, pen holder, stapler, calculator, notepad, and telephone— each placed precisely in the form of an arch. There were no folders or coffee mugs or papers or any sign of "real work." Behind the desk was a matching credenza, dust-free, not a thing on it—no photos, no children's artwork, no computer, no hint of Satterfield's personal life.

Church secretary Barbara Cooley, a heavyset redhead wearing an electrifying blue dress, a necklace of large faux pearls and matching earrings, and thick red lipstick, had led Jack to Satterfield's office and assured him the associate pastor would join Jack shortly. While they chatted, Jack confirmed that Mrs. Cooley had seen Pastor Evan McDaniel the morning of his disappearance. She agreed to speak with Jack when he was finished with Satterfield.

Jack didn't know whether he was shivering because it was freezing in the office or because he was uptight about leaving the girls alone. So much for his simplistic theory about the intruder being a drug addict on a mindless binge; the man had proven himself much more menacing. Now Jack was the one talking about purchasing a gun. He had discussed it with Officer DeVry the morning after the bridge incident. DeVry was neutral on the topic, but this time it had been Pam who hesitated.

"Let's wait," she said.

"Wait ... for what?" Jack said. "For him to kidnap you, or one of the girls? This guy's certified nuts, Pam. He's liable to do anything. If he comes on our property again, we need to be prepared."

It was the same argument Pam had pleaded days earlier.

But something had changed in her since the night on the bridge. Her silence, her quiet determination ... it spoke volumes. It whispered to him that they had all the protection they needed, if they would only believe.

But this guy was crazy ... and he might come back.

Does God not know that? Jack chastised himself. If the guy was insane, did that make God any less effective in protecting them?

The heat gets turned up, and you're going to take matters into your own hands?

Jack pictured the Gadarene demoniac from the Bible, rushing from his home among the tombs to the shoreline where he confronted Jesus. The dude wore no clothes, and no one could subdue him. They tried, but he tore the chains and broke the irons.

Jesus sent the man's demons fleeing into a herd of pigs.

This guy haunting us must have demons, Jack thought.

He envisioned himself squaring off with the stalker in their front yard at night. Could he rebuke the man's evil spirits? Would God give him the power? Or would Jack pull out a semiautomatic, the one he couldn't stop thinking about, and blow the guy to kingdom come? Or would he beat the scum to a pulp with his bare hands?

Jack detected the odor of manufactured nylon and polyester, and determined that the spotless wall-to-wall short-pile maroon carpet beneath his feet must be brand-new. He could still smell the glue and noticed several tiny pieces of cut carpet along the gray baseboard.

A number of framed objects leaned against the walls, waiting to be hung. Two were Satterfield's degrees from Dallas Theological Seminary; another was a Bible verse, penned exquisitely in bold calligraphy: *And let us not be weary in well doing: for in due season we shall reap, if we faint not —Galatians 6:9.* Next was a painting of a fly fisherman wading in a shady river. Last was a painting of a mean-looking Jesus in the sky, surrounded by ominous gray clouds, with hundreds of people cowering on the ground below.

Voices came from a distance down the hallway, getting clearer as they drew closer.

"You have lunch at twelve thirty with the elders." It was Barbara Cooley's voice. "At two you have the contemporary worship director. At three it's Benevolence Committee—"

"Tell me the rest later," a male voice said, just outside the door. "I've kept this gentleman waiting long enough."

Dr. Satterfield blew into the office clutching a black laptop and an eyeglasses case. He wore dark green slacks, a white button-down shirt, and a khaki sports jacket, and he smelled like the antiseptic Pam used to clean her face.

"Hello, hello." He whisked past Jack without shaking hands, curved around the desk, and set his glasses case down precisely in line with the other items on the desk's surface. "You shall have my full attention in *un momento*. I am Five Forks' associate pastor, Dr. Andrew Satterfield."

With his back to Jack, the tall, thin man set his PC on the credenza, leaned back to examine how it sat, and with both thumbs adjusted it ever so slightly so the laptop was in perfect alignment with the front edge. He wore a sleek watch, no rings, and his hands were white and clean, nails trimmed up tight. He turned to face his guest. "And you must be Mr. Crotten—"

"Crittendon." Jack stood and—awkwardly clutching his pad, pen, and list of questions against his thighs—leaned over the desk to shake hands. "With the *Dispatch*."

Satterfield ignored Jack's hand, swung his fake leather maroon chair around, plopped down, wheeled up to the desk, placed his elbows on the surface, and locked his bony fingers.

"Tell me what I can do for you and our friends at the local fish wrapper, Mr. Crittendon."

Ignoring the dig, Jack explained concisely that his editor had learned of Pastor Evan's disappearance via *Faith Line* and that he had interviewed Wendy McDaniel. He let him know he'd obtained a copy of the letter Evan left behind and was there to find out as much as he could about the man's vanishing.

Jack left it open-ended, just to see what kind of a talker he had in Satterfield. He could ask some people one question and they would spill the entire can of beans; others required relentless prying just to retrieve yes and no answers.

"I don't believe I have a great deal more to add," said Satterfield. "The article you ran on the cover of the *Dispatch* the other day adequately summed it up. As that piece indicated, I don't think it's going to end pretty."

"It did surprise me," Jack said, "that the *Faith Line* article came right out and said that coworkers believed the pastor was 'genuinely determined,' I believe it said, to take his own life—"

"Ah-ah." Satterfield held up an index finger as if correcting a child. "Actually, what it said was that coworkers believed he was genuinely determined to follow through on his 'expressed intentions,' referring to the letter he left."

"So you *do* think he intends to commit suicide."

"You said you read the letter, did you not? And you know about the medications he took with him?"

"Not exactly. What more can you tell me about them?"

"Not long after Pastor McDaniel arrived here, I was somewhat shocked to learn that he had been seeing a psychiatrist. He told me he had struggled with long seasons of depression, as well as some anxiety. He said he was trying to get a grip on it with medication. He thought I should know."

"And that surprised you?"

"To say the least."

"Why?"

"Mr. Crittendon." Satterfield sighed and hunched over, as if Jack had zero common sense. "The job of pastor is that of a shepherd. It is a most sacred and sobering responsibility and one that must be held by men of *sound mind*. Is Evan a warm and generous man? Absolutely. Does he love the people of this congregation? Perhaps to a fault. But does he have the alert, sober mind of Christ? Is he prepared *at all times* to preach the Word, correct, rebuke, encourage? That is in question. And I've said as much both to him and our elders."

"It sounds as if you don't feel he's fit to be the pastor here."

Satterfield leaned forward, opened one of his desk drawers, snatched a sanitary wipe, and slathered his hands with it. "It's no secret I think Evan needs time away from the pastorate to deal with his psychological issues." After finishing with his hands, he wiped the arms of his chair, then meticulously rubbed the area in front of him on the desk and tossed the wipe in the trash can.

"When did you see him last?" Jack asked.

"Thursday. Day before he left," Satterfield said. "I saw him toward the end of the workday. He often seemed tired to me, low energy. I noticed nothing unusual. He came in the next day, Friday, early from what I understand, then disappeared."

Satterfield's elbows rested on the arms of his chair, and all ten of his fingertips touched each other. He glanced at his watch. "Now I do have a lunch appointment, so if we're about through …"

"Did he have appointments lined up for the day he went missing?" Jack asked.

"He did."

"Hospital visits?"

"And people recuperating at home."

"And he didn't make it to any of those?"

"Obviously not."

Smug fellow …

"Did he have enemies?"

Satterfield sighed. After a moment he said, "I think it's safe to say that all pastors, at least those who are upholding sound doctrine, are persecuted to some degree." He massaged his temples with two fingers on each side. "We've had our share of resentful, bitter congregants, but in my mind, none of those things are pertinent in Evan's disappearance."

"There was some church discipline invoked recently, involving a man named Hank …" Jack scoured his notes. "Garbenger."

Satterfield's eyes narrowed, and his mouth shrank to a slit. He wheeled backward in his chair. "What about it?"

"Could that have led to anything?" Jack said. "You know, a revenge-type thing against Evan?"

Satterfield closed his eyes and shook his head. "We deal with things like that all the time. That's what we do, sir. This is a hospital, a mending place, if you will. Frankly, I think you're looking for something that isn't there, Mr. Crittendon. In fact, I know you are." He examined his watch and tapped it. "I've really got to be moving along." He stood and came around the desk. "I hope I've been of assistance."

Still seated, Jack said, "If you don't mind, just one or two more quick things while I have you. Do you know what medications Pastor Evan had been taking? And do you know which ones he took with him?"

"Let's see." Satterfield crossed his arms. "Zoloft. Remeron. Effexor ... and good old Valium for the anxiety."

"And how do you know this?"

"He told me." Satterfield threw out his hands. "My first week on the job."

"And how do we know he took these drugs with him?"

"He kept them in a medicine cabinet in his office restroom. They were there. Now they're gone. Honestly, Mr. Crittendon, I'm bewildered at your line of questioning. Has something specific led you to believe Evan did *not* disappear with the intention of taking his own life?"

"Hold on just one second, sir." Jack finished scribbling what Satterfield had said and looked up at him. "His wife is as sure this *isn't* a suicide as you are that it is."

"I see." Satterfield's eyes went side to side, and he sucked in his cheeks. "That sounds like Wendy—blindly devoted to her man. It is indeed a sad case."

"So," Jack said, "is this a private bathroom we're talking about, in the pastor's office—where the medicine was kept?"

Satterfield looked at his watch again and seemed to deflate from exhaustion as he spoke. "It's a small lav right off his office, yes. Now I really must be shoving off."

Jack held up a finger, looked at his pad, and scrambled for a way to phrase his next question with kid gloves. But there was no gentle way. "So you look in his medicine cabinet? I mean, you must, in order to know—"

"Let me say something to you, sir." Satterfield bent over, his sour face within inches of Jack's; he smelled like rubbing alcohol. "I have a sacred responsibility to God and to this body of believers. It is a high calling and one which I hold with unflinching devotion. You can try all you want, for whatever reason, to make this *look* like something it is not, but I have been set apart to assist in protecting this flock, making certain no ravenous wolves sneak in to destroy the sheep. I will do whatever is necessary to fulfill my responsibilities before God. For that reason, I answer to no man, Mr. Crittendon, but only to God. But I don't suppose you would know anything about that."

Jack quickly finished writing, gathered his things in one fell swoop, and stood, feeling dizzy and disheveled from the scolding.

"I apologize." Satterfield wrung his hands. "I did not mean to bite your head off. I just don't think people understand sometimes the responsibility laid upon pastors; the Bible says we will be judged more severely. That's probably why Evan was in the state he was in. Dealing with other people's sins and baggage can be absolutely suffocating at times. I did not mean to insult you. Again, I hope you will accept my apology."

"I understand," Jack said. "This is a difficult time for the whole church." He did not attempt to shake with Satterfield, whose hands were conveniently stuffed in the pockets of his jacket.

Barbara Cooley was nibbling greasy potato chips and a bulky sandwich from her brown bag when Jack found his way back to her desk. "I'm sorry," she said with a mouthful of what smelled like tuna, "I wasn't sure when you'd be done."

"No, forgive me for interrupting your lunch," Jack said, still recovering from the weird session with Satterfield. "If you want, I can go find a place to work until you're finished." He was a bit anxious to call the house and make sure Pam was fine.

"Oh my, no." She giggled and with a napkin and two plump hands wiped her mouth and dabbed at her pink face. "I'm anxious to get this over with. We can go in this conference room right over here." She worked her way out of a little black chair on wheels, her thick legs and ample hips slowing her tremendously. She sneaked one more chip, twisted her brown bag closed, grabbed her can of Mr. Pibb, knocked the crumbs off her chest, and punched several buttons on the massive phone. "I'll set this to pick up for me, and we're good to go. You just follow me. I've been nervous as a cat about this."

Once they were settled in the conference room at a large glass table that accommodated twelve black executive chairs, Jack explained the story he was working on. As usual, he led with an open-ended question—this one about the last time she'd seen Pastor McDaniel.

"Evan and I are almost always the first to arrive." She spoke in an animated, somewhat secretive tone. "The morning he went missing I got here right around eight, and he came in at about a quarter after or so. That's pretty much the norm on Fridays."

"Did you talk to him when he came in?" Jack almost lost his train of thought due to the sucking noises Barbara was making as she polished her teeth with her tongue. "How did he seem to you?"

"That's just the thing." Her bright eyes darted about as if she was searching out eavesdroppers. "He seemed somewhat morose to me. Now don't get me wrong, Evan is never one to get overly excited about anything. He's always very, how do I say it, even-keeled, low-key. But

that morning"—her cheeks scrunched up and she shook her head—
"something seemed to have him in a funk."

"Did he say what was bothering him?"

"We talked just a little while the coffee was brewing in the break
room," she said. "I asked if he was all ready for his visitations that day
and he said he was. I remember, he asked me what I did on my day
off, and I told him my husband, Virgil, took me to the dollar theater
to see Sandra Bullock's new movie. I just love her. And they have a
bottomless bucket of popcorn, all-you-can-eat for $4.99. Anyway,
that's all I really recall discussing."

Barbara was turning out to be a talker, and that was fine with Jack.

"And he left, supposedly to make those visits, at what time?"

"I've been racking my brain about that, knowing you'd ask. I
didn't actually see him leave the building. I must have been away
from my desk, either at the restroom, running copies, or talking to
someone. But I'm guessing it was right around nine fifteen, give or
take a few minutes."

"So there were other people in the office by then?"

"Oh yeah, quite a few. We have a big staff. A lot of people get
here around nine. Patrick Ashdown was here. He's our director of
contemporary worship. He did say hi to Evan. Rhonda Lowe was
here—another receptionist. She saw him briefly as well."

"Can you do me a favor?"

"I can sure try."

"Can you send an email blast to the staff and let them know
I'm interested in communicating with anyone who interacted with
Evan that morning or who may be able to give any insight about his
disappearance?"

Barbara borrowed a sheet of paper from Jack's pad and wrote herself a note. "That I can do."

"Just give them my email address and cell number." Jack scribbled those on her paper. "Tell me," he continued, "who found the note in Evan's office?"

"I did!" Her eyes grew. "I saw it on his keyboard that morning but didn't think a thing about it—can you imagine? Anyway, later, when we started getting calls from his missed appointments, I kind of scoured his desk to see if I could find any hint about where he might be. That's when I opened it."

"What did you make of the note?"

She shook her head, filled her cheeks with air like balloons, then squirted the air through pinched lips to generate the wet noise a child might make. "I don't know what to tell you. They say you never really know a man—and I believe that, Mr. Crittendon. How do you know what a person's like behind closed doors? You know what I mean? What he's going through on the inside?"

She clutched her Mr. Pibb close to her chest. "Evan may well have been struggling more than any of us knew." She glanced around, then whispered, "They say he was on Prozac. But let me tell you something. No matter what anyone says, Evan's the most loving person around here. You get what I'm saying?"

Jack leaned in close. "Wendy McDaniel says there's no way her husband committed suicide."

"Poor Wendy—and those boys." Barbara tilted her head and pulled at her orange hair in different places. "I cannot fathom what they're going through. Just the not knowing."

"Do *you* think this is a suicide?"

For the first time since they had begun to talk, Barbara froze. She stared at Jack and finally said, "I have to say yes, simply because of the letter. And the drugs he took with him. I hate it, but again, we just don't know people. Man looks at the outward appearance, but God sees the heart. I guess Evan's heart was very troubled."

"Did he have enemies?"

Her lips formed a frown.

"Anyone really mad at him?" Jack probed.

"Not really. Not that I can think of."

"What about Hank Garbenger?"

"Oh jeepers." Barbara rolled her eyes. "That was a fiasco. Hank was angry at the whole church—the whole world. The leaders disciplined him for cheating on Audrey, his wife."

"Didn't Evan kind of spearhead that whole thing?"

"Evan was going to handle it privately. Dr. Satterfield, on the other hand, insisted the only biblical response was to take two elders and warn Hank and, if it continued—which it did—to invoke church discipline."

"It *is* biblical, what they did."

"It is. And Evan handled it like a pro. He was firm but compassionate. Anyway, naturally Hank was mad—and embarrassed. Sheesh. If it had been me, I would've moved to Montana."

Jack wanted to ask if Hank was mad enough to hurt Evan, but the notion was just plain far-fetched. Jack couldn't help it; as long as he could remember he'd had a hyper-suspicious mind. Occasionally it empowered him to break the big story, but more often it caused him to waste a great deal of time, fall into trouble and embarrassment, and perform exercises in futility.

"Hmm." Jack contemplated what more to ask.

"Satterfield is always prodding Evan," said Barbara. "Always challenging him to live up to this lofty standard he has of what a pastor should be. Evan takes it with a grain of salt." She leaned across the table and whispered, "He has a lot more patience than I do. Pastor Evan is a humble, wise man. He has his doctorate degree too, you know. But he's just not the type to go around hanging it on the wall and insisting everyone call him 'doctor.'"

Point taken.

"Anything else out of the ordinary going on with Evan? Anything at all?"

Barbara's eyes fell to the table, as if she'd been inches from escaping the interview unscathed only to hit a nasty snag as they drew to a close. She glanced out the door of the conference room, then leveled her gaze on Jack.

"You won't print any of this?" she whispered.

"Not if you don't want me to."

"I don't. This is something I've tossed and turned over. I wasn't going to mention it, but I don't want to regret not saying anything."

"Off the record it is."

She cleared her throat. "Pastor Evan has a heart the size of Texas, okay? He's always giving, always going the extra mile for everyone. But sometimes, well, he's been known to make appointments that could look, if you didn't know him, they could look suspicious."

"In what way?" Jack asked.

Barbara pushed all ten of her bright red fingernails onto the table in front of her. "I'm talking about appointments with women." She tilted her head up to the ceiling and raised a hand. "Lord, forgive me if I'm saying anything I shouldn't." Then back at Jack. "He meets one-on-one with women, to counsel them, and it just doesn't look right. Dr. Satterfield has questioned him on it. He's warned Pastor Evan that it's an absolute no-no in ministry. But Pastor Evan just goes along his merry way. Sometimes I think he's incredibly naive—"

"Where are these meetings?"

"On occasion at coffee shops. But mostly in his office."

"Door open? Door closed?"

Her eyes darted about. "A little of each."

"With any one woman in particular?"

Her hands gripped her elbows and she leaned on the table and rocked back and forth. "I can't say that. I just can't say." Her cheeks flushed like a paper towel absorbing cranberry juice. "It seems so … condemning."

Jack waited and nodded, figuring his silence would be all Barbara would need to continue with her suspicions.

He was right.

"There's a widow who goes here," she said. "Her name's Sherry Pendergrass. Beautiful blonde. Her husband, Joel, passed away about a year ago. Very wealthy people. Anyway, Pastor Evan has been meeting with her for quite some time, following Joel's death, of course."

"How often?"

"Once a week, usually Wednesdays. Sometimes they move it to another day, if there's a conflict. But it's been very regular for quite some time."

"And these appointments are on his calendar? I mean, he didn't try to hide them?"

"Oh, no." She shook her head. "It's all right there on his calendar for anybody to see. Probably completely innocent."

Jack sensed she didn't believe that.

"Since when?" he asked.

Barbara shook her head. "I can check his calendar, but I'd guess five months, maybe six. Look, I'm not insinuating anything. I promise. I just thought, with him missing, who knows? Maybe she can …"

Jack gave her time to finish, waiting, wanting to know precisely what Barbara was thinking. But to his surprise the room fell silent.

"Well, thank you." He reached over and patted her wrist. "This has been extremely helpful. A lot of what I've learned is off the record and can't go in the paper, but as you said, who knows? It might help find Pastor Evan."

"That's what I'm hoping."

Jack compiled his things and stood. He was starving and anxious to get home to Pam and the girls. Barbara folded the note she'd written herself and stood as well, then hesitated.

Call it a reporter's instinct, but Jack knew something else was coming. Something Barbara Cooley could not bottle up one second longer.

"Just a little FYI." She lowered her head, avoiding eye contact. "I mentioned that Mrs. Pendergrass has been on Pastor Evan's calendar each week, and I mean, it's been like clockwork. What I didn't mention was"—she looked at Jack—"she wasn't on it the week he disappeared. And no more appointments with her have been booked—at all."

11

The air in the large, dimly lit auditorium had grown stagnant. The crowded Sunday morning service was almost over. A thin woman wearing a light green dress two sizes too big gave announcements from the pulpit. Pamela shifted uncomfortably in her theater-style seat.

"Antsy, aren't you?" Jack whispered.

"I'm *hot*."

"Reached your limit?"

"My dress is sticking." Pamela wiggled. "It's been an hour and a half."

"Almost over." Jack linked her arm with his and patted her hand. "Pay attention," he jested.

She pinched his finger.

"Ouch." He laughed.

"You better watch it." She squeezed his wrist.

The big joke between them had long been that Pamela was just like her father, Ben, who couldn't sit still for more than thirty minutes. On trips she was worse than the kids about pleading in her whiniest voice, "When are we going to get there?"

She opened her journal and turned to the lyrics she'd penned hurriedly a little earlier in the service as a young African-American woman sang. *If all of these trials bring me closer to you, then I will walk through the fire if you want me to.*

Pamela soaked in each word that had maneuvered its way into her heart during the song, whispering peace into the caverns of her being.

It was as if the sermon had been tailored for her as well. She turned another page and meditated on the verse she'd jotted down from Pastor Dan's sermon: *For <u>Christ's</u> <u>sake</u>, I <u>delight</u> in <u>weaknesses</u>, in insults, in <u>hardships</u>, in <u>persecutions</u>, in <u>difficulties</u>. For when I am <u>weak</u>, then I am <u>strong</u>.*

Never had she thrown herself upon God with such abandon as she had since the night at the bridge. Like a beggar snapping up crumbs, she gathered and clung to the words of Scripture. They had become her sustenance. For the first time she understood what Jesus meant when the disciples urged him to eat, but he only replied, "I have food to eat that you know nothing about."

Pamela had left everything she cared about to God's care: her life and hopes and desires; Jack, Rebecca, and Faye; their home and possessions; their health and safety. She'd left *him* there too, the wicked invader who'd flipped her picture-book world into the air like the spinning house in *The Wizard of Oz*. All of it she had deposited with a great thud of relief into God's capable hands, where it belonged. She'd dusted off her hands and left it there.

Period.

If she could just *keep* it there; if she could just keep that *mind-set*; if she could just know—really know—that she and her family were safe in God's hands. And even if he did allow something to happen to them—even something bad, that involved suffering—she could know it was okay, simply because it was the Master's plan and he did what he wanted.

But once again, the stranger's words weaved their way into her present tense like prickly little gremlins. They visited her at the oddest times, when her defenses were down, like right there in church, of all places. Without warning they swept back in, vividly, like the wind and rain and gut-twisting terror of that awful night.

Pammy.

It was a nickname she'd been called frequently as a child. She rehashed it all again—when it was that she'd insisted others call her Pamela, or if they must shorten it, simply Pam. When had she declared the moratorium on Pammy? Seventh grade? Eighth?

Had this man known her from back then, when they were children growing up on Cleveland's upper east side? He'd used her maiden name, Wagner. And he'd said, "I've never forgotten you."

"You've got goose bumps." Jack rubbed her wrist gently. "I thought you were hot."

She just squeezed his arm hard as the choir started into the last song.

For the umpteenth time she racked her brain, recalling her earliest love interests. Furthest back was Scotty Marmaduke from Mrs. Jones's fourth-grade class at Hodges Elementary School—but he'd had brown hair and skin the color of an Indian. William Rose and Doug DuCharme were her other "true loves" prior to high school, but neither had the skin, features, or hair coloring of the invader.

The guy had mentioned Rebecca and Faye. How on earth had he known their names? And why? She was sure he'd said something like "I want to take care of you."

Pamela tried to shake the whole thing from her mind and found herself actually moving her head side to side. It felt as if she'd fallen asleep, nodded, and woke with a start.

"You okay?" Jack's eyes narrowed.

She nodded.

"Let's all stand for the benediction." Pastor Dan's curly gray hair looked almost blond in the spotlight. He lifted his leathery brown hands and closed his thoughtful eyes behind silver-rimmed glasses. "Now may you go in peace, fully knowing, enjoying, and sharing the love of God, which he shed abroad in our hearts. In your weaknesses, may you be made strong."

Pamela closed her eyes and made the prayer her own.

"May he guard you, protect you, give you wisdom, and fill you with divine power as you go forth from this place, ministering to a world in need. And may he bring us safely back together again very soon. Amen."

The lights came up and it was back to reality as voices arose all over the sanctuary. People bent down to pick up bulletins and pens and Bibles, teenagers high-fived and hugged, old people with white hair shuffled out, leaning on walkers and each other.

Jack clasped Pamela's hand and led her down their row.

A man in the adjoining aisle smiled and nodded. Something about him, the small eyes, perhaps, made her think of the stranger. Clearly, so clearly, she pictured his pasty white skin and recalled the sandpaper-like feeling of his hand nudging her neck and shoulders. She reached behind the base of her neck, rubbed the skin deeply, and dusted off her shoulder several times, as if wiping away the memory.

His filthy, blocky fist had grappled and fumbled and yanked her hair. She patted the top of her head and smoothed her hair all the way to the back, two, three times, as if making sure nothing was in it—a tangle, a fly … *a hand.*

Until the night on the bridge, Pamela had sequestered thoughts of the intruder solely to their home. That's where he'd broken in, taken things, planted things, parked his junky brown car—at their house. Period. Therefore, she had actually felt safer venturing anywhere away from home, because the house was the only place the predator had dared to meddle.

The night on the bridge changed all that.

Now, she realized, he could be any place, following her—around town, at the grocery, the library, the pool, the mall … who knew?

Jack led her into the vast flow of people. Like cattle they slowly made their way up a carpeted runway toward the many sanctuary exits.

He could be here, lurking among all these bodies. Watching.

"How 'bout I get Rebecca?" Jack turned to Pamela.

"Okay," she agreed. "I'll get Faye."

The church had grown immensely during the past decade, with new buildings popping up all over its sprawling campus. Except for two or three, all of the structures attached to one another and could be accessed with a few zigzags via wide, well-lit hallways. Because most of the buildings were three stories, classrooms were everywhere—on the main floor, upstairs, and at the basement level.

"Maybe we'll grab a pizza on the way home," Jack said.

"Sounds good. Can we get black olives on our half?"

"Sure. How about sausage?"

"Ehh." Pamela made a sour face. "Last time it was greasy."

Jack chuckled. "You are so spoiled."

As they walked past some offices, Pamela noticed a computer sitting on a desk beyond a glass wall. Its screen saver flashed a Renoir she recognized of people gaily socializing at an outdoor festival. It faded and a golden landscape appeared, by Claude Monet she guessed. That dimmed, and up came *Starry Night*, the beautiful oil by Vincent Van Gogh.

Interesting …

Just the day before, Pamela had Googled *Van Gogh, self-portraits*, because the intruder's coarse look, his tiny eyes and hooked nose, the thatch of red hair had reminded her of the famous artist. Seeing the very brushstrokes of the Van Gogh self-portraits up close on her computer, in vibrant color—especially the ones that featured him with no beard, pipe, or hat—made Pamela believe that, if a bit of weight could be added to the artist's face, a few of them would have proven more accurate than the police artist's rendering of the stalker.

If all of these trials bring me closer to you, then I'll walk through the fire if you want me to.

Jack and Pamela reached the old sanctuary building.

Jack put a hand on her shoulder and squeezed the back of her neck. "We'll meet you at the car in a few minutes."

The girls' Sunday school rooms were in opposite directions—Rebecca's to the left on that floor, and Faye's to the right at the basement level.

"Okay. Don't forget to get the little Bible homework thingy. Rebecca loves those."

"Pamela!" Freckled and frizzy-haired Dawn Hoganson was rather a mess, as usual. Her arms were stuffed with various crumpled papers, books, a Walmart bag, and a Cleveland Indians cap. She was hunched over, holding hands with the two youngest of her five children. "I just saw your Bible in the lost and found. My Justin lost his favorite cap, and I saw the Bible when I was digging around in there."

Pamela stopped.

Dawn's voice turned to mush in her ears.

Something registered with a *slam* deep and hard in her chest. From the waist up, everything clanged. From the waist down, everything melted.

Jack had heard her too and was already coming back, his mouth open, his eyes burning holes into Dawn. "Are you sure it's hers?" he said.

"Simon!" She pulled one of her children by the wrist. "Don't you dare get that blue piece of whatever it is all over that Sunday shirt. Who gave you candy? Why do they do that? What did Mommy tell you?"

"What did it look like?" Jack stuck his face in Dawn's path.

Dawn drew back, her features scrunching as if she'd just been insulted. "Well, for one thing, it had her name in it. It's red. Maroon, I guess you'd call it. Big old thing."

My Bible. The one the creep had stolen from the house.

That means he had to have been here, at the church. *When?*

The girls!

"Jack!"

He was already in motion. "I'll get Rebecca. You get Faye." There was a slight tremor in his voice.

Pamela pressed a hand to her temple. She turned her head inquisitively but couldn't remember where Faye's room was. Suddenly the church felt like an enormous compound the size of eighteen airports put together, and Pamela felt like a mouse about to get trampled by a gazillion people.

Every gear in her head spun till they rattled. Jack must have noticed a dazed look on her face.

"Pam, go! Faye's class. Basement."

The guy could be here, right in this building.

God, please, let the girls be okay ...

She slammed the brown metal door open and hit the steps to the basement, each one feeling like a slow-motion moon walk.

Every organ in her pounded in unison as she heaved in an enormous breath and banged open the metal door on the bottom level, mentally preparing to see the intruder.

Faye's Sunday school classroom was straight ahead about fifty feet, then left another seventy-five. Taking off, her heart drummed harder, more rapidly, rising to the base of her throat.

She cut the corner hard at the ninety-degree turn in the hall, moving too fast to sidestep the couple coming her way. Her left shoulder bashed the man's chest, and she heard the wind go out of him with an *oomph*.

"I'm so sorry," Pamela cried, regaining her balance, ripping herself from his clutches, and scrambling on. "My child ... there may be something wrong."

She broke into a flat-out run down the long hallway for Faye's room, dodging adults and children, scanning them feverishly for the man in black.

Several parents stood waiting at the closed door for the kinder-garten class to end.

"Excuse me, excuse me." Pamela could barely breathe. She swung open the door and burst into the room. "Sorry ... sorry ... I just need Faye."

Pamela spotted her daughter's head first, the white bow, the stringy blonde hair, then her plump little red cheeks and the blue-and-green-checked dress they'd chosen together that morning.

"Faye!" Pamela dashed to her, slid to her knees, and hugged the child. "Oh baby, thank God you're okay." She locked Faye in her arms, rocking her back and forth, their heads nestled together.

The teachers, Trevor and Cindy Samuelson, looked at each other.

"I'm sorry to barge in," Pamela said. "We've had—"

"What's wrong, Mommy?" Faye pulled back a few inches and set her little hands on Pamela's shoulders. "Did you see the bad man too?"

12

Jack gripped Rebecca's sweaty hand tighter, but he was hurrying so fast that she was pouting and dragging three feet behind by the time they got to Faye's room.

"Have you seen him?" Jack's blood pumped feverishly through his wrists and pounded at his temples.

"No." Pam hugged Rebecca, then yanked Jack's hand, her eyes bulging. "But Faye thinks she saw him."

He did a double take at Pam, dropped to one knee, and took Faye's little hands in his. "Tell me what you saw, Faye." His eyes were just inches from hers. "Do you think you saw the man who broke into our house?"

Jack felt Pam's hand rest on his shoulder and her fingers digging in. That meant, "Be gentle." It meant, "Don't scare the girls."

Faye blinked slowly and nodded. "I told Miss Cindy, but she didn't believe me."

"When? When did you see him?" Jack wiggled her little hands, trying to keep it light, but his neck and shoulders were as taut as the strings on a banjo. "Where were you?"

"We went for a potty break, and I saw him getting a drink. It was him, Daddy. His clothes were black, just like when he came into our house. And he had those pointy boots."

"He was getting a drink at the fountain?" Jack scanned the hallway.

"Uh-huh. He smiled and waved at me, but I didn't wave back."

Jack's head buzzed with static and seemed to lift from his shoulders.

"Should I have waved?" Faye said. "It felt mean not to. He seemed nice."

Pam hugged her hard. "You did the right thing, honey. No, we never wave or get near strangers, especially the man in black. You did so good."

Jack remained kneeling. *Calm ... be calm. We're okay. We're all okay.*

He forced himself to shed the hatred and revulsion that were mixing like toxins in his head. He shook away the dread and wrath that boiled and steamed and threatened to poison the wisdom he knew was in there somewhere.

He drew Faye and Rebecca close. He took in the people walking past and standing in the halls.

There was no one in black.

Faye wore the nonchalant look of a bored spectator at a chess match, but Rebecca's nostrils flared, her lower lip quivered. She was old enough to know something very wrong was going down.

It ticked him off so bad that this, this *demon* was scaring his girls.

Jack forced himself to take in as much air as his lungs would hold, silently trying to invite the Holy Spirit in anew at the same time, then exhaled aloud. He was so mad. He felt so distant from God.

Pam's dark eyes met his and locked. They seemed to pulsate with terror and blaze with rage at the same time.

"All right." He stood, resolving to be steady, unflinching. "Will you take these, please?" He handed Pam his Bible and journal and took the girls by the hands. "What do you ladies say we go get Mommy's Bible at the lost and found then go get some pizza on our way home?"

"Campolo's!" Faye yelled. "I'm starving. We didn't have a snack today. Miss Cindy said Mr. Trevor forgot. He was supposed to bring Tootsie Rolls, but he forgot them."

He nodded at her and gently squeezed her arm. "Come on," Jack encouraged. "You wanted black olives, no sausage, you got it. Everybody up. Here we go."

They stood and smoothed the wrinkles from their outfits, wiped wet noses on tissues Pam produced from her purse, grabbed hands, and headed for the lost and found. Actually, the lost and found wasn't a room at all but a large cardboard box on the floor behind the reception counter next to the basement-level exit.

"Here, give me your stuff." Jack took Pam's purse and the things she had been carrying. "We'll wait for you over by the doors."

While she went to find the Bible, Jack knelt with the girls, found the papers they'd brought from their classes, and asked Rebecca to tell him what she'd learned in class.

"We learned about Shadrach, Meshach, and Abednego."

Jack examined her artwork—a coloring book picture she'd done neatly, in all colors, of King Nebuchadnezzar's three chosen servants wandering about unscathed in a blazing furnace.

"What a great picture. I love the colors you chose." He forced himself to sound calm. "What's the one big thing you learned from the story?"

In the background of Rebecca's picture, but in the fire with the three devoted men of God, was a fourth man. Jack knew from the account in the book of Daniel and from the traditional way in which the man was portrayed—handsome, strong, bearded—that he was Jesus.

"If you believe in God, he'll take care of you, even if you have to go into a really, really hot fire," Rebecca said. "But you have to believe, or it won't work."

"I see." It took a second, but her words registered and Jack pondered them. Funny how, from a child's perspective, everything was so simple, so cut-and-dried. It was as if Rebecca viewed God as some larger-than-life magician. If you believed the magician was real and had power, he knew it and helped you. However, if you said you believed but really didn't, he knew that too and refused to find favor on you.

Jack believed God spoke to people in different ways—through the Bible, through circumstances, dreams, other people. Rebecca's words were a reminder that God was *that* intimate and *that* involved in Jack's life, that he was speaking to him at that very moment through his own seven-year-old daughter.

They were in a fire.

Did they believe Christ was in it with them, able to keep them unharmed?

Really believe?

Something alit in Jack's spirit. The uncomplicated little Sunday school lesson he held in his hand had been custom-tailored specifically for him, in that moment, at that precise second.

With her back to Jack and the girls, Pam drifted into a corner with her Bible.

Jack's eyes found the words above Rebecca's coloring.

Nebuchadnezzar was furious. He ordered the furnace heated seven times hotter than normal. Strong soldiers tied them up and threw them into the blaze. Nebuchadnezzar said, "What god will be able to rescue you from my hand?"

Pam had retrieved her Bible and was peering down at it, leafing through it.

Below Rebecca's picture Jack found the mother lode, the words that had been designed for him in that moment, before the beginning of time:

Shadrach, Meshach, and Abednego said, "O Nebuchadnezzar, if we are thrown into the blazing furnace, the God we serve is able to save us. But even if he does not, we want you to know, O king, that we will not serve your gods or worship the image of gold."

Whoa.

He'd read the account before, but it had never hit him like that—like a Mack truck.

God can save us from this trial, but what if he doesn't? What if the worst happens? What if that's his will? How will you do then? What kind of Christian will you be then?

"Daddy." Rebecca tugged Jack's sleeve and held up a piece of candy in a yellow wrapper. "Can I have this Tangy Taffy?"

"Yes, sweetie, but that's all. We're going to have lunch soon."

"That's not fair," Faye whined. "I didn't get a treat 'cause Mr. Trevor forgot—"

"Or maybe you didn't know your Bible good enough," Rebecca said.

"It's not *good* enough, Rebecca, it's *well* enough," Jack said. Faye's temper flared and she started to protest, but Jack cut in. "And that wasn't a very nice thing to say."

"Sorry, Daddy." Rebecca proceeded to open the Tangy Taffy.

"Tell Faye you're sorry," Jack said.

"Sorry, Faye. Here." Rebecca bit half of the candy and handed the other half to her sister, dangling the yellow glob by one sticky finger.

Faye's eyes lit up. "Thank you, sister!"

From across the room, Jack saw Pam's whole body tighten and sway. Her head swiveled toward him, her eyebrows angled up high above frightened eyes. The horror resonating from his lovely wife's face was bone-chilling.

"You guys sit down." Jack pounded the floor by the wall and eased them both down. "I'm going to see what Mommy's doing. Stay right here."

Pam had three things in her hands when he got to her. In her right was the thick maroon Bible. In her left was a sheet of wrinkled, yellow-lined notebook paper filled with handwriting in blue ink. On top of it was the piece of their wedding photograph that had been sliced out and removed from the frame on their mantel.

Jack grabbed the yellow paper and photo from her hand.

The back of the photo was charred black and portions of the front were burned as well. A frown had been scribbled over his smile with black marker; lines had been scratched over his eyes to make them look closed. A noose was drawn around his neck, leading to a knot behind the neck and a line leading up and off the photograph, as if he'd been hung.

Jack glanced back at the girls, then slipped the photo into the Bible and held the yellow paper. The small, slanted handwriting covered both sides of the page.

Pamela,

I know I shouldn't be doing this. Life has not been good. I don't even know what friendship is. Thinking about you gives me something to cling to.

There was no one like you. You were always gracious when no one else was. You helped me and talked to me. You laughed with me, not at me. I remember you looking me in the eyes and actually listening—and even speaking up for me. Do you remember holding my hand? I will never forget it. I thought we might kiss that one day. I wanted to, but I was too scared to tell you.

Jack read faster and faster in disbelief.

I watched you on your wedding day.

Do you ever think of me? Could it have been me at the altar? Could Faye and Rebecca be our children? I regret not pursuing you. I should have been the one to win your heart. Maybe then my life would have turned out normal.

I am an outcast. People despise me. I feel like the trash they trample in the street. I'll be honest, it's almost as if I have purposefully fueled peoples' hatred and disgust. Probably because I was taught to believe I was a waste of life. Am I, Pamela?

A hailstorm of fury whirled in Jack's head. He had to get a gun … contact Officer DeVry … get Pam and the girls out of the house … track this freak down.

I don't think you realized what your small acts of kindness did for me.

That's why I began thinking of you again. I told myself—it's wrong! But I was so low. It was so black. The memory of you kept me alive. You saved my life—again—just like in school.

Then I wanted more. Just to see you, but it got worse. My mind began playing tricks. I started to believe—really believe—if something happened to Jack, I could take his place. You know, come onto the scene like your knight in shining armor.

Jack let the letter crunch to his side and shot Pam a look, but she was in a world of her own, curling the pages of her Bible with her thumb, probably looking for any more evidence from the nutcase who'd decided to turn their lives upside down. He held the letter up to read the last of it.

It's gotten worse. I'm messed up. I know that. If you could talk to me like you used to. But we are past that now, aren't we?

I want to cry out, help me, Pam, please, won't you help me make sense of this life? Won't you help me get my sanity back?

But now I've gone and done it. The demons are so much louder than the truth. The only thing I know is that you cared, and I want that again. It's wrong. You belong to someone else. You are the mom of two kids. But the voice in my wretched mind keeps screaming that none of that matters. We still have a chance. And even if none of that is true, I believe you are the only thing in this life that will make it worth living.

From the lost boy, with love,

G.M.

13

"I know who it is," Pamela heard herself say, softly, evenly, as if in a trance.

"What?" The letter crumpled at Jack's side. "Who?"

"Granger Meade." She spoke weakly, as if all her energy had been zapped. "He lived in my neighborhood. We grew up together."

"Pam, are you serious? You know this person?"

"No one liked him. I felt sorry for him. I know it's him."

"Are you sure?" Jack's eyes were huge.

She nodded and stared off, remembering the snowy winter wonderland bus stop at the end of her street in Cleveland Heights. Granger would stand there day after day in the predawn chill, so big and awkward with his large, black trombone case, never knowing exactly what to say or do. They'd been in the same elementary school before that.

"He had oily red hair," she mumbled. "He was tall, broad, fair ... It's him." She nodded slowly, looking at nothing, recalling everything from the previous days with chilling clarity.

Jack scanned the basement level of the church, looked over at the girls and back at her. "Okay, we gotta tell the police, now." He rested his hands atop her shoulders. "This is *good*, Pam." He took her face in his hands and fixed his eyes on hers, like a coach attempting to revive a pulverized boxer in the corner of the ring between rounds. "This is really good. They'll get him now. It'll be over soon."

With quick movements and quiet but gentle commands, Jack led Pamela and the girls down the hall and into a vacant children's classroom. He pulled up a small blue chair for her in a corner and a basket of toys for the girls, then got busy on his phone. The odor of dirty diapers enveloped them, but it didn't faze Pamela—and the girls certainly didn't seem to notice.

From the opposite corner of the room, Pamela heard Jack leaving a message for Officer DeVry, explaining the returned Bible, the defaced photograph, the letter. She also heard him mention the name Granger Meade.

Funny, but somehow knowing it was him who'd been behind everything was a relief. That was lunacy, she knew. There was plenty to fear, based on all that had happened already, the letter and the sordidness of it all. As she stared at Rebecca and Faye, each dinging a xylophone as they sat on the red rubber mat in that sour-smelling room, she realized she was somewhat paralyzed by what she could only assume was a combination of disbelief, curiosity, and fear. She would work her way back to sickening reality soon enough.

But for a moment, just a fleeting moment, while she sat comatose in that chair, Pamela allowed herself to drift back to her youth in Cleveland Heights, where indeed Granger Meade had seemed an odd but harmless boy. He had been extraordinarily quiet and was, frankly, somewhat of an oaf. And, although he was uncomfortably awkward and came across as a self-proclaimed nuisance, she had liked him.

Certainly none of her friends understood her kindness to Granger. The crux of it was, he had no friends. That's what had bothered her so. He was a loner. And she had decided to do her small part, whatever she could, to make his life a little happier. So she made a habit of asking him questions—about band, classes, his job as an usher at the theater in the local mall. But never about family. No, no—she'd gone there once or twice, only to be told on both occasions that "My mother and father *hate* me. I'm an anathema to them."

Vividly Pamela remembered going home, heading straight to the living room, and looking up *anathema* in the big red family dictionary. Just as clearly, she recalled several of the words from its definition that had stood out so potently: *detested, denounced ... cursed.*

Although Pamela's own family had been dysfunctional, at least they loved each other, even if it was buried beneath layers of distrust and paranoia. For that reason, because she had thought her family was about as weird as they came, she always assumed Granger exaggerated and said such things simply to gain attention.

There were rumors, however, about Granger's parents being some kind of fanatical fundamentalist Christians. His father was supposedly a church deacon and his mother, who never wanted children and always wanted to be a missionary, was said to despise Granger and told him repeatedly that he was neither planned nor wanted.

Pamela could not conceive carrying a child in the womb all those months, then giving birth and loathing that precious life.

That's your baby.

For a split second, she wondered whether it was pity chewing at her stomach.

One kid from the neighborhood, Tony Givens, said Granger was actually forced to *live* in the woods, anywhere from a few hours to several days at a time, to serve as punishment for his trespasses. Pamela always dismissed such nonsense without giving it a second thought, because Tony was a bully and a jerk.

For the first time since her youth, Pamela recalled a cold, sopping wet morning when she was riding the bus to school. She could practically smell the damp Ohio air. Boys were teasing Granger. Crowding around him. Pointing. Jabbing at his ear. Laughing and yelling that he had ticks or lice or some such nonsense. Poor Granger. There he sat, scrunched against the dew-covered bus window, cowering behind his black trombone case.

Back then she was certain none of those things were true. Certain. Because, when she was a kid—when anyone was a kid—nothing could be *that* awful, could it? That backward? That *sick*?

He was just a shy kid, she figured, like all the other shy kids.

Now she wondered, what *had* Granger Meade been through?

Interestingly, when he did finally speak up, Granger said things that either made uncanny sense or that came across so dryly humorous that Pamela laughed and laughed. When that happened, his head would tilt up and he would smirk, flare his nostrils and kind of look around at everyone else on the bus, proud that he had made Pamela Wagner laugh so hard.

When she saw Granger in the hallways at school, Pamela said hello and occasionally chatted with him. As he'd said in his note, she may have even walked with him to class. She didn't remember that, specifically, but what she did recall was that whenever they were together, Granger was on his toes, quick to notice her needs, alert to open a door, always watching out for her. He'd liked her. Pamela knew that. And now that she reflected on it, she may have even sensed that he had a crush on her. But, as did most such things, it simply went unspoken.

"Hello, hello." A tall brunette woman swept into the church classroom like a whirlwind, dragging a garbage can on wheels, waving a rubber-glove-covered hand to her long nose. "Whew-whee!" she cackled. "Smells like we had some real party poopers in here today. Don't mind me." She stepped on the pedal of a white plastic trash can to pop up the lid, snatched the bag, and replaced it with a new one in a blur. "There, all clean for service tonight. Have a good day, everyone."

She was gone.

"I'll just be another second." Jack held up an index finger. "Gonna try Potanski."

Pamela didn't want to leave that hard plastic chair. Cars maneuvered in the parking lot beyond the window, people talked and laughed in the hallway. She was safe where she was and didn't want to move.

The time Granger mentioned in the letter—when Pamela had spoken up for him—came creeping back. It had been one of their high school's last home football games of the season. Pamela was bundled up and on her way to meet several friends somewhere between the bleachers and the concession stand. It was a frigid Ohio night. People were layered in sweatshirts, heavy winter parkas, wool scarves, and winter hats and nestled close together in the packed slant of stands. Their warm breaths hit the cold night air and rose like chimney smoke in the white glow of the stadium lights.

Pamela walked fast to stay warm along the black-cinder running track that encircled the football field, past the shivering, smiling, pom-poming cheerleaders, past the school's large-headed patriot mascot (who was really classmate Ricky Bogan). With the smell of winter and cigarettes and hot dogs swirling in the wind off Lake Erie, the announcer's voice echoed as he reported the plays.

In the darkest stretch of the walk, beyond the glare of the stadium lights and well before the lines for hot cocoa at the concession stand, where hooligans huddled to sneak swigs of booze and cupped their hands around flickering lighters and joints—she saw Granger Meade. He was down a slope, away from everyone, swaying oddly against the tall chain-link fence, wearing his navy band uniform, boxed in by three dark figures.

Pamela slowed. Her heart quickened.

With a playful, sweeping uppercut, the one on the left sent Granger's white band hat flipping into the air. He did not pick it up. The one in the middle shoved him, and again he wobbled against the sagging fence.

"Granger!" she shouted, realizing as she headed toward him that it did no good to yell from that distance.

She set her resolve and hurried her pace.

They wouldn't hurt a girl.

She just hoped they had no weapons and weren't too drunk.

The three young men harassing Granger didn't look familiar until she drew within ten feet of their little party. The one that had knocked his hat off was the infamous Blake Devonshire, who had either dropped out or been expelled soon after the school year began. Pamela did not know the whole story, only that Blake had been accused of flushing another student's head in one of the school toilets.

Great.

She didn't want to tangle with him or his sidekicks.

The other two boys wore baggy low-rider jeans. White shoes. Silver chains. Dark hoods and baseball caps. Blake wore a denim jacket, a black conductor's cap, and steel-toed boots. The collar of his black shirt was unbuttoned, revealing a bony white chest, a silver skull necklace, and a portion of a tattoo.

Almost simultaneously, the four of them turned to her.

"Stay away, Pamela," Granger huffed, hunched over, a trickle of blood glistening from beneath his nose. "Get outta here, now!"

"Pamela … baby." Blake stepped toward her, invincibly, as if he knew her. Reeking of booze, he reached for her. "Come 'ere, sweetie …"

She swatted his filthy hand. "Where've you been, Granger? Come on." She reached out a hand to him, praying her act would work. "Let's go. Everybody's waiting."

"Wait a minute, baby." Blake seized her arm. "You ain't goin' nowhere—"

The second Blake's fingers sank into her arm, Granger detonated.

With his big head lowered and his blocky shoulder down like a battering ram, he catapulted toward Blake. His massive, chugging, steam-rolling frame struck Blake Devonshire square in the back, smack between the shoulder blades.

Oooomph.

The twerp left the ground for an instant and *bash*, hit the rocks and dirt and grass face first, with Granger crashing down on top of him. The wind left Blake like the last bit of air leaving a wilting balloon.

The other two squared into the ready-for-battle position with knees bent, arms and hands out stiff, ready to rumble.

"Come on, Granger." Pamela scrambled to him and reached a hand out. "Let's go."

Blake looked like a rag doll beneath him.

Granger rose and examined the other two.

They were frozen in place, eyeing each other, checking up the hill for onlookers.

"Take my hand!" Pamela ordered.

He took it.

His hand was large and rough.

She helped him to his feet.

Blake's face must have been a mess. It was straight down against the gritty earth. He wasn't moving.

Shifting her meanest eyes to the other two, Pamela eased in front of them slowly, over to the fence. She bent down, snatched Granger's hat, and dashed back to his side. Without a word, without stopping, she lifted his heavy hand in hers and led him up the slope.

By the time she glanced back, the other two jerks had fled.

Blake's crumpled body lay small and still, like an old pile of clothes one might see along the side of a road.

"You okay?" Pamela looked up at Granger as they walked.

He looked down at her and nodded. "Thanks."

"You got blood right here." She pointed above his upper lip.

He wiped it with the sleeve of his band uniform.

They reached level ground, the cinder track, throngs of people.

"Why were they hassling you?" She let his hand go, stopped walking, and faced him.

He put his hat on, tugged at the lapels of his band jacket, and tilted his head back.

She waited for an answer, but he only dropped his head, as if it was all too much to explain. She dusted his coat off with her hand.

"You can talk to me, you know," she said over the announcer's echoing voice. "I'm your friend. I won't say anything to anyone. It helps to talk, Granger."

"Why are you doing this?" He squinted at her and tilted his head.

"Doing what? Being your friend?"

He shook his head, frustrated. Towering at least a foot and a half above her, he turned slowly from the glowing field to the burning lights to the black sky to the crowd. "You don't understand," he said. "There's no way you could."

"But I *want* to understand, Granger. What happened back there?"

He threw his hands into the air. "What? You think that's unusual? It happens all the time. That's my life, right there."

"I don't understand," Pamela said. "What did you do to get picked on by them?"

"Trouble finds me," he said. "I went under the bleachers to try and find a ten-dollar bill Michael Riggler dropped."

"You went down there to help Michael?"

"He didn't know it. I overheard him tell some other guys he dropped it through the stands. I was gonna find it and give it back to him."

"And what? You ran into those creeps?"

His small mouth sealed shut, his eyes closed, he nodded.

The outside corner of his left eye glistened, and she knew it wasn't from the cold.

Suddenly, Pamela thought *she* might cry.

He looked down at her as if pleading for understanding with those tiny eyes. A tainted concoction of cruel emotion seemed to spill over from his troubled soul. She saw hurt and humiliation; she sensed inadequacy and embarrassment.

Keeping her eyes on his, Pamela reached up and covered his hand in hers. "You are a good person, Granger Meade."

She smiled and kind of bounced on her toes in an attempt to lighten things up by shaking his hand and letting it go—but he held on.

And then she saw something else coming from those small, penetrating eyes. Something desperate. But something she couldn't quite put her finger on.

Until now.

Now, twenty years later, she knew.

Now, as her offspring played on the floor at her feet and her soul mate yakked on the phone about the bizarre, twisted monster who was after her, she realized—it had been love.

The love of Granger Meade.

Perhaps hers had been all the love he'd ever known.

And apparently he wasn't going to let it go.

Not on his life.

14

With the body language of a Secret Service agent, Jack hurriedly and methodically escorted Pam and the girls out of the church, into the hot sun, toward his car. Scanning each person and car in the lot—looking for any figure in black, any brown car—he unlocked the VW, ushered everyone inside, got himself in, and locked the doors.

"He saw you on our wedding day?" Jack started the car and cranked the air-conditioning. "You held hands with this person? Yet you had no clue it was him? What's this about, Pam?"

"Jack." Pam shot a glance toward the girls in the backseat, then gave him a foul look. "Cool down. We'll talk at home."

"How about some music, girls?" Jack jabbed the button for the stereo and started an upbeat CD the girls had enjoyed that morning. "Why don't you tell me now?"

Pam explained who Granger Meade was, how she'd known him as a child ... sharing the same bus stop ... feeling sorry for him ... the incident at the football game. Her speech came in bits and pieces, as if she was doped up on some kind of truth serum.

"It didn't dawn on you till now that this might be the guy?" Jack pressed.

"No, it didn't."

"Never even crossed your mind—"

"What are you implying, Jack? That I *knew* who it was and didn't tell you? Are you sick?"

"It sounds like it was pretty serious."

"I barely knew him. I certainly didn't recognize him, or I would have said so."

"Yet you almost kissed the guy?"

"Don't be a jerk! I felt sorry for him." Pam slipped a trembling hand to her mouth. "Why are you doing this? I can't believe you. You're making it harder than it already is!"

His mind reeled. Dizzyingly, he checked the rearview mirror for the brown car.

"Daddy, don't forget pizza," Rebecca yelled over the music.

He didn't answer, but he wasn't about to stop until they were locked down at home. If the nutcase was brazen enough to wander into their church, he certainly had the gall to make his way back to their house.

"Campolo's!" Faye yelled. "Extra cheese, please. I'm a poet and I don't even know it."

Jack ignored her. That afternoon he would go see Amiel, their friend who owned a small gun shop and shooting range on the square in downtown Trenton City. Whatever gun Amiel would recommend, Jack would buy it.

"Did you hear them?" Pam's voice brought him back.

"What?"

"The girls … pizza."

"We're not stopping," he said.

She shook her head and glared out the passenger window. He could tell she was hurt, and he'd been the one to wound her. On the rare occasions they argued, Pam would sometimes cry silently, just like that—her eyes glassy, her chest hitching periodically but barely making a sound. Holding it all inside.

And it was his fault.

Idiot.

The time she needs you most, and you're driving her away. How can you possibly think she might have known it was him?

Jack couldn't remember the last time he'd allowed his temper to flare. He knew it was pure poison—one of his ugliest flaws.

He drove faster than normal, zipping right past Campolo's, feeling a tinge of meanness for not stopping, yet justifying his robot-like action by reminding himself that he needed to take charge; it was up to him to keep his family safe. He simply needed to get them home, pronto. Pam stared out the window. The music played on.

"Daddy, did we pass Campolo's?" Rebecca said.

You're not fighting a man. This isn't flesh and blood you're up against. This is Satan working through this guy, and he wants you to freak out ... He wants to divide you and Pam ... consume you with rage.

"I'm sorry," he blurted. "I'm letting this thing get to me. I apologize, Pam. Forgive me, please."

Still holding everything in, staring out at the landscape in the opposite direction, she gave a quick nod and sniff.

But he realized the damage had been done.

The people in that car—his bride, his girls—they were *his* responsibility. But things were getting away from him. It was all happening so fast. He felt weak and inadequate, as if he was battling another suitor for the lives of his girls—and losing. Not just being defeated by a little but getting slaughtered.

He would have a security system installed as soon as possible. The girls could get away, perhaps to his parents' house in south Florida. But was that realistic? It was so far. He needed to be close to them, but then again, where would they be safest?

His phone vibrated, and he answered.

"Mr. Crittendon, Officer DeVry."

"Officer DeVry," Jack said. "Did you get my message?"

Pam shot him a watery-eyed glance.

"I did. Good timing too," DeVry said. "Turns out our guys were able to lift two stray prints off that picture frame of yours after all, and guess who they belong to?"

"Granger Meade."

"Yes, sir. One and the same. He was arrested in some sort of brawl outside a miniature golf place in Geauga Lake, but he was never charged."

Jack covered the phone and looked at Pam. "Prints on the wedding picture—Granger Meade."

Pam's head dropped.

"So what now?" Jack said with renewed confidence.

"Let me tell you what else we've found."

"Yes, go ahead."

"The results from your laptop came back."

Jack could almost hear his heart ticking faster, faster.

"The encryption shows that all the pornography was downloaded to your computer on July 11—the day of your home invasion. So your suspicion was correct."

"Thank God." Jack repeated the news to Pam. Both of her hands covered her nose and mouth. Her eyes glistened with tears.

"Something else of interest," DeVry said. "On that same date, same time of day, a number of photographs from your laptop were copied over to some sort of USB device."

"Personal photos, like of our family?" Jack sensed Pam watching him.

"That's right," DeVry said. "Fortunately, our guys were able to restore those to your desktop. This Meade character may have thought he deleted them, or stole them, but they were still there under all the layers. Shoot, everything's still there long after you think it's been deleted. I don't understand how it works, but it's amazing stuff."

"That's probably how he knew what my daughter looked like," Jack said. "I told you he waved at one of my girls at our church."

"Disturbing, I know."

Jack's whole body tightened as he thought of Granger Meade fantasizing over their family photos. He wanted to *kill* the monster. "So what now?" He swung the VW into their neighborhood.

"Well, when all this started hitting the fan yesterday and this morning, I put in for a search warrant. Officers Potanski and Nielson are on duty today, so we're going to pay Granger Meade a visit."

"Today? You have an address?" He gritted his teeth, pumped a fist at Pam, and told her the news.

"Affirmative. We'll be heading his way within the hour. We'll let you know—"

"Where does he live?" Jack eyed Pam, who rubbed her nose with a wadded tissue and stared down at her lap.

"Here, in town. We'll give you all the gory details later."

"Do you plan to arrest him?"

"We're going to search his place and see what turns up. We'll go from there. Don't worry, Mr. Crittendon. We wouldn't be doing this if we didn't consider him a prime suspect in the invasion of your home and the harassment of your wife and family. Hopefully we'll surprise him, confiscate evidence, and make an arrest—at least bring him in for further questioning. We'll see. But don't hold your breath; sometimes these things don't happen as fast as we'd like."

Jack knew it was doubtful, but he asked anyway. "Is there any way I could go with you, or meet you there?"

Pam scowled at him.

"No, sorry, that wouldn't work," DeVry said. "If we need you for anything—an ID or something like that—I have your number. Just sit tight, Mr. Crittendon. We want this guy out of your hair and off the streets."

Jack hung up and explained everything to Pam as they maneuvered their way along the curvy, tree-lined roads leading to the back of their neighborhood. Seeing no brown cars on their street and no sign of anything unusual at the house, Jack wheeled the car into the driveway. The girls skipped out to the street in the bright summer sun to get the bulky Sunday newspaper that had been tossed in the daisies.

"Girls, inside!" Jack yelled, waiting to close the garage door.

They scampered in and dashed off to their rooms to get changed.

With her shoes off, still wearing her black linen dress and the brown pearl earrings and necklace Jack had bought her for a recent anniversary, Pam picked up odds and ends throughout the downstairs, then began cleaning up the morning dishes at the kitchen sink.

After glancing at a few of the day's headlines at the island, Jack approached her from behind, gently and deeply squeezed her shoulders, reached around her, and turned off the water. He then slipped both arms around her waist and nestled his head against her soft hair. She rested her hands on the counter in front of the sink and stood still, looking straight out the window.

"I'm sorry," he said softly. "I know I hurt your feelings. I didn't mean to. It's my fault."

She didn't answer.

"It's my job to protect you," he said. "I guess it felt like this guy had the one-up on me."

Still she said nothing.

"That doesn't excuse what I said—what I implied. I don't know where it came from. I didn't mean any of it, please know that. It was the old me, rearing his ugly head."

"The old you is a *jerk*," she said, and pinched both his wrists, hard.

"Ouch!" He did not pull away, but closed his arms around her.

She dropped her head back against his chest. "Is it going to end today?"

He nodded so she could feel it. "Yes."

"He was always shunned," she said. "I bet no one's ever loved him. Can you imagine how that feels? All I did was show a little interest; we didn't even know each other that well. I listened—that's all. I treated him like a friend."

"That sounds like you."

Pam was too good for Jack. So often, he looked into the mirror of her life and was ashamed at the selfish, prideful man he saw looking back at him. Her words confirmed what an idiot he'd been. But she was always quick to forgive—always. Jack could tell Pam had recognized that his outburst was a character flaw issue between him and God. She'd completely relinquished it. That was her way. Forgive. Leave it with God. Forget.

Jack kissed her head and held her close. Very close. Very quiet.

But as far as Granger Meade was concerned, Jack was dumbfounded that Pam could feel any sort of compassion for the guy. Then again, if what Jack knew was true—that it was the evil powers and spiritual forces at work inside Granger that made him "bad"—then Jack *should* be able to conjure up some remnant of sympathy. His dad always said, "Be slow to judge other people until you know what they've been through."

But Granger had literally busted his way into their private world. He'd stolen their personal things and attempted to frame Jack for a despicable felony. He'd attacked Pam. And he'd dared—*dared*—to enter the unspoken boundaries clearly and sacredly drawn around a man's wife and children. And the sick threat of replacing Jack as Pam's husband?

Jack would destroy him if he ever found him.

Yet Pam seemed willing to be merciful.

"You're a good person." He turned her around, leaned her up against the kitchen sink, and kissed her softly, deeply.

She pulled her head back and searched his eyes. "We're partners, Jack. We're one. I've never doubted that, or you, ever."

He drew her in as close as possible and just hugged her.

"I love you," he said.

She was perfect for him. No other woman on earth could understand him, or put up with him, or uplift him as she did. He rocked her back and forth in his arms, slowly, and banished the thought of ever having to live without her.

"I love you too, Mr. Reporter," she said.

"Don't remind me of work." He groaned. "I really gotta dig into that McDaniel piece. I've had no time."

He needed to follow up with Barbara Cooley to make sure she'd sent the email blast and find out if she'd heard back from any other church employees who may have seen Evan McDaniel the morning he disappeared. He needed to talk to the two people Barbara had mentioned who did see Evan that morning. And he needed to track down that rich lady, Pendergrass, to see what she had to say about her weekly meetings with the pastor.

If the cops can just nail Granger Meade, we can get on with our lives.

"I was thinking maybe I could go with you if you go back to the McDaniels' house," Pam said. "You know, just to kind of be there for Wendy, see if there's anything I can do."

"Great idea." Jack stretched his arms above his head and yawned. "I'd give anything to be at Granger Meade's apartment right now."

"Oh, I'm sure that would be a pretty picture." Pam squeezed him around the waist. "Let the police do their job. Come on, let's scrounge up some lunch and get you your Sunday nap."

He held up his hands. "Maybe you can join me."

She lifted hers. Their fingers intertwined and their palms pressed together.

"Oh, really," she said. "I didn't think you let *anything* interfere with your Sunday nap."

"Anything but you." He guided her hands around his back; she latched them behind him. Smoothly, softly, he leaned in and kissed her, hoping she would feel how very much he loved her. Their mouths melted together. Warmth flowed. Pleasure swirled. And suddenly nothing else in the world mattered but their passionate communion.

15

Hunched over a small, creaky desk in his stifling basement apartment, Granger Meade knew the authorities would be coming for him soon.

He let out a sigh and wiped the sweat from his forehead with the shoulder of his tight black T-shirt.

Nothing ever went right.

Fingering the letter he'd just finished writing, he dropped the pen on the desk and stared up at the dreamy photographs of Pamela taped to the entire cinderblock wall in front of him like a patchwork collage.

Many of the photos—color, sepia tone, black-and-white—he had taken on Pamela's wedding day with a telephoto lens as he sat in his car across the street from the church. There she was, in the poster-size black-and-white at the center of the mix, coming down the front steps of the church, a lovely hand at her forehead, blocking the rice being tossed by well-wishers.

Granger's already-failing heart had been irreparably damaged that windy spring afternoon. His lofty dream of a future with Pamela had been swept away that day, the only genuine friend he'd ever known claimed by another. It didn't matter by whom. It could have been Jack Crittendon or Brad Pitt; the fact was, she was now officially off limits. At least by moral standards, and according to the Christian doctrine to which she adhered.

A flash of rage alit within him. His mother and father had called themselves Christian. They'd played their roles at church, putting on masks of piety and righteousness on Sundays and Wednesdays and every other day the blasted place was open. Yet they were hypocrites of the worst kind. Miserable. Hateful. Self-seeking and self-righteous. In their own deceived minds, they were above everyone else, yet in reality they were the lowest of low.

Scum.

Bottom-dwelling *scum*.

He'd almost put an end to them, that one Christmas night.

What stopped me?

Little had his father and mother known how close they'd come to being smothered to death by their oddball son, who'd stood over each one of them as they slept. The pillow had been in his sweaty hands, inches from his father's gaping, snoring trap, within a foot of his mother's poisonous, scorn-filled mouth.

Oh, how he'd longed to shut off the flow that beat him down and weakened him like the melting desert sun each day of his rotten life.

They'd sung in the choir Christmas Eve, his mother and father. Candles burning. Faces glowing. Wreaths smelling of pine. They took Communion. They hugged their friends and handed out their cheap little gifts.

When they arrived back at the close, warm house, Granger gathered blankets, thinking they might allow him to sleep inside. It had been a good evening, his parents' favorite time of year.

"What are you doing?" Mother's grating voice pierced him to the wall.

"It's Christmas Eve," he said softly.

Mother and Father stared at each other.

Father looked as if he might concede, but not Mother.

Not even close.

Her ghostly face broke out with burning red splotches, and she lit into Granger once again for not paying attention at the service, for not singing right, for sitting alone like some "retard," for embarrassing her and Father by being such an "awkward oddity." One night in the shed would be his punishment.

He retreated to the cold, damp mattress in the tool shed. Late into the night he lay awake, damp to the core, wrestling with the mythical Christmas story, listening to the mice scurry about, hating himself, his parents, the classmates who bullied him—the whole world.

On Christmas morning he'd crept inside, frozen to the bone, and curled up on the heater vent on the kitchen floor to thaw out before his parents awoke. Father made cocoa and handed him a cup. They sat by the manger scene and tree, and with great anticipation he gave his parents the gifts he'd saved up for—a new Bible for each of them, both with genuine leather covers. Mother's turned out to be the "wrong version," and she insisted the print in Father's was too small.

In the back of his mind, Granger had known the gifts would be wrong; some way, somehow—wrong. But still, her ugly comments hollowed him inside and made him feel inadequate, clumsy, and sick to his stomach.

Granger received two pairs of wool socks in a Walmart bag and a blue-and-gray-checked flannel jacket that used to be Father's and smelled of Old Spice. Gifts that would keep him warm when he was forced outside, away from them, where he belonged.

Later that night he almost choked the life out of them.

He was glad he hadn't, for one reason: he didn't want to look bad in Pamela's eyes. After all, it would have made national news.

Sitting there at the desk in the glow of the computer light, he laid the letter down, gave a hard cough, and reached for the ratty-looking pack of Newports sitting next to a box of saltines and a can of Red Bull on the floor. Knocking one of the smokes from the pack, he tapped it on the back of his hand, flipped it to the corner of his mouth, lit, and inhaled mightily till the tobacco glowed orange.

Look at her …

He exhaled, blowing a stream of smoke up toward a photo of Pamela in which her full lips curved into a mischievous smile. Some of the pictures had been lifted from the husband's laptop, reprinted, and enlarged. Her marble-brown eyes were dazzling. She had soft, bouncy blonde hair, worn in many different styles over the years, and her figure was curvy and full—a dream.

Did she know he was not "after her" in a physical way? Not yet, anyway. She must know. She knew him back then. She knew he would never hurt her, the one true source of joy he'd ever discovered. The thought of coming across to Pam as some kind of sexual preda-tor felt so villainous.

He was always misunderstood.

But you smashed your way into her home. You tried to frame Jack. At the bridge, you pointed the knife at her and slashed the tire …

Messed up, messed up, messed up.

His whole life was a mistake.

Why had God let him be born?

He slid the ashtray over and flicked the cigarette with his thumb, knocking a few flakes of ash onto the pile of a dozen butts. Shoving his chair back a foot, he buried his sweaty head in his hands.

Why couldn't you just let her be? Let her live her life …

You're tormenting her—and her girls.

The kiddy porn he'd dumped on the husband's laptop wasn't his. He'd bought it off some pervert at the bowling alley where he worked.

She's going to hate you, you know that, don't you? She thinks you're some sadistic, psychotic goon.

"It's not true," he moaned. "That is *not* me …"

But it was. Although he didn't want to live like a monster, he was going through the motions, almost like some kind of programmed demon.

Maybe he was just a bad seed, as Mother had always declared.

"There are vessels of honor and vessels of dishonor," she would say. "You, my son, are clearly a vessel of dishonor. I don't bother to ask the Potter why. We do not question the Potter. We are simply the clay in his hands. I can't help it if he stuck your father and me with a bad lump like you."

Maybe he was a hideous, ugly mental case with no brain. Maybe he was destined for destruction, a lawbreaker who would spend the rest of his life in some concrete prison with peeling paint, fighting off rapists and felons and eating slop.

Maybe that's where you want to be.

Maybe it's the safest place for you, for everyone.

He sat up, leaned back in the chair, and—*puhhhhhhh*—took a deep, loud hit of the smoke, wishing it would give him instant cancer and he'd die in that hot, cramped apartment.

A handful of the photos on the wall were childhood keepsakes he'd hung onto all those years, including class photos and yearbook pictures. There to the right was Pamela's seventh-grade picture—the friend and confidant whom he remembered so vividly. He'd thought of her night and day while growing up as a boy and young man in their Cleveland suburb; much more than she'd ever realized.

But now she knew. Now she knew he had her on his brain.

And so did the police, he was certain.

The cat was out of the proverbial bag.

Granger hadn't meant to scare her by breaking into her house through the front door. He was panicked himself. The sight of her had snapped something within him and driven him into a blazing frenzy. And then the night at the bridge, he'd just wanted to talk, that was all. Oh, to talk to her again like when they were kids. That's all he'd wanted, he'd have sworn it on his mother's no-good Bible. He hadn't meant to pull her hair, to hurt her. That was the last thing he would ever want. But Pamela hadn't recognized him. She acted as if he was some kind of fiend.

Then she tried to run me down.

He took one last drag, let the smoke drift out of his O-shaped mouth, and inhaled every last gray vapor up his nose. It burned, and he liked it. He wished again that it would kill him. His fat, yellowish fingers warmed as he mashed the cigarette in the ashtray. His soul felt stained, just like his fingers.

If he could just think clearly, make a few more good, sound decisions—keep the Devil at bay. He knew one thing: he needed to make things right with Pamela. That was the only thing that mattered now. He couldn't think beyond that.

The brown cardboard box he'd prepared earlier sat on the yellow Formica table in the dinky kitchen beneath a cheap hanging light. It contained Pamela's jewelry and the girl's locket.

This is good. You're doing what's right. Just hurry up and see it through.

It would be dangerous to deliver the box and letter to her home, but that was the next move on the agenda. He knew he could not come back to the apartment. Cops would be there within twenty-four hours max, he guessed. He would throw his clothes and essentials into his leather duffel, do the deed at Pam's house, and ditch the car somewhere.

Then what?

He couldn't last much longer in that town. When they ran the sketch of him in the paper—even though there wasn't much resemblance—he was forced to quit his job at the bowling alley. Someone was sure to recognize him or put two and two together—probably already had.

Granger needed to get away from there. Out of Ohio. Far away. That would be the best way he could show his love to her.

What was love, anyway?

He had no idea.

The only taste of it he ever got was from Pamela, back in the day.

Now he could return the favor—by letting her go.

Yes, go away. Far away. Leave her alone. Never interfere in her life again. Set her free.

That would be love.

The sheer separation would make him—force him—to let her go.

As long as he could continue on this train of thought, keep thinking clearly, being pure, doing the right thing …

But he knew it wouldn't last.

No, don't think that way …

The Devil always returned.

Always.

Just like Mother said: "You sweep the house clean. You try to be good, morally. But if you ain't surrendered your life to him, the Devil will come back with a vengeance, and he'll have all his rowdy, rat-pack hooligan demons with him. Then they'll really make a mess of things."

How else could he show his love for her?

Take her.

No. You mustn't. That's not what she wants.

Show her what life could be like.

It was the Devil knocking, see? He was right there. He was always right there. He was in Granger's head. Granger could only do what was right for so long, and then …

Hurry. Get going. Return the stuff before it's too late. Before you change your mind. Before you start thinking and planning and dwelling on how to take her.

There'd been a plan.

It will be messy at first. I'll have to take her by force. But she'll get used to me. She'll see I'm not going to hurt her. Then she'll come around. She'll love me again.

He made his mind go blank; then he stood, folded the letter, walked it to the box, and slipped it inside. He taped the box shut and fetched his leather bag.

"The spirit's willing," Mother would say, "but the flesh is weak."

Keep moving.

Get your stuff in the bag.

Get the box to Pam. Don't think about her. Just deliver it and get away.

Far away.

Before you change your mind.

16

A calming breeze blew down on Pamela from the ceiling fan, and the smell of fresh-baked cookies drifted into the family room from the kitchen. The girls, in their oversized flowered aprons, had helped her bake several batches of oatmeal–chocolate chip cookies and were enjoying their bounty on the screened porch. They sat across from each other at a small table, sipping tea and, of course, wearing their long dresses, bonnets, and plastic high heels. She didn't know how they could stand the heat, but they seemed content, gabbing like young marrieds.

The girls were so enthralled in their conversation, Pamela didn't think they even noticed when she meandered out and latched both screen doors. She was still in hyper-security mode and probably would be for a long time. At that moment, she hoped Granger's apartment had been raided and he was in custody—above all, for the girls' sake. How it would play out from there—if there would be a trial, whether Pamela would need to testify—was anybody's guess.

As usual on Sunday afternoons, Jack had fallen asleep long-ways at the foot of their king-size bed upstairs. They had made up sweetly and enjoyed some peace and quiet together before he drifted off. He'd listened as she explained everything there was to know about her history with Granger. She had a feeling, however, that Jack was a lot more understanding than he would have been if the police had not been on their way to apprehend the man.

She put her bare feet up on the ottoman and opened the Sunday *Dispatch*. As always, she looked first for anything with Jack's byline. This week he had a piece about parents who had lost one or more children to death. Seventy percent of those bereaved couples ended up getting divorced, the story read.

Pamela loved Jack's feature articles. As opposed to hard news like crime and politics, feature stories gave him the opportunity to be creative and showcase his emotions and sensitivity. The story she'd just finished was about Compassionate Friends, a national group of volunteers comprised of parents who'd lost children through death and helped others make it through similar grief.

Pamela couldn't fathom losing Faye or Rebecca. It was one of those unspokens she always tried to prepare herself for in the recesses of her mind, yet couldn't imagine actually living through. She knew if it ever happened, it would be God's plan. She knew that in head knowledge, but losing one of them would be earth shattering. Would she have the faith to endure such an ordeal? Part of her feared she wouldn't be able to overcome the bitterness toward God that would surely come in the days after.

If it happened, it would be meant for a purpose.

But, oh, the suffering it would bring.

You would be forced to deal with it. You would cope, because you would have to.

But the constant wishing, longing, yearning for a smile, a kiss, a hug.

Life would never be the same. You would live waiting for heaven.

Did other people think about such things? Or was all of her fear simply a behavior she had learned from her mom? She thought about confronting her mother in hopes of finding out why Margaret was so afraid—was it a behavior her mother had learned from her parents?

Pamela wanted more children; she envisioned them growing up, loving and encouraging each other, from childhood to adulthood. But maybe she wanted more, too, because she was afraid; afraid of losing one of them, or two. Afraid of what God might allow for whatever reason.

The back door opened, and Rebecca led Faye in by the hand, both holding up their dresses, ankles wobbling on pink high heels.

"Mommy, can we each have one more cookie?" Faye asked. "That will be all."

Sometimes Pamela was certain Rebecca put Faye up to such stunts, thinking Mommy would more readily say yes to the littler of the two. Sometimes Rebecca was right.

"Por favor, señora?" Rebecca added in her most sophisticated tone.

Pamela sat up, trying not to smile. "Two more, that's it."

She began organizing various sections of newspaper, sorting out the ads and classifieds. She glanced at a front-page story about a thirty-seven-year-old family man who'd been beaten almost to death by two thugs the night before at a convenience store. He was clinging to life, and what kind of life he would have if he lived was yet to be seen.

There were bad people out there. So many. All around.

Granger Meade had become one of them.

How Pamela wished she could turn back the hands of time and share with him the only thing that made her any different from him, or even different from her mother, for that matter, who was afraid to walk out her front door in the morning. It was the only thing that made *anyone* safe or unafraid or sane or somewhat stable in that chaotic world: a relationship with Jesus. Pamela was going in, in, in. Deeper inside the High Tower than she'd ever been. He was the creator of the universe. The one who gave the seas their boundaries, kept the snow in its storehouses, and told the lightning where to strike.

She was safe with that kind of God.

How could anything harm her in that place?

But what if it did?

What if he allowed it?

She recalled the words of a song Jack loved. *On the road marked with suffering, though there's pain in the offering, blessed be your name.*

Could Pamela bless his name if tragedy struck?

Bad things *did* happen, yes, to good people and bad. Scripture said that God caused the sun to rise on the evil and the good; he sent rain on the righteous and the unrighteous. In Proverbs it even said God made everything for its own purpose, *even the wicked for the day of evil.*

Such mysteries were terribly difficult to reconcile. The innocent guy in the paper who'd been beaten—what about his wife, his children, his job, their future? What if he was brain-dead? What could possibly be the good in it? Was there good? The thousands of bereaved parents, all this stuff with Granger, why did any of it have to happen? How did people cope? What happened to their faith, or lack of it?

Truly awful things *did* happen. People *were* shaken to the core. There *was* suffering. It was bizarre madness. How could one endure such trials?

When I am weak, then I am made strong.

That was the whole point; she couldn't endure anything on her own. God wanted Pamela to purify herself of any hint of reliance upon herself. She'd come to think of it as an *indelible knowing* that God was in control—and she could trust him completely.

A wellspring of emotion came up from her insides to her eyes and spilled over. She slid to her knees, swept the newspapers from the ottoman, and leaned on it, burying her face in her folded arms.

"Lord, thank you," she whispered. "Thank you so much. Blessed be your name."

Silence fell.

Be still.

The house was quiet.

Then, there it was, out of nowhere.

Pray for Granger.

God had been doing things like that since she'd begun fasting—just bringing things into her mind.

"You are so radical," she whispered. "Your love was so radical. So many hated you, but you gave your life. The least I can do is love Granger."

The word came like a hard, refreshing rain.

Yes.

"Then I lift him up to you. Have your way in Granger's life. I'm not in charge, you are. This isn't up to me … Your will be done. Draw him to you, Lord."

Perhaps God's plan would be to save his soul in prison.

"What you want, I want to want. Help me, Father. Help your desires become my desires."

A thump at the front door startled her.

She stood and walked toward the door.

There was something leaning at an angle against the vertical window beside the door. A package.

It was a brown cardboard box the size of a shoe box.

She got closer, thinking she would see the FedEx man or UPS lady heading back to the delivery truck, but then realized it was Sunday—no delivery.

She stopped five feet from the door.

Heading away from the house, almost to the street, was a large man, wearing black. He looked both ways, a bounce in his stride, wearing black. He quick-stepped around the back of a … brown car.

"Jaaaack!" All of her energy and breath and strength drained from her with the scream. "It's him!"

Granger must've heard Pamela's terror-ridden scream. He stopped, hand on the driver's door handle, staring back at the house, back at the front door—as if peering into the depths of her soul.

Can he see me?

She wanted to step back, out of sight, but was frozen there in the foyer. She wanted to look at the box. Was it a bomb? A dead animal? What had he left? But she mustn't take her eyes off of him.

From upstairs she heard the blinds rip up, then the boom of Jack's footsteps coming toward the top of the stairs. "Coming!"

Outside, still at his car, Granger looked up at the master bedroom window where Jack had opened the blinds, then back at the front door. His big hands went up in the air, palms to the sky, and he shook his head and frowned.

"Where're the girls?" Jack barely hit a step as he plummeted down the staircase.

"Back porch," she managed.

He fumbled with the big locks on the front door. "Get 'em inside. Lock it. Call the police."

"Jack, don't go out there!" Pamela screamed, still seemingly stuck in concrete. "I'll call DeVry. Come back."

The door banged open and swung back. Jack was tearing so fast toward the brown car, Pamela thought he might bulldoze the whole thing if it was still there by the time he made it to the end of the driveway.

She locked the door, turned, and made for the back porch. The girls played on cluelessly, music blaring from a small boom box. Pamela stopped hard at the back door. They would be so scared if she rushed them in and locked the doors, exposing them to the fact that the "bad man" had returned.

Maybe she should leave them out there, so they wouldn't have to know.

She changed course and went back toward the front door.

Jack was on top of Granger, his knees pinning the large man down like a vise. Pamela's whole body flushed as she saw a blur of white knuckles grasping, tearing, bashing; taut necks and faces; blood splattering and glistening in the sun.

The girls would have to be okay where they were. She snatched the phone from the kitchen, grabbed Officer DeVry's business card from the side of the refrigerator, and punched his number as she headed for the front door.

17

Jack cut loose punches to Granger's stomach and face before he was lashed with a surprise left backhand that felt like a two-by-four. The blow laid Jack on the street, and before he had a chance to rebound, Granger's damp body smothered him. His large fists twisted Jack's collar until he was locked down.

Jack maneuvered one of his arms around the creep's enormous elbows and skimmed his forehead with a punch, but it didn't faze him.

"I don't want to hurt you." Granger was out of breath, pushing painfully harder on Jack's chest and arms. Blood trickled down Granger's puffy face from a gash beneath his eye. "I returned your stuff. I'm leaving—for good."

No, that wouldn't do. He couldn't let Granger haunt them anymore. Jack was the gatekeeper of the home sixty feet away, and his girls were in there. He arched and kicked and butted. They were both breathing like worn-out dogs. Suddenly Granger seemed to hoist an extra forty pounds he had been hiding onto Jack's stomach and shoulders.

"Just let me go," Granger grunted from clenched teeth. "You'll never see me again. I promise you."

"You're gonna pay." With all of the fury churning inside him, Jack loosened an elbow and jacked it toward Granger's face. It cracked his nose, and his assailant's eyes closed. He shook his head, conveying the oddest look of, what, humiliation? Blood dripped from his hooked nose, over his lip, onto Jack's chest.

"Don't make me tie you up." Granger twisted his knobby fists tighter, and Jack's collar cut into his neck, making it difficult to breathe.

"Leave him alone!" Pamela's scream came from the front of the house. "Get out of here. The police are coming!"

Granger's posture straightened, his neck seemed to telescope three inches, and his wide head turned toward Pam's voice. His mouth opened. His eyes enlarged. He drank her in.

"We know who you are," Pam called. "You won't get away. Leave him alone."

"Those are your things." Granger panted, nodding past Pam toward a box at the front door. "Everything's there, Pamela."

Jack's stomach soured when he heard his wife's name come from the freak's mouth.

"Get out of here, now!" Pam said.

"I'm trying." Granger squeezed Jack's collar. "He won't give up."

"Let him leave, Jack." Her voice was close now, within ten feet. "He won't get far."

"Stay away, Pam!" Jack yelled. "Get inside!"

"Granger, please, leave!" Pam barked.

It made Jack boil even more that Pam addressed him by name and that she had to be the one to coax him off their property.

"I'm sorry, Pamela." Granger stared at her while riding Jack. "I never meant it to be like this. I ... I wanted to talk to you, like we used to."

Pam finally came within Jack's sight, arms crossed, clutching the cordless house phone in one hand.

"It got out of control." Granger's voice broke, his face twisted, rows of lines deepened above his eyes. "Sometimes I …" His head dropped. "I would never hurt you."

"Good, now just go." Pam pointed toward his car. "Jack, let him go!"

Lying there beneath the strange, heavy body, Jack felt weak and incompetent, as if he was the outsider looking in on the love of his life and this … this stronger man who had once attracted Pam's sympathy.

"Okay, get outta here." Jack allowed his body to go limp, but meanwhile alarms of rebellion screamed in his head and sent tremors throughout every fiber of his being.

Let the pig think I'm giving up.

Jack huffed, "We better never see you again." He closed his eyes and inhaled deeply, feeling Granger's grip release.

Wait, just wait for the right moment. Be ready to explode …

Granger grunted as he hoisted himself up and turned to face Pam. "I'm sorry for what I've put you through." He wiped his sweaty, bloody face with the back of his thick wrist. "I won't bother you anymore. Please, I hope you can forgive me."

With that, he repositioned one of his legs and looked as if he was going to walk toward his car. In that instant of shifting, Granger's tree-trunk legs formed a perfect upside-down V almost directly over Jack's right leg.

From complete stillness to a blur, Jack thrust his right foot upward with all the adrenaline-laced venom he had been storing up since his home was invaded.

With a dense thud, the kick landed squarely in Granger's crotch. The air left him with a grunt and he bent over, his surprised face within three feet of Jack's.

Rolling onto his right shoulder to gain momentum, Jack exploded with a right fist to Granger's face and nose, following through all the way to his left side. The blistering pain in the back of Jack's hand told him the punch must have scored some damage, although Granger did not fall.

Pam screamed and ran full out for the house.

"You shouldn't have done that." Granger's muffled voice came from behind one of his mitt-size hands that covered his bleeding nose and lip.

Like a missile leaving earth, Jack propelled himself from the ground toward Granger, head lowered, with the intent of sticking him in the gut and driving him like a tackling sled into the side of the brown car.

Jack made it to his target, but Granger only staggered backward a step or two. With surprising power, he bear-hugged Jack and slammed him into the parked car, bashing his lower back against the side mirror. Jack's legs lost all strength, and he collapsed to the street, realizing that the wind had been knocked out of him. His head whirled.

A glance at the house revealed that Pam had made it inside.

Good.

Rolling to his elbows and knees, Jack stopped and focused on breathing. Everything flipped to slow motion, and he saw Granger's black boots approaching from the side.

"Pamela." Granger took a step toward the house. "I did not mean any harm."

The pain in Jack's back was searing. He was dizzy. But he was catching his breath, trying to gather enough steam for one last burst.

"You planned it all," Pam yelled from the door. "How could you be so hurtful?"

Jack realized she was trying to stall him till the cops arrived.

"I'm messed up. I know that." Granger's boots moved another three steps toward her. "Sometimes I'm okay and other times ... I do things I don't want to."

"You need help, Granger," Pam said. "Sit down where you are and wait for the police."

He laughed. "The police are going to help me?" He moved toward her again, wiping the blood from his mouth.

"Don't come any closer!" she screamed.

Jack had to muster one more attack. It didn't matter what happened to him.

"You were the only person who ever cared about me." Granger continued slowly toward the front door. "And now it's too late."

"There are people who can help you." Pam's upper body leaned out the front door, her fingers poised to slam it shut if he got too close. "God can help you."

"Would that be the same god my mother and father claimed to follow?"

"Your parents had problems," she called. "They weren't right. You've got scars from that, but God can make you new."

"It's no good, Pam." Granger was within ten feet of her. "I've read the Bible. I know all about it. My parents lived and breathed religion, but they poisoned me with their evil."

Clutching his back, Jack forced himself to his knees. His tail-bone felt cracked. DeVry wasn't going to make it in time. Jack had to take Granger until the cops arrived.

Granger glanced back and spotted Jack on his knees. In a flash he dashed over, booted him sprawling to the pavement, and ran for his car.

Through the pain, Jack worked his way to his feet, but only in time to see the brown car bend around the corner and speed out of sight.

18

Now I'm in for it.

Although he didn't see any squad cars or uniformed officers, Granger felt as if the police were closing in on him as he drove, windows down, under the speed limit, into the city limits of Trenton City. Creeping past the Nicoma Café, past Butch's Barber Shop, past Sun Appliances, Granger realized life as he knew it was about to change dramatically.

He'd said what he'd had to say to Pamela, and that was that. There was no more he could do to clear the slate with her. Part of him wanted to pull over along the city sidewalk and simply wait for the cops to converge on him.

Could penitentiary life be that bad, compared to the life he'd lived? Shoot, he knew it would; it'd be as bad as the day was long. But his whole life had been bad; it had been a prison with walls not made of bars or razor-wire fences but of condemnation and disapproval, criticism and gloom.

He was so alone.

Always had been.

His world was dark and sad and seeping with the heaviness of insecurity and loneliness. Except for those times with Pamela, those fleeting moments from his youth—the only times when he ever really felt free or alive or worth anything.

He'd seen fear in her eyes at her house, to be sure, but there was something more. Behind all the tension, he saw that Pamela still cared; she was still concerned about him.

Stopped at a light on the corner where the Home Spun restaurant filled up with a lunch crowd of fried chicken lovers, Granger admitted that he did not have the skill, knowledge, or prowess to dodge the law for long. Fugitives never remained on the lam very long. They were always tracked down, bagged, and booked.

The toot of a horn from behind made Granger aware of the green light, and he hurried along in the sweltering car, whose air-conditioning had failed long ago.

Everything he owned was in the black bag in the seat behind him. *Sheesh.*

Do you realize what people would think of that? Of you? To think that you have resided on this planet more than thirty years and what you have to show for it fits into a two-by-three-foot satchel?

A disgrace.

Waste of breath.

Detriment to society.

Who would care if he was gone?

If he did not exist tomorrow, what difference would it make?

Would it impact one single thing?

Would any great task or project or mission that impacted lives fail to be completed?

Would anyone cry out in mourning or miss his presence so much that they actually hurt inside?

Not even close.

What would they do with his body? Cremate it? Bury it? Who would pay for the casket? Would there be a funeral? No one would come.

Would Pamela come, if she knew about it?

The romantic part of him cried, *Yes, she would be there!* She would insist on getting dressed up and going alone. She would kneel at his graveside and drop flowers on the casket after it was lowered into the ground.

Some guy was right on his tail in a humongous pickup truck. All he could see in the rearview mirror was the guy's dang grill. Probably some little five-foot dude with a Napoleon complex.

Granger flipped his blinker and pulled into one of the angled parking spaces in front of the Second Chance Thrift Shop. The pickup roared past with the rigged-up muffler you would expect from such an idiot. Granger put the car in park and turned it off. He had saved up a good bit of money from the job at the bowling alley, but not enough to buy a decent car. If he was going to avoid the police for any time at all, he needed a different vehicle.

He didn't want to steal one, didn't know how to jump-start one. The fact was, he didn't want to take someone else's car. But the clock was ticking and so was his heart. This was it.

Subconsciously he knew why he had parked in that spot. There was a gun shop several stores down.

Why do you need a gun?

Granger didn't want to go to prison. If he had a gun, that gave him more options.

Like what? Shooting anyone who closes in on you? Are you really going to do that?

He knew he probably didn't have it in him. Perhaps he would draw his weapon and let the police fill him with lead.

Or maybe you'll kill yourself.

That was just words, a blip on the screen, a flash in the back of his mind.

You probably don't have the guts to do that either.

Or maybe he needed the gun to take Pamela. Maybe that's what this was all about.

All of it was just a rush of thoughts.

His nose felt broken. He checked it in the rearview mirror and wiped away the dried blood.

Had the police put out some sort of bulletin about him? If so, he would be dead meat if he tried to buy a gun, because he'd have to show his driver's license. If not, they were sure to do so within minutes, since Pamela and Jack were probably explaining everything to the police right now, while he sat sweating like a pig in that roasting car.

He made up his mind, got out, and headed for the gun shop. Bells tinkled above his head when he entered, and the cold air-conditioning sobered him.

"Hey there," came a voice somewhere in the crowded store.

Granger finally spotted the small guy at the far end of the long glass counter. He had long, shiny brown hair and was wearing a black Who T-shirt. Granger nodded and quickly found the used guns within another long glass counter on the opposite side of the store.

"Is there anything I can show you?" The little guy with the Who shirt was headed toward where Granger stood, scanning guns and price tags.

"Yeah, can I see that little Jennings? That one for a hundred and twenty?"

"Sure."

There were a couple other customers in the shop, a tall guy in a cowboy hat and a middle-aged lady with a tattoo of a cat on her wrist.

"That's a handy little gun," the kid said as he worked hard to push the slide back, checked to make sure it had no ammo, and gently handed it to Granger. The kid's front teeth were badly out of whack, and he was extremely thin. Granger felt comfortable with him.

"This is probably a dumb question, but what is this, a .22?" Granger felt the weight of the little piece.

"This is actually a .380, so the ammo is slightly larger than a .22, but it's still nice and compact. Great for the glove compartment. Fits in your pocket. We just got that in a day or two ago on a trade."

"I'll take it."

The kid laughed. "Well, that was easy. Where's my easy button?" He laughed some more, locked the back of the counter, and headed around to where he had originally been standing. "Can I get you a couple boxes of ammo for that?"

The bells on the front door jingled, and two cops walked in. Granger lost his breath for a second. He looked away, took in a deep breath, and told himself to keep cool. He had been going to ask the kid how many bullets were in a box, but now, the sooner and more quietly he got out of there, the better.

"That'll be fine," he said to the kid.

"Two boxes?" the kid called.

Granger nodded and glanced at the cops. One was off looking at heavy artillery across the store. The other was giving him the eyeball. Granger knew he must look ratty after the fight with Jack and wondered if he was bleeding somewhere.

He quickly turned back to the counter where the kid had stacked the gun and ammo boxes.

"Do you have a carry permit?"

"No," he whispered and shook his head.

"That's fine," the kid said. "Just fill this out and we'll get you going." He pushed a paper on a clipboard to Granger and handed him a pen.

Now you've done it, you idiot.

He could feel sweat forming at the top of his forehead.

If he filled out the form and the kid got some kind of red flag when he did the background check, the cops were right there.

How could he get out of there?

He'd tell the kid he forgot his wallet, that it was in his car. Then he could make a break for it.

You never do anything right. Even this …

"Whatchya gettin' there?"

Granger flinched and turned, quicker than he should have.

It was the cop who'd been watching him. "That a little nine?"

"Ah, no, actually it's a .380." Granger swallowed hard and wiped his forehead with the palm of his hand.

"I like them two-tone jobs." The cop pointed to a copper-and-black-colored gun in the glass case. "They're makin' 'em sharper and sharper these days."

"Yeah, they are," Granger said.

With pen in hand, he bent over the paper on the clipboard. He had to start writing something, but his mind was a jumble. He thought he might drip sweat right onto the paper. Should he fill out a false name, say he forgot his ID, and get out of there? Or fill out his real info and take his chances?

Head buzzing, Granger scanned the form. Beyond name, address, and social security number, it asked:

___ Are you a fugitive from justice?

___ Are you under indictment?

___ Have you ever been convicted?

By that very moment, he was probably considered a fugitive. There must have been twenty yes-no questions on the forms. There was no way he was going to stand there, fill that thing out, and take the risk of being grabbed.

"Man, I don't know what I was thinking," Granger said softly, taking several steps toward the kid, who had wandered ten feet down the counter. "I left my wallet in my car. Lemme go grab it. Be right back."

"No worries," the kid said, as he walked toward the gun and ammo Granger had been about to purchase. "I'll put this behind the counter till you get back."

"Great."

Granger turned and headed for the door, his heart thundering.

He sensed the cop, still way too close. Saw his dark uniform out the corner of his eye.

Just keep going.

Within three feet of putting his hand on the door to push his way out of that hornet's nest, Granger took one last glance back.

The cop stood frozen, brazenly staring at the bulge in Granger's back pocket, precisely where his wallet was situated.

Like a flash, the cop's brown eyes flicked up to meet Granger's. He squinted, as if taking a mental photograph.

Granger practically fell out of the store, losing his balance on the two steps leading down to the sidewalk. He found his feet and fought his way through the wall of sweltering heat that engulfed him. He was tempted to peer back through the store windows, but instead made a beeline for his car, moving as fast as a man could move without running.

19

Pamela turned on the lamp next to her in the den as the evening shadows filled the room. The police had finally gone, except for the one watching the house from her patrol car out front, and Jack was upstairs giving the girls their baths and getting them ready for bed.

She looked at the old driving directions she had just dug out, the ones she always used to get to her parents' home on Cleveland's east side. There were a few stretches of Ohio freeway where she always got confused.

She had not told Jack she was planning to take the girls to her parents in the morning. She knew it might not go over well, but this was a battle she was prepared to fight, because she was convinced it would be the safest place for them until Granger was captured.

Pamela tried to imagine Granger's basement apartment and the photographs of herself that Officer DeVry said they had found plastered all over the walls. Photos from old yearbooks, pictures he'd taken on her wedding day ...

How could she mean so much to him? She had simply been nice to him. She'd noticed someone shy and odd and wanted him to feel like he fit in, like he had some friends.

Jack was not the least bit sympathetic, but that was between him and God. She didn't have the time or energy to be his spiritual voice.

In the box Granger left at the front door they found Rebecca's locket and Pamela's jewelry. The police took it all with them as evidence, including the letter Granger had enclosed in the box.

In that cryptic, slanted handwriting of his, he'd written a lot of the same things he'd said in the confrontation out front. He was sorry, realized he had gone too far, and felt as if he was losing touch with reality.

The letter was depressing and pitiful. He was a man showing obvious signs that he had been mentally abused his entire childhood. He had no one in the world and viewed himself as a worthless loner who never should have been born.

Those were his words.

How could his parents have been so cruel? It was their fault he'd turned out this way. What had gone on in that house around the corner from hers when they were in high school? The house wasn't visible from the street but was grown over with trees, thick brush, and weeds. Did his parents still live there?

DeVry and the other officers involved in the case insisted Granger wouldn't get far. They thought he was driving the same brown car. One Trenton City officer thought he spotted Granger in Amiel's gun shop on the square, trying to purchase a gun. Pamela wondered why he wanted it. To kill himself? He seemed desperate enough, and he had to know the police would track him down soon. To hold someone up for a car or money?

To come back and torment them?

She heard Jack's footsteps on the stairs.

"Cop still out there?" he asked.

"Last I looked she was," Pamela said. She heard him open the slats.

"Yep."

"From what I can tell, she looks tougher than any of the guys who were here today," Pamela said, trying to soften him a bit before broaching her trip to Cleveland.

He plopped down next to her on the couch and groaned. "I wonder where he is right now."

"How's your cut?" She reached toward the bandage a paramedic had put on the gash at the back of his head.

"Can't even feel it."

"How do the girls seem?"

"If only I had that kind of faith," he said.

"Why? What happened?"

"Just the way Faye prayed. So much confidence God will protect us 'from that Granger man.'"

They both laughed.

"She prayed for my boo-boos to heal and for God to help the police 'catch the man.'"

"Aw. What about Rebecca?"

"She's quieter about the whole thing. She's either scared or feels sorry for the guy."

Pamela watched as Jack found the directions lying next to her on the couch.

"What's this for?" he said.

"I want to go to my folks' in the morning. Take the girls. Just for a few days, till they catch him."

"What for? We have police protection here."

"You heard the police, though. They said he's not going to get far in that car—"

"He can change cars, Pam."

"But I feel like he's still around here."

"He's going to be on the run!" He shifted uncomfortably. "He knows exactly where your parents live."

"I just have a feeling we need to get away from here, out of town."

"What about my folks' place in Florida?"

"I thought of that, but it's so far."

"I know."

"This is what I want, Jack."

"I could work from the house, you know? We could all be together that way. It's going to be over soon."

She wanted to remind him that they had all been together that day, and look what had happened, but she didn't want to make it worse than it already was.

"If it is over soon, then we will have had a great couple days letting the girls be with my folks. Something in my spirit is telling me to go."

"What are you going to tell your folks?" Jack said. "Your mom will have an absolute conniption."

"I thought I'd just say we came to visit," Pamela said. "That you're putting in a lot of time at the paper, working on Evan's case."

Jack leaned forward and stuck his elbows on his knees. "I want to protect you. That's my job," he said. "Do you understand that?"

"I do." She rubbed his back gently. "Of course I do. But I'm not comfortable here right now. Between the break-in and him showing up today, I just need to get out of here. I need to get the girls away. Maybe you could come too?"

"I can't do that. I've got work to do. I'm way behind."

"Well, this way you'll have time alone to concentrate and get caught up."

He sighed. "You're probably right."

"DeVry said they'll have police on the lookout up around Cleveland Heights too," Pamela said.

Jack stood, crossed to the window, and stared into the dark.

"Honey," she said, "it's not you I don't want to be with—it's here. This house. Trenton City. I just need to get away."

He turned to face her. "I understand."

Pamela got up and went to him. He rested his hands on her shoulders and looked down at her.

"I'm ready for this to be over," she whispered and leaned her head against his chest. "I'm running out of steam."

"You're strong, Pam." Jack ran a hand up the back of her neck, fingers into her hair. "You've been a trouper. You need to go."

Oh, the relief.

Yes.

Leaving her head where it was, she squeezed him tightly, and whispered, "Pray for us, please …"

20

By eight the next morning, Jack was pleased with how right every-thing felt about the girls being on the road for Cleveland. Pam had risen when it was still dark, packed the muffins she'd made the night before, and thrown some things into one big suitcase. She woke the girls and had them in the car and on the road by seven, which should get them to Cleveland Heights by ten at the latest.

There was no reason for Jack to sit around the house. He had showered and gotten dressed for work early when Pam was still scur-rying about. The girls had been amazingly chipper for that time of morning. They were giddy about making the trip and anxious to see MawMaw and PawPaw.

Sitting at his desk in the sprawling, quiet newsroom, Jack scratched out a list of things he needed to get accomplished, in no certain order, most dealing with the Evan McDaniel story.

He had let DeVry know the night before that Pam and the girls would be making the trip to Cleveland. DeVry wasn't concerned and once again comforted Jack by explaining that, because Granger had returned their belongings and knew the police were after him, his most logical move would be to disappear.

Of course, Granger Meade had done nothing "logical" yet.

Jack remembered that Barbara Cooley got into work early at Evan's church, so he started by phoning her. She hadn't heard back from any other church staff about seeing Evan the morning he went missing, but Jack assumed they would contact him directly. Although his email box was brimming with thirty-nine new emails, none of them pertained to Evan.

"I did get one odd email back almost immediately, from Dr. Satterfield," Barbara said.

"Oh? Can you tell me what he said?"

"Here, let me find it," Barbara said. "Here we go. 'Mrs. Cooley, obviously Mr. Crittendon convinced you there was some sort of mischief surrounding Pastor Evan's disappearance. Please, let's not stir up the troops. This is far-fetched media hype at its finest and will result in nothing positive. On the contrary, it will only generate innuendo and gossip. From now on, kindly restrain from sending out any more such correspondence. In Pastor Evan's absence, please run any such communication by me for approval first.'"

"Barbara, I'm sorry about that," Jack said. "It sounds like I got you in trouble."

"Don't you worry about it," she said. "That's nothing unusual for Dr. Satterfield. I thought it was a good idea, and I was happy to do it, for Evan's sake; I just hope it gets some results."

At Jack's request, Barbara gave him cell and home phone numbers for Sherry Pendergrass. She also told him that Patrick Ashdown and Rhonda Lowe were due into the church office soon. Jack planned on going to the church unannounced that morning to speak with them. He could do it by phone, of course, but he preferred to be able to see their facial expressions and body language.

"There is one more thing, Mr. Crittendon."

"Please, call me Jack."

"Jack, okay," Barbara said. "Since you asked for Sherry's numbers, I thought you should know, I haven't seen her at church at all."

"That would be since Evan's disappearance?"

"That's right. Remember I told you—"

"They met weekly like clockwork, but suddenly nothing was on Evan's calendar with her for the week he disappeared, or any other week."

"You have a good memory."

"That's my job."

"Right, well, I know it's only been ten days or so, but you have to understand, Sherry is a fixture here—Wednesday night, Sunday morning, Sunday night, and she comes to a women's Bible study Friday mornings."

"She hasn't been to any of those things?"

"No. And she wasn't on campus at all Sunday—morning or evening."

Jack was searching his notes for days and dates, but Barbara was a step ahead of him.

"I've looked back at the calendar and checked the attendance sheet," she said. "Sherry was not at the ladies' Bible study the Friday morning Evan went missing either."

"Hmm." Jack made a note of it.

"Them fish don't fry, do they, Jack?" She *click, click, clicked* her tongue.

Boy, was she a character. And she had a point. Evan could have run off with Sherry Pendergrass.

"I'm going to try to contact her," Jack said. "Hopefully she can provide some insight."

"Anyway," Barbara said, "you know I'll be watching like a hawk for her at this end."

Jack thanked the secretary and told her he would be seeing her soon.

Next he called the home phone number for Sherry Pendergrass but got only endless ringing. He tried her cell next, and it went straight to voice mail.

"This is Sherry. Please leave me a message."

"Mrs. Pendergrass," Jack said, "this is Jack Crittendon, a reporter with the *Trenton City Dispatch*. I am writing a feature story about Pastor Evan McDaniel and his disappearance. My wife and I attended a marriage seminar Evan and Wendy did at the church, and I know he is a good man." Jack considered himself fairly deft at knowing what to say to get people to call him back. "Please give me a call. It shouldn't take more than a few minutes."

Pam and the girls should have been well into their trip to Cleveland by the time Jack put the phone down. He began packing up his leather satchel to head for Evan's church when his office line rang. It was Wendy McDaniel.

"Is it too early?" she said. "I was just going to leave you a voice mail."

"Not at all," Jack said. "I'm hard at it. How are you? What's the latest?"

"Oh, gosh, where do I start?" Wendy took a deep breath and exhaled. "Well, first of all, thank you for the fine story in the paper. I thought it was well done."

"You're welcome," Jack said. "I wanted to let you know a couple things. One, it was not as detailed as I planned, or as you might have expected, simply because my life has been chaos the past week. Two, I had Derrick Whittaker help me with it, for that reason. But I gave him all my notes and approved the story myself. I'm hoping the next piece will have my full attention."

"Perfect," Wendy said. "And I want to know more about what's happening with you and Pam and the break-in, but I've got some news I'm bursting to share."

"Tell me."

"The police believe Evan's car was spotted on I-75 southbound by a traffic cam."

"That's great news, Wendy. When was this?"

"Friday. Three days ago he was alive."

"Could they tell if he was alone?" Jack regretted it the second he said it.

There was a pause and a sniffle.

"Alone?" Wendy said. "They didn't say. What makes you ask?"

"Oh … I don't know." Jack hesitated. "I guess it's just the news-man in me."

"Jack, have you found out something you're not telling me?" Wendy said.

When are you going to learn to keep your mouth shut?

A dozen answers and ways to explain raced through his mind.

"Wendy, no," Jack said.

"There's something …"

He stood and silently cursed himself.

"Please, Jack, I need to know everything," Wendy said.

"Look, this is nothing," Jack said. "In my interviews, the name Sherry Pendergrass came up—"

"Ohh ... I get it," Wendy said. "People are telling you there was an affair."

"No one has come out and said it," Jack said. "The only thing that I felt was important was that she had a weekly counseling meeting with Evan, and the week he disappeared there was no meeting on his calendar."

There, it's out.

He wasn't about to twist the knife by telling her Sherry hadn't been at church since Evan disappeared.

Wendy said nothing.

"It probably doesn't mean anything, Wendy, I've just got to cover—"

"Okay," Wendy said, "here it is. Sherry Pendergrass is a lovely, beautiful, very rich widow who is extremely lonely—I would say, to the desperation point. She's leaned heavily on Evan since her husband's death. But to my knowledge she is a very faithful, generous, God-fearing woman."

"Okay ..."

"Evan has counseled her every Wednesday for five or six months," Wendy said. "He's an excellent counselor. That's his spiritual gift. People are comfortable with him. He listens. He asks the right questions. He prays. He gives wise, biblical counsel. She's not the only woman he meets with one-on-one, and I have never had a problem with it. It's other people who have a problem with it, Andrew Satterfield being chief among those. I swear he's trying to get rid of my husband."

Jack sat back at his desk and scribbled some notes.

"But the funny things is"—Wendy was getting revved up now—"Satterfield has *encouraged* Evan to meet with Sherry Pendergrass. Can you guess why the double standard?"

"Why?"

"What's always the bottom line?"

"I'm not tracking with you."

"Money, Jack. Sherry likes Evan. She trusts him," Wendy said. "Over the months she's almost come to depend on him, to a fault. Evan and I have discussed this. There's nothing romantic going on, he assured me of that. But the thing is—and all this is off the record—her giving has increased dramatically since Joel died. Satterfield attributes it to her relationship with Evan. And he may have something there. She's given special gifts to the church-planting fund, which is especially dear to Evan's heart."

"So, Satterfield thinks it's wrong for Evan to counsel one-on-one with women, *except*—"

"Except when it's with a rich widow who happens to be the church's cash cow."

Okay, Jack understood that, but was Wendy completely naive?

What kind of man was Evan McDaniel? From what Jack had seen of him at the marriage retreat, Evan was rock solid, and so was his marriage.

But where was Sherry Pendergrass? Could she have run off with Evan? Jack imagined them driving to Miami and taking off on a flight to who knew where.

"Does Evan have a computer at home?" Jack asked. "And have you gone through it, extensively?"

The further this thing went on, the more Jack felt like it was a ministry project rather than an assignment for the *Dispatch*. He had a chance to help Wendy and her boys find their man.

"I did that the first day he was gone," Wendy said. "The police have it now. They said they'd bring it back within a day."

"Did you find anything?" Jack asked.

"No." Wendy paused. "That's what's disconcerting."

"What do you mean?"

"His computer was clean as far as I could tell," she said. "No history. Emails gone. Most of his files cleaned out." After a moment of silence, she began to weep softly.

Jack's heart broke for Wendy as more doubts arose about her husband's disappearance.

"I didn't tell you that before. I don't know why. I wanted you to believe he hadn't run off. He hasn't; I know he hasn't!"

"But because his computer was recently purged you're upset," Jack said, "because it looks like he was preparing to leave. Is that it?"

She cried openly. "God … my boys. My boys. What are we going to do?"

Jack buried his head in his hands, closed his eyes, and remembered Rebecca's coloring of Jesus in the fire with his three devoted servants.

"Wendy, my seven-year-old daughter Rebecca recently told me something when Pam and I were going through a really, really hard time. Can I share it with you?"

"Yes." Her breath hitched.

"'If you believe in God—*really believe*—he'll take care of you. Even if you have to go into a really, really hot fire.'"

She cried openly.

"Now get this part," Jack said. "Only from the lips of a child: 'You have to believe, or it won't work.'"

Wendy's sudden laugh blended in with her sobs.

Jack breathed a sigh of relief and vowed to find Evan McDaniel.

21

Granger was fighting sleep while driving the speed limit northbound on a two-lane Ohio freeway. As the sun dissolved the morning mist, he could better see for the first time the car he had stolen from the old man with the limp at the gas station the night before.

The vehicle was medium blue outside with a light gray interior; totally average, older model, four-door sedan. He glanced over at the logo above the glove compartment: Chevrolet. He'd never been big on Chevys. This was an Impala, he guessed. The smell of cigarettes was deep in the seats and butt-filled ashtray. The windows were smudged with the same tar-and-nicotine coating that covered the windows of his old brown ride, which he had left at the gas station in Trenton City.

He punched the lighter, dug in the seat beside him for the crumpled pack of Newports, fired one up, and reflected on the last twenty-four hours. After bailing from the gun shop, he had driven out of town, into the Ohio countryside. Its curvy, hilly, little-traveled roads—its green pasturelands, leaning barns, and stark blue skies— reminded him of the places he used to escape to when he was a youth in northeastern Ohio.

He would light out there to the country in his old Charger, wind blowing back his hair, Springsteen cranking about those two lanes that could take him anywhere. And he would just drive and sing with the tunes about escaping, finding a girl, making something of his life.

Sometimes he would pull off and park in the cinders up there on the ridge. It was so quiet. He would turn off the music. The breeze comforted him. The air was alive with the smell of grass and animals. Enormous white clouds enveloped him. Something inside told him God must certainly have created the landscape out there in that beautiful countryside, yet that same God seemed to have penned such a cruel script for his life.

He would sit up there and just think, about the most recent berating by his mother, the rats that scurried about him in the shed at night, the most recent humiliation with the bullies at school, the fact that he was overweight and unattractive. He wished, oh how he wished, his parents would change, that he could live in a loving, uplifting home.

He reflected on many of those same things after he fled the gun shop and town the day before and drove out through the middle-Ohio farmlands, which were not a whole lot different from those at home. His heart ached. Having seen Pamela, something mysterious and powerful was pulling him back to her. If he could just spend a few hours talking with her. But he knew better than to go back—her house would have been swarming with police after his fight with Jack.

So Granger had just sat in the old brown clunker out in the country—thinking those same crummy old thoughts from his youth, and trying to figure out what he was going to do.

When dusk came, he had crept back toward the city limits of Trenton City to get gas and a bite to eat and figure out where he was going to spend the night. He hadn't planned on stealing a car at the gas station, but the perfect opportunity presented itself. The man must've been eighty-five. He shuffled ever so slowly.

It was pitiful, what you did.

Granger had watched the old gentleman limp from his car. His thin arms shook like crazy trying to get the gas nozzle back where it belonged. Quickly Granger moved in, explaining that he was sorry, but he was desperate and needed to "borrow" the car. The old guy's mouth just hung open and he looked up at Granger with sagging, yellowing eyes through crooked glasses. Never uttered a word. Didn't seem to have an ounce of energy to protest. Just shuffled backward a step, got out of the way, rubbed the gray stubble on his hollow face, and watched Granger get in and drive off.

After having driven around for some time that night, he parked the Impala in the Sterling Business Park, where it looked like many dozens of night-shift employees parked their cars while they worked. He slid into a space several spots away from any other cars, turned it off, and went for a brief walk and a smoke. He thought about getting on the road and just driving into the night, anywhere. He thought about driving back by Pamela's house. Eventually he just climbed into the back of the Impala, locked the doors, and fell asleep.

He awoke before dawn and got on the road, any road. He heaved a phlegmy cough that made him see stars as he always did in the morning, rolled down the window, and spat. Setting the cruise control just below sixty-five, he worked out the kinks in his legs. He wasn't proud of himself for taking the old man's car; he was ashamed. But as he looked out over the fog and rolling, tree-filled hills and leaned back against the headrest, he did feel a sense of accomplishment for letting Pamela go.

You've given her back her freedom.

Now if he could just escape from the cops, maybe he could start over.

Did Pamela want him in jail?

He hoped she didn't think he was a monster.

But he *was* a monster, of sorts, wasn't he?

Maybe behind bars was where he belonged.

Like he always said, no one escaped the long arm of the law forever.

Where are you going?

He told himself he didn't know. But the fact was, he was heading straight for home. Yes, home sweet home, where those two witch doctors raised him to be the loser he had indeed become.

It made him sick.

Sick, sick, sick.

He grabbed another Newport, lit it, sucked the menthol smoke deep into his chest, and enjoyed the cool burn at the base of his throat. Then he cracked the window and blew out into the wind.

He would pay his dear parents a visit before he was captured, give them a proper thank-you for all they had done for him.

He pictured Pamela's childhood home, not far from his own. Last he knew, her parents still lived there. He would slide by it one last time. Who knew how long it would be before he would see it again.

Pamela had aged so beautifully. After seeing her the day before, he swore she was prettier now than ever.

Jack Crittendon was a lucky man—in more ways than one.

Lucky he's not dead.

He flicked the butt of the cigarette out the window and watched in the rearview mirror as it sparked orange and danced in the road behind him.

Where did those hideous thoughts come from?

You're sick, you know that?

He would never have hurt Jack—would he?

His mother had told him repeatedly that he had a demon.

"You were designed for the Devil's use, Granger Lawrence Meade," she would say. "Just a puppet of the prince of the power of the air."

Perhaps he would not stop to see them.

Perhaps he would just keep driving, right on up to Carvers Cove on Lake Erie.

There was a place he knew where he could sit on the enormous rocks right where the waves broke, mighty and unforgiving. And with the weight of the world—and all the badness and meanness of it on his shoulders—he could slip right into the water, and just keep going.

Cleveland's Monday morning rush hour had dwindled by the time Pamela, Rebecca, and Faye blazed the trail up I-90's Innerbelt Freeway and into the gritty old city.

Buckled up in the backseat—which was now scattered with muffin crumbs, crayons, books, and papers—the girls lifted themselves as high as they could, peering wide-eyed like panting puppies at men and women in suits bustling to work, a homeless person holding a cardboard sign, a messenger on a bicycle, a newspaper blowing across the street. Passing the familiar intersections of Carnegie, Euclid, and Prospect in the cool shade of the tall, ancient brown and gray buildings, Pamela let out a sigh, relieved to be "home." She could finally relax.

They passed the concrete campus of Cleveland State and zipped on out past Superior and St. Clair to the lakefront. There was a shorter way to the Heights, but she wanted the girls to see the lake—and she wanted to see it too.

"Look, an airplane!" Rebecca pointed north at one of the small planes taking off from Burke Lakefront Airport. Heading out I-90 east gave the girls a beautiful view of Lake Erie, whose water was dark, choppy, and vast. They passed runners and walkers, bikers and skaters, and people walking dogs on leashes.

She viewed the people of her hometown as warriors of sorts for braving those frigid, snowy, gray winters when the sun rarely shined. Between the lake-effect winds and the freezing temperatures, it was brutal, both physically and mentally. When spring finally bloomed and summer blossomed—after what seemed like nine months of winter—so did peoples' hearts and souls. They came out of hibernation to relish the thick green grass, to absorb the penetrating heat of the long-missed sun, and to stand between hedges in front yards and talk to their neighbors again.

She'd phoned Jack ten minutes earlier to let him know they were safe and almost to her folks' house. They'd stopped once at a Starbucks along I-71 for a potty break and tea for Pamela. She felt rather proud they'd made the trip so efficiently. Jack had no news from the police on Granger's capture. Surely it could only be a little longer.

Heading out Cleveland Memorial Shoreway, Pamela realized she was actually feeling sympathy for Granger. Who knew what it was like to be bullied as he had and to grow up in that home, with those parents? How difficult it would have been for anyone to overcome all of that mental baggage.

And now what? He would be going to prison.

For how long?

Would he dare invade her life again when he got out?

"Will PawPaw take us on that boat again?" Rebecca asked, refer-ring to a boat tour of Lake Erie that Pamela's dad had taken them on the last time they visited. That was when her mother had pitched such a fit about making sure they all wore life jackets; her dad had almost strangled her.

"I'm not sure how long we're going to be here, honey," Pamela said. "We'll see."

Of course, Pamela's mother had not gone on the excursion. She'd said she felt sick that morning and, indeed, had probably made her-self ill with anxiety. Of what had she been afraid? The water? Other boats? Drowning? It never failed—she always found something to fear.

Don't even go there. Just keep it positive. Be a light.

They passed the picturesque green setting at Lakefront Park. It was spectacular. The sky was a piercing cobalt blue. The sunlight danced on the water.

"How long till we get there, Mommy?" Faye asked.

"Not long, sweetie," Pamela said. "You girls have been so good on this trip. I am so proud of you. What good travelers you are."

"I've got to go potty," Faye said.

They would come back out to one of the parks along the lake sometime during the trip, after they got settled in at the folks' house.

"Okay, sweetie," Pamela said. "Just hold it a few more minutes. We'll be there soon."

In a few blocks Pamela took a right and headed inland toward her neighborhood in the Heights. The old streets, sidewalks, trees, buildings, and residences never changed much. It was the same where they lived in Trenton City. Not so in Atlanta. When they had lived there, the landscape changed constantly—roads being widened, new plazas going up, new schools being built, orange barrels everywhere. She didn't miss it a bit and in fact loved Trenton City as a place for raising the girls.

They curved around Providence Parkway down into the valley. Granger's street was just off to the left. She was tempted to drive by his house, which, last she remembered, was covered up by trees and had a deep, damp, slanting backyard enclosed by a chain-link fence.

The next street was Pamela's.

"Almost there," she said.

She took the familiar turn and felt a tug of apprehension as they glided along the shady, tree-lined street with spots of sunlight dotting the way.

"This is my street," Pamela said, "where I grew up."

The middle-class, two-story homes sat one upon the other, separated by abutting driveways and manicured shrubs.

"I remember this!" Rebecca said. "Oh, I love this place."

Pamela had decided not to tell her parents that she and the girls were coming. It was a bit out of character for her, but she knew from talking to them recently that they were going to be home for the week, and with all of the emotion of the past days, she didn't want to get on the phone and accidentally spill her guts. Plus, she thought they would be blessed by the surprise.

"I remember too!" Faye called.

Pamela swung the red Accord into the driveway and stopped next to the sidewalk leading to the front door. Both of the girls' doors bounced open, and they were flying for the front porch before Pamela could even get out of the car.

Pamela's dad's little gold Ford wasn't in the driveway. He was probably walking at the mall or having his fifth cup of coffee with his cronies at the food court. The mall was his refuge. It was only two miles from the house, and four or five of his boyhood buddies congregated there almost daily.

She got out, gathered some trash from the car, and headed up the sidewalk. Meanwhile, Rebecca had already dashed to the front porch and, with her hands cupped against her face, peered in the front window, while Faye rang the doorbell and knocked at the front door.

Pamela assumed her mom's car was in the garage out back, but she could be at the store or running errands. That would be fine. It would give them a chance to get their things in and get settled. She made her way up the steps to the wide front porch.

"MawMaw isn't answering." Pamela said.

"She must not be home." Faye now did what her big sister had done, blocking the reflection with her hands and looking in through the glass in the front door.

Pamela walked to the far side of the porch and got the key that was hidden behind the shutter. She crossed to the front door.

"Here, sweetie." She put her hands on Faye's little shoulders and gently guided her out of the way. "Let Mommy get in there. I have a spare key here."

"Yay, yay!" Rebecca bounced. "I thought we were going to have to sit out here till they got home."

"Yay!" Faye yelled and tugged on Pamela's shirt.

Pamela unlocked both dead bolts, pushed the old door open, and entered the dark living room. The floor creaked, and the air was still and stale. As she had noticed her past few visits, the house smelled ever so slightly like a nursing home, even more so as she drew further inside.

Old age was old age. The carpet was spotted because they weren't as with it as they used to be. She remembered Mom telling her when they were together last that it was becoming more difficult to keep her breath fresh. Her mother had bouts with yeast infections, and she was fighting a low blood platelet count. Daddy's hygiene had been slipping of late as well, Mom had said. He didn't shave or get his hair cut as often as he used to, and she often had to nag him about putting on a fresh shirt or pants instead of wearing the same things repeatedly.

"Mom?" Pamela headed into the kitchen. "Anybody home?"

"MawMaw!" Rebecca yelled. "MawMaw, surprise!"

"Surprise, PawPaw!" Faye cried. "Anybody home?"

"I don't think they're here, girls," Pamela said.

She noticed something shiny on the kitchen floor and stopped cold. "Don't come in here, girls." She knelt down over shattered pieces of one of her mother's broken dinner dishes.

"Mom?" She stood. "Are you here?"

"What's wrong, Mommy?" Rebecca was holding Faye by the shoulders now, just outside the kitchen.

Pamela scanned the room, thinking her mother might have passed out. She looked for blood from the shattered plate but saw nothing.

"I heard something." Rebecca's eyes shifted to the ceiling. "Upstairs."

Faye looked up.

Pamela went past the girls. "Follow me, girls. Not too closely. Just stay where I can see you." She climbed the steps quickly, her adrenaline kicking up a notch with each step.

This can't have anything to do with Granger.

Maybe Mom had hurt herself or had a heart attack and was somewhere in the house.

The doors in the upstairs hallway were never closed, but one was now: her mom and dad's bedroom at the end of the hall. Should she call the police?

You're paranoid. It's just a closed door.

"Yoo-hoo," Pamela called as she walked gingerly toward the closed door. Her heart ticked rapidly, but she was trying to be light-hearted in front of the girls. "Mom, Dad, anybody home?" She got to the door, stopped, and knocked. "Mom? It's Pamela. Surprise." She knocked harder. "You in there?"

Someone was. Pamela heard movement.

"Mommy, I'm scared," Rebecca said.

"Me too," said Faye.

Pamela could barely catch a breath. "Don't worry," she managed. The top of her head buzzed. It all felt surreal. But she had to get a grip for her children's sake. Quietly she tried the doorknob, but it was locked.

Granger came to mind again, but she pushed the thought away.

"Mom!" She called loudly this time. "Open up; it's Pamela. I brought the girls for a surprise visit."

After a time of silence, the lock clicked loudly, jolting Pamela. She grabbed the knob and pushed the door open. Her mother was walking away into the dark room, arms wrapped tightly around herself, toward a window where the shade was pulled down.

Pamela held up a hand toward the girls. "Stay here for a minute," she whispered.

"Mom?" She walked slowly into the bedroom, overcome by the smell of liquor. She squinted in the dark, scanning the room for any sign of trouble, for her dad, for Granger—but there was no one else. "Mom, did we frighten you?"

Her mother nodded as she stood facing the window.

Pamela touched her shoulder from behind. Her mother was shaking.

"I'm sorry, Mom," Pamela said. "We wanted to surprise you. Bad idea, huh?"

Her mom didn't look back, just nodded more aggressively. Her breathing was rapid and irregular, somewhere between laughter and sobs. Pam leaned around to see her face. The fear and paranoia and bitterness of a lifetime showed in her brittle white hair and deeply creased face—which was highlighted almost grotesquely by swollen, dark purple bags beneath her sagging eyes.

"It's okay, Mom." Pamela gently turned her around, wondering if she was doped up on some kind of medication. "Is that what it was? We just frightened you?"

Again her mother nodded heavily then stared with sunken eyes past Pamela, toward her granddaughters. Her eyes were glazed. Her mouth hung open. If Pamela didn't know any better, she would think her mother didn't recognize any of them.

22

Following Barbara Cooley's advice, Jack made his way to the enormous sanctuary of Evan McDaniel's church in hopes of finding worship leader Patrick Ashdown. Entering the cool, dark sanctuary was like going into a sports arena before the fans arrived. It featured two decks of steep, stadium-style seating all the way around, with a round white stage on the floor at the center—all of it lit by dramatic indirect lighting.

He followed the beating of the drums to the sophisticated-looking drum kit off to one side of the stage but could not see the person making the noise due to the reflections shining off the Plexiglas surrounding the drums.

"Hello," Jack called as he approached.

The sound stopped and a man stood from behind the drums, raising a hand to cut the glare of the lights. "Can I help you?"

"I think so, if you're Patrick," Jack said.

"I am." He put his sticks down and made his way around the equipment and down the steps.

They shook hands and made introductions, and Jack explained the reason for his visit. He turned down Patrick's offer for coffee, and they sat in two cushy theater-style seats in the front row.

Probably about forty, Patrick wore navy Dockers, a pink button-down shirt, with a shiny brown belt and shoes. Based on the man's long, straight blond hair, which was parted in the middle and tied back in a ponytail, Jack assumed the dressy clothes must be part of a staff dress code. Patrick was about six feet, with sunburned cheeks and dark brown eyes and eyebrows.

Jack learned right off the bat that Patrick and Evan were close friends who had worked together for years and known each other even longer.

"I knew something was not exactly right that morning," Patrick said. "Evan was down. His color wasn't good. He looked exhausted. I thought he might be sick." He shifted in his seat. "He seemed absentminded, which isn't like him. When I asked what was wrong, he said he'd tell me later. But looking back on it, there was a look in his eyes … I should have picked up on it and tried to dig deeper."

"What did you see in his eyes?" Jack asked.

"Desperation?" Patrick said. "Anxiety? I'm not sure. Hopelessness? He was obviously not himself. Evan is always all about people, church stuff, ministry, all that. He'd do anything for anybody. But his mind was a million miles away that day. He was consumed with something."

"What? Any idea?"

Patrick shook his head. "Don't know." He squinted and scanned the large room. "Are you aware he struggled with depression?"

"Yes, I've heard that," Jack said.

"He was under a lot of pressure."

"Anything in particular?"

"There's a small contingency in leadership who don't think Evan is fit to pastor."

"I've heard that also—especially Andrew Satterfield."

Patrick looked uncomfortable. Jack explained that he had interviewed Satterfield and had discussed the situation with Wendy McDaniel.

"That guy …" Patrick pursed his lips and waited an extra moment before speaking. "As if there wasn't already enough stress being head pastor, Evan's had to deal with all this infighting."

"This can be off the record," Jack said, "but what do you think about the talk of suicide?"

Patrick chewed the inside of his top lip and again hesitated before speaking.

"It's possible," he said. "But I can't fathom him leaving Wendy and the boys. I just can't. The only way that could be possible is if he was in such a state of depression—worse than any of us knew about."

"I guess that's possible," Jack said.

"From what I know, Evan was fine when he was on his medication. But Satterfield made him feel so inadequate, as if Christians can't struggle with depression, especially those in leadership. That's why Evan quit taking his meds from time to time. If he did take his own life, Satterfield's going to have to live with it."

"Okay …" Jack hesitated. "I'm going to be straight up about this next thing. It's something that's bugging me."

Patrick just stared at him.

"I've been told Evan sometimes counsels women one-on-one," Jack said. "There's a lady named Sherry—"

"Pendergrass," Patrick interrupted. "I'll tell you right now, Evan was not having an affair with her or anyone else. That's that. Next question."

"Okay." Jack nodded and retreated to his notes, pondering where to go next.

"I'm sorry," Patrick said. "That sounded rude, but Evan is committed to God and to the vows he made to Wendy. They lead incredible marriage seminars."

Jack didn't have time to explain that he had been to one.

"Look." Patrick sat on the edge of his seat and clasped his hands in front of him. "He's either gone off because of the pressures and intolerance here at the church, or something's happened to him."

Jack let that register. What did he mean? Could he finally have someone here with as suspicious a mind as his own?

"Like what?" Again, open-ended was always best.

"I have no clue."

"Do you mean foul play of some kind?"

Patrick's mouth shrank to a slit, and his shoulders bounced. "I don't know of anyone who would want to hurt him. Maybe it was something random."

Jack probed, trying to see if there was the slightest chance Patrick might think Satterfield or the disgruntled Hank Garbenger might have had something to do with Evan's disappearance. But Patrick wasn't tracking with him.

Only your mind could conjure up something so dramatic.

The two men finally stood and shook hands. When Jack mentioned he would be looking for receptionist Rhonda Lowe, Patrick offered to walk him to her area.

As they strolled along the wide, plush maroon-carpeted corridor, Jack wanted to check in with DeVry to see if Granger had been captured, but he didn't want to be rude. Besides, DeVry would have let him know.

Jack checked his watch. Almost noon. He pictured Pam's parents, especially her mom, doting over Rebecca and Faye, offering them anything they wanted for lunch, from chips and cheese balls to Ding Dongs.

Rhonda Lowe, it turned out, was one of three receptionists at the church. She was situated in a cramped cubicle plastered with family photos, baby pictures, and Bible verses. Wearing a silver headset and sipping constantly at an iced coffee in a huge Starbucks cup, Rhonda was bone thin with harshly cropped black hair. Her dark purple lipstick stained the top of her straw, and she pecked rapidly at the buttons on the massive phone in front of her while handling calls.

When Patrick apologetically interrupted her to introduce Jack and let her know what he wanted, Rhonda popped up, whipped off the headset, and grabbed her drink.

"I need to take five anyway." She ducked around the corner and told Barbara Cooley she was going on break.

Barbara looked back. "Hey, Jack." She stood, holding a bag of chips. "Do you have a second?"

"Sure," Jack said. "Rhonda, can you give me a minute?"

Rhonda was a step ahead of him. "I'll meet you in the conference room when you're done, right over here." She pointed to the room where Jack had interviewed Barbara.

"Let's just go over here." Barbara led him to a well-appointed waiting area with a glass coffee table, large plant, and several leather chairs. She remained standing and faced him, munching chips as she spoke.

"I've only got a minute," she said, "but I just learned something that I thought you might want to know."

"Okay."

"It's about Sherry," she whispered. "She's always been a big giver, you know, tithes and offerings. The months she counseled with Evan, it went way up."

"Okay." Jack nodded, but wasn't going to tell her he knew that.

"Well." Barbara looked around, then back at Jack. "About a month ago, her giving went way down and then just stopped. It's the oddest thing. I don't know what to make of it."

"Hmm." Jack made a mental note of it. "That is interesting."

"I knew you'd think so," Barbara said.

"Thank you for telling me," Jack said. "Anything like that is very helpful."

"Sure thing." Barbara turned to go. "I'll talk to you soon."

Jack entered the conference room.

"I wanted to be a reporter," Rhonda said, curling a leg beneath her in one of the large swivel chairs and spinning around. "I studied journalism for a while. Then I fell in love and got married. Never did finish college. Now we need the money; that's why I'm working here."

They made small talk for several minutes. Rhonda was married to a guy named Jesse, a bass player on Patrick's worship team. They had two children under the age of three. The kids were in child care there at the church, provided for all employees who wanted it.

Rhonda did not know Evan extremely well, she said, but they were familiar with each other and their family situations, and she had crossed paths with him the morning he went missing.

"Hardly anyone was here yet," Rhonda said. "I came in early to keystroke info from visitor comment cards; I was behind, as usual."

CRESTON MAPES

She sipped her drink and rocked in the chair. "Jesse was home with the kids. He had hurt his back the day before helping a buddy move. I told him no more heavy lifting; it happens every time. But he's got to keep up that macho image, if you know what I mean."

When she finally cut to the chase, Rhonda said she had met up with Evan in the hallway early that morning, near his office. She smiled, said hello, and slowed down, expecting him to do as he always did—inquire about her children, her work, Jesse's music.

"But he scooted right by," Rhonda said. "He kind of nodded and gave a half smile but just kept going. It was totally out of sync with who he is. You have to understand Evan, he's the friendliest person. Always has time for everyone. Never talks about himself; he's always asking how *you* are."

"Was that your only contact with him that morning?" Jack asked.

"Yeah," Rhonda said. "I saw him again twice, but he didn't see me. I mean, we didn't talk or anything."

"What was he doing the other two times?"

Rhonda sipped her drink, quickly wiping her chin where she dribbled some. "Once he was on the phone. He was sitting hunched over with his back to the door of his office. All very hush-hush."

Jack made a note.

"It sounds like I'm an eavesdropper," Rhonda said, "but the copy machine is down past his office, so I'm by there all the time."

"What about the other time?"

"It was just a few minutes later," she said. "He was kneeling over a bag. I saw a windbreaker, dark blue, and one of those miniature umbrellas. He was kind of organizing things in the bag."

"What kind of bag?" Jack asked.

"Black. Looked nice, like leather. An overnight bag."

"How big?"

Rhonda held up her hands two to three feet apart.

"Was that the last time you saw him?"

She nodded and sipped. "Yep."

Jack's phone rang, and he glanced at it. It was DeVry.

He apologized that he had to take the call and thanked Rhonda for her time. She smiled, waved, and bopped out of the conference room.

"This is Jack." He walked toward the tinted floor-to-ceiling windows that overlooked the woods; same view as Satterfield's office.

"Jack, Dennis DeVry. Wanted you to know we found Granger Meade's car at a gas station in Trenton City."

Jack's wheels spun. "And?" Everything else evaporated from his mind. The full weight of his world leaned on the next words that would be spoken.

"He stole a car from an elderly man right there at the pumps," DeVry said.

Jack's head dropped, as did everything within him.

"We have a full description of the car, the plates. There's an APB out. He won't get far."

The officer answered all Jack's questions: it happened the night before; Granger was not armed; the elderly man was unharmed; the car was a 2000 medium blue Impala; it had not been spotted since.

All Jack's attention swung like a wrecking ball to Pam and the girls.

Surely Granger was on the run, getting as far away from Trenton City as possible—but where?

He could be in Cleveland Heights right now!

Finding Pam's number on his cell, he cursed himself for letting them go.

You should have made them stay.

Throwing pad and pen in his shoulder bag at the large conference room table, Jack listened as Pam's phone rang three, four, five times—then went to voice mail.

23

As Pamela wandered the bright aisles of the Giant Eagle in Cleveland Heights, shopping for cereal, grapes, and a few other things for the girls, she looked around for Faye and Rebecca. Not seeing them, she spun frantically, on the verge of screaming their names—then deflating as she remembered they were at her parents' house in the Heights.

Phew. The girls had become such a fixture at her side, it was just a habit to make sure they were there. But now Pamela was alone at the grocery. She told herself to enjoy the freedom of the moment and concentrated on making her neck and shoulders relax.

She admitted once again that she scared easily, a behavior she'd learned from her mother. And after all these years, she had some insight into why Margaret lived in such fear. Soon after their disastrous arrival, when her mom had thought someone was trying to break into the house, Pamela called her dad on his cell phone to get him to come home.

Looking older and grayer, he'd knelt down to give the girls big hugs then walked Mom to the back porch where he helped her prop her feet up beneath the breeze of the ceiling fans. He brought her a cup of chamomile tea, an English muffin, and two extra-strength pain relievers. Soon she was smiling with Faye and Rebecca on her lap, asking them all about their summer and swimming and life in Trenton City.

"Her blood sugar drops this time of day," Dad had said to Pamela when they were alone in the kitchen. "She doesn't eat anything."

"She may not have *eaten* anything," Pamela said, "but she's been *drinking*. I can smell it."

Daddy basically ignored the comment.

"She's drinking in the morning now?" Pamela persisted.

"Honey, I don't know what to tell you," Daddy said. "You know your mom. She has a hard time coping."

"Coping?" Pamela said. "You're both retired. You live in a beautiful home in a safe neighborhood. You have good neighbors and friends. I don't understand what there is to 'cope with' that's making her drink during the day."

He had persuaded her to go to a local AA meeting one time, he acknowledged, but she never went back. To some extent, he seemed to blame himself for her discontentment.

"It's not you, Dad," Pamela said. "She needs God in her life."

"We go to church every week. We never miss."

"Dad, the act of going to church isn't what I'm talking about. Does Mom ever read her Bible? Does she get alone with God? Pray about her issues? He can set her free of her fears."

Dad's silence reminded Pamela of her parents' older, war-Depression-era generation. Many of their friends seemed to think all Americans were Christians and, beyond that, they didn't want to talk about it. If anyone dared mention Jesus Christ or salvation or being born again—or, God forbid, hell—they thought you were a fruit loop who should be avoided at all costs.

"Pam." Daddy broke the silence. "It's time we had a talk."

He sat Pam down very close to him at the kitchen table, looked her in the eyes, and began to speak very softly and concisely. "When your mom was in college, something happened to her."

Pamela's stomach flip-flopped, and heat consumed her face.

"A man broke into her dormitory room one weekend when her roommate was away. He kept her there all night—she couldn't get away."

Pamela's heart was pounding. "Oh, Daddy … did he hurt her? … Rape her?"

"She's never been able to talk about it," he said. "He slipped out in the morning, and she never saw him again. But she never reported it or told anyone about it at all for years, until she finally broke down one night and told me that much."

He shook his head slowly. "It changed her life, Pammy. We need to be patient with her."

And now, as Pamela put a box of chewy granola bars in the cart along with the other items and headed for the checkout, she thought about her mother's fearfulness.

You judged her—wrongly.

She would be more patient now, just as her father said. She would set her mind to loving her mom through her troubles.

Pamela had debated whether to even leave the girls with her folks that day, especially knowing Mom had been drinking. But Daddy was always extra attentive when Faye and Rebecca were in his care, so she had grabbed an apple to munch on the way and told them she'd return in a while.

Once outside the Giant Eagle, she walked the shopping cart to her car and let the July heat soak in and thaw the chill that lingered from the freezing store. She put the groceries in the trunk, wheeled the cart to the cart bin, and found herself scanning the parking lot for Granger's brown car on her way back to the Accord.

Was she being paranoid, like Mom? Or would anyone be thinking the same thing after what Granger had put them through?

She wondered why she hadn't heard from Jack with news about Granger's arrest. It had been a whole day since he had shown up at their house. Certainly the police must have tracked him down by now.

She got in the car, shut the door, and dug in her purse for her cell phone, thinking she might have missed a call or text. Jack often asked her in jest why she even had a cell phone, because so many times she failed to answer it. But she couldn't find her phone.

Uh oh.

She dumped the contents of the purse in the passenger seat.

Nope.

She must have left it somewhere in the house after calling her dad, probably in the kitchen.

Jack would be ticked if he knew she was bopping around town without her phone. What if he called her cell and Mom or Dad answered, or one of the girls?

He's going to have to get over it. Besides, he knows we made it safely.

She started the car and put the windows down.

She'd been gone less than an hour.

Working her way out of the large parking lot, she wondered what people did before cell phones.

They had faith and a lot more time to themselves.

She sometimes wondered if the invention of cell phones and computers and iPods was some devious plot by Satan to busy people's minds so there was no time or space or quiet left for hearing God's voice. They made everyone so codependent.

The day was picture-perfect. Blue and clear. Sunny. So good to be back in her hometown. She still called it that, even though their lives were in Trenton City now. But everything was familiar—the streets, the businesses, the memories of youth—and she loved that. She sometimes wished Jack would apply for a job at the *Cleveland Plain Dealer* or *Akron Beacon Journal*. They could find an affordable place in any number of towns near the city—Euclid, Eastlake, Maple Heights.

Still debating what to do next, she headed in the direction of the house but also toward the lake and several shopping options.

Relax.

The girls were fine.

But Mom and Dad don't know about Granger.

He could sweep in there and snatch one of the girls before the folks knew what hit them.

But it wasn't the girls he was after, it was her.

You are so paranoid.

Even if Granger was in the area, he didn't know Pamela and the girls were.

Quit this!

She made a quick left on Neff Road and swung up toward the lake, singing aloud. "Give to the wind, your fear. God hears your sighs and counts your tears … God will lift up your head."

Approaching Lake Erie, Pamela felt like a kid pulling up to an amusement park as she wheeled into the gravel lot leading to a small green area where she and her parents used to picnic. She pulled right up to a rope, beyond which were some steps leading down to the grassy area, picnic tables, and farther out a concrete pier.

It was beautiful. Dark and cold and vast, yet shimmering as far and wide as she could see. God's utter power and majesty were spilled out there before her. It looked more like an ocean than a lake. Several boats dotted the endless horizon. A few cars were parked nearby, no one in them.

She got out to gaze at the water and feel the breeze whip her hair. Yes, waves and clouds and storms would roll in, but God would be the lifter of her head.

Everything. Everything. Everything must be thrust onto him.

That's what he wants.

In weakness he makes you strong.

Nothing can separate you from his love.

Nothing.

Not Granger Meade.

Not anything.

Back at his desk in the newsroom—now bustling with reporters, photographers, and editors—Jack was slightly miffed, his head beginning to buzz with anxiety. It had been more than an hour since he'd left Pam a voice mail telling the latest about Granger, and she still hadn't called back. "He could be anywhere," Jack had warned. "Call me as soon as you get this."

He knew Faye and Rebecca were safe, because he'd phoned Pam's parents' house immediately after failing to reach her. Pam's mother had laughed and said they had heard Pam's cell phone ringing somewhere in the house but didn't answer because, (a) they didn't think they should, and (b) they "didn't know the first thing about operating that contraption." He wondered if, (c) Margaret might have been nipping at the peppermint schnapps.

Pam had told her folks she would be gone awhile, grocery shopping and driving around the old town; she'd obviously forgotten her phone, which frustrated him and left him tight as a drum.

She's fine.

Jack was 98 percent sure of that. It was the 2 percent uncertainty that nagged him.

He sifted through the notes on his desk and glanced at his computer screen. He'd pounded out almost all of a new story on Evan's disappearance, mainly just to stay busy. But it still had holes, and he was a bit hesitant because it didn't deliver a lot of new information.

Pam didn't know Granger had stolen a car and was still on the loose. Even though she had forgotten her phone, she probably figured it didn't matter, since she had called Jack to let him know she and the girls had made it to Cleveland Heights. He envisioned her driving around town, happy as a lark, probably hitting the Goodwill to see if there were any treasures for the girls. *Lord, please … let her be fine. Let them find Granger. Bring this thing to an end.*

His computer dinged, then his desk phone rang.

The email was from Wendy McDaniel. He ignored it for the moment to answer the phone.

"Jack Crittendon."

"Jack, it's Wendy McDaniel. I just sent you an email." The tone of her voice was hurried and high-strung.

"It just popped up," Jack said.

"Don't read it yet," she said. "Please. It's a letter from Sherry Pendergrass. The police found it on Evan's computer."

Jack wanted to read it right then, but he focused on Wendy. "Tell me more."

Wendy sniffled. "She's in love with Evan."

Ouch. That was what Jack had dreaded.

"You'll see when you read it," Wendy said. "I just wanted you to have the latest. Not for print, of course. Just so you know."

"I'll read it when we hang up." He moved to the edge of his chair, wanting to help but not sure what to say.

"I don't know if Evan feels the same about her," Wendy said.

Poor Wendy, hanging on to every last hope. She had to suspect, as Jack did, that Evan and Sherry had run off together.

"Jack," she said. "I think I know where Evan's going."

"Where?"

"Englewood, Florida."

"That place in the picture I saw at your house, where your family always goes? What makes you think so?"

"I just have a feeling."

"Have you mentioned it to the police?"

"Yes, but I can't get any help from them. It's so frustrating."

Jack had a good hunch what was happening. Evan was a grown man. The police had no evidence of foul play. If he had run off in an affair or to commit suicide, that was his choosing. They had criminals to catch.

Like Granger Meade.

"Does the letter suggest … I mean … do we have reason to believe they might have gone off together?" There was no easy way to ask it.

"No, no way," Wendy said.

She was in total denial, especially if the letter said what he assumed it did.

"She may have feelings toward Evan," Wendy said, "but that doesn't mean it was reciprocal."

"Have there been any more sightings of his car?"

"I don't think so. I can't reach anybody!" Wendy began to cry. "This woman's fallen in love with him. Church leadership is driving him out, making him feel guilty. His mind is messed up from stopping the antidepressants. All he ever wanted to do was love people, help people. And this is what he gets."

Sometimes the best way to calm a person was to ask a question, to get the person's mind going in another direction. Jack had an important one; the trick was framing it right.

"Wendy, I talked with Patrick Ashdown and Rhonda Lowe at the church." He let that sink in and gave her a chance to pull herself together. "They both sensed something was wrong the morning Evan went missing, that he wasn't himself. I remember you saying you saw him off to work that morning, but did you speak to him after that—on the phone?"

Wendy quieted. There was a pause.

"No," she said. "Why do you ask? What do you know?"

"Nothing—"

"Please, Jack, don't play games. I need to know everything you do. The police aren't telling me anything. If you have information, I need to know, please …"

"Rhonda Lowe saw him in his office that morning," Jack said. "He was on the phone, that's all. I wondered if he was talking to you."

Wendy said nothing.

Jack realized if he were Wendy, he would want to know everything. He looked at his notes from Rhonda.

"One more thing," he said. "Rhonda saw Evan with an overnight bag that morning. She said she saw him packing a windbreaker and umbrella."

"I'm afraid he's going to hurt himself." Wendy spoke in a quiet monotone.

"I pray that doesn't happen."

Silence.

"Well, that's all I have." Jack tried to relieve the awkwardness.

He heard Wendy take a deep breath.

"Wendy …"

"Thank you, Jack. Please call me the second you hear anything."

She hung up.

Jack drew closer to his screen and opened the email to read the letter from Sherry.

Dear Evan,

Ever since Joel passed away, you have allowed me to call on you and count on you as my counselor, helper, guide, sustainer, and friend. I literally do not know how I would have survived without your presence and help.

The scripture you've given me, the advice, the listening ear, it has all served as balm to my aching soul. In the process of learning to cope with the loss of my beloved husband, I have made a new friend in you and that has truly been a Godsend.

I hope you will agree with me in thinking that the time we've shared together has been not only soothing for me, but enjoyable for both of us. Getting to know you, your hopes and passions, your wisdom, your sense of humor ... it has been a complete surprise and thrill for me. You are such a sensitive man. Each week when we part ways, I never want it to end. Then I think of you often and smile as I anticipate our next session.

The reason I'm writing is to say thank you for being there for me, Evan, for being such a selfless servant. Also, I hope as we continue to meet that you will give me some sort of sign that you are feeling the same way I am about the feelings and emotions I've described in this note.

Warm thoughts and regards,
Sherry

24

Granger perked up and drummed the steering wheel as he rolled back into Cleveland Heights, his old hometown. Appropriately, Kiss was blasting "Rock and Roll All Nite" on the Impala stereo as Granger seemed to float over the hilly road leading to Carver High School.

Other than the large parking lot having been freshly black-topped and the bleachers newly painted in red, white, and blue, the brick school buildings looked exactly the same. He rolled past the outdated two-story middle school, Carver Junior High, and glided through the empty parking lot, coming to a stop at the tall chain-link fence at the football stadium.

Over where a leathery brown Hispanic man in work boots was mowing at a high rate of speed on one of those stand-up riding mowers—that was where Tim Lingoli had teased him in front of the others. Knocked Granger's books from his arms. Poked. Prodded. Called him filthy names. Spit on him. "What are you gonna do about it, Granger Ranger? Huh, Granger Ranger?"

Granger had gone off by himself without a fight.

If you were here now, Lingoli, I'd show you what I'd do about it.

Beyond the thick green grass of the playing field and the black-cinder running track was where the band used to congregate. He had loved being part of it. No, he didn't have friends, but he had made himself so good and strong on that trombone, they had come to need him. Whether they knew it or realized it or cared, he was part of the team—the team that made the music.

The bleachers were the old wooden kind, with slats beneath the seats. People used to drop money through down to the ground all the time. He would walk beneath the bleachers, looking for money as a kid. That night came back to him, when he trudged under there to find a bill Michael Riggler had dropped through the slats.

Granger had always been desperate to make a friend. Just one true friend. Someone who would listen. Take him seriously. Not laugh. Someone he could trust.

Pamela had been the closest thing to a friend he had ever had.

Granger peered down over the hill at the portion of the chain-link fence where Blake Devonshire and his buddies had knocked his band hat off his head and tried to mess him up.

What guts Pamela had, barging down into that scene.

Granger had shown Blake who to mess with.

He'd skidded that loser's face into the stones.

Blast him.

And that special moment with Pam minutes later—she'd held his hand and looked up into his face, those big eyes glistening in the cold. "You're a good person." And she had said his name.

Sitting in the Impala alone at the school, he looked down at the hand she'd held and shook his head.

But you're not good. You're a bad seed.

The mess he'd gotten himself into pressed in on him like a stifling, shrinking cage.

They're coming.

He knew it wouldn't be long.

You're in for it now.

This was his parents' fault. His despicable life was *their* doing. He was fully aware he had been mentally abused growing up, but knowing it was not enough to help him.

He imagined it was like being an alcoholic or shoplifter or gambling addict—fully aware of what led to the condition, the symptoms and effects, but completely unable to pull out of its grip.

The thought of his mother and father made his mind, his whole being, turn inside out.

He could go home one last time. See if they had changed. Try to make amends.

Why do you want to go there?

The police would be watching for him.

You're doing it again.

He drifted into a daze, seeing blue duct tape being wrapped tightly around and around and around his mother's shocked face.

Stop it.

His father's handgun …

Leave them alone.

A smoky, surreal, chaotic confrontation in the living room.

Get away while you can.

Still staring at the hand Pamela had held, his view of it blurred, then flooded, and it dawned on Granger Meade that he was doing something he had vowed long ago never to do again.

He was crying.

❧

Driving by a stately red brick courthouse on the square of a small town somewhere in North Carolina, Evan McDaniel knew he had to get rid of his car. He squeezed his right bicep, which was twitching again. Highway cameras along I-75 hours back had made him diverge from his planned route once again.

Those cameras would spot him for sure—if they hadn't already.

That mustn't happen.

He could not subject himself or his family to any more humiliation than would already be coming.

In Knoxville he'd turned the tables and headed southeast on I-40 a long way to Hickory, North Carolina. Once there, he picked up 321 down to Gastonia. Although there were no highway cameras along those routes, there were local cops and speed traps—a lot of them.

That's when Evan decided to ditch the car.

He could not string this thing out any longer; he had to disappear. It had been days since he'd left Sherry in that cabin. He'd been on and off highways, through small towns, on country roads, and in and out of shabby, backwoods motels—trying to decide where to go and what to do.

All he could think about now was being gone.

Leave no trace of this defective, contaminated life.

His GPS had shown a Greyhound station in the nondescript town of Fort Prince, North Carolina, so he'd taken his chances and gotten back onto I-85, a main thoroughfare that would have taken him down through Atlanta if he'd remained on it. Instead, he'd exited and taken the main road into the town square of Fort Prince, where the battery in his GPS went dead. Because he knew he was close, he didn't bother to dig the charger out of the console, thinking he could find the station on his own.

So much was wrong.

Too much.

He reached into the baggie full of orange pill containers in the passenger seat, several of which were open. He found one of the light blue Valiums with the heart shape knocked out of the middle and threw it to the back of his mouth, but it stuck there. It had been weeks since he'd last had any. He coughed it to the front of his tongue, opened the door, and spit it out. The residue left in his mouth was bitter, like poison. He would kick that junk if it was the last thing he did—which it would be.

His life was strewn with rotten baggage. He'd crossed a line. Like Judas. He'd fallen so short of what a Christian was supposed to be. And he was a pastor. *Held more accountable.* Satterfield had seared it into his head. *Judged more severely.*

And what about the boys? Those handsome, robust, innocent young men. He took a moment to picture each one: Nathaniel … Zachary … Silas.

Bible names.

You worthless hypocrite.

Evan's face, his whole body, burned with guilt and hopelessness.

He'd talked about God as they had grown up, read them the Bible, told them how a Christian should act, taught them how they needed to be boys of integrity, showed them how to minister to people—and what had he become? A feeble, pathetic, drug-dependent weakling.

That was the example he'd set. That was what he had shown his sons a life with Christ would get them. And on top of all of that, now they would think he was an adulterer as well.

How will they get through this?

Likely, they would rebel.

The sins of the fathers …

You've not only ruined your testimony, you've probably ruined their walk with God—showing them there is a cheap way out of marriage, teaching them it's okay to give up on life.

Is this just the easy way out for you? Wouldn't it be best for them if you went back, confessed all your faults and shortcomings, spilled your guts about Satterfield, and hung on? How difficult is it going to be for your precious boys to grow up knowing their father took his own life?

It was too late. There was no going back. He was too tired. It was all too overwhelming.

Each time Wendy came to mind, he immediately forced her out. He could not even go there. His life was a lie. He'd failed her and God, the boys, his family, the church …

Once again, he questioned whether he was even a Christian, whether he would even go to heaven. If there was a heaven. How could God let him fall to such depths? Nothing was supposed to be able to separate him from Christ.

But he was clearly separated. Cut off. Prayers unheard.

There it was—the neon Greyhound logo, half lit on a marquee above several empty metal benches and a set of dirty glass doors. Driving past and turning up the block, he would find some place to hide the car.

The sooner he vanished, the better it would be for Wendy and the boys. They could put this behind them, forget, start over, and live a whole new chapter of their lives. That was the most optimistic game plan Evan could figure out. It was the only plan left.

Sherry.

What had that even been about? He'd entered it innocently, wanting to help. She had begun to fall in love with him.

You brought it on. You teased her. Yes! In your quiet, meek, devious way, you flirted. Why? To prove you are still handsome? Desirable? You'd been looking for something like this. Yes, you had. Slyly throwing the bait out there, not expecting some tiger fish to chomp on to you like Sherry had.

But no, Evan had not made advances toward Sherry! That was a lie. It was all in his mixed-up head. He'd just wanted to help. He felt compassion for her, having lost her spouse and best friend of so many years. He had put himself in her shoes and tried to imagine losing a spouse. That's why he had agreed to counsel Sherry. He only tried to guide her closer to God, knowing there she would find comfort.

But what about that passionate email she sent?

The electricity was there in the room each time they met—like two college kids getting to know each other for the first time.

No, that is not true! You are doing this to yourself. That's what Satterfield wants! For you to feel inadequate, rotten, unrighteous. Nothing you ever did was right in his eyes. That's because he was railroading you out—because you found out too much!

There had been nothing wrong between Evan and Wendy. She'd given tirelessly of herself to their marriage, the boys, their home, and the ministry. And she was more attractive than ever to Evan. Although they rarely made love anymore, because the antidepressants tended to throw a cold, wet blanket over his libido, they were still best friends. But even in that respect, Evan fought terrible silent bouts of guilt because of his lack of ability to be the man he knew Wendy needed.

Yes, Evan had agreed to meet Sherry that day he left. And they *had* met—at a cabin she and Joel owned, nestled on a tree-filled ridge adjacent to a state park in Springfield, Ohio. Sherry had told Evan he needed time away, alone, to sort things out. She said she would simply let him into the cabin, show him where everything was, and the place would be his for however long he wanted it.

In his mind, Evan was thinking that was where he would finally muster the guts to kill himself. That's why he'd left the suicide note. Finally, he would spare his family; spare his congregation all the dirty laundry he knew about Satterfield but had failed so miserably to do anything about. Why? Why hadn't he acted or spoken up? He was so depressed, so consumed with himself—and too inattentive to focus, to rise up, to stop him!

Evan had been barely functioning as it was. He didn't have the mind or stamina to hire auditors to prove Satterfield was embezzling money from the congregation. He'd failed to report the suspicious activities of several elders. He was the leader, the pastor, the shepherd of the flock—living in a chronic state of depression.

"Face it, *Pastor*," Satterfield had said. "You are unfit to shepherd this flock."

And now the world was going to think he was a womanizer too. *Lies.*

Sherry had stayed on at the cabin that day, changing into shorts and a skimpy top, trying to make Evan believe that somehow God had predestined them to save each other. Evan told her to go, that it wasn't right, that he didn't want her there. But she stayed, and he was too miserably weak and self-consumed to do anything about it.

The days he spent at the cabin were like gravel in his mouth.

He knew.

Every fiber in Evan's being cried out that it was wrong that they were there together, even though she was gone for long stretches and nothing physical unfolded between them. It was the "appearance of evil" that mattered in his soul. It *looked like* he had escaped with her. It was wrong because there was a God watching. Wrong because Christ had died for them and they were now killing him again.

Sherry came and went. Evan slept heavy and deep most of the time, with blankets over the curtains so it remained pitch black in his bedroom. The times he did awaken he was dizzy and nauseated. He had stomach pains and uncontrollable crying spells. On that fourth or fifth day, whatever it had been, Evan threw his things in his duffel. Sherry had returned and was out for a walk. When she came back, he sat her down by the stone fireplace and told her he was leaving, that the whole cabin idea had been dead wrong and that he had failed her as a pastor, counselor, and friend.

It was as if a lightning bolt had blistered the place. She knew it too.

Suddenly, the two of them sat there, stone-cold sober in their separate worlds of sin and humiliation and humanness—and they cried. Sherry's trembling hands reached for Evan's shoulders and he pushed them away, as they awkwardly touched hands and separated. She cried out repeated apologies for what she had done to his family and marriage and ministry.

The repulsive lie of their fictional relationship pounded in Evan's head and rib cage as he gathered his things.

"I'm going," he had said.

Mascara running rivers of black down her face, Sherry shook her head, reaching out for him again, but Evan bolted for the door.

"Where?" she cried.

"It doesn't matter," Evan said.

She nodded, almost uncontrollably. "I'll go too. I'm so sorry. I'll go away—somewhere far, right now. You go back to Trenton City, make things right … I'll move away for good if I have to, to clear your name."

Evan blew out of there, leaving the door banging open and Sherry babbling in the wind.

Now, driving about the red brick, red clay, single-story town of Fort Prince, North Carolina, Evan cruised past a deserted auto garage for the second time and turned around to go back. It was his best bet. If one of the three huge bay doors was open, he could back the car in and it would go unnoticed for quite awhile. Pulling up to the broken-down garage, he parked, hopped out, and tried each of the three bay doors, but all were locked.

So be it.

He hurried back into the car and headed for his second choice, a midsize library about three blocks off the square.

It doesn't even matter, just go.

If he had to leave the car out in public, the library was the best spot he could find. He figured no one would notice it had been abandoned for several days. That would be all the time he needed to get where he was going, to the ocean where things had once been the way they should be. There, he would finally do what had to be done.

25

Pamela felt so refreshed to be driving around the familiar streets of Cleveland Heights. No phone. No girls. No responsibilities—just alone. Warm breeze. Memories of youth and times when life was carefree.

She couldn't be out of contact with the girls much longer. And she knew Jack might have tried to reach her again. She figured he might have even called her folks' house, since she wasn't answering; he was so protective. Mom or Dad would have explained that she had forgotten her phone and was running errands.

Just a little while longer, then back to reality.

Back to her parents' house. Back to being a full-time mommy and daughter—and wife. Back to the routine that sometimes got to feeling like a deep rut of repetition, but one she wouldn't trade for the world.

A new Starbucks had gone into the plaza where Dominic's Pizzeria used to be. The car wash across from the bowling alley stood vacant, weeds sprouting through the broken concrete. The tux shop was now a smoke shop, and the mall had undergone a facelift, complete with a big fountain at the main entrance.

It was time to get back.

She took Ravenna Boulevard east toward her neighborhood, past the shoe store, the dry cleaner, and a bunch of little bars and ethnic eateries. Much of the area was blue collar—the skyline not far from there comprised steel mills, smokestacks, and rubber manufacturers. But people were moving south because of plant closings. The area had changed.

Wearing shorts and tank tops, black and Hispanic children, whites and Asians skipped, rode bikes, and skated along the uneven sidewalks. Little girls danced and laughed in a front-yard sprinkler with a beagle nipping at their heels. An elderly man in dark blue denim overalls sat in a rocking chair on his front porch, staring off into nowhere.

Old age was sad. Her parents had changed so.

They would die one day.

Who first?

Would they go to heaven?

Death took everyone.

But what about the innocent?

Babies who died at birth or mothers *giving* birth? Cancer victims? Children starving? Why were some kids severely handicapped and others abused? Even more difficult to reconcile—why did God allow children and young adults to be kidnapped, sexually abused, and murdered by complete strangers?

It happened. Sometimes Christians were the quickest to attempt to excuse God from the equation. "I don't believe God *caused* that plane to crash," they would say, "but he *allowed* it."

But in Pamela's estimation, God was either in control or not.

Somehow, some way, he was in charge of everything—every circumstance. She recalled the words she'd found and pondered so deeply during her fast: *he has made everything for its own purpose, even the wicked for the day of evil.*

She slowed down and made a sudden left on Broussard Boulevard, telling herself it was the quickest route home.

What had Granger been through all those years? How did he turn out the way he did? What had gone on in that house?

Why had God allowed Granger to torment her?

What was the purpose?

Was there one?

Were his parents still alive? Still in that house?

She was curious, that was all.

Without warning or blinker, she made a quick right on Shady Meadows, precisely in the direction of Granger's childhood residence.

❧

Jack had been surprised when Hank Garbenger agreed to take time out of his workday to meet him for a late lunch at Jimmy John's. The sub shop was nestled in a busy plaza near where Hank worked as a foreman in the distribution center of a large dairy manufacturer.

"I got painted the villain over there at the church, but there's more to the story," Hank had spouted on the phone. "I don't know if it has anything to do with Pastor Evan's disappearance, but something fishy's going down over there."

All Jack wanted to do was keep busy until he heard from Pam and, if possible, fill in his story about Evan with some fresher content. Having arrived at the bustling restaurant ten minutes early,

Jack grabbed a roast beef sub and was formulating some last-minute questions as he waited for Hank in a booth.

DeVry had told him on the phone on the way over that there had been no sighting of Granger but that the APB had gone nation-wide. The Cleveland Heights PD and police at several other potential destination spots had also been put on high alert for Granger and the Impala. "To tell you the truth, Jack," DeVry had said, "my gut feeling is that he's a long way from Ohio or any of the other obvious destinations by now."

Maybe it was just his reporter's instinct, but Jack didn't take a whole lot of comfort in DeVry's words. Or perhaps his unrest had more to do with the impassioned look he had seen emblazoned on Granger's face when the creep laid eyes on Pam during the brawl in front of their house.

He was a man possessed.

Jack had tried to reach Pam again from the restaurant but got her voice mail. He did not leave another message; she would see that he had called. Although the last thing he wanted to do was to get her parents riled up—especially her basket-case mother—he decided if he hadn't heard from Pam by the time he finished with Hank, he would call her parents and tell them about Granger and the stolen car. He wouldn't give them all the gory details about the break-in and how Pam was being stalked but just enough to put them on alert.

He made the decision right then that the safety of Pam and the girls was more important than sparing her parents from a few hours of worry.

The man Jack guessed was Hank Garbenger got out of a white van and walked through the crowded parking lot with long, forceful strides, sunglasses atop his head and a bulky white plastic Walmart bag swinging from a big fist. He entered, stopped, searched the room, and made eye contact with Jack, who stood to greet him.

After spreading the vast contents of the sack in front of him on the table, Hank scrunched up the bag and put his head down for a silent prayer. It reminded Jack to do the same, so he took a moment, requesting that God station his guardian angels around Pam and the girls. Then he looked up at the middle-aged man across from him, who had a long, thin, rough-looking face, the kind of guy you might bump into running the merry-go-round at the county fair. He had a head full of curly brown hair and a pack of cigars in the breast pocket of his green-and-white plaid short-sleeved shirt.

Hank said he had read Jack's stories about Evan's disappearance in the *Dispatch*. He seemed genuinely concerned about Evan, the very pastor who had disciplined him in front of the whole congregation for cheating on his wife, according to Wendy McDaniel and Barbara Cooley.

"What is your hunch about where Evan is?" Jack got to the point quickly.

"Oh, shoot, I have no clue where he is," Hank said, taking a mammoth bite of the huge turkey sandwich he'd brought from home. "I for one feel sorry for the guy. I just hope he don't hurt himself; I'm afraid that's where it may be headed."

When Jack asked if Hank had heard about a possible affair between Evan and Sherry Pendergrass, Hank shrugged and got rather loud. "That guy was under a microscope," he said with his mouth full. "Everything he did got scrutinized by the higher-ups. He's the most upstanding person at that church. Even the way he handled my whole mess, he was civil, wise … Some of them pastors and elders had it out for me after the mistakes I made—"

"You're talking about a relationship?"

"Yeah. I admit I made the worst mistake of my life, and I'm paying for it; and I'm trying to fix it. Me and Audrey got counseling, from Pastor Evan, in fact. He did it privately, on his own dime, because the church board wouldn't allow him to counsel us. He met with us every other week for months, and it really helped. Those vultures made the whole situation worse; just scorned us. It figures they'd chase him out. Bunch of Pharisees."

"Do you really think they want him out?"

"It's a fact, okay? Trust me."

"Who, specifically?" Jack had a hunch.

Hank did not hesitate. "Andrew Satterfield. He wants to be the pastor over there—everybody knows it. Now he's getting his wish. He's convinced at least a few of the elders that Pastor Evan is weak. Needless to say, we don't go there no more. But I think Satterfield has major issues."

"I've met him," Jack said. "Issues like what?"

"He's a control freak." Hank dug into a bag of pork rinds. "Just ruthless. You know, Pastor Evan didn't hire him. Pastor Evan was brought in by the board later. Satterfield has always been peeved he didn't get the job as senior pastor."

"I didn't know that."

"I think the whole reason he forced Evan to handle the church discipline on me was because he didn't think Evan would go through with it; thought he'd quit or something. Otherwise he would have loved handling it himself, trust me."

Evan's depression, Hank said, was just another excuse Satterfield used to try and force Evan out the door.

Hank looked around the sub shop, as if to make sure no one was listening too closely. "I'm gonna tell you something, Jack, but you didn't hear it from me. You can write about it, but you can't say where you got it from."

Getting to the good stuff.

"Okay, tell me."

Hank looked around again and leaned over the table, closer to Jack. "I admit when I had the affair and all the bologna was hitting the fan, I was a jerk, okay? I know that now. And there are things I'd do differently."

"Yeah …"

"I was so ticked off." Hank smashed up all the trash from his lunch into a wad and stuffed it into the bag he'd brought it in. "I was mad at Evan for the church discipline, although in the end that turned out to be a good thing." He laughed. "I was mad at the elders. Shoot, I was bitter at the entire congregation, really. But most of all, I had an issue with Satterfield, because I knew he'd put Evan up to it—and it was so humiliating. I knew he wanted me out, and I suspected he wanted Evan out too. So I started following him."

This is getting interesting.

Hank leaned back and took a big breath, then exhaled. "I don't know if I was looking for dirt on him as payback, or if I was hoping he might even notice me following him so I'd scare the tar out of him …"

"And?"

"The guy has a lake house in Lincolntown and a twenty-five-foot sport boat." Hank said it with the force of a howitzer. "It's on Lake Hudson. I've seen it."

"Who knows about this?"

"I'm not sure," Hank said. "But I know that cruiser has twin Volvo engines and goes for a sweet chunk of change."

"Really …" The goal was to keep him talking.

Hank closed his eyes and nodded slowly. "Yep."

Jack waited.

"He ain't married." Hank leaned on the table, close to Jack. "So there's no other income. And he has a house right here in town, but it's middle income at best. That's where he wants people to think he lives, but he spends most a' his time at the lake."

Jack shook his head and scribbled everything down as fast as he could.

"I don't know if he's renting the place on the lake or what," Hank said. "But how can he afford all that on an assistant pastor's salary?"

"Inheritance maybe?" Jack said.

Hank shook his head. "Two elders count the tithes and offerings every Sunday afternoon; the same two. Satterfield meets those two elders every other Thursday, twelve thirty, at Aqua Terra, fine food joint on Fourth Street."

"I know of it."

"Expensive."

Jack nodded.

"Satterfield picks up the tab."

"Could be a legitimate church write-off."

"Could be a scandal." Hank looked at his watch. "I gotta get back."

Jack wrapped up his trash, hoping for more information. But Hank was on his way.

"Will you tell me the names of the two elders?" Jack said.

"Ryan Seeger and Bruce Trent." He spelled the names, and Jack wrote them down.

They made eye contact as if to wrap up, then Hank turned and headed for the door. Jack followed. They walked outside, stopped, and faced each other.

"I called Archer Pierce at TV-10 News, you know? The investigative reporter?"

"I know Archer. He's a friend."

"Okay, so I told him all this, anonymously of course. I'm done with it. I've moved on. But I think he's putting together a story."

"Wow." Jack's wheels were turning. He wondered if or how the Satterfield stuff fit into his series about Evan. If it didn't, he might need to talk to Cecil about doing a separate piece on it but only after the whole Evan saga came to a close.

The two shook hands, and Jack gave Hank his business card. "Please, if you find out any more on any of this stuff, or if Archer sheds any more light, let me know, will you?"

Hank said he would and headed for his van.

Hank was an okay guy.

It wouldn't be an easy thing to put the pieces of one's marriage back together after an affair. Jack's thoughts turned to Wendy and Evan, their boys, and his unanswered questions about Evan's involvement with Sherry.

On his way to the car, Jack took out his phone.

No text or call from Pam.

Dang it.

He got in the car and sat there, dreading the thought of getting Pam's parents all stirred up about Granger being on the loose.

He just wanted Pam to call him. Then he could speak with her about it alone, give her the heads-up, and her folks would never have to know.

You're being paranoid. Just wait for her to call. She will, soon.

Like DeVry said, Granger was probably as far out of Ohio as he could possibly be by now.

Jack wanted to believe that.

But something pushed him, made him look down at the number for Pam's parents—and call.

26

Granger took one last hit of his cigarette, dropped it out the window, and pulled the Impala ever so quietly around the back of his parents' house where it couldn't be seen from the road. He brought it to a stop beneath the now huge sycamore tree, about thirty feet from the dilapidated shed in the backyard where he had spent so much time as a kid.

Although Granger had his own bedroom in the house, his mother had made him spend the night in the shed for certain transgressions. He'd grown up thinking this was normal. She would sequester him out there, quoting what he'd done wrong from Scripture. In his early years he'd read the Bible himself, trying to learn right from wrong, so he would stop frustrating her. But as he grew older, he realized that some of the things she punished him for were not even in the Bible. Once he accidentally dropped and shattered one of her favorite bowls and received two nights in the shed. Other times he would earn a night out there simply because she was in a bad mood and didn't want to see his fat face.

His stomach churned. He hadn't eaten all day, not to mention that he hadn't seen his parents in years. He stood there by the car half frozen, staring down at the leaning shed with its rust-streaked metal roof, remembering how the rain sounded when it slowly began to pang, pang, pang. Then the skies would open and the downpour would clang and bash and echo so loud it would make his ears ring and threaten to drive him mad. And then the leaks would start, and he would drag the mattress wherever he could find a dry spot.

He looked up at the dining-room and kitchen windows but saw no one. The old chain-link fence that boxed in the backyard was leaning, vines overtaking it in places. Having been out on his own for so long, seeing how the world operated, watching other people, being out from under the tyranny and oppression of that prison, Granger realized how miserably he had been treated when he was growing up. It wasn't fair.

Why did you even come back?

He didn't know for sure what he was going to do.

He could have gone anywhere in the country, and here he was at one of the most obvious and dangerous places.

All he knew was that he planned to sneak into the house. From there, he wasn't sure. Perhaps he would give his mother and father a little dose of their own mental-abuse medicine; put the shoe on the other foot for a change.

Or maybe he had come to say good-bye—for good.

The windowless garage door was closed. He tried the side door next to it. With a good shoulder nudge it came unstuck, like always. He stepped into the darkness. The smell of dampness and grass clippings from the mower were immediately familiar.

What's this?

Instead of the old Buick sedan his dad had driven forever, there sat one of those boxy conversion vans, an older model. Granger made his way along his dad's long workbench, past the big vise and the large silver toolbox, and to the steps. Up he went, taking each gently, like a cat, avoiding those that he remembered creaked.

Silently he turned the knob to the door at the top of the steps and opened it several inches. He saw no one in the kitchen but smelled soup or chili cooking, which reminded him that they usually ate dinner extremely early, like three thirty or four. The audio from the TV projected loudly from the den. If it was anything like old times, he would bet his life his mother was watching soaps and his dad was either napping or doing the crossword from the day's newspaper.

Quickly Granger swung the door open, crept into the kitchen, and peeked around the corner into the den. The room looked odd, rearranged, cluttered. From what he could see, his mother sat hunched, staring at the TV with her mouth open, her hair more gray than black now. His father was lying on his side, asleep. Sure enough, a Botox blonde was pitching a fit on the bulky old TV that still sat awkwardly on the fireplace hearth.

Granger turned and headed for the bedrooms in back, passing what turned out to be chili simmering on the stove. He would get some of that before he left. He tiptoed across the wood floor in the dining room, down the dim hallway to his bedroom.

Or was it?

He did a double take in the hallway, then stepped into what used to be his room. There was a new bed, much bigger, made neatly with a thick, dark brown comforter and beige pillows. A sleek nightstand was situated by the head of the bed, with a nice clock and a lamp he'd never seen. He walked farther in. The carpet was thick and also new. An impressive desk and lamp were against the wall to the left.

They'd completely redecorated his bedroom.

A new guest room for the guests they never have.

Clearly, Granger hadn't been worth the time, thought, or expense for such nice things when he had lived there.

He crossed to the closet, spread open the accordion doors, and scanned its contents. He jerked the old jackets and women's sweaters and dresses that were now on his hangers. Not one thing of his remained.

Quickly, his glance shifted to the shelves above—for his comics, car models, music books, snare drum, the old box of baseball cards. But the only things he found were an old sewing machine and several empty picture frames, which he recognized as those that had once displayed his band photographs.

Granger realized his teeth were locked so tightly together they were aching.

My trombone.

He dropped to his knees and swept back the clothes on the right—it wasn't there. He shifted and ripped back the clothes hanging on the left—nothing.

If they got rid of my trombone . . . I paid for that thing with my own money!

He stood, taking one last look for any of his things.

Leaving the closet open, Granger exited the bedroom and stopped in the hallway; but hearing the TV and seeing no sign of movement toward the front of the house, he slipped into his mother and father's bedroom.

Where his mother's bed used to be, there was a new one, like a hospital bed, the top half tilted up, with silver rails on each side.

One of them was sick.

He could smell it. Seven or eight orange bottles of pills dotted the bedside. Everything else in the room looked the same, just messier than they normally kept things.

Granger ducked into the small bathroom, closed the door, and urinated. As he stood there, he took deep breaths and tried to relax. His whole body ached.

You need to get the guns.

The police were sure to drive by there sooner or later. They might even come to the door.

Whatever you're gonna do, you need to move!

Every trace of Granger had been swept from the house. Truly, they had never wanted him.

Couldn't they have faked it? At least pretended to care?

They were weird, cruel people—people with serious issues. That was what the shrink had implied. And that was what he had always reminded himself to try to make himself feel better, to try to explain the temptations and fears and evils that lurked within.

They deserve to suffer.

He rinsed his hands, watching the dirt swirl down the drain, figuring it had been a day or two since his last hot shower at the apartment. Splashing water on his face, he snapped out of it, grabbed a towel, and leaned close to the mirror as he dried. His orange hair was a mess and his ridiculously small, bloodshot eyes were underlined with dark half-circles. His face was puffy—just plain fat is what it was.

He'd always been ugly. It wasn't just his weight. He was just plain unattractive. He knew it by the reaction of virtually every person he'd ever met. No one gave him the time of day. People would look at him and their eyes would roll off as if they'd never seen him at all.

Pamela had been the only one who made him feel worth anything.

You've poisoned that now.

He left the bathroom and ducked quickly to the floor of his parents' closet. One of his father's two guns—the smaller caliber of the two—was hidden in the Rockport shoe box, where his father had always kept them. Perhaps he'd sold the other or hidden it elsewhere; its clips weren't there either. Granger pushed a button on the side of the handle, and one full black metal clip dropped into his palm. He clicked it back into the gun and grabbed the extra full clip lying in the box.

Stepping quietly to the window, he moved the curtain slightly with the back of his hand, peered out, and saw no cars. The gun was heavy. The gun gave him authority. Control.

Respect.

He inhaled deeply through his nose, held it for a long time, and exhaled slowly. Then he made his move down the hallway. It was time to greet his beloved parents.

Jack had to concentrate, so instead of getting back on the road, he remained seated in his car at Jimmy John's as the phone rang at Pam's parents' house.

Margaret picked up. "Hello."

She was who he *didn't* want.

"Hey, Margaret, it's Jack."

"Oh, hi again, Jack." She was her giddy self.

"Is Pam back yet?"

"You must really miss her!" Margaret giggled. "Not yet, but she should be here soon. You know her, she goes from one place to the next—loves being home."

"Listen, Margaret," Jack interrupted, "would you mind getting Ben on the other line with you? I need to tell you guys something real quick."

"What is it?" Her voice immediately sobered, and she yelled for Benjamin to get on. "What's going on, Jack? Is it your parents?"

"No." It always amazed him how Margaret could go from normal to freak-out mode in under two seconds.

The line clicked. "Hello?"

"Hey, Benjamin, it's Jack. I need to tell you and Margaret something. Now listen, this is most likely no big deal. In fact, it's nothing, I'm sure. But I need to give you a heads-up, just in case."

"Good Lord, Jack, what is going on?" Margaret was almost out of breath already.

"It turns out there is a man on the run right now—he's probably going to be caught any minute by police—"

Margaret shrieked.

"Go ahead, Jack," Benjamin insisted. "Margaret, *calm* yourself."

"He's kind of had his eye on Pamela—"

"Pamela!" Margaret moaned, then sounded as if she was hyper-ventilating.

"Margaret!" Benjamin said. "I can't hear him. *Please!*"

"He stole a car here in Trenton City last night," Jack said. "He's running from the police. He could be anywhere. He's probably half-way across the country by now. But since—"

"Is Pam is danger right this second?" Margaret blurted. "Is she okay? Do you know she's okay right now?"

"The only reason I'm even telling you this is because she doesn't have her phone with her. I wanted to call and tell her and leave it at that. There's a very small chance—"

"Is he here?" Margaret blurted. "In Cleveland Heights?"

"Please, Margaret, let me finish," Jack spoke over her. "Let's not make this worse than it is. Since you have Rebecca and Faye, I wanted you to be aware that this guy is at large—"

"The girls!" she screamed. "Ben, are they with you?"

"Would you stop?" Ben barked. "They are right here."

"It's most likely he's long gone out of Ohio," Jack said, "and there's nothing whatsoever to worry about. I just wanted you to know that, for now, you should probably keep the girls inside and keep the doors locked."

"Doing it now, Jack," Benjamin said.

"Do you know he's here and you're not telling us?" Margaret's voice quivered. Her breathing was heavy, as if she was pacing. "Tell the truth, Jack!"

He wasn't about to tell them who it was or that Granger had gone to school with Pam and lived within blocks of them.

"Jack." Benjamin ignored his wife. "Should I try to find Pam?"

"You are not leaving me!" Margaret yelled. "There is no way you're leaving this house!"

Jack seethed. That's why the woman lived in such a pathetic state of fear, because all she thought about was *herself*.

"Just stay put for now, Ben," Jack said. "I want you there with the girls. I'm sure Pam will be back any minute. Have her call me the second she gets there."

Jack heard someone slurping at a bottle, and he knew it wasn't Benjamin. "Margaret, can I talk to Ben alone for a minute?"

"What are you not telling me?" Margaret said. "Let's have it all, Jack."

"Get off the phone *now*, Margaret," Benjamin said evenly.

The line clicked.

"Please, Ben," Jack said, "just keep a close eye on the girls."

"Don't worry. We're all locked up, and they are right here with me."

"I know you have a gun in the house," Jack said. "You may want to keep it with you, but please, make sure it's out of reach of the girls."

"Who is this guy, Jack?"

Jack paused.

Maybe it would be best for Benjamin to know. That way there wouldn't be any confusion if Granger did show or if somehow the police got involved.

"Please don't tell Margaret; it will just freak her out," Jack said. "It's a friend of Pam's from high school. Name's Granger Meade—"

A gasp came from the other end of the line.

Margaret had never hung up the phone.

27

Standing in a dusty corner within the old Greyhound station with its yellowing tile floors and tired cream-colored walls, Evan was deflated to learn from the reader board that the next bus heading for south Florida didn't leave until late that night.

He peered up at the board again—the old-fashioned kind with the black felt background and white plastic letters and numbers—then picked up his bag and approached the ticket window. The old gentleman with white beard stubble and a checked conductor's cap sitting low behind the glass assured Evan that the bus he was interested in would depart at 10:40 p.m. and arrive in Venice, Florida, the closest stop to Englewood, the next afternoon, with many stops along the way—*too many*.

Evan purchased a ticket and quietly thanked the man. He walked to a nearby wooden bench where he set down his bag and gazed through the dirty, crooked blinds into the motionless street.

He looked at his watch and figured he had something like seven hours to wait.

He was so tired. His stomach burned with hunger, but he wanted no food. In fact, Evan actually wanted to suffer. He wanted that unanswered hunger to burn off all the fat and dross and sinfulness, to quicken him, to bring him close to the bone.

He slid onto the bench, elbows on knees, head in hands. He could change his mind, walk back to the car, fill it with gas, and take back roads all the way to south Florida; the GPS would get him there.

But he just didn't have it in him. Besides, his car would be spotted. Then he would be apprehended, brought in, possibly charged, and there would be press coverage. Wendy and the boys would go through endless humiliation—as if they weren't going to face enough already.

The tips of his fingers tingled. He opened and closed his hands numerous times to make it go away, but it wouldn't. He felt like a guinea pig that was being poked, prodded, and drugged in some miserable testing lab. He contemplated the weirdness of all the different side effects popping up since he quit the antidepressants. If they were capable of causing all those visible effects, what had they been doing to his brain?

Why hadn't he killed himself already? He'd had plenty of time alone at the cabin. Could he do it? Would he go to hell for it? He eyed the black duffel. The gun was right inside. He'd gone from one cheap motel to another, the gun in the room with him each time. One time he had even taken it out and, with hands sweating, pushed the slide back and inserted a bullet into the chamber.

You don't have the guts.

Yes he did.

He stood, caught his balance, snatched the bag, and headed for the doors and the sidewalk beyond. He would go to the car and decide what to do from there.

All this time he had been determined to visit the cottage in Englewood one last time. Something was calling him back to that particular slice of life and sand and ocean where everything had been so right.

As he walked along the sidewalk toward the library where he had parked, a breeze kicked up and with it came memories of the cottage where he and Wendy had slow-danced countless times on the screen porch and even out on the dock, beneath moonlit skies and shimmering seas. They'd gone to that same cottage since before any of the boys had been born. They'd made passionate, fun, breathless love in most of its rooms. Later they even determined that Nathaniel, their oldest, had been conceived at the cottage during one of their vacations.

Evan took a turn on Bell Street. The gun made the bag heavy. The library was down just a ways.

He and the boys had always bonded in Englewood. They would fish and fly kites and ride bikes, while Wendy read book after book. She even had a membership at the local library. Most of all, Evan and the boys would laugh and love and ride the pounding Gulf waves until their bodies collapsed beneath the gold umbrella stuck in the sand, where Wendy waited for them with towels and sandwiches and ice-cold sodas.

He'd thrown it all away—his precious marriage, his life as father to those three wonderful sons, his reputation, his ministry.

Because of the depression, there was no going back or making things right. His life was controlled by it. He'd battled it for years and lost. Yes, lost. Period.

Many days were so heavy and bleak he didn't want to get out of bed. But he had to. So he would end up fighting, fighting,

fighting—just to keep his sanity, to somehow find some light—just to live the kind of day a "normal" person lived without even thinking about it.

Why?

Why was he like this?

So weak and hopeless.

He dug out his remote, unlocked the car, and headed toward one of the back doors.

Why had God made him so frail?

Oh, it wasn't as if he was actually asking God those questions, because he and God weren't on speaking terms. Whenever Evan thought about communicating with God, he sensed some sort of invisible ceiling above him. It wasn't that God didn't hear him; God was just silent. An observer. Evan's prayers were hindered, a thought he was sure old Andrew Satterfield would have appreciated.

But he was good at helping people.

Were. You were good at helping people. Your reputation is ruined.

Right there! Who planted that thought? Satan? God? He didn't know the difference anymore. Everything had blurred. He'd lost the moorings on which he had once built a life.

Evan pulled open the back door on the passenger side of the car, stood there, and looked around the shady parking lot to make sure no one was watching. A mother and three boys entered the library. Pushing back thoughts of Wendy and his sons, Evan tossed the duffel to the floor of the backseat, got in, shut the door, and lay down.

After looking at his watch and trying to get comfortable—finally nestling his head in the crook of his crossed arms—he closed his eyes.

He would sleep.

Sleep till the bus came.

Or until someone found him.

It didn't matter. Nothing mattered …

The harsh taste of the pill he had spit out came back up his throat, into his mouth.

The lyrics of an old James Taylor song whispered into his drifting mind. *Set me free, sleep come free me, please, please, please …*

❧

Granger noted the heft of the gun in his right hand as he crept down the hallway back toward his parents' den. Man, were they in for a surprise. For once, he would be in control. For once—perhaps one last time—*they* would have to listen to *him*.

What exactly he was going to do, he still didn't fully know. Whatever it was, he needed to move swiftly. The cops could be nearby.

It was his deranged mother he wanted a piece of. She was the one—

"The prodigal returns."

Granger froze at the entrance to the dining room. Slowly he turned to his right. There stood his father. Calm. Older. Smaller. One arm comfortably at his side; the other, bent at the elbow, pointing at Granger's heart with the bulky, dark gray .45 caliber that had been missing from the Rockport box.

"The police were here," Father said quietly. "Said you might pay us a visit." From behind smudged glasses, Father's cataract-glazed brown eyes flicked to the weapon at Granger's side. "Give it here."

Granger did not move but looked directly into those hypnotic eyes. "You wouldn't shoot your own son." He too spoke softly but sarcastically.

"I have an excuse," Father said. "You're wanted. You broke in. You're armed. Give it to me."

Granger came within a second of lurching for the man and bashing his lights out with the metal in his hand, but he was a bit too far away, maybe four feet. His own gun wasn't cocked, or he might have tried to beat the old man to the draw.

Although his father was slight and seemingly tranquil, he had a ferocious side when heated to a boil. As Granger eyed the gun pointed at him, then his father's unflinching face, he realized the man might just blow a gaping hole clean through his stomach.

Figuring he could overtake the old man as things played out, Granger slowly handed over the gun.

"Smart," Father said, taking the gun in the palm of his other hand, turning his back on Granger, and walking toward the den. "Your mother's not well. Come see her. And give me the other clip."

Granger debated tackling the old man from behind; it would have been a piece of cake. But the confidence with which his father had turned, the curious words about his mother, and that familiar, mesmerizing spell that seemed to make Granger fall into submission caused him to simply follow his father toward the den, handing him the spare clip as he entered.

Granger thought it odd that his mother wasn't whizzing about, all up in his business. But as he approached her, he realized why. What he hadn't seen before when he had peeked into the den was the wheelchair in which she was seated. He approached her from behind.

Even from that angle he could tell something was very wrong. She leaned awkwardly to one side, facing the TV but slumped. As he came around her side, he saw the knot of severely bent wrists and fingers locked in grotesquely shaped fists.

This was serious. And it was permanent.

His heart seemed to weaken. She was a sad and hideous sight. The ramifications were too much to grasp in that split second. At the same time, however, a strange and somewhat deranged sense of elation—perhaps relief—settled into Granger's bones.

"Can you turn that down?" he said to his father.

The volume on the TV cut in half.

"Hello, Mother." Granger knelt at her side.

Her watery yellow eyes and piercing blue pupils stared straight ahead at the flickering TV. Her small mouth hung open an inch; he wanted to reach up and close it. Her putty-colored skin looked soft and fuzzy and was tightly stretched against her bony face. The thick, straight hair was now a blend of silver and black. He could tell Father had tried to brush it and part it the way she liked but had failed miserably.

"Mother." Granger was within ten inches of her face. "It's Granger. I've come to visit."

She was like a statue, the eyes unblinking, fixed on the boob tube.

While on his knees, Granger shifted around to his father, who was seated on the ottoman with his knees wide apart, handing the big gun back and forth from one palm to the other. The other gun rested between his legs on the ottoman.

"Massive stroke," Father said. "Back in April."

Granger looked around the room, which he now realized was cluttered with dirty dinner trays, rags, adult diapers, medicine bottles, and old newspapers. "Do you have any help?"

"Nah." Father stared down at the gun.

"What about when you have to go somewhere—the store, errands?"

"Van has a lift."

"That'll wear you out," Granger said.

"What're you gonna do?" Father's shoulders jumped. "It's the plan."

Some plan. This is what their religion has gotten them.

Granger didn't say it aloud; his father would have detonated. Instead he said, "How does she eat?"

"I feed her."

"Tube?"

"Mouth," Father said. "She can eat."

"You mean she's okay from the neck up?" Granger said. "She's not ..."

"Brain-dead? No son, *you're* the only one who suffered from that around here. What'd you do in Trenton City? They wouldn't tell me."

"What'd you do with all my stuff—my trombone ... my keepsakes?"

"You've been gone how long?" Father said.

"So you just threw it all away?"

"We figured if you really wanted that junk you'd have gotten it by now," Father said. "Are you kidding me? It's been years."

"Does she know I'm here?" Granger said.

"She knows," Father said. "What'd you do, kill somebody?"

Granger thought of Pamela. How he wanted to blurt out that, no, he hadn't killed anyone—he'd gone back to find the only person who'd ever loved him.

He turned back to his mother, whose head had moved slightly toward him. Her eyes were wide open, fixed on his face, burning into him now. She flinched. Her head and shoulders began to shake. The pace of her breathing kicked up. Her face went pink, and a strand of drool spilled over her bottom lip.

"Uh oh, she's mad now." Father laughed. "She wants to know what you did. She's upset you're gonna ruin our good name."

Mother's fiery eyes continued to lock onto Granger's face, even as he used the rag on her shoulder to remove the drool, and she shook so bad the wheelchair began to rattle.

Granger stood and stared down at his father.

"I think she's reminding you," Father said, "once a vessel of dishonor, always a vessel of dishonor." He smirked. "We've always expected this. In the back of our minds, all these years, we've been waiting for the day you would self-destruct. It was inevitable."

To heck with this.

Granger walked into the kitchen, got a bowl and spoon, found a ladle, and served himself some chili. He grabbed saltines from the pantry, broke two fistfuls into the bowl, and took it back into the den.

"Help yourself," Father joked.

Granger had forgotten the power of the awful words spoken under that roof. How deeply they penetrated. How much they hurt. But he remembered quickly how he had trained himself to let the words roll off, as if he'd never heard them. It was a battle of the mind.

FEAR HAS A NAME

Figuring this might be the last time he would see his parents, Granger pulled a chair up next to his mother, sat down, and began to eat.

"You say your prayers?" Father quipped.

Granger stopped with the spoon at his mouth and stared at the old man. "No, I didn't. I never do."

Mother's head turned to face him, her eyes burning into him like lasers.

"'Raise up a child in the way he should go,'" Father said, "'and in the end he will not depart from it.' You ever hear that?"

Mother seethed.

"Didn't work in my case, did it?" Granger said.

"Who knows, maybe in prison you'll come to realize your need. Although your mother has always said you were destined for hell from the day you were conceived."

"You know what I think?" Granger talked with his mouth full, looking back and forth at them. "I think you didn't raise me in the way I should go. I think you *poisoned* me. You two call yourselves Christians, but you're nothing but hypocrites. I don't see how you sleep at night, knowing what the Bible says about love, yet knowing how you treated me all those years. It's a sick lie. You're deceived, Mr. Meade." He pointed at his mother. "And you too, Mrs. Meade."

Her mouth closed and shrank to a slit. Her eyes ballooned to twice their normal size, and her face lit up like a burner on a stove.

With mouth clamped shut and jaw jutting out, Father pushed himself to his feet, pointed both guns at Granger, and gritted his teeth. He hesitated, then jammed the guns into his front pockets. They stuck out clumsily as he walked to Mother and set his hands softly onto her shoulders. Bending just above her head, he spoke loudly. "It's okay, dear." He patted her. "Calm down. Granger's leaving now." He eyed Granger. "Aren't you."

Granger got to the bottom of the bowl and purposefully made a loud, repeated clacking noise with the spoon, pretending to scrape up every last drop, which he knew grated on his father's nerves.

Still bending over the back of Mother's wheelchair, Father stared at Granger as he took the bowl to the kitchen, set it in the sink, and let the faucet run till the bowl overflowed.

It was looking doubtful Granger could get one of the guns. He'd wanted one desperately—for what, he still wasn't certain. He could take their van, but it would be easier to spot than the car he had. Plus, they needed it.

He dried his hands on a kitchen towel, walked back into the den, and looked at his mother and father.

He'd come there for what? Revenge? Revenge for the piece of garbage he had become?

But look at them. They're pitiful, just wasting away in their bitterness. You just need to go.

"We've got something for you." His father left the room.

Mother stared at Granger. He knelt in front of her again, wanting to touch her. But the fury in her glare—those eyes—she wouldn't take them off him. They almost spoke, as if to say, *Even in my state, you are still lower than me, boy.*

Father entered the room holding a maroon Bible. "This is for you."

Granger recognized the Bible he'd saved up for and bought for his mother for Christmas all those years ago. It was still like new. He opened it and found the note he'd written to her.

Although she was stiff as a board, Mother watched everything, alert as an owl. There may have even been a hint of a cruel smile at the corner of her mouth.

"Take it." Father stepped back behind Mother. "Read it."

"I got this for her."

She flinched.

Father interpreted. "It was the wrong version. You're gonna need it where you're going. Now get out of here. Hurry up. The police are coming back."

"What?" Granger started. "Since when?"

Father took the big gun from his pocket and nodded toward the room from where he'd just come. "I just called 'em."

"Why? Why would you do that?" Granger took several anxious steps toward the door. "Why couldn't you have just let me go?"

"I would have." Father racked the slide, sending one of the .45s into the firing chamber. "But the problem is—there's been a murder at this address." He pointed the gun at the center of Mother's head and smirked. "And *you* did it."

28

Pamela drove down Granger's creepy, overgrown street and slowed way down along the stretch where he used to live. Trees and shrubs and weeds and vines had so encroached the place, all she could see was one corner of the white house, some of the roof, and a small brick chimney.

Out of curiosity she eased the car past the leaning rusty green mailbox and turned into the driveway, figuring she would pull in ten or fifteen feet just to see if anyone still lived there. She rolled in slowly, coming to a spot a quarter way down the driveway where she could see the whole house. She stopped. There were no cars in sight. The siding on the old place was warped and buckling, and shingles were missing in various patches on the roof. One of the gutters had broken and was swaying in the breeze.

She wondered if they still lived there, if anyone did.

No name on the mailbox.

It looked like no one was home.

Jack would be furious if he knew where she was at that moment. *You need to go.*

She shifted the car into reverse and took one last look at the house.

A flash lit up a wall inside, then it went dark.

POP.

Pamela's heart clicked and everything inside revved. The car seemed to wobble.

Get out.

She started to back the car up but couldn't take her eyes off the room where she'd seen the flash.

What had she just seen? Her insides felt sickeningly hollow.

Gunshot?

Heart spinning, head buzzing, Pamela turned back, arm stretched across the passenger seat, and started to navigate her way back out the driveway when she heard something.

Screaming.

She hit the brake, strained to hear.

She zeroed in on the house, the grounds, looking for any movement—anything.

Although the landscape was frozen, Pamela *sensed* motion, tension.

Thud.

What was that?

It had come from the house, maybe out back?

Then it registered somewhere at her very core.

Car door.

"Oh dear Jesus!"

She looked back, found the driveway, and punched the gas. The car lurched, faster than she'd intended—too fast! Her stomach shrank to a knot as the car banged over a hump at the side of the driveway.

No!

She slammed the brake through the floor, and the car did a half spin, skidding, sliding, bumping down an embankment. It banged to a stop at an awkward angle, the front up high on the slope, the rear down at its base.

The house and driveway were no longer visible from the dip she was in. Instead, when she looked forward, she was pointing up at a green canopy of trees.

Pamela took a deep breath in the stillness.

It was okay. She was only fifteen or twenty feet from the level surface of the driveway, and she was pointing right at it.

She shifted into drive and started up the slope.

Thank God, she was moving. Moving ...

A few feet from leveling off on the driveway surface, she felt the anxiety of the moment and pressed harder on the gas, but then ... she wasn't moving.

Go!

The car was getting louder, louder, but it was no longer climbing. It was listing, barely moving side to side. The engine roared, the needles on the dashboard vibrated upward. Pamela's body and mind felt like the car—overheating to the bursting point.

Crazed with fear, she smashed pedal to metal.

The car jumped uphill slightly.

Yes.

The noise was deafening ...

But no. The car dropped back and, although roaring, was barely moving. Smoke rolled up from behind and filled her nostrils, as did the smell of burning rubber.

She was scared and losing it.

Back down, back down and gun it.

She put it in reverse, took her foot off the gas, and let the car roll back down the slope until it pushed into thick weeds and underbrush and stopped on level ground.

Please get me out of here.

She gripped the wheel tight in the ten-two, took a deep breath, exhaled, and hit the gas hard to get that sucker moving fast up, up the embankment.

It was going, going.

This time she wanted to keep the speed steady so the tires didn't spin.

She was still climbing, almost there.

Don't gun it.

She blocked out every thought except keeping the gas pedal pressed exactly as she had it. *Steady.*

In a second she would be out of there, free, Granger's house in the dust, headed home to the girls.

Up, up … the level surface was right there.

The front of the car made it over the edge and began to level.

Thank God!

Movement to the right, out the corner of her eye.

Crunch.

Everything spun.

Eyes closed, she heard herself scream.

Down, down, sliding, turning, tipping?

The car stopped its free fall at the base of the embankment. She barely moved, opening her eyes, examining her body. Seeing no cuts or blood, she looked up, straight ahead, into thick green woods and a rolling cloud of dust.

The engine had shut off.

She turned the key off anyway and sat as still as she could, trying to get her bearings.

The right front hood was mangled.

She wondered if the car was drivable.

Wait ... someone had hit her.

Shaking feverishly, she unbuckled her seat belt, fumbled for the door latch, and opened it. Her body ached as she swiveled and grunted to get out of the car. But she couldn't stand yet. She thought she might pass out. She sat there with her feet in the weeds, trying to shake the fuzziness.

"Pamela?" a man's voice called from above her.

Who?

Granger's dad?

But he wouldn't know her.

She looked up, almost directly into the afternoon sun, toward where the driveway leveled. All she could make out were silhouettes— one of the car that had hit her, parked level up on the driveway; the other of a large man, sidestepping, slipping, kicking up dirt as he made his way down the embankment, directly toward her.

Jack's head felt lighter, freer, to be driving out in the country, toward nearby Lincolntown and Andrew Satterfield's supposed house and boat on Lake Hudson. Jack figured he needed to keep as busy as possible until DeVry finally let him know Granger was apprehended.

The car radio was off. The windows were down. Jack was relieved to have told Pam's parents about Granger. Now he just wished Pam would hurry up and call so he could be certain she was safe. Although he wanted to let her have it for not carrying her phone, especially with Granger on the loose, he reminded himself to keep his cool when they talked; the important thing was that she was okay.

His phone vibrated, and his heart spiked. But it was just Wendy. Between intermittent static and dead spots in the call, he deciphered that she was trying to farm the boys out to some friends. She was planning to fly to Englewood, Florida—certain that's where Evan was heading.

Having reflected on the letter Sherry had written to Evan, Jack had a feeling no matter how the Evan-and-Wendy situation played out, it wasn't going to be good.

He asked if she knew anything about Satterfield's lake house or the two elders with whom Hank implied he might be in cahoots. Wendy was so classy. She said no, and that was that. No bitter or malicious words about Satterfield, even though she strongly suspected he was spearheading the charge at the church to oust Evan. All Wendy cared about was finding her husband—alive.

Lake Hudson was a few miles past Lincolntown University, which was at the center of the preppy, upscale college town that shared its name. There was big money in Lincolntown, a brick square with tree-lined streets, cobblestone crosswalks, awning-covered shops and eateries, gas-torch street lamps, a park, amphitheater, and bell tower.

Lincolntown was where Trenton City's money was—attorneys, physicians, investors ... and associate pastors.

Jack had been to Lake Hudson several years back for a picnic with reporters from the paper. He could tell he was getting close, as the ground became sandy and he spotted docks and bait shops, marinas, boat slips, and patches of water.

He drove over a rickety bridge and wound around the lake, along a shady road carved out of a thick pine forest. He hit a clearing and came to Satterfield's street, Edgewater Cove, which took him directly toward the vast lake.

When Jack came to the address Hank had given, he drove past it, turned around, and pulled slowly to the edge of the street about a hundred yards shy of the house.

Although it was far from enormous, the house was bright, immaculate, and situated like a dream in a valley of thick, rich green grass, almost level with the water and surrounded by huge, ancient trees. Just feet from the house was a spacious wood deck complete with high-end furniture, an enormous silver gas grill, and a cozy, extra-wide white hammock swaying in the breeze.

"Holy Toledo," Jack whispered.

The gleaming one-story white house looked like something out of an architecture magazine. The heart of the house was simple, small, and square. But it featured three stone steps leading up to double-glass doors, flanked by two dark windows. Around the sides were floor-to-ceiling windows, also tinted. A wide shady porch wrapped around the entire house and featured white wood columns and rockers, hanging plants, and a bench swing. The lustrous green metal roof gave the house a clean, contemporary appeal.

A black Saturn with tinted windows was parked in the circular drive; behind it sat a silver Chevy pickup with its windows down. The landscaping was simple and beautiful, designed to highlight the picturesque lake house.

Jack popped his trunk from inside the car, scooted around back, grabbed his Nikon, and returned to the driver's seat. His longest lens was already on the camera. He didn't know what he was expecting but figured he would be better off having the camera in hand than not.

His thoughts wandered from Pam and the girls at her parents' place, to Wendy and her boys and her upcoming journey to find Evan, to Granger Meade somewhere in the stolen blue Impala.

His phone vibrated at the same time he noticed movement on the lake. In the distance he saw a white boat with red trim rounding the wooded bend and heading straight for Satterfield's comfy cove. Jack glanced at the phone. It was Wendy. He made it go to voice mail, turned the camera on, and quickly set it to motor drive.

The boat seemed to tower over the greenish-blue water as it leaned, straightened, and left a curved trail of white water behind it. He peered through the camera and zoomed in on two men perched near the wheel.

Jack recognized Satterfield immediately—squeaky clean in a white short-sleeved polo and aviator sunglasses; he was driving the boat. With him was a much shorter, stocky man with black hair that looked like a toupee. This man could be one of the elders Hank had mentioned—or not.

Jack zoomed in on the men as the boat's engine wound down and Satterfield guided the vessel gently up against the dock. Jack held the shutter button down, and it clicked off multiple frames, but he chastised himself for having forgotten to turn off the volume. He sounded like the paparazzi.

The men climbed out of the boat, laughing. The shorter man hoisted a brown leather bag over his shoulder as they left the dock and walked toward the house. It was quiet with the boat off, but Jack continued snapping away. Instead of entering the house, the men circled around the side nearest him, through the green grass and shade of the towering trees. They got to the circular drive, closer than Jack had anticipated. He dropped down in his seat and stopped shooting, afraid Satterfield would recognize him. The short man put his hand out to shake, but germ-freak Satterfield simply waved and hopped up the steps to the double-glass doors; the other man headed for his truck.

With Satterfield entering the house, Jack zipped off a few more noisy frames, and the short man stopped and swiveled around. Gingerly Jack set the camera in the passenger seat. Having spotted Jack's car, the short man stood glaring at him and called out something to Satterfield, who was just inside the door. Jack slipped his car into drive, spit some gravel, and rolled out of there.

As he drove back to Trenton City, he listened to Wendy's voice mail. Sherry Pendergrass had contacted her, saying she had insight on Evan's disappearance and was requesting a meeting. When Jack returned her call, Wendy said that Sherry would be at her house in a few minutes, and she'd convinced her to allow Jack to be present at the meeting. She'd assured Sherry that Jack was a friend and advocate for her in Evan's absence and that as much of the conversation as they wanted would be off the record.

287

Jack checked his watch, then his phone. Nothing on Granger. And Pam should have called him! It was totally unlike her to leave him hanging like this. She had to be back by now. Maybe in all the excitement she had just forgotten to call him. She was probably showing the girls all the things she'd found for them while she was out shopping.

Jack dialed her parents' house again.

He didn't care if he was a nuisance.

He just needed to know his baby was safe.

29

Granger's mind was blown. *Blown.*

Here he was, flying down the interstate with Pamela by his side—*Pamela Wagner.* He'd basically kidnapped her. But think about it, she had actually driven by *his* house. *Granger Meade's house!* Why would she do that if she hadn't been thinking about him? There was something there. She might not be acting like it now. Of course she was distraught. But there was something there.

He hoped she was almost done crying. It was tapering off, as the enormous sobs and gasps from earlier now turned to sniffles and quick, jerky breaths. She'd fought with everything she had back there, just like the night on the bridge—kicking, clawing, screaming, hitting; like a tornado. And Granger had a heck of a time dragging her up that hill and had the scratches to prove it. When he first got her in the car, he was sweating like a pig. He didn't see how Pamela could possibly be cold, but her teeth were chattering.

His mother was dead, at the hand of his father, and Granger would be blamed for it. His prints were on the gun. Sure, his father's were too. But Granger was the fugitive. He was the black sheep. His psycho father had planned to blame it on him, and the sentence would come down on him—*if* they caught him. But he didn't plan on letting that happen. No way was he going to prison.

Never.

He only wished he'd gotten one of Father's guns.

He couldn't believe his mother didn't exist anymore. He would never interact with her again, never again cower before her and suffer the wounds from her nasty, belittling words. It was like a heavy net had been lifted from his life. But it was also weird. She was his mother. She'd carried him in her womb. They were connected genetically. Now those ties were severed.

He was glad he hadn't seen the shot. How gross it must've been—everything splattered all over the place. Once it had clicked in his mind what Father was about to do, Granger had bolted. He'd been on the steps leading down to the garage when the sound of the gunshot seemed to erupt in his own chest. He couldn't remember if he screamed or if he just imagined that part. How could his father have done it? They were sick people.

As far as Granger knew, Father had simply waited for the police to arrive, amid all that gore, and blamed it on Granger.

Imagine the manhunt now.

Granger was driving south with an ultimate destination in the back of his mind—someplace of which Pamela would assuredly approve. But it was far, far off; he would have time later to zero in on specific directions. For now he knew he couldn't spend a lot of time on the freeways, so his plan was to get on and off, use back roads, distance himself as much as possible from that house.

"This isn't your car." Pamela was shivering and slouched and did not make eye contact.

"Had to make a change." Granger looked over at her.

Goose bumps covered Pamela's tightly crossed arms. She wore a plain black short-sleeved shirt and jeans, the low-cut kind, with a thick black belt and flimsy black shoes that looked like slippers; they were dirty from trudging up that hill. Her blonde hair was fluffy, soft, and short, and she had on dark lipstick. That lovely mouth ...

Granger had found her one of those mini tissue packets in the glove compartment, and she'd gone through almost the whole thing. The used tissues were strewn on the seat and floor, and several new crumpled ones were wadded in her fist.

"Where are you going?" she said.

"*We*, where are *we* going." Granger laughed. "Driving for a while. We're going to get caught up. Just you and me. Like old times."

Keeping her shaking arms crossed, Pamela wiped her eyes and nose with the tissues as she carefully watched every sign and land-mark. "I need to call my husband," she whimpered. "Do you have a phone?"

"Don't you have one?" Not that he planned on letting her use it.

Her face and mouth and eyes scrunched as if she'd just eaten a lemon. "No."

"You want a blast of heat?" Granger turned the heater to low. "This'll make you feel better."

"I need to call him." She looked sideways at Granger with those gorgeous watery eyes. "Please. Then we can get caught up all you want. They need to know I'm okay."

Granger didn't like it that she was so focused on *them*, on easing *their* minds and returning to *that* life. It made him feel temporary.

Like he was just some stupid obstacle whom she would falsely pacify, toss aside, then get back to what really mattered.

"I am safe," she said, "right?"

∽⌒⌒

Jack pulled into Wendy's driveway and parked behind a sleek white Mercedes, which he figured must belong to Sherry Pendergrass. He had just hung up the phone after talking with Faye and Rebecca, who were having the time of their lives listening to PawPaw read stories and playing games with him.

"What about MawMaw?" Jack had asked.

"She's in her room," Rebecca said. "We haven't heard a peep out of her."

"Yes, and the door is bolted locked and she won't come out," Faye chimed in.

Jack blocked Margaret out of his mind, grabbed his camera and notes, knocked at Wendy's front door, and waited. After quite a pause, he heard Wendy call for him to come in.

He saw himself into the room where he had met her several days earlier. It was dark and quiet now, and he could immediately sense that the two women had been deep in a conversation that was probably both awkward and highly emotional. There weren't tears, but the tension was palpable.

The two ladies stood. Wendy introduced Sherry, who was almost as tall as Jack. She was tan and striking in white shorts and sandals, a shiny silver top, and a light sweater—with lots of silver jewelry. Jack guessed she was in her late forties, but she looked more like thirty. Her skin and the firmness of her body radiated good health, and she had the broad shoulders of a swimmer. She seemed meek as she shook Jack's hand and quietly said his name.

When they all sat down, Wendy and Sherry were positioned in chairs that angled toward one another. Wendy took the lead in a businesslike way, explaining to Sherry that Jack had become a fast friend and partner in her search for Evan. Then, just above her emotions, Wendy explained to Jack that Sherry had offered to let Evan use a cabin in Springfield that she and her former husband owned.

"I knew Evan was under a lot of stress," Sherry chimed in. "That's why I offered him the cabin—a private place where he could go to sort things out."

Wendy's body stiffened. She crossed her arms and peered outside.

"I've been frank with Wendy," Sherry said to Jack. "My motives were wrong; they were impure. After all of the weeks we spent in counseling, I began to have feelings for Evan. The day he went missing, I drove up to meet him at the cabin—to let him in, show him where everything was and, well …" She reached over and touched Wendy's arm. "Let me make it clear again—Evan wanted nothing to do with me. He was in despair, but he made it clear—you will always be the only one for him, Wendy."

Wendy turned slowly and stared into Sherry's eyes, her mouth a slit.

Sherry continued, admitting she stayed on at the cabin that day but that her presence added even more guilt to Evan's already frazzled state of mind.

"He became terribly distraught," Sherry said. "And he was very upset with me, that I had … tried to be more than friends."

"How long did you stay?" Jack said.

"I was in and out the first several days he was there," Sherry said. "Really, I was just checking in to make sure he was okay, trying to get him to eat something. He didn't feel well. His stomach was terribly upset. I thought it might be an ulcer or something. He was sleeping a lot—day and night."

Jack wondered if Sherry knew about Evan's antidepressants, the suicide note, or the gun, but he wasn't about to bring those things up if Wendy wasn't.

"He kept saying it was too late to turn back," Sherry said. "He was tortured inside. But it was his … goodness …" Sherry dropped her head, took a deep breath, and looked up again. "It was his desire to be right before God that shocked me back to reality." She snatched a tissue from her purse and patted her eyes. "I'm so sorry, Wendy; so, so sorry. And I don't expect your forgiveness, that's not why I'm here. I just want to help you, and help Evan."

Wendy frowned and fought back tears, her head shaking ever so slightly.

"I found these tucked inside my front door." Sherry pulled an envelope from her purse, opened it, and produced a handful of photographs. "Someone followed Evan and me to the cabin. They took these pictures."

The photos showed Evan and Sherry walking side by side on a dirt path in the woods, sitting close to each other on a porch, sharing a meal …

"I can assure you we were not intimate," Sherry said. "We were both just trying to figure out how we got into this mess and where we were going to go from there."

Amazingly, it sounded to Jack as if Sherry were telling the truth—that Evan had not wanted her there. In fact, if Evan had already been suffering from life-threatening depression, Sherry's presence and the guilt that came with it might have indeed been the nail in his coffin.

Wendy's eyes were tired, and Jack noticed creases in her pretty face he hadn't seen before. She quietly examined each photo, tucking one behind, moving another into view. Jack waited for Sherry to continue.

"I got a call late this morning," Sherry said. "It's blackmail."

"What do they want?" Jack said, feeling like some kind of legal representation for Wendy.

"Three hundred thousand dollars," Sherry said, "wired to a foreign account."

"And if you do it?" Jack said.

"I know it's not true, but he said the original digital photos will be destroyed."

"Right," Jack said sarcastically. "And you'll never hear from them again."

"By paying the money he said my name would be protected, and Evan's too."

"Evan's name is already ruined!" Wendy said.

"Who could have known you were going to meet Evan in Springfield that day?" Jack said. "The exact time and place?"

Sherry's eyes closed and she inhaled deeply, shoulders back, holding in a chest full of air—then she opened her eyes and let it out. "This is Andrew Satterfield's doing," she blurted. "I think he was having Evan followed. To what end? I'm not sure." She looked directly into Jack's eyes. "I've come to believe Satterfield is capable of anything—I mean *anything*."

30

Pamela was still struggling desperately to calm herself. They were on a wide-open two-lane back road, driving at a good clip. The sun was arching toward her right, west, so she figured they were heading south.

Be still. Know he is God.

Granger smoked with his window down four inches. His whole body had smelled like a mixture of old cigarettes and body odor when he had manhandled her, wrenching her in those viselike arms and forcing her up the hill into the car.

He was a huge man, a husky, immovable mass in that driver's seat. His head and neck were enormous, as were his arms, which, thanks to her, looked like a cat's scratching post. As Pamela recalled from high school, his nose was hooked and his eyes were small and shifty. He wore the same black clothes. Several spots of what looked like tomato sauce dotted the front of his black T-shirt.

At least he was a good driver.

Funny, the things you thought of when you were kidnapped.

"There goes a Smoky." Granger watched the gray-blue-orange cruiser go north in his rearview mirror. "Right past us. How do you like that?"

He was constantly eyeing the rearview and side mirrors.

He must've stolen the car. She wondered if he had hurt or killed someone to get it.

Did he have a gun?

She didn't see one.

What happened back at his house?

Dare she ask? Would it send him into a rage?

Would he hurt her? Rape her? Leave her dead somewhere, not to be found for months?

She'd heard of cases where the psycho male didn't want anyone else to have the woman, so he would kill her, then take his own life. That would leave Jack alone to raise the girls. Thank God they had life insurance; her policy was smaller than Jack's, but they'd made it just substantial enough to allow Jack to get a full-time nanny and give the girls a good education.

They had hoped to have at least one more child—probably more.

Would Jack remarry?

The needle on the gas gauge showed they were below a quarter of a tank; they would have to stop soon. She had to go to the bathroom and he would have to go too. Could she quietly tell someone in the restroom she'd been kidnapped? Should she try to run? Beg the mercy of anyone near them?

Would he let her call Jack from a pay phone? If so, perhaps she should not try to escape but ride it out.

Was he planning to drive all night? Where were they going?

All Pamela could decipher for certain was that he was set on heading south.

"Old Jackie boy's gonna be worried." Granger took a hit of the cigarette—which was burning almost down to his fat fingers—and breathed the smoke swirling out the window.

"Yes," she said. "He is."

A large maroon Bible sat on the floor at her feet amid a bunch of used tissues; she wondered what on earth it was doing there.

As the silent minutes ticked past, Pamela was getting the feeling she needed to revert back to her youth. She needed to get her mind off herself, the fright, the turmoil, and get to a place mentally where she could treat Granger as she had when they were kids—friendly, outgoing, encouraging, nonchalant, fun.

But there was no way she could do it.

She'd barely said a word and was stiff as a board, not wanting to move, feeling locked to the seat. Her body was tense to the core and everything in her was burning with fear—every organ from her chest to her stomach to her bowels felt as if it was being wrung out like flaming hot rags.

Now she had a taste of what her mother had experienced.

That Scripture came to mind, of Jesus telling his followers, "Don't worry about what you'll say—my Spirit will provide the words."

She reached for the Bible on the floor. "Do you read this?" she managed, her hands trembling.

He pitched the butt out the window, rolled it up, and eyed her. "I don't know what that's doing here."

"It's not yours?"

"Huh uh."

It was like new. She opened it, turned several pages, and found an inscription in bold, slanted handwriting.

Dear Mother,

    I know how much the words in here mean to you. I hope you will use and enjoy this for many years to come.

With love from your son,
Granger

"You got this for your mom?" Pamela said.

Granger looked straight ahead and nodded.

"If you got it for her, why do you have it?"

"I didn't mean to take it," he said. "It was just in my hands when I left."

Pamela racked her brain, trying to come up with the right thing to say. Having heard the shot, asking Granger if his parents were both still alive after all these years, or how they were doing, didn't seem the smartest approach.

"Do you want to talk about what happened back there?" She held her breath and stroked the soft, thin pages of the Bible.

"No matter what anyone says, or what you hear, I'm no killer." He looked over at her. "Will you believe that?"

Oh, Lord, they were dead. Or at least one of them was.

But his eyes seemed innocent, virtually harmless. She searched them for darkness and evil but saw only sorrow and dejection.

"I'll be honest," she said. "I don't know what to believe. You've put my family through hell."

"I don't want to talk about your family!"

So much for harmless.

"This is *our* time," he snapped. "Probably our *last* time. And I refuse to waste it talking about your *other* life."

"Let's talk about you then." She forced herself to stand up to him, to sound upbeat. "Do you still enjoy music? The trombone?"

"No." His small mouth shrank, and he shook his head. "I don't have it anymore."

"Well, where have you lived all these years?" Pamela heard the quiver in her own voice. "What have you been doing for work?"

He looked at her, silent for a moment. "I've lived around Ohio, different spots. Favorite job, I know it doesn't sound like much, was running a putt-putt course in Geauga Lake. It was basically mine. Cleaned it. Took care of all the repairs. Waited on customers. Real family-oriented joint."

"That sounds really good," she managed, still trying to keep her teeth from chattering. "How long did you do that?"

"Two and a half years. It was rewarding, because you felt like you were providing something nice for families. That was about the best I've ever been."

"What happened to that?"

He sighed. "One night a big group a teenagers showed up. Couple big shots in the crowd—football players. Acting crazy. Messing with the windmill. Cussing around families." Granger stared at the road in front of him, as if he was reliving it in his mind. "I warned them once. Then it just got worse." He looked at Pamela and shook his head. "I liked that job."

"What happened?"

"I kicked them out. That's what the owner told me to do if anyone got unruly, and they were. I mean, they were getting obscene in front of these families …"

"And?"

"The guys were waiting for me in the parking lot when I closed. Told me I'd made 'em look bad in front of their girls. They'd been drinking. One of them had a bat. What was I supposed to do?" He pounded the steering wheel. "Let them abuse me like they did in school? Let them bash my skull in? I wrung their scrawny necks is what I did. The ringleader ended up in the hospital with broken ribs. That was the end of the job."

They rode in silence.

Every now and then, Pamela could sense him studying her.

She would not be afraid.

She would heave it all at God's feet and trust.

This was *his* will. She was meant to play this part.

"It helps to talk," he finally said. "I've never had that."

"It does help. We all need friends."

She wanted to give him hope, suggest he get involved in a church where people would love him and accept him for who he was; but who knew what he had done back at that house? And all the things he'd done to her—including kidnapping.

Maybe if she could get him to turn himself in, she and Jack could drop the charges—he could start over. But the odds were so against him. His whole life was marred. He would likely never change. That was the hard truth.

But God *could* change him. After all, why was she there, riding next to him in that car? Why had he been so obsessed with her all those years?

Pamela leafed through the Bible and found one of her favorite verses. "'Peace I leave with you; my peace I give you,'" she said, feeling an incredible sense of rightness about reading the words aloud.

"'I do not give to you as the world gives. Do not let your hearts be troubled and do not be afraid.'"

As they rode on into the waning afternoon, Pamela silently prayed those words and asked that such supernatural peace would permeate Granger's soul—and hers.

"We're stopping up here," Granger announced.

He took exit 6, a town called Selby, but Pam wasn't sure if they were still in Ohio or in West Virginia. Once off the exit, he headed right. Soon he flicked the blinker and the car slowed as it approached a convenience store and gas station. There were a few cars in the parking lot—and a vacant pay phone.

"I'm gonna let you make one call," Granger said, "but I'm gonna be right there. All you're gonna say is, 'I am okay. The more people who try to find me, the worse danger I'm in.' That's it. No more, no less."

"Thank you." Pamela's insides raced. "Thank you so much."

"You're staying in the car while I fill the tank." He eased the car up to one of the pumps, put it in park, and turned it off. "After I fill it, we're pulling up to the store and going in, arms linked, like a nice happy couple. We're sharing a restroom. We're getting some food. We're back on the road."

Granger opened his door, and the car rocked as he got out. Then he bent down and looked back in at Pamela. "Don't say a word to anyone." He patted his waist beneath his T-shirt where a gun might be tucked. "Not one word."

Jack checked his phone again: nothing. A heavy mass of dread sat hard in the pit of his stomach. He had done all he could—phoned Pam's parents and let DeVry know he hadn't heard from her and was worried. Beyond that, he was helpless. If he didn't hear from her soon, he would throw some things in an overnight bag and drive up there. Then, if she did call, he could always turn around and come home.

As the tense meeting with Wendy and Sherry continued to unfold, Sherry told them that Evan believed Satterfield and the two elders were purposefully attempting to railroad him out of the pulpit, and would stoop to doing anything to achieve their goal. Evan realized Satterfield paid more than a colleague's natural attention to the senior pastor's schedule and activities and had even once caught Satterfield snooping through his files.

"But you know Evan," Sherry said. "He always gives people the benefit of the doubt."

Jack saw Wendy wince at the other woman's implied knowledge of *her* husband and was about to redirect the conversation when Sherry spoke again.

"There was more going on than just some kind of professional jealousy or a personal vendetta. Evan suspected Satterfield and two elders of skimming money from the church."

That aligned with what Hank Garbenger had said. Jack rifled through his notes and found the names Hank had given him. "Would those elders be Ryan Seeger and Bruce Trent?"

Sherry nodded.

No wonder she'd stopped giving to the church.

"What I didn't realize before," Sherry said, "is that Evan blames himself for allowing those funds to be taken. He was in such a state of depression, he just couldn't mount any kind of counterattack." Sherry looked from Wendy to Jack. "You know he'd stopped taking his antidepressants?"

Jack nodded.

Wendy deflated and settled back into a silent daze. It was obvious she felt even further wounded by the personal things Evan had confided in Sherry.

"Evan knows he's called to a higher account, being the pastor," Sherry said. "He feels he failed because he let all this happen on his watch, and he was too sick to do anything about it. He had even begun to believe Satterfield was right, that a pastor shouldn't have to rely on medication."

Wendy shook her head and covered her mouth.

"Evan was distraught," Sherry continued, "that he had allowed Satterfield and two of the men under him to be led so far astray. He said he could never prosecute his own elders—"

"The darn elders should know better!" Wendy said. "They have a responsibility to God, not just Evan. This whole thing is sick." She stood and paced and chewed at a thumbnail.

There was a long silence.

"There's something else," Sherry said.

Wendy sat down hard. "What?"

"Satterfield has a rental house on Lake Hudson, and a boat," Sherry said. "He's using church funds to pay for both. He justifies it as a second office, a place to study and pray. He makes it look like he lives at the little house he has here in Trenton City, but he spends most of his time at the lake. Evan thinks he's going to milk the church for as much as he can and disappear—do it all over again someplace else."

"You have got to be kidding me." Wendy tilted her head in wonder and peered at Jack.

"I just came from there," Jack said, nodding. "Hank Garbenger told me about it."

"Evan thought only Seeger and Trent knew about it," Sherry said.

"Apparently not," Wendy said. "How do *you* know about it?"

Sherry looked down at her hands and twisted her rings. "Evan found out a few days before he left. In his mind, that was just one more thing that blew up under his nose."

"He blames himself again," Jack said.

Wendy nodded. "That's Evan."

"I think Satterfield knows Evan is onto him about the money laundering, the lake house, the boat—everything," Sherry said. "I think he had Evan followed to the cabin and realized the photos of us would give him all the evidence he needed to oust Evan as pastor."

It made sense. Satterfield knew Evan was in no condition to put up a fight or press charges against him. In fact, for all Satterfield knew, Evan was indeed going to see his plan through to take his own life.

And wouldn't that play right into Satterfield's scheme ...

Just then Jack received a call from his friend Archer Pierce, the investigative reporter for TV-10 News, and excused himself to talk to him.

Hank Garbenger had phoned Archer to let him know Jack was working the missing pastor story. Archer was about to broadcast an in-depth piece of his own on Evan's disappearance and wondered if they could compare notes.

When Jack told Archer where he was, Archer asked if he could join them, for he had yet to manage an interview with the missing pastor's wife. He also had some information he thought Jack and Wendy would find of interest and hoped to confirm some things he had discovered. Wendy agreed to the meeting—with the TV coverage, perhaps someone would spot Evan and notify the authorities.

When Sherry stood to leave, they all meandered out to the driveway. It was then Jack realized he'd forgotten to show the women the photos he'd taken of Satterfield and the other man on the boat.

When he turned on his camera, shielded the screen from the sun, and directed it toward the ladies, Sherry said, "That's Ryan Seeger."

Wendy nodded slowly. "He's an elder."

"Hank told me he's one of the ones who counts the offering; is that right?" Jack said.

Once again Wendy nodded as she crossed her arms and inhaled deeply.

As Jack moved his car out of Wendy's driveway so Sherry could back out, Archer pulled up to the curb in front of the house. He was driving the white TV-10 News van, complete with the recognizable yellow-and-blue News 10 logo on the sides and the mast and microwave dish on top.

With Sherry gone, Jack made introductions between Wendy and Archer, and the three of them sat in white wicker furniture on Wendy's front porch. Archer was a slight man with brown hair that resembled Bobby Kennedy's—cropped close on the sides, longer on top. Although Archer could be fiercely intense when questioning people for his stories, Jack knew him to have a wonderful sense of humor and to be thoughtful and strongly committed to his family.

Wendy offered lemonade, but everyone seemed to want to get down to business.

Jack started by leafing through his notes, touching on some key main points, and conferring with Archer to see if he had similar information.

When Archer inquired about the note Evan left behind before he disappeared, Wendy admitted he had done so but gave no further details, and Archer was enough of a class act not to pry. Wendy made it clear that her story now—to Archer, Jack, and all of the media—was going to be a plea for help for her beloved husband who struggled with depression and had run off.

"We know he was heading south several days ago," Wendy said, "and we beg the public to be vigilant in helping us find him and get him safely home."

"I would like to have you say that on the air," Archer said. "After we're finished here, we can tape a brief interview and you can say what you want, make an appeal. I can assure you, a lot of people will be watching."

Wendy agreed.

Jack gave an inward sigh of relief that Archer seemed to have found nothing about Sherry Pendergrass.

Then the newsman spoke again. "So … do you think it possible anyone else was involved in your husband's disappearance?"

Wendy's eyes immediately shifted to Jack.

"Why do you ask?" Jack said.

Jack and Wendy looked at each other and waited.

Archer combed his thick hair with his fingers repeatedly, then looked at Wendy. "I keep stumbling over this Andrew Satterfield."

Wendy cleared her throat. "Go on."

"Well, in addition to the accusations I've heard about his suspicious activities at the church," Archer said, "I just found it so screwy that he went public about Evan taking meds with him and leaving behind what he blatantly called a suicide note. I would have thought they would have kept that under wraps as long as possible."

"Tell me about it," Wendy murmured.

"So I did some research on this guy," Archer said. "Did you know Satterfield was let go from his last job at a church in Denver?"

Jack looked at Wendy, who sat frozen, eyes locked on Archer.

Archer continued. "What I came up with via email and a few phone calls was that they let him go for reasons"—Archer made quote marks with his fingers—"in the best interest of the church."

"I hadn't heard that one yet," Jack said.

"Sounds like he was on a power trip–greed trip type thing," Archer said. "They actually caught him embezzling funds. I have reason to believe the same thing might be going on at Evan's church. I'm not sure if Satterfield is after Evan's job, or if he wants to skim as much money as he can and skip town."

"Did they file charges against him in Denver?" Jack said.

"Nope." Archer leaned back and clasped his hands behind his head. "Didn't want the negative publicity. Ran him out of town on a rail instead."

31

Something startled Evan. *What?* Rapping at the window just above his head. He remained still, blinking, stirring himself, getting his bearings. He'd slept, but had no idea how long. He was in the back-seat of his car somewhere in North Carolina, waiting for a bus to take him to Florida. The knock came again, and he was wide awake but stayed still. He felt someone looking down in at him.

Police?

His gun was in the duffel on the floor.

The sun had shifted. It was close to evening.

He was sickened at the prospect of being taken in, of facing Wendy, the boys, the people back home. If he remained still and it *wasn't* the police, maybe whoever it was would move on.

Not if it was a library employee—they might call the police.

He continued to pretend he was asleep, frozen, hoping the knocking would stop, waiting, panning through all his options.

The knocking came louder now, and a voice with it. "Git yer bones up or they gonna take you in." It was the shrill voice of a woman. "I ain't gonna stand here all day."

Evan propped himself up on his elbows and found himself squinting into the large brown eyes of a very small, elderly black woman. She wore a saggy woven hat with a curled brim all the way around and a dark purple wool overcoat.

"What you thinkin'? You tryin' to land yerself in the big house?" She motioned across the parking lot. "Po-lice was just here. If you ain't got no manners, I'll be on my way."

Her use of the word *po-lice* made Evan scramble upright and open the door. When he swung his feet around to the ground to face her, he realized he had kicked his shoes off while sleeping and was now sock-footed.

"Well, ain't you a sight."

Evan looked her up and down and wondered why on earth she had winter clothes on in the heat of summer. Beneath the oversized coat she wore gray sweatpants, white socks, and black vinyl shoes that looked too big.

"Ain't you got nothin' to say?" she said. "What's yer name?"

What could it hurt? "Evan," he said. "You?"

"Valerie," she declared. "Valerie Belinda McShane."

"Good to meet you." Evan shook her hand, which was small and rough. "Did you say something about police?"

Her head craned around. "They cruised through here real slow-like. Not sure if they noticed those out-a-state tags a' yours. One thing's fer sure, if they'd known you was sleepin' in there they'd have rousted you for certain. The Fort Prince po-lice do not stand for no loiterin', nope, not 'round these parts."

Evan figured if they had run his plates, it would have been finished; they never would have left. But he didn't feel safe staying there much longer.

"How did you know I was in here?" he said.

"My belongings is right over yonder." She pointed to a black metal bench beneath some large trees. A mixture of white plastic bags and brown shopping bags with big handles dotted the bench. "I don't miss much. You slept a good bit. What brings a Yankee from Ahia south a' the Mason-Dixon?"

"Just a little summer trip," Evan said, leaning back into the car to get his shoes. "What town is this?"

"Fort Prince," she said. "That's not what I was told."

Evan pulled his socks up, slipped on a shoe, and tried to figure out what she was talking about.

"You ain't on no summer trip," Valerie said. "You's in trouble."

Evan stopped. "Someone told you that, you say?"

She crossed her arms. Her mouth sealed into a smirk and she nodded big and slow.

"Who?" Evan said.

"Never you mind who," she said. "You think you kin outrun yer problems?"

Evan stared at her with one shoe in his lap. She was either slightly off in the head, a prophetic bag lady, an angel, someone who liked to hear herself talk, or a combination of the above. When he had been closer to God, Evan would never have ignored a "chance" encounter such as this; he'd try to figure out what God might be trying to tell him. But now he just wanted to get out of there.

"Look." He put on the other shoe and tied it. "Thanks for letting me know about the police. I'm going to be on my way. But I really appreciate you watching my back."

"You took a vow, did you not?"

Evan's whole body ached as he stood and examined Valerie.

Her eyes were fixed on his left hand—his wedding ring.

"For better or worse?" she said. "In sickness and in health?"

"What's your point?" Evan didn't know what else to say, but he knew he wanted her to stop. The whole thing was confounding.

"Just that you made a vow."

For a second it was like he'd been dazed by a verbal stun gun.

A promise ... to Wendy ... before God.

And the boys ...

Evan shook it off. He didn't have time for this. Who was this Valerie, anyway? If she were so holy, so close to God, she certainly wouldn't be homeless; God would have blessed her more than that.

Listen to you.

You are so messed up.

Deep within, Evan knew—or at least he had been taught—God didn't operate that way. Rich or poor, God played no favorites. Valerie could be an angel. Evan knew God did not look at outward appearances; he bypassed all the obvious stuff the world judges and fixed his eyes on the hearts of men.

Evan's head was so screwed up. It was as if he'd had a lobotomy. There was no feeling ... He just seemed to go thirty miles per hour, never slower, never faster. His stomach ached and his fingertips tingled.

"You can either keep yer vow or try to play God yerself," Valerie said. "That's what yer doin', you know. It's selfish. So what if ya made mistakes? Sometimes ya gotta pull up yer britches, be a man—face the music."

Okay, Evan was out of there. He felt for his wallet, then keys. He shut the back door and opened the driver's door. He found a ten-dollar bill and handed it to her.

"We kin put my belongings right in the trunk." She ignored the money, pointed to her things, and began walking toward them. "Just pull right 'round over yonder."

Evan stood there. His hand with the bill dropped to his side.

No way was she going to manipulate him.

He put the ten back in his wallet, got in the car, started it, and sat there.

Valerie arrived at her things, plopped down on the bench, and did not look back at him.

Of all the nerve … she's going to try to put me on a guilt trip.

Evan didn't have time for her.

Then again, what was he going to do until the bus came later that night?

He should just leave. That would be the safest thing. She'd be forgotten in five minutes.

Valerie sat on the bench with her back to Evan, kicking her dangling feet like a little kid and looking all around at the sky and shady streets of the town. Evan thought he could hear her singing.

Good for her.

There sat a lady who had virtually nothing in the world yet had cared enough to reach out to help him. She seemed so content, sure of herself, carefree.

A homeless bag lady was in better shape than he was.

That about summed it up.

Evan put the car in drive and swung out the back entrance, as far away from Valerie Belinda McShane as possible.

FEAR HAS A NAME

Granger stood thick and immovable just outside Pamela's car door. She could hear the hum of the fuel and feel it splashing into the gas tank.

Taking her predicament one second at a time, which was the way she'd determined she must play it, there was no getting away from her captor at the moment. She would have to dive over the driver's seat, hit the unlock button, fling the door open, and run. She could scream, she could try to blurt out to the people at the next pump what was going on, she could sprint for the inside of the store. But what would stop Granger from drawing his weapon and marching right after her?

There were a few people getting gas, meandering in the store, but no police, no one with the authority to stop a madman. For now, for that moment, she would need to sit there and be obedient.

But that didn't mean things wouldn't change. When she got out of the car, into the store, into the restroom, on the phone, who knew? A chance to escape or send up a warning signal could present itself at any second. She had to be ready, right there on the edge, alert, prepared to run or scream or whisper something to someone, or do whatever it took to get away.

She had to be smart. *Be smart.*

No one was on the pay phone. That was good. Pamela wondered who even used them anymore, with cell phones so prevalent.

She heard the pump click off and turned to watch Granger remove it from the gas tank, hang it up, and rattle the gas cap into place.

The beat of her heart quickened.

He opened her door.

"Come on," he said.

"I thought we were pulling up."

"I changed my mind. Come on."

She got out. He pushed the door shut and linked her arm with his at the elbow. A homesick feeling overwhelmed her.

"Remember." Granger nodded at a heavy middle-aged man with a ruddy face waddling from the store to his car with a huge drink. "Not a word."

Pamela nodded. Each step felt odd and unbalanced, as if the ground was farther away than it was. If he had the audacity to touch her like that now, what would come later?

Granger held the door for her. "Pump three," he said to the olive-skinned cashier, who wore a white turban with a fake diamond at the front. The register area was packed with cheap gadgets and doodads, from Confederate flag lighters to anti-drowsy pills to miniature flash-lights and girlie magazines.

"That vill be thirty-seven dow-lare," the man said as he eyed the scratches on Granger's arms.

Granger retrieved his wallet and let Pamela's arm drop.

That feeling, right then, was indescribable.

She could run. She could be free. But she knew it would only be temporary. And then he would be angry.

Granger handed the man two twenties, got his change, and before Pamela could blink, they were in the men's restroom with the door locked.

Granger walked her to the lone blue stall, let go of her, and went in. "Just a second," he said.

She heard a bunch of toilet paper roll off the spool. Then a pause. The loud flush made her jump.

"Okay, all clean." He left the stall. "Ladies first. I'll be right outside the door."

He left her locked in the restroom alone, which surprised her; she thought he was going to stay. Although Pamela had desperately needed to go, it took forever. She examined the yellowing Styrofoam ceiling tiles and thought about trying to get up there. Maybe she could climb the sink, then the wall of the stall. If she could somehow hoist herself up into the rafters of the ceiling, Granger wouldn't be able to get up there. She could scream until help came.

It wasn't realistic. She could never get up there. He'd open the door and be on her like a goon in seconds.

She finished. The hot water and foamy soap felt good. She splashed her face, dried with paper towels, shook her head, and fixed her hair with her fingers. Looking at herself in the mirror, she wondered if her mom and dad remembered what she was wearing so they could put it on the news.

When she opened the heavy blue door of the restroom, Granger slipped in and locked it.

"You get in the stall and lock the door," he said. "I'm going to go right here." He nodded toward the urinal on the wall. "Don't try anything."

She remained silent in the stall, plugged her ears, and prayed for safekeeping.

He knocked. "Come on."

She left the stall and watched him as he washed and dried his hands but never once looked in the mirror.

Out in the store he said softly, "Get whatever you want. Get enough to last awhile."

How long? she wondered. *What does he have planned?*

She really believed he didn't know, that all he knew was that he wanted to be with her. She must become the world's best actress. In her mind she must revert back to the Pamela Wagner he knew in high school, who reached out, showed compassion, wanted him to be one of the gang.

Her stomach ached. She wasn't hungry, but she knew she must eat to stay strong and alert. She walked down the aisle nearest them. Although Granger wasn't holding her arm, he was right there in her shadow, looking himself for food.

She picked up a good-sized bag of cashews and several crunchy peanut butter bars while he grabbed a package of teriyaki beef jerky and a can of potato sticks. At the refrigerated section, Pamela got several yogurts, a package of string cheese, and a bottled water. Granger got a tall can of Red Bull.

"Ready?" He eyed her.

She nodded.

He took several items out of her full arms, and they walked back up to the man in the turban. They set all the things on the sliver of available counter space.

"And two packs of Newports—soft," Granger said. "Not the box." He turned his head to the side and muttered, "If you can understand English."

A young couple entered the store. He was black, tall, and built, wearing navy nylon warm-ups and a flat-brimmed Reds cap. She was white and chubby, possibly pregnant, a bleach-blonde with a tiny diamond stud in her nose. Everything in Pamela wanted to make eye contact, signal somehow. She thought of making a horizontal slashing sign at her throat and pointing at Granger. If she only had a small sign she could hold up, with 9-1-1 written on it. She could put a finger to her lips as if to say *I need help but keep it quiet.*

But again the opportunities flew past. Before she knew it, Granger had paid, clasped her arm, and they were exiting through the sticker-filled glass doors. Her thoughts flipped to Jack and the pay phone. Granger hadn't forgotten. He turned right out of the store, toward the phone.

But a man was standing there, bending over slightly, dialing or putting money in.

Granger stopped.

Pamela kept going, like a homing pigeon that would not be denied, but Granger's arm locked down, hurting her.

"At the next stop." He turned and headed for the Impala.

"Please, no." She craned back toward the man on the phone but kept moving with Granger away from it. "I have to call now. I've been good. Please, wait."

Granger continued walking, forcefully pulling her. "Get in my side." He opened the driver's door.

Pamela stopped and looked back. The man was still at the pay phone. She faced Granger, short of breath. "If you care for me at all, you'll wait. Please."

Granger's tiny eyes shifted from her to the pay phone, then back to her. "He's off."

"Thank you!" She hurried toward it.

"Stop," Granger grabbed her bicep.

"Ouch!"

His big head swiveled eighty degrees right, then left. "Keep your voice down!"

"I'm sorry," she said. "That hurt. And it scared me."

"I'm sorry." He was flustered and blinking. "I'm going with you."

They walked quickly through the parking lot.

"Here." Granger pulled his hand out of his pocket and opened it. There must've been twelve quarters there.

She looked at him and froze for a second. She hadn't even thought of needing change. But he had. She put out both hands, tiny compared to his. "Thank you."

He nodded.

She tried to recall exactly what he had told her she could say … that she was okay, and the more people who tried to find her—

Pamela stopped cold and almost got sick as her eyes fixed on the words scribbled on a small white piece of paper taped crookedly over the coin slot.

OUT OF ORDER.

32

Jack was home, and the house had never been quieter. He couldn't remember the last time he had been there alone. Amid the late sun and shadows that fell long in the family room, he sat on the ottoman where Pam liked to spread out books or newspapers or knitting. He could hear the faint hum of a mower somewhere in the neighborhood—someone getting the grass cut before dark. How he wished his life were still that simple.

He had gotten home that afternoon from his meeting with Wendy and Archer and pounded out an updated story on Evan McDaniel, with volatile and incriminating references to Andrew Satterfield and his shady past at the church in Denver. He emailed copies of the story to Cecil and Derrick, suggesting that Derrick try to confirm the new information with several of Archer's contacts in Denver.

Although Jack could not mention the photos of Evan and Sherry in the story or the pending blackmail, because he'd assured Sherry the information was off the record, he did subtly imply that Satterfield might be after Pastor Evan's job. Jack realized there was much in the story that his editor might reject, but he'd written it as truthfully and powerfully as he could, sent it in, and left it at that. They could water it down if necessary.

Jack tried to reach Archer to let him know he was handing the story off to Derrick, but his call went to voice mail. He would try again later; right now he had more weighty issues to deal with—like finding his wife. Something was terribly wrong, so wrong it was sickening. Pam had not returned to her parents' house in Cleveland Heights. Granger had not been apprehended. Those were the surreal facts. The room seemed to rotate like a spooky merry-go-round from the power of all the horrifying what-ifs.

He stood with force and crossed to the front door where that creep had broken in.

Calm down.

You don't know anything's wrong.

But if Pam were okay—if she were well, healthy, free—she would have been in touch with him long before now.

That was a fact.

Prayer crossed his mind, but he needed to *move*. He headed upstairs to the master bedroom, dug a small suitcase out of the closet, and opened it on the bed. He would let Tommy and Darlene know he was leaving, gas up, and head for Cleveland Heights. He could make contact with DeVry, Pam's parents, and his folks on the way.

Hopefully, amid all that, he would hear from Pam and everything would be okay again. This would have all been just the beginning of a wicked dream, and things like cutting the grass before dark would once again top his list of priorities.

He gathered T-shirts, boxers, socks; set out his toilet kit and packed it with a razor, shaving cream, toothpaste—

His cell rang. It was Archer Pierce.

"Hey, Archer," Jack answered.

"This Satterfield thing is turning into a powder keg, Jack."

"What's up now?" Jack went on packing with the phone to his ear.

"An anonymous source in Denver just told me the amounts of money Satterfield ripped off from the church there; we're talking *major* funds, *major* scam artist."

"Does anyone know this besides you?"

Jack just couldn't pack with one hand. He stopped over the bathroom sink to focus.

"I don't think so," Archer said. "This whole thing's gone under the radar. I'm talking with my station manager now about doing Satterfield as a whole sidebar to the McDaniel story. I'm ready to go with it, if they let me."

"Great job," Jack said. "Listen, Archer, I've got a favor to ask. I'm in the middle of a family emergency and am going to be out of pocket."

"Wow. I'm sorry. Okay ..."

"After we met, I updated my latest story with a lot of the new info from you and sent it to my editor, Cecil Barton, and another reporter, Derrick Whittaker. Can I have them keep in touch with you on this thing?"

"Sure, give 'em my cell."

"I'll do it. Thanks, man. I owe you."

"There'll be more coming out of the church in Denver," Archer said. "People are starting to talk; they want justice. If it heats up like I think it's going to, Satterfield's gonna be facing serious charges."

"Okay, man. Derrick will be calling you on all that."

"No problem," Archer said. "I hope everything works out for you."

After ending the call, Jack went on stuffing hairbrush, tooth-brush, mouthwash, and other familiar items into the toilet kit, sure he was forgetting things. He made a mental note to call Cecil to give him Archer's cell number.

He threw a travel clock into the suitcase, flip-flops ... what else did he need?

The ping of the doorbell echoed through the still house.

What now?

He hurried to the steps, quickly got down to the foyer, and peered through the slats. Officer DeVry stood in uniform with his back to the door, hat in his right hand.

Jack's heart lurched.

"Officer DeVry." He opened the door and stepped out. "What's going on?"

DeVry turned to face him, but the expression on his face was sober, emotionless, unfamiliar.

"Cleveland Heights PD was called to Granger Meade's child-hood home this afternoon by Granger's father," DeVry said.

Jack's insides twisted.

"I hate to tell you this, Jack, but a red Honda Accord reg-istered to your wife was found down an embankment along the driveway; she has not been found. We think Granger's abducted her. We've—"

"Wait, wait." Everything spun. "Pam's car, at his house?"

DeVry nodded. "The father says Granger showed up there this afternoon. Local PD had stopped earlier in the day to warn the par-ents he was wanted and might be in the area. When he showed up, the dad phoned it in."

"Wait, what was Pam's car doing there? What about the girls?"

As the reality of each bad scenario became worse, Jack's brain wigged out. He turned, entered the house. He had to get his things and get up there.

"Jack." DeVry's voice came from behind, then a hand on Jack's shoulder. "Jack, calm down. Your girls are fine. They're still at Pam's parents' house; they're all fine."

"Pam never got back there?"

"No, Jack."

"Do they know? My girls?"

"I don't think the girls know," DeVry said. "When I called to check on them, I spoke to Pamela's mother, Margaret. I did tell her what was going on. She … well, she broke down. Her husband had to take the call."

Jack almost collapsed. He gripped the back of the couch, nodded, and breathed, just focusing on deep breaths, getting air to the brain, lungs.

"What was Pam doing at that house?" He realized he was hoarse, almost whispering.

"No idea."

"Was there any sign of injury at her car?" He was thinking blood.

"No," DeVry said. "Nothing to indicate she was hurt."

"How'd her car get down there?"

"Well, it was dented—"

"This keeps getting worse," Jack snapped. "Just spill it!!"

"This isn't easy, Jack. I'm getting there, okay? I'm not going to hide anything from you. The car tracks indicate she tried to get back up the embankment several times. They think she might have just

FEAR HAS A NAME

barely made it back up when Granger came down the driveway and bumped her right front quarter panel, sending her back down."

Jack's face whooshed like an inferno. "Then what?"

"It looks as though Granger went down the embankment on foot and forced her to go with him, in his car."

Jack gave a cry as he swirled and smashed the wall, just beneath a mirror, with a crushing right fist. A fissure of pain sizzled up the top of his wrist. He covered it with his other hand and turned away. "Why?" he yelled to God. "Why would you do this?"

"Jack." DeVry's voice came near. "We've got nationwide alerts out. We're gonna find them."

Jack ripped around, still sheltering his aching right wrist and arm. "You've been saying that for how long?" he screamed and distanced himself again. "What did we do to deserve this? What did we *do*?"

Without giving DeVry a chance to reply, Jack stormed out the back door and cried out in anguish to the heavens.

Evan had driven and parked at various nondescript spots around the small town of Fort Prince, snoozing, moving the car each time he awoke, watching evening turn to night. His heart was as black as the streets beyond his window.

He was parked diagonally on the town square in front of a sandwich shop that had closed hours ago. The bus station was a five-minute walk. He would leave the car there and head for the station in another ten minutes, no longer caring if his vehicle was found soon or not. That would get him to the station about thirty minutes before the bus left for south Florida and the place where things had always been right with the world. It would be the last place he would ever see.

What had happened to him?

Who had he become?

He sat there, useless and pitiful, so unlike what he used to be even five years ago. Back then, his care and concern for others had brought him such joy and contentment—and he had been able to help so many people. Now the rug had been pulled out from under him. His church was in a hopeless downward spiral. Satterfield had done irreparable damage. At least two of his elders were crooks, and he couldn't fix it or save them. He and Sherry had gotten way too close. And he knew if he even tried to go back and raise his boys, it would be a disaster.

The life had been sucked out of him.

The only thing that mattered was disappearing.

The dim, yellowish light from the street lamps filtered into the car. The baggie and many pills and orange plastic bottles shined back up at him from the passenger seat.

You got burned out. The ministry took its toll. You were spending more time helping other people—strangers, in many cases—than loving your own wife and boys.

When he finally refused to get out of bed one morning, Wendy had insisted he go for a physical. His doctor, after performing a battery of tests, announced Evan was struggling from a combination of stress and depression; he suggested an antidepressant. "Why not?"

Wendy had said. But something in Evan had told him not to get going on them, to try to work through it. After three weeks fighting that battle, he had never felt so sad and hopeless. He called his doctor and asked him to phone in the prescription.

Years and several different prescriptions later, there he sat, nothing more than a dismal blob, a sack of potatoes, a hypocrite who had ruined the lives of a woman who had dedicated her life to him and three fine boys who would each deal with his demons as they became men.

What was most depressing, most sickening of all was that he was the pastor. He was supposed to be the spiritual one, the one nearest to God, the one guiding others through their minefield of problems. Little did they know, Evan faced a bomb-riddled battlefield of his own. His failure and depression became an enormous secret, an albatross that wore him to the bone. He had become vulnerable and weak. A failure before God and his congregation.

He reached around to the floor of the backseat and hoisted the duffel bag into his lap. Undoing the zipper, he reached in and found the cold steel of the semiautomatic. He got it out and held it in front of him in both hands, as if it were a valuable artifact.

Would he be able to do it?

He'd always believed it was deeply sad and disturbing when people took their own lives. He'd thought it a selfish and cowardly act. Who was anyone to declare when his or her life would start or end? That was up to God.

Yet now, sitting there with the reality of it—the possibility of it—resting in his hands, he understood with clarity why a person would end his own life.

Hopelessness, that's why. Utter, bleak despair.

If God was still listening to him at all, if he would look down on the situation and grant one last request, Evan would ask that he spare Wendy and the boys from ever hearing of the cabin in Springfield and what he was sure would become his supposed "affair" with Sherry Pendergrass.

Lightning illuminated a gray sky whose ceiling was low and packed with thick, menacing clouds. Evan braced for the thunder, which jolted him when it cracked loud and long, making the car shimmy. No rain on the windshield yet.

Time to roll.

He took the keys out of the ignition and removed the silver keychain with "#1 DAD" engraved on it—the boys had given it to him one Father's Day. He slipped it into his pocket. He removed the car's remote so he would be able to lock the car then placed the rest of the keys in the glove compartment.

Evan got out of the car. There was no one around. The night was thick with humidity, and a stiff wind assured him rain was coming. He leaned in for the duffel and hesitated as he examined the bag of pills.

He left them, got out, threw the duffel over his shoulder, slammed the door, and locked it. Turning to the sidewalk, he lost his balance but steadied himself. Noticing a large metal grate on the ground by the curb, he stepped over it, stopped, held the remote in front of him and dropped it clanging through the grate into the dark sewer system below.

No turning back now.

Another fissure of lightning ripped open the sky. Thunder boomed. One by one, raindrops snapped at the sidewalk and pelted his head and shoulders.

It would be an uncomfortably long bus ride if his clothes were sopping wet.

He contemplated running but only sighed.

Why bother?

He began to walk.

And he wished for the lightning to come closer, much closer.

33

Now that it was completely dark, Granger and Pamela were blazing a trail. Late on a Monday night was proving to be a darn good time to take a trip south.

Granger was sticking mostly to highway roads now, I-77 to be specific. They were in the hill country of West Virginia. First Parkersburg, then Ripley, then winding past the romantically lit gold dome of the capitol in Charleston. Every time he had ever driven past, Granger always thought he could live there. It looked like an old mining town. Friendly. Peaceful. Blue collar—like him.

He was doing about seventy as the green signs for Princeton and Bluefield and Wytheville shot by one at a time over the miles.

"I remember one time when I was a kid," Granger said, "we went on a vacation right around here somewhere. Galax was the name of the town; I'll never forget that name. My old man rented this little junk camper. It was gonna be a real family love-in type thing." He chuckled. "Man, did it go sour."

Pamela was hunched low in the passenger seat, but looking right at him, with her pretty mouth closed. Her body looked rigid. He wished she would relax.

"We went to my cousin's house," he said. "The first night we got there, they had a big tent revival in Galax; you wouldn't believe what happened."

Pamela just kept staring.

"Some huge dude wearing a big old silver belt buckle and a leather cowboy hat got up in front of everybody and handled what they said was a poisonous rattlesnake. It was huge. My father was out of there so fast. He was furious at my aunt for taking us. We packed it in and took off, drove all night, all the way back home. The whole way he harped about that snake handler, how he was a wolf in sheep's clothing."

Pamela's expression didn't change. She'd eaten a few cashews earlier and sipped her water, but that was it.

Missing that husband.

"We're only gonna have a little time together." Granger eyed her. "Can you just talk to me? That's all I want."

"I told you I need to let Jack know I'm safe." Pamela didn't move in her seat. "I'm worried because I know he's worried. Can't you understand that?"

"Okay, look, I told you we're gonna stop again. It's only been a half a day—"

"Have a little sympathy, okay?" She sat up, crossed her arms, and glared out the passenger window into the blackness. "I have a family. Little girls. Parents. They're worried sick."

She turned to him for a reaction. He drained the last of his Red Bull, tossed the can into the back, punched the lighter, and reached for the pack of cigarettes in the visor above his head.

"Your problems are small, Pamela." He put a fist to his mouth and belched silently. "Your world is small. You don't know what it's like to suffer—to be tormented in your mind. To be raised by tyrants."

It was dark and silent in the car for perhaps a mile. He opened his window, lit the smoke, inhaled deeply. He was about to mention his plan to stop at one of the upcoming exits so she could call, when she spoke.

"I know you had it rough." Pamela turned and looked straight ahead. "I heard different things. I don't think anyone really knew what you went through."

"You're darn right they didn't." He could almost feel the cold, damp mattress beneath him and smell the wet, frigid nights in the shack behind the house.

"Bottom line," he said, "they never wanted me."

The highway hummed beneath them.

"But because they *did* have me, out of spite they decided to make my life miserable. Most of it was mental. 'Thou shalt not lie. Thou shalt not steal.'" Granger imitated his mother. "They were so good at it, they made it seem like they didn't even know they were doing it. I'm still not sure how much of it was done to purposefully hurt me and how much of it they really believed was true religion. I learned to let it roll off."

"What about once you left home?" Pamela looked at him. "Were you able to lead any sort of a normal life?"

Her hands were trembling. At least she was trying.

"I had a good job," he said. "Had my own car, and place."

"What happened?"

"Pffft." He paused. "Relationships. People skills." He spewed the words as if spitting in his parents' faces. "Nobody taught me any of that stuff."

"But you *know* you have issues." Her whole body turned to face him, and she curled a knee up on the seat. "That's the important thing. You realize your parents mentally abused you, and you know you need help. That's everything."

He looked at her. Even in the dark, her lovely face was radiant.

She would have been so good for him. She would have made the difference—the difference between a good life, and this.

"I went to see a doctor," he said. "Not too long ago. Paid an arm and a leg. Was ready for help."

"And?"

"Oh, we talked and did tests and looked at pictures, the whole nine yards; took a whole day. The entire time I was trying to figure out if what she was doing was truly scientific, if it would help, or whether it was all just a sham. Still haven't figured it out."

"What'd she tell you?" Pamela twisted open her water and sipped.

"Ah … that I was emotionally abused," he said sarcastically.

"What else?"

"That my parents ignored me when I needed to express myself. They isolated me from healthy relationships."

Pamela shook her head.

"She said that's why I'm withdrawn … why I'm not good at relationships."

"In high school sometimes you seemed okay. Even funny."

She looked away when he tried to make eye contact.

"I knew you weren't popular," she said.

The faces of the jocks, the incidents with the bullies seemed to come at him like obstacles in the road. "That stuff left scars, you know?"

She looked over at him in silence.

"It was bad enough I got it at home, but then at school—from everyone? And it was like a disease. Once the others saw or heard you getting harassed, they assumed that gave them the freaking license to do the same."

His voice broke.

Stop it, you baby.

"Granger, do you believe in God?"

"Don't even go there," he snapped. "My parents lived and breathed that garbage."

"But you've got a skewed view of it. They weren't true Christians," she said. "I'm a Christian. Any compassion or interest I ever took in you was because God used me, that was God reaching out to you. Your parents might have ruined your concept of Christianity, but I can tell you for a fact, nothing will change you more than this book on the floor right here."

"I'll tell you something." He took a painfully deep hit off the Newport. "You are the *only* person on earth I would still be sitting next to after hearing that pitch. Now let's cut it."

"If you read this book" —she picked it up and set it in her lap— "I guarantee it will pierce your heart and change you—if you're open to it. Come close to God, and he'll come close to you."

"I've read more of that thing than most people. I've *tried* to change."

Pamela shook her head. "It's not about trying. It's about *not* trying. It's about letting go of life as you know it. Falling into his arms. Trusting him to carry you—and to supernaturally change you."

"That all sounds real good," Granger said.

"It can be."

"The truth is, Pam, the way I really feel is totally worthless—undeserving of anyone's love or care—yours or God's or anyone else's."

"That's because your parents rejected you!"

"Yeah, they did." He slammed the steering wheel. "I was never good enough."

"Everyone needs to be loved and feel they're important and wanted and listened to. You never got that. It's no wonder you're—"

"A freak?" he said, looking straight out at the road.

"That you have big challenges you need to work to overcome," she said.

Granger stared ahead as far as the headlights reached.

"That's what the shrink said. 'Every individual needs to be nourished with human contact.'" He turned to Pam. "I can't remember touching my parents. I'm not talking about hugging or kissing them; I'm talking about *never touching them*."

His own statement pierced him. Sorrow or relief or regret, something foreign, rolled up in his throat and behind his nose.

He drove, wishing so badly that his life had been different. Wondering why, if there was a God, he had allowed Granger to grow up in that wicked, rotten home and with such torment at school.

"One time I dared to raise my voice to my mother. I told her she and my father were abusing me with all their mental voodoo. She got so ticked she turned purple." He laughed out of sheer frustration.

Pamela even chuckled, and her eyes glistened.

"She said, 'We've never once hit you. You have no idea what it's like to be abused. You keep it up and you'll find out.'"

Pamela opened the Bible. "It's not too late to start over," she said quietly.

"Oh yes, it is." Granger nodded. "My mother's dead back there. My prints are on a gun. And here I am on the run with you—add kidnapping to the murder rap."

"The evidence will prove your father did it," Pamela said. "You'll get an attorney. A jury will hear the case—"

"And who do you think they're gonna believe? An upstanding, longtime member of the Cleveland Heights community and a deacon in his church—or a wacked-out thug like me who's tormented an innocent housewife and mother?"

"We could drop all the charges," she said, realizing that was probably a lie. "Then it would just be a matter of getting you off the murder rap."

"No how, no way would your husband ever go for that."

"Look, I'm not making any promises," Pamela said, "but if you stop running, let me go—I'll talk to him. I'll plead with Jack to drop all charges in order to give you a clean slate. I promise you that."

That was the Pamela Wagner he once knew.

He wanted to reach over and softly touch her hand, take it in his.

He wanted to nestle her close to him and ride through the night with her head resting against his arm.

But he knew.

Yes, he knew none of that was to be.

This would be the last time he would ever travel that road. Everything behind him was gone and forgotten.

Blank.

He would remember or revisit none of it ever again.

All that was left was a little more time with Pamela, his only love, on the gray highway whose white lines stretched out before him like a ribbon unfurling in the night.

And then what?

He felt like opening that Impala up to a hundred miles per hour and driving it off a cliff into the ocean wherever the map ended.

They would go out together.

The sky far off to the right burst open with lightning, revealing thick, mean clouds.

Appropriate, he thought. *Bring it on.*

"What do you say?" Pamela's soft voice brought him back. "Will you stop this? Will you let me go home to my little girls? They need me, just like what we talked about. I promise I'll do whatever I can to help you."

He didn't look at her. "You can't help me."

"But you can help me," she whispered. "You can give me my life back."

He pushed down on the accelerator, not wanting that, not wanting to give her up.

The car roared, pinning his shoulders to the seat, jarring Pamela.

And he wanted it to roar, louder, more deafening—to drown out the knowledge of right and wrong; the confusion and chaos firing like sparks, chugging like pistons in his messed-up head.

✎

Evan sat shivering alone on a bench in the dimly lit station, waiting to board the bus that sat just beyond the window in the rain, its orange and white lights glistening and passengers stretching beyond its dark windows. Halfway to the station he remembered he'd packed an umbrella. It sat on the floor still soaked and open next to him. His clothes and body were wet and cold to the touch; inside he was numb and nauseated.

"Sir, did you want me to check that bag for you?"

Evan slowly looked up at the short female attendant in the navy pants and white short-sleeved shirt. Her nametag read *Ann*.

"I'll keep it with me," Evan said.

"That's fine," she said. "You can go ahead and board now." She hesitated, then removed her blue cap and scratched her head of frizzy brown hair. "I wasn't sure if you heard the announcement."

"No." He stared at her and gave a dazed chuckle. "I must've been daydreaming." He stood with ticket in hand and bent down to get his duffel bag and umbrella.

"Just give the driver your ticket when you board," she said.

He nodded, made sure he'd left nothing behind, and headed for the door.

"Safe travels." She waved as she went through a swinging door leading behind the counter. "Might be a little slow going. There are weather issues."

Evan stopped at the door. "Really?"

"Yeah." She straightened a stack of bus schedules along the front of the counter. "Radar's showing a big line of storms in Alabama and Georgia, moving our way. This is just the beginning of it."

He nodded toward the bus. "So we'll be heading right into it?"

"'Fraid so. It's showing severe thunderstorms and some tornado watches all the way. Don't worry. Our drivers are the best."

Evan pushed the door open and went out, but Ann's words settled there at the front of his mind. He stared at the large, wet bus, idling now and being pelted by rain. He smelled the gas fumes.

Is it up to a human being to keep this thing safe?

What do you believe anymore?

Even in his toxic condition, Evan knew—as well as he knew his own name—that God was in control of that enormous hunk of metal. What happened to it or any other car on the road, in storms or sun, was God's doing.

All things were his doing; the good and the bad.

Even the predicament he was in, who knew? Maybe good would come out of it. Wendy might remarry some guy who would turn out to be great for the boys, better than he could have ever been.

The sidewalk by the bus was covered from the rain by a metal awning, so he closed the umbrella. Coming down the steps of the bus was a well-built, middle-aged African-American man wearing a uniform similar to Ann's—the driver.

"How are you this evening, sir?" His nametag read *Bernie*.

"Tired, to tell you the truth," Evan said. "Do I give you my ticket?"

Bernie set his coffee cup on the sidewalk, took Evan's ticket, examined it, tore it, and gave half back to him. "You got a long ride ahead of you," Bernie said. "Plenty of time to catch up on your sleep."

"I'm going to do that, if the weather doesn't keep me up." Evan started up the steps of the bus.

"We'll be fine," Bernie said. "Enjoy the trip, sir."

Evan squinted down the long narrow aisle, and the whole setting seemed like a dream. The fluorescent-lit bus was dotted with yawning, heavy-lidded passengers of all ages and ethnicities. Some were reading and doing puzzles while others slept or listened to iPods. There were probably thirty rows with two seats on each side of the aisle.

About halfway back Evan found two empty seats on the right. He set his bag and umbrella in the aisle seat, took off his jacket, swayed from a wave of dizziness, and eased into the seat by the window. A reading light shone down from above. He found a switch for it on one of his armrests and turned it off.

He was so exhausted.

Stuffing his jacket and umbrella into his bag, he patted around for the gun. It was heavy and dangerous in his hand.

Soon the bus hissed and rocked and steamed. Its doors closed.

"Next stop, Prospect, North Carolina." Bernie hung up the microphone, and the bus lurched forward.

Evan released the weapon, zipped up the duffel, and pushed it beneath the seat next to him.

The fluorescent lights along the overhead bin flickered and went off, darkening the whole bus except for reading lights here and there.

He leaned back, closed his eyes, took a deep breath, and exhaled silently.

Relax.

His body was rigid, cold.

He shivered and crossed his arms, wishing he'd gotten a blanket from the overhead, as some of the other passengers had.

But he wasn't about to get up. He was too sleepy.

The bus turned, shifting him against the cold window.

He moved away from it and nestled in, recognizing the familiar half-conscious feeling he always got when he was about to drift off.

You're in control … of all things … this bus … the good and the bad.

34

Talk about helpless. There was Jack in that one little Volkswagen Jetta on a blank highway in wide-open America, whose roads could take a person anywhere. He felt like an ant in a desert searching for one red grain of sand, and that was Pamela.

The many gruesome possible scenarios—with which he was all too familiar, working in the news business—flashed before him: Pam being taped or tied, without food, in a car trunk or filthy hideaway, unbathed, gagged, beaten, bruised, raped, worse …

He put the windows down and let the night wind blow away the images. He examined each oncoming car, thinking he could get lucky and spot the Impala—if that was what Granger was still driving.

They could be anywhere.

Anywhere!

According to DeVry, Pam's abduction happened between two and four p.m., which meant Granger could have her as far away as Iowa by then—or Manhattan, or Nashville, or DC, or the Upper Peninsula of Michigan.

Jack was doing the only thing that made sense—heading toward the last place she'd been seen, Cleveland Heights, which he thought he could make in two and a half hours, maybe less, if he flew. He

needed to be with the girls. Ben and Margaret would be totally dev-
astated, especially Margaret. Jack just hoped they were keeping it
together in front of the girls.

On the seat between his legs was wedged Tommy's .40 caliber
Taurus pistol, which his neighbor gave him on his way out of town. It
looked almost snub-nosed: blue steel, black rubber grip, and loaded
with a clip containing ten rounds—which he vowed to use on that
sick punk once he tracked him down.

Jack's right hand still ached from bashing the wall. And he was
still seething.

Why are you allowing this?

"Do you realize this has me completely doubting what I ever
believed?" He spoke aloud into the night. "You let this … this *demon*
into our lives. Why? Why don't you protect us? Are you even there?"

Nothing in the world felt important anymore, except finding
Pam. Everything else—Wendy and her boys, Evan's disappearance,
Sherry, Satterfield, Archer, the *Dispatch*—it all vacuumed back and
disappeared into thin air.

What would Jack do without her? How could he work and raise
the girls?

They'll have no mother. Pam can never be replaced.

But Pam was smart. She was quick. And she could be tough.

*If that monster leaves one little opening, she'll take it. She'll escape.
She'll call me or 9-1-1.*

He felt for his phone and checked it. Nothing.

What if he kills her? This kind of sicko did it all the time:
murder-suicide.

The phone rang in his hand: Cecil Barton.

Jack waited.

He was in no mood to talk to anyone, unless it had to do with Pam. Although Cecil was likely calling about the Satterfield story, there was a small chance he might have heard about Pam's abduction and have some kind of information from any number of news sources.

"Cecil." Jack rolled up the windows so he could hear.

"Jack, I know about Pam," Cecil said. "I'm sorry."

"It stinks, man."

"Is there anything new? What's your game plan?"

"On my way to Cleveland Heights. That's where she was last seen," Jack said. "Our girls are there, at her folks' place. That's where I'll set up base for now."

"We're running a story and Granger's mug shot tomorrow, front page," Cecil said. "What else can I do?"

"Try to get it picked up by AP," Jack said. "Keep your ear to the ground. Let me know if you hear anything at all—from police, DOT, whoever."

"I'll do it. I heard there's a nationwide crime alert about Pam's abduction; we're trying to confirm it."

"It's gonna be impossible to find her unless we get help. Someone's got to spot them and call it in."

"I'll have Derrick keep on DOT."

"Okay," Jack said.

There was an awkward silence.

Jack needed to change the subject. "Any word on Evan McDaniel?"

"Nada," Cecil said. "Derrick told me Wendy decided to drive to Florida, you know, down to where she thinks he's headed. Instead of

FEAR HAS A NAME

flying, she wanted to drive the route the family always takes in hopes she might find him. It's not looking good."

There was a pause.

"Jack, I've got other news," Cecil said. "Better brace yourself."

"What?"

"It's about Archer Pierce."

"What about him?"

"He's dead."

Jack's mind blinked and teetered and threatened to shut down.

The road seemed to come at him like a high-speed video game.

"He and Jerry Kopton, his video guy, were mugged and shot. Their equipment, notes, all that stuff: taken. I've got Derrick working on the story full time; I told him to go around the clock if he has to. Sheets is helping too."

"I can't believe it … I knew Satterfield was a sleazebag, but a murderer?"

"We'll find out," Cecil said. "We're going to blow the lid on this thing. Derrick's got a good in with the Trenton City PD; he thinks they might be making an arrest soon. I didn't want you to hear it someplace else."

Jack realized he was barely breathing. "I don't know what to say." He cracked the window and forced in a huge, deep breath.

"Don't say anything, just go find your wife," Cecil said. "And know that you got friends trying to help. Heck, I'm even praying."

They hung up.

Cecil Barton was praying.

God made no sense.

Jack knew that. He knew, from life and the Scriptures, that God was mysterious, his ways lofty, often incomprehensible. Jack was aware that bad things sometimes happened to good people. He always prayed against such things ever befalling him, unsure how he would handle such an ordeal, how his faith would stand up.

But now, on that summer night, on that lone freeway, so helpless and undone, Jack was face-to-face with it, with him, the God unleashing havoc in the whirlwind. Pam was gone. Kidnapped. Possibly dead. Archer and Kopton murdered.

This was the work of the God he had never wanted to meet.

This was another whole plane, another whole dimension of life. He'd seen others go through such torment, but deep down, in many of those cases, he'd wondered if they were being chastised or disciplined for some secret sin.

How wrong you were to judge; how utterly wrong.

He rested his aching hand on the gun.

Why do you need this?

Who's in charge?

"Are you in control?" he yelled. "Why is this happening? It's too much!"

The vast distance Pam could be from him at that moment and the danger she certainly faced made him gag. He took his foot off the gas and almost pulled off the road to throw up. But he took in a deep breath of night air and vowed to keep going.

He wanted to kill Granger Meade.

His phone rang again: DeVry.

"Officer," Jack said.

"Jack, the Impala was spotted at a convenience store in southern Ohio. A customer recognized it from the alert."

Jack eased his foot off the gas again. "When?"

"We're not sure yet."

"What about Pam?" Jack bumped his car off to the side of the highway. "Was she with him?"

"We think so," DeVry said. "A man fitting Granger's description was seen in the store with a woman fitting Pam's. We're trying to get our hands on the store video."

"Where was this, specifically?" Jack said.

"Quicky-Mart in Selby, Ohio. Just off Interstate 77 near the West Virginia state line. We think they're heading south. If so, they're heading into big storms. The whole southeast is a barrage of lightning and tornadoes."

Jack craned his neck and, seeing no headlights behind him, eased the car back onto the highway. He took it into the left lane, slow, searching for a place to turn around. "Do we know how Pam was? How she looked? Whether he had a gun on her? Anything like that?"

"I think we would have heard if anything looked bad or really out of place," DeVry said. "Again, we gotta get our hands on the video to know for sure."

"Is that it?"

"For now."

"Okay, I gotta go. Thank you, Dennis. Let me know the second you know more."

Jack mowed down high grass and weeds making a speedy U-turn and bumped onto the southbound lane of the freeway, figuring he would backtrack and take I-70 over to 77 South. He wasn't that far behind them; anywhere from two to four hours, depending on what kind of time they were making.

Jack punched in Pam's parents' phone number and let it ring, hoping it wouldn't wake Rebecca or Faye. Benjamin answered quickly, and Jack explained the latest.

Benjamin let out a whimper of relief when he heard Pam was alive. Although Rebecca and Faye were not aware their mom had been abducted, Benjamin said they knew something was wrong, because Margaret had secluded herself in her room again.

It wasn't a healthy environment for them, but Jack had no options.

"Ben," Jack said, "I was thinking maybe you should bring the girls to our house in Trenton City. They'd be so much more comfortable there. You and Margaret could pack some bags and make yourselves at home."

Ben sighed.

"Is that a problem?"

"It's just Margaret." Ben hesitated. "She's not going to want to leave here. I could bring them myself, but—"

"Okay, listen. Just talk to her," Jack said. "It's not a must. I'd just feel better if they were in their own home, familiar surroundings. You get me, don't you?"

"I understand," Benjamin said. "And your place is closer to where Pam was last seen anyway."

"Can't you just get her to the car and—"

"She's paralyzed with fear, Jack. You wouldn't understand till you saw it. But I'll work on it. I'll do my best. Tell me what you're doing. And the police—are they on this? Tell me they're on it."

"Officer DeVry is driving down there as we speak, and I'm on my way." Jack almost mentioned the gun in his lap and his intent to blow Granger's head off. But he stopped short, realizing that was not the man he was.

Or was it? ...

35

Hours had passed since Granger and Pamela last stopped. Granger had drawn eerily within himself. It was as if a switch had been flipped. The car was silent for long stretches of highway.

Granger had ignored her repeated requests to stop so she could phone Jack and use a restroom. Instead he'd driven them barreling smack-dab into a wall of rain that drummed so hard on the roof and hood it was almost deafening. With the wipers slapping on high, he followed about fifty feet behind the glowing red taillights of a semi truck that forged unflinchingly through the storm. Pamela found herself gripping the seat and armrest as they coasted through the slippery night.

Before hitting the downpour, they'd rocketed down I-77 beneath an ominous sky, made their way around Charlotte onto I-85 southwest across the South Carolina border, directly into a gray-black night filled with flashes of lightning and thunderclaps so loud they made Pamela jump. Granger seemed to know where he wanted to take her.

She had to go to the bathroom so badly she was starting to have visions of wetting her pants—and the sound of the rain was not helping. But Granger just kept driving, leaving her to wonder what was going on in that troubled mind of his.

Had he murdered his mother? Pamela didn't know what to believe. It was quite possible that he was such a good liar he'd convinced himself he hadn't done it.

In the dark, she squinted once again at his waist—the spot where he had patted earlier, indicating he had a gun. She saw nothing protruding beneath his black T-shirt. All she could make out was his hard, massive stomach hanging over the waist of his black jeans. He'd said his fingerprints were on a gun back at the house where his mother was killed. Was there a gun with him? Pamela just wasn't certain.

The only thing she knew for sure was that she had to get away.

He'd had no sleep. The confines of the car smelled strongly of cigarettes and body odor. Granger was getting quieter and creepier with each tick of the clock.

"I need to ask you something." He looked straight ahead, leaned toward her, and spoke loudly over the splattering rain. "Will you be mine?"

Everything within Pamela twisted and shriveled.

Calm … be calm.

"Let's just say there is no Jack," Granger said. "I know it's difficult, but just imagine he doesn't exist. It's a game."

This was exactly what Pamela had been trying to keep him from doing—floating off into some twilight zone.

"Rebecca and Faye can or can't exist, I'll leave that up to you," he said. Just hearing their names coming from his mouth made her ill. "But the question is, if there is no Jack, would you be mine? Would I be … is there any way we could be a couple? Seriously."

This was sick. Did he intend to kill Jack? She felt numb and freezing and outside of her own body. Somehow she had to play his game, not give him any false hope yet keep him diffused.

"Granger," she managed, "I'm your friend. And I'm going to do all I can to help you get back on your feet—"

"Don't treat me like some mental case, Pamela! Just answer the question, yes or no."

"No. I am your friend," Pamela went on, half expecting him to explode. "But it's not too late for you. You can find someone like me. But I'm happily married. God's given me—"

"You know, we were just playing a game," he said. "But you can't even do that. You've changed. You're not like you used to be. Forget it."

"Granger, I'll be honest with you. I'm not in the mood for games."

What was she thinking? She felt her insides burning now, everything in her, rising up, rebelling.

"I have a husband and two girls who need me. I have a *life*. You've taken that from me. You say you care about me, but do you? If you do, you'll stop this and turn yourself in, let me go. I will plead with Jack not to press charges, I promise—"

"So the answer's no." He shot her a glance. "You won't be mine, willingly, ever—even if you have no husband."

Was that a question?

What was he going to do, swerve the car into the side of a mountain? Off a cliff?

"Say it!" he screamed.

She flinched, crossed her arms, tried not to tremble.

He extended his right hand in front of him and lowered his voice. "I just need to hear it. The truth. Straight from you."

The next words out of her mouth could kill her, or allow her to live.

She pleaded silently for the Spirit within her to speak.

"I will be your friend." She shivered, and her breathing quickened to little hitches.

"You will be my friend, after all I've done to you."

She nodded repeatedly, looking at him. "Yes." She swallowed. "I will try to help you however I can."

"Why? After all this—*why*?"

"You've had it rough," she said. "That's what friends do."

Her words seemed to seep into him.

Before she could stop herself, more flowed from some hidden wellspring. "I'm no better than you," she said. "We're both full of sin. Different sin? Yeah. But sinners all the same. That's who Christ came to help, sick people like us who realize we need mercy."

Granger was silent. As if on cue, the rain came even harder, louder. He followed the truck, clinging to it like a beacon in the blackness of a port.

"If we'd ever have gotten together," Granger said, "you probably could've convinced me to be a Christian."

What?

Pamela heard it, but didn't. She let the words repeat themselves in her mind.

She was stunned, as if one of the lightning bolts had zapped her. And she knew, indelibly, at that precise moment, that God loved her and that she was his blessed child, even amid her storm.

And she suddenly knew why all of it had happened.

Her life was a testimony.

For him.

For the despicable Granger Meade.

∽◦◦

Evan awoke but did not open his eyes at first. The foam seat, dull hum, and slight vibration reminded him he was on the bus, heading south. Heavy rain pelted the window next to him. He could hear the wind, gusting at times, and could feel the bus sway like a large tipsy man trying to walk a straight line.

The interior of the bus seemed even darker than before. Everything was still. Most people slept. It was the middle of the night. All he could see out his window were splatters of rain against the glass, a few reflections from inside the bus, and a light here and there in the distance, each resembling a different-sized snowflake through the wet glass.

He had slept several hours and probably through several stops. His stomach growled, and he looked around to see if anyone had heard it. He wondered if they were in Georgia yet. All the stops were going to make it a long journey to south Florida.

Lightning flashed to the right, and a faint collision of thunder rumbled just above the noise of the bus engine and air-conditioning.

Evan pictured Wendy sleeping alone in their big bed, and the boys in theirs. But he pushed the images away, got to his feet in the dark aisle, stretched, and yawned. Only three reading lights remained on throughout the bus. He headed toward the back in search of the restroom, noticing the sleeping passengers, many of whom had found the navy blankets he'd wished for earlier. He would get one down when he returned.

"Why didn't you pick me up?" came a high-pitched female voice from a seat in the dark. "We wasn't through."

A reading light clicked on, and way below it, by the window, sat little Valerie Belinda McShane, the bag lady from the library parking lot.

Evan stopped. All around Valerie, dotting the seat next to her and the floor, were the plastic bags that had been on the bench at the bus stop. She wore the same dark purple overcoat and sagging black hat whose curled brim was pulled way down by her eyes.

"Yes, I'm talkin' to you," she said. "Sit down here." She moved three bags from the seat to the floor in front of her.

Evan dropped into the seat, staring at her, dumbfounded.

"You must be starved." She dug into the bag in her lap. "You want a banana? I got a good ripe one here." She produced a beautiful, fresh-looking piece of fruit like a magician pulling a bouquet from a hat, and handed it to him.

Without a word, thinking he must be hallucinating, Evan simply began peeling the banana as he waited for the show to continue.

"That was rude of you back there," she said, "after I woke you up and saved you from the po-lice."

He snapped out of it and whispered, "I'm sorry. I just needed to be alone. It was nothing against you."

"Yeah, bein' alone is doin' you wonders, I see."

He took a bite of the banana. Nothing had ever tasted better.

"I know where yer goin', you know," Valerie said.

Evan ignored her comment. "How far are you heading?"

"Just far enough," Valerie said. "Your wife needs to talk to you—one last time."

She's one of those senile bag ladies who just wanders and babbles.

"Your work ain't finished." Valerie struggled to open a small bag of almonds. "Can you get this?"

Evan opened the bag and handed it back to her, wondering what she meant by "one last time."

Valerie shook several almonds from the foil bag into her hand and popped them into her mouth. "You need to make this one phone call at the next stop. Find the pay phone; it'll be outside a log cabin–looking country store, just down the street from the bus station, on the left. Call Wendy's mobile phone. When you—"

The banana dropped into Evan's lap, and his head tilted to examine the apparition two feet from him. "How do you know my wife's name?"

She tossed several more almonds into her mouth, crunched them, then raised her hands. "Don't make no diff how I know, what matters is, I know. And she needs to hear from you one last time."

Evan scowled at her, then looked around the bus, thinking he must be dreaming; or perhaps his quick withdrawal from the meds was toying with his mind. "Who are you?"

He thought someone must have put her up to this, but no, this was definitely the bag lady from the town back there, Fort Prince. That was her town. She lived there. She'd gotten on his bus … It was all coincidence.

The microphone clicked several times over the loudspeaker. "Next stop, Lake Serenity, South Carolina," Bernie announced. "ETA five minutes. There are some flash-flood warnings, so if you are getting off in Lake Serenity, be careful."

"That's your stop." Valerie stuck the bag of almonds in his chest. "Here, take these. You need some protein, Lord knows."

"Look." Evan sat frozen, holding the bag of almonds and the banana peel. "I'm not sure who you are, but—"

"Yes, you are, Evan. I'm Valerie Belinda McShane, and I'm as real as that .40 caliber in your bag up there." She nodded toward his seat. "So don't get any big ideas about dodging this like you did me back in that parkin' lot. Pull up yer britches, be a man, and do what you need to do. One last call; you owe it to her."

That was it—she'd gotten into his bag when he was sleeping! That would explain how she knew about the gun—but not about Wendy's name or any of the other truths she so uncannily announced.

"How do you know about Wendy and where I'm going?" He stuffed the banana peel into a small trash bag hanging between the seats.

The reading light shining down on her went out, and for a moment Evan couldn't see her.

"Shhh," Valerie quieted him in the dark. "Would you stop fighting this?"

Evan could just make out the whites of her eyes.

"I'm the voice no one usually hears." Valerie was completely still now and spoke ever so softly. "I'm the message, the whisper in your spirit, telling you to press on. I know it's been difficult."

"But just tell me how you know—"

"Forget all that. Is the Almighty on his throne, or not?"

What the …?

Evan was silent, questioning why he should even bother reasoning with a hallucination.

"I hate to say this, Evan, at a time when you're so down, but you are thinking only of yourself. Does the enemy desire to sift you like wheat?" she whispered vehemently now. "Of course he does! The destroyer wants to take out every good soldier. One of the ways he does it is by playin' yer mind like a puppet on strings. Don't let him do it, Evan. No more. Your work isn't finished. You'll see. You'll see very soon."

With both hands, Valerie gently shooed Evan out of his seat. "Go on now."

Evan stood, still trying to see her in the dark.

A booming, rippling display of lightning and thunder engulfed the bus. Evan grabbed the closest headrest to steady himself and reached over to make sure Valerie was okay. But as the lightning illuminated the seats, he could only stare in disbelief.

There were no bags scattered about.

There was no Valerie Belinda McShane.

He stood frozen, then looked around the sedate bus.

You're losing it.

He wished he had a Valium.

Feeling as if he'd been sucker-punched, Evan scanned the dark bus again. Had anyone seen him? They'd think he was nuts. He shook his head and walked the last few rows to the restroom.

Vacant.

Need to throw some water on my face …

He unlatched the door and squeezed into the tiny lav.

As the light flickered on, he realized there was something in his hand.

But he didn't look down at it. He knew what it was.

A foil bag of almonds.

36

Granger drove and smoked and chewed at his cuticles, which Pamela hadn't seen him do before. Was he formulating a plan? The lightning had become almost constant, revealing even more foreboding clouds. They seemed to be driving even deeper into the heart of the storm. The semi remained in front of them. Pamela had begun to view it as a sign from God, as if he were whispering, "I'm right here. A fortress. Guiding you. Don't worry. I'll get you through."

My rock.

She had to pee so badly she didn't even want to speak or move. She kept forcing herself to relax from head to toe, trying not to think about it. Although she had to convince Granger to stop and find a restroom, she didn't want to lose sight of the truck; it was not only serving as a lead car through the torrential downpour, but it was also forcing Granger to keep his speed down.

She wondered if the police had found her car down the embankment at Granger's house, and whether they'd indeed found the body of Granger's murdered mother. Was there a manhunt? She hoped to heaven there was, but it would be difficult to find anyone in this rain.

Jack and her father would be out of their minds. And her mother, well, Pamela couldn't even go there. She just prayed

Rebecca and Faye were sound asleep and that somehow Jack had managed to keep it from them. She was afraid, however, that Margaret's uncontrollable fear would alarm the girls and force Jack to tell them she had been taken. Pamela found herself longing to be with her mom, to make up for lost time, loving her in a more understanding way.

Ever so gently, she leaned over and peered at the gas gauge.

"We're getting low on gas," she said quietly, her bladder about to burst. "I really have to go, bad."

Granger shot her a glance, as if coming back from a dream.

"We'll stop," he said. "I didn't want to lose this truck."

"I know," she said.

He took one last drag on his cigarette and flicked it out the window. He opened the tin of potato sticks and threw a handful into his mouth, several dropping onto his shirt and into his lap.

"You know what I think we're gonna do?" he said through a mouthful.

Pamela stared at him, her heart lifting in her chest.

"I think we're gonna get through this storm, and we're gonna drive till we find a beautiful little beach community on the gulf of Florida, where there are pastel-colored houses and a huge, long pier jutting right out into the ocean."

He swept his greasy hand in front of him, left to right. "Maybe there'll even be a rainbow. And we can go to dinner at an expensive restaurant; I still have plenty of money. A seafood place, right on the water. We'll have a candlelight dinner and walk out to the end of the pier and watch the sunset. Does that sound like someplace you know of?"

He examined her, anticipating, as if she'd better say yes.

She felt sick deep in her stomach—sick because he somehow knew—

"Does it sound familiar?" he repeated in a gruff tone.

"It sounds like a place my family used to vacation," she said.

"Seaside," he declared. "You told me back in school you used to vacation at a dreamy little beach town called Seaside. In the Florida panhandle, right? Between Pensacola and Panama City?"

She nodded, shocked he remembered such things; shocked she had ever confided such things to him!

"You described it in the most romantic way," Granger said. "Yellow and pink and blue pastel houses, gleaming white porches overlooking the turquoise gulf. Quaint shops. A tiny post office. Soft golden sand. And the most beautiful sunsets on earth. I think those were your words."

She nodded again, at a total loss for what to say.

"Does that sound like a plan?" he said.

Pamela fumed. *How dare you.*

"Then what?" she blurted.

Granger scowled. "Look, can't you just enjoy the picture I just painted? Does it always have to be what next? What next? What next? Back to you and Jack, you and Jack, Rebecca, and Faye? Can't you see this is *it* for me? Can't you get your eyes off yourself and Jack and your stupid family long enough to just help me see this thing through to the end? Shoot, Pamela, I didn't think it was going to be this way."

"What did you expect?" she said. "You kidnapped me! You *took* me from my—"

"Stop!" He cupped her mouth with his huge, greasy right hand. "I don't want to hear it. Don't say that again. That is *not* the way this is gonna be. That is not the way I'm gonna go out. No ma'am."

He shook the hand hard against her mouth, then removed it and jabbed a big index finger into her arm. "We are going to be a couple for the rest of this day," he said. He looked at the clock on the dash. "It's almost two. Until dinnertime tonight, we are officially a couple. Come here."

Granger's enormous right arm engulfed her and forced her toward him. She pushed back, her bladder aching, the smell of him swirling into her brain, sickening her.

"Don't you make this ugly, Pamela, or I swear …" The car swerved as his arm braced her like a vise and slid her close. "If you just go along with it," he whispered through clenched teeth, "make it good for me, you *might* get to live."

That was what she had dreaded ever since he'd forced her into the car—crazy talk of her being his, of life and death.

Never until that very second had Pamela been convinced he might force himself on her and even kill her.

Now she was sure he had it in him.

He nestled her close, damp with perspiration, smelling of beef jerky.

Her bladder hurt so badly, once again she feared she would pee right there in her pants.

The rain coming off the semi swirled back at them like a fairy throwing magic dust.

She fixed her eyes on that enormous gray truck, the bolts on its back doors, its bright red taillights, the way it steadily powered through the sheering rain and gusty wind—staying its course.

She closed her eyes.

A tear ran down her right cheek.

She quickly wiped it away so he wouldn't see.

She envisioned her mother in similar circumstances, how many years ago?

She rested her head back and recalled the song she'd heard in church: *Just because you love me the way that you do, I'm gonna walk through the valley if you want me to.*

꩜

DeVry had been right about the storms. Almost the second Jack hit 77 South, his car was pummeled by violent rainstorms and heavy winds, and the lightning was like nothing he'd seen before—almost constant.

All he could think about was Pam riding with that creep in the storm, worried sick about ever seeing Rebecca and Faye again.

Driving in the left lane, he pushed the VW as hard as he safely could, whizzing past dozens of cars and trucks that crept along at twenty or thirty miles per hour with their flashers on. Makeshift waterfalls poured over the sides of flooding bridges and overpasses, beneath which cars and trucks were parked bumper to bumper to escape the deluge.

Several miles before reaching the exit of the Quicky-Mart where Pam had been spotted with Granger, Jack phoned DeVry and asked if it would do him any good to stop.

"No, it would be a waste of time," DeVry said. "We're doing all we can with that."

"I'm going to keep heading south then."

"Be careful, Jack. There're tornado watches and warnings all over the place."

Was he backing out?

"You're sticking with it, aren't you, Dennis?"

"Of course, but we're just not able to move at the speed we'd like."

"They won't be able to get far fast either," Jack said. "Any more visuals yet?"

"Jack, the DOT cameras are …" DeVry hesitated. "They're not very helpful in this storm. Between the rain and fog, we can't get any kind of good pictures."

DeVry's words plunged into Jack's heart like a dagger.

A spasm of rage and helplessness became words. "Where do I go, Dennis?" Jack cried. "I don't know what to do. This is so bad."

"Jack, hold on—"

"Poor Pam, she's so innocent."

"Jack, hold on. Just hold on." DeVry raised his voice. "These storms won't last. Light will come. The sun will shine tomorrow morning. We're not giving up, okay? You need to—"

Jack's head floated like the huge puddles swirling on the highway in front of him. It was all too much. He was a dot on a map, a tiny raft in the middle of a raging ocean. How would he ever find her?

What will that animal do to her?

Jack dropped the phone and, like a dam breaking, let go, crying out, sobbing, heaving for air, tears flooding his eyes.

He heard DeVry calling his name but couldn't see the phone in the dark. He pushed the button for the reading lamp near the rearview mirror and looked down. There it was. He bent down, snatched it, turned it off, and looked back at the highway.

A puddle the size of a lake was coming at him like an oil slick.

His speed was seventy-three.

Too fast.

He ripped his foot from the gas pedal but knew it was too late.

The car seemed to leave the ground, like taking off in a jet.

No control.

Careening.

Spinning.

Jack fought to steer, to brake, but the car was unresponsive.

It was going to do what it was going to do.

Jack grimaced, shut his eyes, and braced for impact.

37

Evan was one of only a handful of tired passengers who staggered off the Greyhound at the still, low-lit bus station in Lake Serenity, South Carolina. Although he carried his duffel bag with him, he had every intention of reboarding before the bus departed in twenty minutes.

He flat-out did not want to call Wendy. In fact, the sooner he became only a memory to her, the better off she and the boys would be.

But Valerie's premonition vexed him.

He'd told the driver, Bernie, he would be right back and had gotten off the bus with the intention of stretching, using the restroom, and perhaps checking to see if the pay phone Valerie mentioned really existed. But it was an absolute mess outside, complete with a monumental thunder and lightning show.

A tall, thin man wearing old leather work boots and an army green jumpsuit, the kind mechanics wear, buffed the speckled linoleum floor with a large, heavy-looking silver machine that seemed to float on air. Evan approached him. The man made eye contact, bent down, flicked a switch, and faced Evan as the machine whirred to a halt.

"Thank you," Evan said. "Can you tell me where the general store is?"

The man looked at his watch. "It closed a long time ago." He pointed to his right. "We got drink and snack machines around the corner."

"I was told there was a pay phone in front of the general store," Evan said.

"We got a pay phone right here." The man walked toward where he had pointed. Evan followed him around a corner of nicked and scuffed beige walls. "It'll save you from going out in that rain."

Sure enough, there were vending machines, restrooms, a water fountain, and a pay phone. "Thank you," Evan said.

"My pleasure."

Out of curiosity, Evan picked up the scratched receiver and put it to his ear. There was no dial tone. He clicked the silver hang-up bar repeatedly but got nothing.

Valerie knew …

That did it.

He went back around to the man in green, told him the phone was dead, and got directions to the general store, which was several blocks from where they stood.

"Hope you got an umbrella," the man called as Evan headed out the glass door.

He set his bag down on the sidewalk beneath the breezeway, bent to one knee, and dug out the umbrella. The heavy gusts of wind and splatters of rain felt cool and refreshing after all the time confined to the stuffy bus. Rainwater gushed loudly from a nearby downspout, and several portions of the overhang overflowed with waterfalls.

Evan stood, took in a deep breath of moist air, hoisted the duffel bag onto his shoulder, opened the umbrella, and surveyed the rain-filled streets and town. Trees and lampposts dotted the sidewalks. The storefronts were covered by different colored awnings, and the sidewalks were flanked by diagonal white lines and parking meters.

A lone station wagon, missing a headlight, splashed by and stopped at a red light.

Evan saw no one else around.

Your wife needs to talk to you—one last time.

Evan frowned. The rain was roaring down.

Your work ain't finished.

He shook his head and sighed, knowing he had to go, had to do this one last thing.

Why?

Because he still believed. In God. In another realm. In angels and demons and fate and things happening beyond the curtains, the likes of which simple humans could not comprehend.

Without another thought he ducked into the downpour and ran.

The heavy bag bounced against his hip. He dodged puddles but couldn't help hitting some. Each drain he ran past howled with runoff. He went in and out from awning to rain to awning, huffing past darkened businesses—an antique store, a fine jeweler, a coffeehouse. He crossed a dead intersection without slowing. His heart flickered and sparked as thoughts of Wendy and the boys seeped into his bones like the unavoidable dampness around him.

He spotted the general store from fifty feet away because of its unique reddish wooden facade, which resembled a log cabin, just as Valerie had said. The pay phone was to the left of the door.

Evan slowed to a walk beneath the large copper-looking awning that covered the length of the Lake Serenity General Store. Catching his breath, he slid his bag beneath the phone and set the umbrella down open on the sidewalk.

He wasn't going to beat around the bush; his bus would be leaving soon. He would call Wendy's cell one time. She would likely be sound asleep; the phone might not even be nearby. However, based on the percentage Valerie was batting, Evan realized anything could happen.

The phone took coins and credit. Although he had change, he didn't want to run out in the middle of the call, so he swiped his MasterCard and punched in Wendy's number. He did it quickly, without hesitation, not knowing or thinking about what he would say, not really planning to hear her voice at all.

The phone rang just once.

"Hello." Wendy sounded completely alert, as if it were first thing in the morning.

He couldn't say anything. And it was then he realized—he hadn't planned to. He was such a coward.

"Evan, it's you, isn't it?" Wendy said. "I knew you'd call. I knew it. I've been trying to think of what to say."

The connection was fuzzy, as if she were browsing in a store or driving, but it was after two in the morning.

"I'm on my way to Englewood, to our rental place on Lemon Bay; I reserved it for us," she said. "I forgive you, Evan. Do you understand me? I *love* you. Sherry told me everything—that she came on to you and you wanted nothing to do with her."

His brain short-circuited. She was driving all the way to Florida, in that storm? Through the night? What about the boys? She'd talked to Sherry ... forgiven him?

The spark inside flared.

But he could not speak. He was a two-faced hypocrite. He'd abandoned Wendy and the boys, disgraced them and the people in his church, let corruption spread like cancer right under his nose, and failed miserably at living up to the morals he'd espoused. He was no man at all.

"There are things you don't know," she continued. "Satterfield's got a bad past—worse than you thought. He's played others like he played you. He's in trouble with the law. He might even be a killer. It's not your fault, Ev, trust me ..."

Her words rattled him on so many fronts.

"Evan, what's happened to you isn't out of the ordinary for someone who stops taking antidepressants suddenly. It's dangerous. It causes you not to think right. It would do that to anybody! Do you hear me, Ev? It's okay! We'll find a doctor who can fix all that."

Evan's head dropped. He shivered and began to cry, then quickly covered his mouth so she would not hear.

"Honey, the boys need you," Wendy pleaded. "*I* need you. I know you're going to hang up ..." She began to weep. "I need you to live for me, Evan. There are others who need you. You can come back. You don't have to be in ministry." She laughed through hitched breathing. "You can work at the car wash for all I care, or McDonald's. Just live, Ev. Promise me ..."

He wanted to cry out to her, to gush with love and sympathy and gratitude. But he was so utterly humiliated. He did not want to live—could not.

"I don't care if you don't say a word." Wendy's voice found resolve. "I don't care if we have to spend five years in counseling. Just promise me you'll meet me at the beach."

He pictured the small white cottage they'd rented forever, the screened porch out back, the mangroves and narrow fifty-foot dock leading out to the dark blue and turquoise waters of Lemon Bay. He could see the yellow-orange sun creeping up over the drawbridge in the distance, see himself riding waves with the boys in the surf until he collapsed on the blanket with Wendy.

It will never be that way again …

"I farmed the boys out," she said, "but we can put them on a plane and bring them down."

Listen to her.

Somehow she'd known he was going to call. She was okay with his not saying anything.

How can she forgive?

He could not even forgive himself.

She was still speaking when he mouthed the words *I love you* and ever so gently hung up the phone.

Cold now, he crossed his arms and walked to where the awning stopped. The unforgiving rain came down sideways, like huge curtains of water dancing in the wind; he could see it in the lights from the lampposts across the street. There along the sidewalk was a green sign: Lake Serenity.

He grabbed his bag and umbrella and entered the storm. As he walked across the street, even though he covered himself with the umbrella, the rain knifed in at his lower body, soaking his jeans and shoes. He walked on, right toward the sign, then followed the sidewalk beyond. Lanterns about a foot off the wet ground lit his way. He followed them, sensing the sky opening up, feeling he was getting closer to a large body of water.

The lanterns led him winding downward to a wide dock. He stepped from concrete to dark, wet wood. Careful not to slip, he crossed to a rope at the edge of the dock and peered out. In perfect timing, lightning flickered and glowed white, illuminating a vast body of choppy black water. Thunder boomed and echoed across the lake.

He could almost feel the gun in the bag on his back.

His life could end right there, right then.

Lights out.

He could drop right into the water.

Wendy had set her mind on driving more than twenty hours to their dream spot.

He shook his head and blurted out a laugh, which quickly evolved into tears.

Thunder rumbled, and the massive walls of rain created dazzling patterns on the surface of the lake.

He imagined a man walking on such water, in the middle of a night eerily similar.

Come back to me.

It was nothing more than a whisper in the wind.

No.

His mind and body and spirit were riddled with guilt's poison. There was too much against him; mountains of obstacles.

I move mountains.

He wanted to scream at the voice, his conscience, the Presence—whatever it was. He wanted to cry out that he had tried everything, knew the Bible, understood what was expected, and had failed—irreconcilably.

But he was too tired and distant to utter a word.

FEAR HAS A NAME

As Wendy said, there is a reason. Trust me.

"You don't understand!" Evan yelled with everything in him. "Things can never be the same!"

He waited, still, exhausted ... listening for something, anything.

Gold must be refined, Evan.

A lightning bolt cracked deafeningly close, flashing like neon across the dock and water, leaving the disturbing taste of electricity on his tongue.

Silver must have its dross removed, only then can the silversmith produce a vessel.

Evan sighed and turned back toward the town.

He was so very drained.

Wendy's voice came back, as if she were standing right next to him: *What's happened to you isn't out of the ordinary for someone who stops taking antidepressants suddenly.*

Putting his head down in the wind, he began to walk, on a different sidewalk this time, not lighted, but heading back toward the main street.

"Your work isn't finished," Valerie had said. "You'll see."

Evan believed Satan was real. If he gave up, the demons won.

The sidewalk took him back up the slope more gradually and bent left around a small, dark brick building. Dim light flickered from within, revealing beautiful multicolored stained-glass windows.

He got around front and stopped at a sidewalk leading to the cozy building's heavy-looking double wooden doors. Wind and rain bent the trees that dotted the manicured yard, and torn branches were strewn everywhere. Beyond the trees, a golden spotlight on the brick sign by the street lit up the words: Redeemer Church.

Evan made a spot decision. If the doors were open, he would go in and sleep and decide what to do when he awoke. If they were locked, he would hurry back to the bus and figure out his next move en route to Florida.

Walking toward the doors, he half chuckled at himself for still clutching the umbrella over his head, because his whole body was waterlogged.

Up the brick steps he walked. Weary. Wanting to collapse.

Wet hand on cold silver door handle. Eyes closed.

Here we go ...

38

As his car floated and spun out of control in the thick rainstorm, a surge of sheer panic took Jack's breath away. Not because he was about to die, but because he was about to leave Pam in the hands of Granger Meade. The car was taking forever to hit something, so Jack opened his eyes. His headlights whirled like a flashlight spinning on a table, illuminating blurry, wet woods and pavement and headlights and weeds and taillights and guardrail.

The impact catapulted him forward like a rag doll, smacking him against the steering wheel and dashboard. Still in motion, the car lurched sideways, and for a split second Jack thought it might roll. But it hit something again, bashing him against the door. Metal scraped metal with earsplitting clarity, and sparks exploded like fireworks just outside his window as the car melded with the guardrail.

The whole mad dream slid to a halt.

Jack did not move. Everything was still, almost peaceful. A loud hissing noise mixed with the rhythm of the rain. Smoke billowed from beneath the hood, which was crunched like an accordion. The stench of antifreeze filled his senses.

Okay, you're okay ...

The top-left corner of the windshield was splintered like a spiderweb. Both sides of the steering wheel were bent toward him; the air bag had not deployed. He looked around outside and saw no other vehicles involved; a relief. Blood glistened on the dash and steering wheel. His left hand felt cold and torn but did not hurt. He looked at it. His knuckles and the backs of his fingers were sliced and bleeding.

He patted his face with his clean right hand. To his left, the window was busted, and blood diluted with rain amid shards of glass. He reached up with his right hand, felt around, and found wetness along the side of his head; blood came away on his fingers.

He had to get out. Pam needed him.

Reaching around to undo his seat belt, he cried out in agony. His chest felt as if it had collapsed. Something was terribly wrong inside.

He tried to open the door, but it wouldn't budge.

Leaning his head as close as possible to the broken glass in his door window, he realized his car was wedged against the guardrail so tight it seemed as if it had been soldered. He would need to slide over and get out the passenger door. It was going to hurt, but he had to keep going.

DeVry would be there soon, wouldn't he?

The engine spit and popped with sickening, dying noises.

He smelled fuel.

Could this thing blow?

Gently, he managed to unbuckle the seat belt and scan the interior for his phone.

It was in your hand.

And the gun, where was it? He tried to reach down to the floor, but his rib cage objected with searing pain; there was no way he could do it.

He looked around outside for help, but no one had come by, or at least no one had stopped. The cars were few and far between.

If he could get out the side door, perhaps then he could lean in and find the gun and phone. But he just sat there, shaking. The rain was coming harder, tapping annoyingly at his left side through the broken window. His teeth clattered. His mind was fuzzy and his head weightless. A light blue film covered everything, like a filter over a camera lens. He just needed to take some deep breaths and keep going. But his rib cage was in a metal vise that just kept tightening and tightening.

Pam.

He hoisted his legs to the passenger side.

God, why are you doing this? Where are you?

Jack pressed his shoulders to the back of the seat and gently shimmied toward the right, but the pain was excruciating.

Breathe.

Keep going.

He looked down for the door handle on the passenger side and saw three of them, circling in vertigo. He blinked. His mind was prickly and fading to white. He tried to shake the haziness, but it was getting worse.

Don't you dare pass out.

He leaned back against the passenger seat, patted for the door handle, found it, and pulled. It hurt incredibly just to get the door open a few inches, but he did. Then he mentally prepared for the agony that was about to come and rolled out.

"Ahhh!" To the sopping pavement he collapsed. Every inch of him cried out in pain—his knees, arms, hands, head, and chest. His lungs felt like they'd been wrenched back and forth, his heart bruised.

Headlights arose like the sun on the car, the guardrail, him. A black SUV whizzed past within ten feet of him in a swirl of rain. Was it traveling the wrong way?

No, wait . . .

Jack lay there, the water on the pavement seeping into his clothes, and he realized his car was facing backward, the crumpled engine still steaming and spewing.

He heard something else too—wheezing? He held his breath and the wheezing stopped; it was coming from *him*.

He had to get help.

Gingerly he rolled onto his knees and elbows, soaking up the cold rain, trying not to think about the distress in his body.

He would get to his feet, find the phone, call DeVry.

Headlights came up and settled on him. The vehicle seemed to slow, yes, it pulled off to the side of the road, facing Jack and his backward car.

It hurt to breathe. He couldn't get a full breath.

A car door slammed, and a young man jogged toward him.

Jack got up to one knee.

Dizzy.

He froze, unable to take any more pain or spinning.

"Are you okay?" The kid from the car got down next to Jack. He had a mop of blond hair and a bottom lip packed with chewing tobacco. "Is there anyone with you?"

"Alone." Jack panted. "Hydroplaned."

More headlights. A second vehicle pulled up close, turned at an angle to block oncoming cars, and parked.

Good.

Jack was having difficulty getting air into his lungs.

"Take deep breaths." The young man wore baggy shorts and a sweatshirt, and he smelled like beer. "You're totally pale, man—and your head is bleeding. Dude, we need to get you an ambulance." He was dialing 9-1-1 before he was finished talking.

"My wife was kidnapped." Jack's head spun even more when he spoke. "I've got to keep looking."

"Dude, right now we need to get you to the hospital."

A lady appeared, right down in his face. She had shiny black hair and a pointy nose and chin. "I'm an EMT," she said. "Can you tell me your name?"

"Oh, thank God, dude," the kid said. "That is so epic you showed up!"

"Jack."

"Where do you hurt, Jack?"

"Chest," he managed. "Really bad."

The kid turned away, talking to the 9-1-1 operator.

"Do you know where you are?" The lady's eyes scanned every inch of him, as well as the scene around them.

"Seventy-seven."

"Do you know what day it is?" She placed her warm fingers on his neck.

The kid returned, and Jack eyed him.

"My wife's missing," he said. "Can you get my phone? In the car ..."

"Jack, can you tell me what day it is?" the woman said.

He was so tired, and his eyelids were getting heavy. But he would stay awake—had to.

"Ouch." He was startled by a firm pinch to the skin on the back of his right hand.

"Sorry," she said. "I'm trying to get a read on how you are."

The lady had a small flashlight. She probed around his head and pulled his eyelids open; the obtrusive white light danced and burned and left purple impressions.

"Can you come here?" she called to the kid. "What's your name?"

The kid came over. "Connor." He had things in his hands. "Man, his steering wheel is bent bad. No air bags. I wonder if he hit it."

"I need your help, Connor." She nodded at a bag on the ground. "Get the scissors out of my kit. And give me your sweatshirt."

"I found his phone—and a gun." Connor stripped off his sweatshirt, revealing an orange Journey T-shirt.

"Let me call someone—" Jack reached toward the kid, and even that hurt.

"Jack, I need you to be very still," the woman said. "Can you sit up for me, over here, against the guardrail? Do you think you can do that?"

"Yeah." Jack started to get up. "Ohhh!" Everything whirled, and he dropped back down.

"Okay. It's okay." She gripped his shoulders. "Whatever is comfortable for you, that's how I want you to get, okay?"

"Nothing is." Jack rolled slowly to his back and let out another cry of pain. "I can't be hurt. This can't be happening."

"Shhh." She stuffed the kid's sweatshirt beneath his neck. It felt dry and good. He let his head relax.

"Her name's Pam," he mumbled. "Pam Crittendon."

In several quick swipes, she sliced the front of his shirt open. "I want your neck and head still, please. I'm checking for other injuries and your breathing."

"My wife," Jack moaned. "I've got to find her."

He realized he was fading, clenched his teeth, battled to stay awake.

Oh, Pam …

The pinch came again. "Stay with me, Jack," the lady said.

"Find DeVry … in my phone. DeVry." It took every bit of strength in him to expel the words. "He's a cop. Please."

"What was it?" The kid bent closer. "DeVry?"

Jack could only nod. His body was going limp.

The lady's movements were quick and precise. Her warm hands were on his forehead. "I need your head back and your chin up, Jack," she said. "Stay with us now, okay? I need you awake and breathing."

Pam. I'm failing you. I'm so sorry …

He heard talking, something about keeping him warm.

A truck rocketed past, leaving a roar in Jack's ears, then a wave of spray and wind made everything wobble. A faint siren wailed in the distance. Jack envisioned a lone ambulance struggling through the hilly terrain from some country hospital.

The black-haired EMT was talking, but Jack couldn't see her anymore.

No, no, no …

He was passing out.

"His pulse is rapid …" he heard the woman say.

A phone rang. It sounded like his, but there was nothing he could do.

He felt something cover him, maybe a blanket or a coat, but he felt no warmth.

Pam …

No.

You can't help her anymore.

He was going to have to let go and trust these people.

Pam is in God's care.

He let it all slip away.

39

"We're not gonna get far when it gets light," Granger said. "That's the reality." Thinking aloud, he finished eating the string cheese Pam had given him and found a cigarette. The rain continued, hard and steady. He lit up.

"If you don't like the smoke," he said, "you can move."

In silence Pam scooted all the way over to her door and stared at the semi that continued to plow through the rain in front of them.

The whole situation stunk.

How could he have ever thought this would make him happy?

The one person he'd ever loved—who'd ever loved him—hated his miserable guts. He wished he could go back, back to when they were teens. But that was impossible.

He cracked his window and exhaled. The breeze and specks of rain awakened him.

"If you just stop the car," Pam said, "I'll go off to the side of the road. I don't care anymore. I have to go *now*."

"Oh, and you're not gonna run?"

"Where would I run? Please stop."

"We will soon."

"You've been saying that forever!"

Granger looked in his rearview mirror, then straight ahead. Besides the semi, there was one set of headlights in a cloud of rain, far behind them.

He wanted to make as few stops as possible. And he needed to get them a different car by the time the sun came up.

"You'll get soaked if we stop here," he said.

"I don't care. It's either that or I'm going to go right here."

The semi's brake lights suddenly glowed red, and the big truck slowed.

"Whoa." Granger got in the left lane. "Looks like our friend's getting off."

"Oh my gosh!" Pam sat straight up, her eyes huge and fixed straight ahead.

"Holy crap!" Granger took his foot off the gas, and his stomach flip-flopped.

From left to right, all across the freeway ahead, blue and red lights flashed in the mist. They were still far away, but Granger heard sirens and could make out fire trucks, police cars, and at least one ambulance and a tow truck.

He flipped on his right blinker and eased back behind the semi. "*Now* it's time to get off. We're not having any part of *that*."

The semi had its right blinker on too, so Granger slowed and kept behind it.

"What exit is this, did you see?" he said.

"No," Pam said quietly.

He suspected she did; she'd been watching every sign and mile marker like a hawk. So now she was lying to him. He was getting sick of her attitude.

The semi went extra slow around a sharp curve that wound them around and around, past a green sign advertising four different gas stations, then another promoting a bunch of fast-food joints.

After stopping at the end of the exit, the truck slowly chugged off to the right.

Granger followed, scanning the puddle-ridden landscape, which was cluttered high and low with bright lights, truck stops, blinking signs, burger shops, and convenience stores. His best bet to get another car would be at a gas station, someone fueling up, like the old man from whom he'd snatched the Impala.

He stuck close to the semi and laughed. "I'll be danged if this guy's not gonna lead us directly to our next mode of transportation," Granger said. "Get ready, Pammy, my girl. We're about to pull a Bonnie and Clyde."

❧

The moment the semi had slowed on the rain-soaked freeway and Pamela had seen the misty horizon lined with police and emergency vehicles, her senses heightened. It had not fazed her that Granger had chosen to get off the highway to avoid the police. What mattered was the semi—the truck that had been her anchor, a godsend. It had exited at a town called Lake Serenity, and as far as Pamela was concerned, the moment of her escape was coming soon.

Granger followed the truck right off the exit, and Pamela's heart drummed like that of Rebecca's or Faye's after they had been running;

pitter-patter, pitter-patter, pitter-patter. Her mind and senses were sharp as a razor. From head to toe her body pumped with adrenaline, like a racehorse at the starting gate. Her assignment now was to watch—to watch and be ready.

⁓☙

Jack wasn't sure if he was asleep or awake, but he understood he'd been in a wreck and that he was now jiggling around on a squeaky stretcher in the back of a hot, bright ambulance whose repetitive siren was wearing on his last nerve.

He sensed the presence of at least two EMTs, one on either side of him. Needles and tape were stuck to his arms. His whole body was warm, but his chest felt like an industrial-size toolbox had been dropped squarely upon it. A bothersome plastic mask covered his mouth and nose. Although it was making his throat sore, he guessed it was also what was generating the cool air that was allowing him to breath.

He'd given up trying to save Pam.

It wasn't up to him anymore.

God knew the circumstances; he'd written the script. And he could do a better job of taking out Granger Meade than Jack could.

Bring him down, Lord.

Put your angels around Pam like a wall.

Sweep down from on high, set her free …

In complete peace, Jack drifted, letting the road take him where it may.

∾✑

"We've followed this good ole boy all this way," Granger said. "We may as well keep at it; he's our good luck charm."

Pamela couldn't agree more but sat still and told herself not to make a peep.

Her heart leapt when Granger followed the semi left into a spacious, well-lit concrete parking lot lined with trucks and cars at gas pumps. The thunder and lightning had ceased, but a steady rain continued.

"First stop, restrooms," Granger said. "Then we do the deed."

Pamela said nothing.

"See, I take good care of you." Granger wheeled the car into a tight parking space to the right of the entrance to Jen's Truck Stop & Diner. "You couldn't be in better hands."

Pamela was sick of Granger Meade but reminded herself to stay calm and wait for just the right moment.

Be smart.

Granger hurried around her side, unlocked the door, and opened it. "Together like a couple in love now, you hear me?"

She nodded and got out. Her whole body ached from sitting so long, and her bladder rolled painfully inside her like an overfilled water balloon. Granger took her arm in his, and they walked fast to get out of the rain. The truck they'd followed all those miles was parked about sixty feet away. Its windows were tinted, and she couldn't tell if the driver was in it.

They went through the same routine as at the last stop. Granger checked the men's room, made sure it was clean and clear, locked

Pamela in, and stood guard outside the door. She hurried into the first stall. She'd never been so relieved to go her whole life. There was no way she could have tried to get away with her bladder as full as it was.

She doused her face with hot water and dried off. Looking in the chipped mirror, her eyes were sore and tired, but they were the size of nickels.

She was ready to take her life back.

As she pushed the heavy metal door open, Granger's back was to her.

Another man stood hesitantly outside the door. "Am I in the wrong place?" He smiled and peered up at the men's sign above the door.

"No, no." Granger chuckled nervously. "My wife was just using it. Excuse us." He pinched Pamela's arm hard above the elbow and began to lead her out.

The man looked down at Pamela, then at Granger's scratched arms. Did he notice the tight grip Granger had on her arm or that Granger wasn't wearing a wedding band?

Something inside her shouted *This is it!*

With Granger leading to Pamela's right, she came within a foot of the man, looked up at him, scrunched her face in the most exaggerated, worried expression she could muster, and mouthed one word: *Help!*

The man stopped. His head pulled back, and he squinted at Pamela. His mouth formed an O, as if he was going to ask, "What?"

Granger's head turned, and his eyes bore into Pamela.

She relaxed her facial muscles, praying the frantic expression had vanished from her face.

"What?" She squared off with Granger.

He turned and fixed his eyes on the man, who was stopped at the door.

The man scowled suspiciously at Granger, took one last glimpse at Pamela, and entered the restroom.

Granger squeezed her arm till it must have bruised. "If you did anything," he whispered through clenched teeth, "I'll kill you." He led her into an aisle crammed with assorted candies. "The second he comes out, we're going back in," Granger said. "I've got to go. Stand here and do not move."

He released her arm and pretended to look at the candy. "You like Milky Ways, don't you, dear?" he said.

Fire raged within her. She wanted to scratch his eyes out.

She scanned the people in the store and quickly dismissed each one as tired and ineffective. The man in the men's room was by far her best bet. The door to the restroom opened, and he looked around as he walked out. When he found Pamela, he locked eyes with hers.

Granger stepped in their path, his face inches from Pamela's. "I'm not taking my eyes off you," he seethed beneath his breath. "He is going to walk right out of here and your eyes are going to be on *me*, smiling now. *Smile!* You hear me, Pam. Lovey-dovey eyes on me, and smiling."

Pamela had no choice but to keep focused on Granger and pray the man in the blue T-shirt recognized trouble.

"For one quick second, check. Is he gone?" Granger's face was sickeningly close to hers.

She glanced. The man was standing outside the store beneath an overhang, looking in at them. "He's standing outside."

Granger turned to look.

In a flash Pamela looked too, found the man, and mouthed the word *Help!* again, with the same frantic expression.

Granger's head jerked back to Pamela, and he leaned close to her ear. "He knows," he whispered. "Whatever you did, it was very stupid, Pamela. It's going to mean your life."

He locked her arm in his and walked them toward the door.

Just then a black-and-white police car rolled into the parking lot. The man from the restroom, carrying a cell phone in one hand, waved to get the attention of the driver.

He called 9-1-1!

"I'll be a ..." Granger grabbed Pamela by the collar with two huge fists and shook, all teeth and eyes of madness. "You just killed Granger Meade—and yourself."

Like an acrobat, Granger spun her around and locked a bulky, immovable arm around her neck from behind. He pressed against her, and something hard and small drilled into her lower back. Pamela almost vomited. Cries and shouts rang out. People scurried for cover, some scooted out the exit.

He faced her toward the door leading to the parking lot. There were two officers in black raincoats, a male and a female, each with a gun drawn and crouching behind their respective car doors.

"Now see what you've done?" Granger spoke in a high-pitched voice, inching Pamela toward the door with those powerful legs, the object still hurting her back. "This isn't how it was supposed to be."

He has a gun after all?

"Let me go! Help!" She screamed and tried to shake loose, but he was completely overpowering.

"Don't, or I'll drop you dead right here myself. That's what it would have come to anyway."

The cops must have insisted everyone clear out. The people outside, most with umbrellas and ponchos, stood deep in the parking lot.

Amazingly, the man who'd helped her looked on from the open passenger door of his semi—the one that had guided them.

Granger didn't hesitate. He busted Pam through the door and stopped at the sidewalk beneath the overhang.

"Let her go, sir," the male cop ordered. "Nice and easy."

"No!" Granger yelled. "I'll tell you how it's gonna be, copper. If you don't go along, I blow her back out right where we stand. I promise. I got nothin' to live for."

"Drop your weapon!" the female officer yelled.

Granger's whole body was smothered up against Pamela's back. He dropped his keys onto the wet pavement, shuffled Pamela away, and barked orders at the cops.

"Start that car." He nodded toward the Impala.

"Not a chance," the first officer yelled. "Let her go, *now!*"

"I'm gonna let her go," Granger screamed, "but only if you let *me* go. Start my car and back it up, facing out. I'll get in the driver's side, holding her till I get in. Then I'll drive out of here. No one gets hurt. Hurry up!"

Granger ratcheted his grip on Pamela's neck and shoved the hard object deeper into her back.

"Move now!" Granger yelled. "Or I swear, I'll shoot her."

The officers spoke to each other, but Pamela couldn't hear what they said.

With her gun pointing directly at Pamela and Granger, the female officer moved slowly toward the keys, made her way to the Impala, and got in. All the while, her partner kept his gun drawn on them.

The Impala revved to life. She backed it up, curled it behind the squad car, pulled it forward a few feet so it faced out of the lot, and put it in park. She started to reach for the ignition.

"Leave it running," Granger yelled, hurting Pamela's ear. "Get out, leave the door open!"

She turned to her partner, who nodded. She got out, left the door open, and returned to her position.

This was it.

Would Granger pull something? Still try to take her?

Or was she almost free?

Tears swelled in Pamela's eyes, and she swallowed back a barrage of emotions, from sickening fright to utter elation.

Without a word Granger nudged Pamela into the rain, shoving her with small, forceful steps toward the Impala. The officers stood slowly, following them with weapons fixed but remaining protected by the squad car. As Granger moved toward the vehicle he shifted Pamela's body so it was constantly between him and the officers; they would never have a shot.

He backed Pamela closer and closer to the driver's seat as the rain and wind kicked up. The officers repeatedly yelled for him to let her go.

"Stay with me," Granger said. "When I say *now*, I'm going to sit. You sit with me. Don't try anything."

She could only pray he would keep his word.

"Now." Granger led and, simultaneously, they bent and sat. Pamela was on his lap. They faced the officers' guns.

"I'm turning," Granger said. "You stay right here."

He swung his legs into the car and forced her bottom onto the edge of the wet driver's seat.

"Toss your guns away from you," Granger yelled.

Both officers shook their heads. "No way," the man said. "Let her go, now!"

The object that had been drilling into her back released.

The arm Granger had been locking tight around her neck eased but remained there.

"I am sorry, Pam." His warm cigarette breath spoke against the back of her neck. The big arm squeezed gently once, twice. "You're free." He rocked her gently. "Good-bye."

Granger shoved her hard from behind, and the car roared into motion. She rolled to her freedom on the hard, wet ground, laughing and crying at the same time.

The car rocketed forward, its driver's door slamming shut from the force of the takeoff.

"Stay down!" the officer yelled. "Take him!"

Their guns exploded and recoiled, exploded and recoiled.

Pamela covered her ears and strained to watch.

Granger's car goosed and swerved through the parking lot as if it were floating on air. One after another, it was peppered with bullet holes, as if a small army was taking target practice on a junk car. *Poof.* Glass exploded in the rear window. *Pop.* The passenger window exploded.

She saw Granger looking back.

Pamela told herself to breathe.

The car bounced out of the parking lot, onto the open road.

You're free.

You're going to be a mommy again—and a wife.

40

Rain swept through the shattered windows of the Impala. Glass was everywhere. The car was maxed out as it flew and banged over the hilly two-lane South Carolina road. Granger had said from the outset he would not go to prison, and he would not.

You should have let them hit you back there.

But he might not have died, then he would've gone to jail.

The wind made his eyes blurry.

He patted the seat, found the Newports, and hit the lighter.

He had to ditch the car and hide.

Get another car … get a gun.

Welcome to Lake Serenity. The sign blew past.

Another sign was coming: Reduced Speed 25.

The lighter popped; he snatched it and lit the cigarette with a shaky hand.

Slowing way down at a City Limits sign, the car was still traveling at a good speed as it whizzed past nicely lit, well-manicured homes on each side of the street. As the estates got larger and more elegant, with circular drives leading up to sweeping curved stairs, he knew he must be getting close to the town.

He thought he heard a siren far off but wasn't sure.

Where would they *not* look for him?

He saw a sprawling white plantation-style funeral home with a big fountain out front, then Marty's Hardware, The Book Nook, Other Place Pub, and on and on.

Granger took a right to go around the town square, then he saw it: Redeemer Church. Somehow he knew this was the best place for him. They would never look there—if he could ditch the car.

He swung into the narrow driveway and pulled around back of the small brick church, where the blacktop parking lot expanded. A lone floodlight lit up the clean lot. There were no cars, only a huge maroon dumpster. Beyond it, an expanse of woods.

He zoomed the car over to the Dumpster and pulled up alongside it, his headlights showing about three feet of space between the bin and the branches of the encroaching trees. He could squeeze it in there. The Dumpster was long and tall enough to hide the Impala.

He took a look around. Seeing no one, he drove forward slowly. Metal from the right side of the car scraped against the trash bin. Branches and leaves poked and scratched the entire left side. He gave it more gas and finally wedged the car in there like a hand in a glove.

With a big left shoulder he bashed, bashed, bashed his door, forcing it open against the thick branches. Once out, the door shut from the force of the trees. He could hear a siren in the distance. Belly against the car, he shimmied and pushed his way along the wet vehicle all the way to the rear and out into the open air of the parking lot. He was scratched up from the brush.

It had almost stopped raining.

It was deathly quiet except for the siren. Of course, it was the middle of the night. But he thought he heard something else, like water lapping against a shore. Lake Serenity?

Hustling across the puddle-filled lot, beneath the floodlight, and up two steps, he tried unsuccessfully to open the back door.

Churches were supposed to be open.

He got his bearings, decided which way around the building would be fastest, and took off. Halfway around, he stopped. The sirens were getting louder. Closer. A soft light from inside lit up red and blue and green and yellow and orange stained-glass windows. It looked warm inside.

How he wished none of this would have ever happened.

Loser.

His mother was dead.

You're going to take the rap—if they catch you alive.

He dashed around to the front of the building, stopped on the walkway leading to the front doors, and squinted up at the bell tower and cross atop the church. The building was only two stories. Maybe he could hide up there someplace, perhaps in the attic. Who knew, maybe he would find some rope. Wouldn't that be a sight for parishioners: Granger Meade hanging like a rag doll from the sanctuary rafters.

He hurried to the double doors and pulled.

Yes.

It was dark in the close vestibule, where his whole body immediately warmed to the core. A small white candle burned on a tall stand by some kind of guest book. The little room was like a fortress, with walls made of thick, almost black wood beams. The uneven wood floor creaked as he entered.

A tier of candles greeted him to the right as he came to the sanctuary, whose vaulted ceiling was layered in caramel-colored wood. Beams crossed overhead with track lighting, set dim. He could sleep so easily on one of those wood pews with the dark red cushions, but there was obviously no time for that.

As he hurried up the carpeted center aisle, he noticed the stained glass along the sides didn't shine as it had from outside, but fell dark. A gas flame danced in a bowl hanging from chains high to the right behind the pulpit, casting a golden glow over the entire room.

He noticed a tall doorway to the left of the altar, beyond the organ, and headed for it. Up the three steps, past the pulpit—

What the …

He halted.

There was a man on the floor, curled up, sleeping. He was nestled down by the organ pedals, like a baby in a womb. A jacket was bunched under his head for a pillow, and a black duffel bag sat on the floor next to him.

Granger looked around the peaceful room, dropped to one knee, stared at the man for a moment, and ever so quietly unzipped the bag. Unable to see its contents, he gently dragged it several feet and shifted his own big frame so the light from above could shine down on the contents of the bag.

The sirens were getting closer.

Opening the bag wide, he dug in and fingered his way through T-shirts, jeans, a cap, umbrella, shaving kit, boxers. What was that in the bottom? Shoes. Okay, so much for that. He stuck his head down close for one last look before moving on. Something caught the light for a split second. It looked like a flashlight, which could come in handy if he were to make it to the attic.

He reached in and grabbed it, but the heaviness surprised him. This was no flashlight. He knew before seeing it that it was a gun. He took a quick glance at the man, then examined the heavy black semiautomatic in his palm.

"Hah."

Talk about cruel irony.

So God gives you a gun in a church to end it all.

Oh, how his mother and father would have howled at that.

It was fitting, wasn't it, for a life that had been such a complete joke?

He pressed a button on the side, and a magazine clicked into his hand. It was stacked with shiny gold bullets, probably .40 caliber.

That'll do the job.

He replaced the magazine quietly with a click, zipped the bag closed, and dragged it back over where he'd found it.

The sirens wailed.

Still on one knee near the man, he froze. His head swiveled to the sound of cars near the building.

Had they found the Impala?

He dived and crawled to the altar, slamming his back to it.

Above him hung a cross.

You created me, now you can have me back.

Granger racked the slide on the gun, resolving to fire a shot to his head if the doors of the church opened.

The lone shot would wake the stranger lying there. If he was in as bad straits as Granger, maybe he would follow suit.

One last sick joke.

He was not going to think about this. It was going to be quick and easy.

Things will just end.

The torment of living would finally be over …

More sirens arrived—*whiz, whiz, whiz*—darting up against the building.

Granger inhaled deeply and raised the shaking gun to his temple.

"Don't do that."

The words startled him.

The sleeping man's head was raised. He spoke softly. "Please … don't."

Granger scowled and cursed and realized he was trembling. His hands were damp; he wiped them on the carpet. It was almost like he'd been awakened from a dream. He pointed the gun at the man. "This is none of your business."

"That's my gun," the man said. "That makes it my business."

"I'm gonna borrow it, okay?" Granger said sarcastically. "You can have it back in a minute. I'll leave you some change for the bullet."

"My name's Evan." The weary man spoke evenly, calmly.

"Well, Evan, I wish you would've just kept snoozing. This whole thing might be over by now."

"I was going to do that too." Evan nodded at the gun.

"Chickened out, I see."

Granger heard loud static and clicking and the sound of voices on police radios.

The man named Evan sat up slowly and crossed his legs as if he were relaxing in his living room. "My wife forgave me tonight. I put her through sheer agony, and she forgave me."

"Huh. You're lucky you have a wife."

"Yes." Evan nodded. "A very good wife. And I have three boys, whom I've let down terribly."

"You should be thankful you have a family." Granger lowered the gun and dropped his head. He was beyond tired.

"I'm going to give it another try," Evan said.

Granger just shook his lowered head. There was no way to explain it.

"I'd like to help you," Evan said. "I'd like to be your friend."

Granger laughed, jerked his head up, and stared at the stranger, thinking he himself had never been that calm or at peace his entire life. He yearned for acceptance, longed for a friend, but he was afraid—so afraid of being hurt, deceived, mocked!

Death was within his reach ... seconds away.

He's just talking, saying words to stop you ...

"Where do you live?" Evan said. "Are you from here? I'm not."

The blaring sirens chirped oddly, wound down, and died one at a time.

It wouldn't be long.

Granger had no dang home. He was a no-good drifter. The idea of this man becoming his friend was unrealistic and far-fetched. But oh, how he wished it could be true.

He shook his head. "I'm in bad trouble." He fought not to cry. "Real bad."

Evan looked deeply into his eyes. "I'm supposed to help you," he said. "We're in this crucible for a reason."

Granger shook the gun. "Yeah, the reason is ... I'm gonna use your crummy gun to end this miserable existence."

Evan shook his head. "Listen, I know you need a friend," he said. "I'm not gonna try to tell you everything will be okay. But I am here for a reason. To help you right now. I know I am. I know I'm supposed to live; I didn't know it till right now. Please, will you do something for me? One thing?"

Granger just stared at the weirdo.

The running footsteps of a growing army could be heard all around them.

He was going to be arrested, sitting there listening to this nutcase.

"Make a pact with me." Evan crawled over to him and put forth his hand.

Granger looked at it, then into the man's piercing eyes.

"We will live." Evan nodded. "Just say it with me: we will live another day."

Voices, yelling outside.

Footsteps thudding on concrete, all around them.

Then through a megaphone: "Granger Meade."

His name pierced the night and stung his heart with reality.

"You are surrounded. You have sixty seconds to come out of the church with your hands up high where we can see them."

Evan examined Granger and nodded encouragingly. "We will live another day," Evan repeated. "I will try to help you."

Slowly, gently, Evan removed the gun from Granger's right hand. He set it down. He put his hand in Granger's and squeezed. It was warm. It was true.

They looked at each other.

They shook hands.

Granger watched Evan's lips and began to speak softly, in unison with him: "We will live … another day."

The doors busted open.

Granger turned to see a team of officers swarm in, weapons held high, jogging in unison in two lines down the center aisle.

EPILOGUE

Evan squeezed his arms around Wendy, who lounged in his lap in one of the comfy rockers on the back porch of the little white cottage in Englewood. They both faced the small yard out back, the mangroves and pier and long shadows falling over Lemon Bay. The setting sun behind them cast a reddish-orange hue over everything. Their three bronzed boys, clad only in shorts, backward caps, and untied tennis shoes, stood with waiting fishing poles at the end of the dock.

"Maybe we should move here." Wendy stared out at the dark moving water and three of the four men in her life. "Or buy the place and rent it out; then we could come all the time."

"But then it might not be like this," Evan said. "We'd have stuff to do all the time, like painting and maintenance and all that."

"Yeah … you're probably right."

"We could try to retire here—later. Although it would get pretty hot in the summer."

She leaned her head back on his chest. "What are we going to do now, Ev?"

The boys' voices and laughter drifted up with the breeze, filling him with comfort.

"Be a family," he said. "Be a couple." He brought his hands up and combed them through her hair. "I met an old homeless black lady while I was gone. A real firecracker. Valerie Belinda McShane."

"Yeah?"

"Yeah. I think she was an angel." He told her about his various encounters with Valerie. "She seemed to know everything. She was like a guide in the storm. I really believe God sent her."

"What made you think of her?"

"She said my work wasn't finished."

Wendy squeezed him.

"I'm going to get my house in order," Evan said. "I'm going to be a friend to Granger Meade."

Evan wondered if Wendy thought he was weird or wrong for making the pact with Granger—to be his friend, to try to help him. He had learned that Granger would be held at Mansfield Correctional Institution, which was just a little more than an hour from their home in Cool Springs. He planned to invest in Granger, convinced that was the main reason they had been brought together that night.

"What about the church?" Wendy said.

As it turned out, Archer Pierce had given his wife a copy of the show he had produced, implicating Dr. Andrew Satterfield on embezzlement charges in Denver, and the show was aired. Satterfield, Seeger, and Trent had been arrested for money laundering and embezzlement at Evan's church, and charges were pending for the deaths of Archer Pierce and Jerry Kopton.

"There's a big hole now," Evan said. "I'm concerned about the people. But to tell you the truth, I don't have it in me to go back yet. I don't know if I ever will."

Wendy patted his leg. "We're going to take as much time as you need."

Almost constantly, one at a time, the boys would drop to their knees, hoist up the dripping yellow shrimp bucket, put a snapping shrimp on the hook, and recast as far as they could. Evan just hoped one of them didn't get snagged. Their neighbor Sam, who lived there year-round, had told them the red fish were hitting big, but so far no luck.

"I've got a conference call scheduled with the church leaders tomorrow," Evan said. "I'm going to tell them I'll be gone indefinitely. It will probably turn out to be a good thing."

"Everything works out for a reason, doesn't it?" Wendy said.

"Yes. It does."

"I was terrified when you were gone," she said. "It was the worst thing I could ever endure. I kept thinking, this has got to be a nightmare; it was madness. I kept asking God why we had to go through it."

"Why did we?"

Wendy interlocked her fingers with his. "To get closer."

When Evan said nothing, she sat up on his knee, put an arm around his shoulders, and leaned close. "After all these years," she said, "I'm still learning, he just wants us to know he's God. He's in charge. He does what he wants—what he needs to do."

"And we just hold on," Evan whispered.

Wendy nodded, threw her other arm around his neck, and buried her head in his chest.

They hugged tightly and rocked.

"I got one! I got one!"

It was Silas, their youngest, legs braced, reeling as hard as he could, his pole bent as if he had landed a whale. His brothers jumped up and down, smacking him on the back, holding the pole with him, making sure he held on.

⁓❧

Jack laid his head back on the leather chair in the family room. He closed his eyes for a second, breathed in as deeply as he could with a severely cracked sternum, and cherished the sounds and smells and joy of being home among family and friends.

Since arriving back in Trenton City from the hospital in West Virginia two days earlier, Jack had worn lounge clothes—sweats, T-shirts, and moccasins—as he moved slowly about the house. He felt a bit ridiculous clutching his big pillow in front of Cecil, DeVry, Derrick, and Pam's father as they sat chatting all around him; but since the accident, he refused to go anywhere without it. The pain was so great it had come to feel like a necessity to have something against his chest, especially when he laughed, coughed or—God forbid—sneezed.

Rebecca and Faye, in their long dresses, high heels, and beads, danced and pranced in and out from the back porch to the kitchen to the family room, carrying trays of snacks and refreshing people's beverages. They relished having company, as each guest became their new victim and playmate.

Somehow Benjamin had managed to corral Margaret the morning of Jack's car wreck and bring her and the girls back to Trenton City. Jack imagined Ben must have had to tranquilize her to get her to come, but it was a huge help having them there to watch the girls and assist with meals.

Pam had told Jack about her mother's experience with the intruder in her dorm room back in college. So now, oddly enough, Pam and her mom shared similar nightmare experiences, and Jack envisioned that ultimately those haunting events would draw mother and daughter closer.

Margaret functioned much better when she had something to do, like now, as she helped Pam in the kitchen and kept an eye on Rebecca and Faye. Of course, it didn't hurt her frame of mind to know Granger was in custody.

"So what happens to Granger now?" Benjamin said.

The family room fell silent.

Pam walked in, wiping her hands on a kitchen towel. Her mother acted busy setting the kitchen table, but Jack knew she was tuned in.

"Well, the formal charges pending range from breaking and entering and robbery to trespassing, stalking, auto theft, and kidnapping." DeVry took a swig of his drink. "He's being held without bond, obviously."

"But no murder charge after all?" Benjamin said.

Jack wondered what Pam was thinking. She just stood there silently. She had come to know Granger better than anyone. Certainly she was relieved he'd been captured, but she'd told Jack that in many ways she had sympathy for him. That was a pill Jack still couldn't swallow. But he was determined to be open about it, thinking if Pam of all people could forgive the monster, surely he should be able to.

"That turned out to be just another sick ploy by the parents," DeVry said. "Granger showed up at their house that day. He was going to take a gun or two, possibly hurt them; we're still not clear on his motives. Anyway, the father fired a shot into the floor as

Granger was leaving. He wanted Granger to *think* he had murdered the mother and was going to frame Granger for it."

"I wish he would have been framed for it," Margaret said from the kitchen. "He deserves death, or at least life behind bars."

"Think of how he grew up." Pam whipped the towel to her side and faced her mother. "You don't know what it was like in that home—the head games and mental anguish they put him through, all under the guise of Christianity. They hated him and let him know it since the day he was born. He had no friends. None of us knows what that would be like."

"Well, he should have gotten himself some help …" Margaret's voice trailed off.

Pam opened her mouth to retaliate but ended up exhaling loudly and disappearing into the kitchen. Soon cupboards slammed and pots clanged.

"The extent of his sentence is going to have a lot to do with the charges you and Pam end up pressing." DeVry looked at Jack. "We've discussed that briefly. I know Pam had some reservations."

"We still have a lot to talk about," Jack said. "And pray about."

"Wait a minute." Cecil sat up on the edge of his chair and eyed DeVry, then Jack. "What are you saying?"

DeVry raised an eyebrow toward Jack and waited.

"Pam's not sure she wants to press charges," Jack said.

Cecil almost dropped his drink. "Why on earth not? The guy needs to be put away. He could've killed her."

Jack shrugged, somewhat embarrassed. "It would reduce his sentence a lot," Jack said. "And he would still do time for the auto theft and other stuff."

DeVry chimed in. "His father is indicating he is going to press charges for the break-in at their place."

"Jack." Cecil turned around toward the kitchen, then back, and spoke firmly. "You need to talk some sense into Pam. Who's ever heard of that, not pressing charges? That's ludicrous. This guy deserves every year he's got coming to him. He deserves to rot; he's a menace."

There it was—in a nutshell.

It was something Pam had come to grips with long before any of them.

They were all guilty.

All deserved judgment. Sentencing. Imprisonment.

Yet someone had chosen to love—radically.

That's what Pam wanted to do.

Jack lowered his head.

Perhaps that was why all this had happened.

To show a man mercy.

To show a man Christ on the cross.

*"Evil is a departure from the way things ought to be.
But it could not be a departure from the way things ought to be unless
there is a way things ought to be. If there is a way things ought to be,
then there is a design plan for how things ought to be.
And if there is such a design plan, then there is a designer."*

R. Douglas Geivett

*"Thus it is not like a child that I believe in Christ and confess him.
My hosanna has come forth from the crucible of doubt."*

Anne Fremantle

CONNECT WITH THE AUTHOR

CrestonMapes.com
Facebook.com/Creston.Mapes
Twitter.com/CrestonMapes

... a little more ...

When a delightful concert comes to an end,
the orchestra might offer an encore.
When a fine meal comes to an end,
it's always nice to savor a bit of dessert.
When a great story comes to an end,
we think you may want to linger.
And so, we offer ...

AfterWords—just a little something more after you
have finished a David C Cook novel.
We invite you to stay awhile in the story.
Thanks for reading!

Turn the page for ...

- **Excerpt from Book 2 in the Crittendon Files:** *Poison Town*

EXCERPT FROM BOOK 2 IN THE CRITTENDON FILES: *POISON TOWN*

CHAPTER 1

Jack could see his breath even inside the car as he dodged potholes on the Ohio interstate and maneuvered his way into Trenton City at daybreak. He blasted the heat, but was getting nothing but cool air. The gun he'd bought three days earlier still felt bulky and foreign strapped to his ankle.

Wiping the moisture from the side window, he glimpsed one of the city's sprawling industrial plants, its web of mechanical apparatuses and smokestacks silhouetted by the dawn's red-orange glow. He didn't like keeping the gun a secret from Pam, but with Granger Meade out on parole, it was for her own good—hers and the girls'.

Jack put the windows down to clear the windshield. It was below freezing outside. "Shoot!" He laughed at how cold he was and how ridiculous he must look with the windows down in the dead of winter. Cars hummed alongside his, covered with clumps of snow and ice and white stains from the rock salt on the roads.

He'd been taking the cars to Randalls' garage for repairs on the east side of Trenton City for years. Galen, the elderly father, and his two fortysomething sons, LJ and Travis, knew cars like a cardiologist knows chest cavities.

He glanced at the digital clock in the dash: 7:17.

The fact that Granger had returned to Trenton City made Jack sick to his stomach—especially when it was time to leave Pam and the girls each morning. The man had come to Trenton City to track Pam down a year and a half ago, because she was the only person who had ever cared two cents about his life. She had paid for that compassion—they all had.

Jack rested a hand on his chest. His sternum had been severely cracked that night when he slammed into the guardrail. The bone had eventually healed, but his heart had not. But Jack didn't care. It was his right to despise Granger. He had zero sympathy for the man, even though Pam—the real victim—had mustered the mercy to forgive.

He recalled driving hopelessly in the dark, through sheets of torrential rain, in search of any sign of his wife—then spinning out of control. Jack realized he was clamping the steering wheel like a vise. *Ease up.* He tried to relax his hands, neck, whole body.

He shook away the disturbing vignettes of that night.

At the last second he spotted the Tenth Street exit sign, shot a glance back, and veered off the interstate. When Granger got into his head, the memories possessed him. Just like that—almost missing the exit.

He looped around the exit ramp, past the new soup kitchen, which was lined with dark figures—standing, sitting, sleeping— trying to stay warm on sewage grates billowing clouds of steam. He

hit green lights for several city blocks. Once past the library, thrift
shop, and triple set of railroad tracks leading to the east side, he
slowed along the narrow streets.

The houses were shoeboxes whose colors had faded long ago.
Many were trailers, yet almost every one supported a monstrous,
leaning antenna or satellite dish. Smoke chugged from tiny chim-
neys, and he imagined the warmth inside. Beater cars and trucks
were parked at all angles in the short driveways and right up against
the shanties and shotgun shacks.

Jack's phone chirped. He knew without looking that it was a
reminder to attend an editorial board meeting at nine thirty. He had
tons of work on his plate. He took a left on Pell Lane and a quick
right at the Randalls' place, easing the Jetta up to the large doors of
the auto shop. It was a leaning, rusted silver metal building the size
of a barn, sealed up tight with no windows or sign.

A hint of snow fell as Jack turned the car off. The Randalls' one-
story house was situated about fifty feet from the shop. It was faded
green with a big metal awning over the back. Next to it was a rusting
white propane tank that looked like a giant Tylenol capsule. Out
back were a red tool shed, an ancient doghouse, and a broken-down
sky blue Ford Pinto.

The Randalls' orange dog with the corkscrew tail was lying on
the back stoop, which led to the rear entrance of the house. A cozy
yellow light shone from inside. The instant the mutt saw him, it
bolted upright and howled.

"Hello, Rusty." Jack continued toward the back door. "It's okay.
I'm here to see the boys. Are they up?" Rusty quieted and sniffed at
his coat.

Jack went up the steps slowly, still not used to the feel of a gun on his ankle. Through the screen door he could see Travis sitting hunched over an enormous plate of food at the small kitchen table. Jack knocked at the leaning screen door, and without any change in facial expression, Travis lifted a hand and motioned him inside.

Jack nudged the tightly sealed back door, scaring a gray cat away as he slipped in. "Morning, Travis."

The kitchen was small and toasty warm, permeated with the smell of cigarettes and dotted with NASCAR posters, hats, and paraphernalia.

"Jack." Travis nodded casually, as if Jack lived there and had just meandered in for breakfast. He sat with his right leg crossed and his right foot gently bouncing. He was distinctly bony, like a caveman, from his large hands and sinewy arms to his long, sculpted face. His fork tapped and cut and diced its way into a pile of yoke-smothered eggs, bacon, grits, grilled potatoes, biscuits, and white gravy.

"Could it be any colder?" Jack took his gloves off.

Travis continued to work on his breakfast, his elbows resting on the Formica table. "I guess it could, but I wouldn't want it to be." He chuckled at his own joke. "What's the word at the *Dispatch*? Any new scandals? You can wipe your feet right there on that rug."

"Nothing earth-shattering." Jack wiped his feet.

"You still doin' the city hall beat?" Travis spoke slowly, in a deep voice. He wore faded jeans with a small rip above one knee, a soft brown T-shirt, and thick gray socks.

"Yeah," Jack said. "And I'm the features editor now, so I've been doing some personality profile stuff. We ran a story about a neighbor of yours recently—Jenness Brinkman."

"They live right 'round back, I think. Jenness is the handi-capped girl, right?"

"Yep. Top of her class at East High. Got a full ride to Yale to study criminal law. Wants to work with the FBI in Washington."

"I'll be," Travis said. "I missed that one."

"The features usually run on Sundays."

"Well, that answers that. Bo's always runnin' off with the Sunday paper. Uses it to clean car windows. You hear he's detailin' cars now?"

Bo was Travis's seventeen-year-old nephew, who was always into something new.

"No, I hadn't." Jack heard a sound from the other room.

"Yup. Ask him 'bout it. He's startin' off really cheap."

"I might do that."

"You want somethin' to eat? Biscuit? I got some a daddy's home-made sawmill gravy over there. A little go-joe?"

It all sounded good, but he'd had fruit and eggs with Pam. "No, thanks. I appreciate it, though."

The smell of a freshly lit cigarette wafted in from the next room, but Travis didn't seem to notice.

"What brings you out this mornin'?" Travis scratched his dark, sparse beard, which was peppered with gray.

"I've got my '98 Jetta out there. The fan is barely working and there's no heat. Plus the muffler's sagging."

Just then LJ rounded the corner from the dark room, a lit cigarette dangling from the corner of his mouth, the usual black eye patch covering his left eye. He wore dark blue jeans, a white T-shirt, an unbuttoned blue-and-red flannel shirt, and white socks. "You want the good ole boy fix on the muffler, Jack, or you want me to get the parts from Volkswagen?"

"Hey, LJ," Jack said. "The good ole boy fix, if you can."

"What you doin', boy?" Travis suddenly came to life. "Sneakin' round here in the dark." He looked at Jack. "He's been doin' that since we was boys. Ears like radar. Stickin' that crooked nose into other people's beeswax. Ain't no such thing as a private conversation 'round here."

LJ smirked as he stirred the grilled potatoes in the frying pan above a blue flame. With the cigarette pinched at the end of two fingers, he took a heaping mouthful. "Momma used to call me Ghosty. Remember, Trav?"

The most prominent feature on LJ, besides the eye patch, was his Adam's apple, which protruded an inch from his long, skinny neck. He was about six foot four and balding. The blond hair he did have on top was long and thin; on the sides it was full and flowing.

"Momma had your number," Travis said. "Remember how she got onto you for spying on Daddy's customers? Hey, don't smoke around the food!"

"How long ago did your mother pass away?" Jack asked.

LJ ran his cigarette under water, threw it away, and got into the eggs, eating right out of the pan. "Two thousand and seven," he said with a mouthful. "These need salt. Want some grub, Jack?"

"I already asked him ... but now that you've gone and stuck your grea-zee grubs into everythin' ... Sorry, Jack. LJ, mind your manners."

"Same thing's gonna kill Daddy that killed Momma." LJ shook the big spoon toward the window as he spewed the words: "Demler-Vargus."

"Is something wrong with Galen?" Jack asked.

"He's in the hospital." LJ tossed the spoon in the sink. "They's callin' it emphysema, and maybe it is, but we know what caused it." He jabbed a finger toward the window. "That plant. It killed Momma and it's killed others. But nobody wants to listen to us poor east-siders. We got no voice in this town."

Travis calmly tapped and scraped at the remains on his plate.

Jack knew that Demler-Vargus, the massive fiberglass manufacturing plant that employed half of Trenton City, had been the recipient of complaints in the past for emitting hazardous pollutants.

But as far as he knew, the corporate giant had only received several slaps on the wrist from the EPA.

"How bad is he?" Jack said.

"He's gonna be okay." Travis didn't look up. "Passed out the other night. Wasn't gettin' enough oxygen to the brain. Scared the starch out of us."

"I thought he was dead." LJ came over and stood by Travis. "He was purple. Sprawled out yonder in the TV room."

"Lucky there was no brain damage, they said." Travis picked at his teeth with his upside-down fork. "It's my day at the hospital, so LJ will be takin' care of your car." He looked up at his brother. "You hear all his Jetta needs when you was listenin' in?"

"I heard. I gotta take care of the fuel filter on that Volvo first, then I got that little day-care bus out back, door's busted—"

"But you gonna get to it today, right?" Travis said.

"I might could. But it might be tomorrow."

Travis craned his neck toward Jack. "That okay?"

"That's fine."

"You need a ride to the paper?" Travis stood and took his dish to the sink.

"That would be great." Jack put his gloves on. "You know, we just ran a feature story about the CEO of Demler-Vargus. He was voted Trenton City's Person of the—"

"That is *the* biggest load of horse manure." LJ scowled and pulled at his thick brown mustache that reached to the bottom of his chin. "Don't get me started, Jack. That man is nothing but a murderer, plain and simple."

"No, please don't git him started." Travis finished rinsing his things and put them in the dishwasher. "I can take you to the paper on my way to the hospital."

"Great." Jack guessed LJ was frustrated and looking for someone to blame for his parents' struggles, but his own curiosity was piqued. He'd come away from his interview with Leonard Bendickson III thinking the fiberglass CEO was intelligent, cocky, and filthy rich. "Why are you so sure Demler-Vargus is hurting people?" he asked. "What do you know?"

"Whatever that plant is spewing, it's killing people," LJ said. "It's in the air and the water. I've heard *plenty.*"

"Like what, specifically?"

"Uh oh," Travis said. "Here we go."

"You know what fiberglass is, Jack?" LJ whirled around like a raging pirate, with his arching brown eyebrows and long, crooked nose. "It's tiny slivers of actual *glass*. We breathe it in day in and day out in this crummy neighborhood. Momma and Daddy been breathin' it in they whole lives. Some days we can *see it* on the cars and houses. You know what that does to your innards? That plant shouldn't be anywhere close to any neighborhood."

"What did your mom die from?" Jack said.

"Lymphoma, eventually," Travis said as he hoisted on a heavy blue-and-yellow parka. "But she had respiratory problems the last three years."

LJ slammed things in the sink. "Her mouth was covered with sores." He stopped, gripped the sink, and stared out the window. "She had a sore throat for years. Used an oxygen tank."

"Did she smoke?"

"All her life," Travis said.

"That ain't the point!" LJ kicked away the gray cat that was poking around the dishwasher. "Smokin' don't make you twitch and break into hives till you itch yerself raw!"

Travis snatched his keys from a wooden key board. "We know people who work in there whose health is broken down somethin' miserable. They's some horror stories, how it affects the central nervous system."

"Big joke at the plant is, none of 'em collect on their retirement 'cause they all dead shortly after they retire," LJ said. "If they last *that* long."

"I've heard things from time to time at the paper," Jack said. "But it always sounded to me like when there was any wrongdoing, Demler-Vargus complied and cleaned things up."

LJ closed the dishwasher with a bang. "Jack, this is dirty, filthy politics and greed and cover-up. Nobody wants to do nothin' about it 'cause Demler-Vargus employs the whole town. It would cripple the entire city if they got shut down. That's yer bottom line."

"Daddy got us a big-shot lawyer." Travis knelt to pet the cat. "Says we're gonna pursue it hot an' heavy. Lawyer says we got a good shot at winning some big moolah."

"Other people have gotten payoffs from Demler-Vargus, but you wouldn't know about that down at the *Dispatch*," LJ said. "Probly wouldn't write about it even if you did."

"Sure we would."

LJ shook his head like a spoiled child. "No sir. I'm tellin' you, Jack, this here is a can a worms. The *Dispatch* don't cover it, and neither does AM 550; Demler-Vargus is too powerful. They're Goliath. No one's got the guts to call 'em out and say what's really goin' on."

"That's enough, LJ." Travis headed for the door. "Jack's gotta get to work and I gotta get over to see Daddy. Oh, that's right ..." Travis rattled around in a drawer until he found a brown bag. "I told him I'd bring him some biscuits." He dropped three in the bag and wrung it closed. "That'll do it. You ready?"

"Yep." Jack followed him to the door. "Look, I'm not promising anything, but if I can get my editor to agree, would you guys be willing to give me names and details?"

"Shoot, yeah. Daddy's got all the facts. You need to talk to him." LJ stretched his long arms, touched the low ceiling, ran his fingers through his thin hair, and snapped the elastic band that held the eye patch in place. "But I bet you a six-pack you won't do nothin'— beverage of your choice."

Jack reached his hand out and it was engulfed by LJ's massive, calloused paw, clean except for the dirt beneath his fingernails.

"You're on."

CHAPTER 2

It was getting light and snowing when Travis dropped Jack out front of the big *Dispatch* building downtown. From there, Travis rocked and rolled his dark green Jeep Wrangler through Trenton City slush puddles and back streets, on over to visitor parking at Cook County Hospital.

Up on the modern fourth floor, he quietly entered the dark, sterile-smelling room. Daddy was upright in bed, sleeping. Travis set the bag of biscuits down, then went to the window and pulled up the blind, knowing his father would want to see out when he awoke. His color looked better, more like the ruddy brownish-reddish color he usually was.

Travis ducked back out into the hallway, keeping the door open with his foot. "Excuse me—Candace, is it?" He addressed a plump young nurse in aqua scrubs, whose shiny brown hair was pulled back in a ponytail.

"Yes?" Her eyes shifted and cheeks reddened, as if she was surprised he knew her name.

Shoot, they'd been there how many days now?

"Has Galen Randall eaten breakfast yet? Right here in 411?"

She looked at her watch. "It should be coming soon. You're one of the sons, right?"

"Travis." He nodded. "I know I asked this before, but can he have waffles 'stead of eggs?"

"They should know that by now in the kitchen."

Travis smiled and went back into the room, doubting they would get the order right. People didn't care about their jobs anymore. Not like Daddy had taught LJ and him—to do your job well, respect others, please the customer, go the extra mile.

Travis sat himself down in the green vinyl chair. His father was fit as a fiddle for seventy-eight. He only stood about five foot nine, but he was lean and stubbornly strong. His forearms were thick and his hands were small and tough as metal. He could reach unreachable places on an engine, unscrew things, bend, clamp, tighten, and manipulate a motor like most people couldn't do with a full set of tools. And nothing ever seemed to hurt those hands, or him—until now.

His father's face was full of gray beard stubble. He looked older. Of course he had to be fatigued from all this hospital business. They still had the oxygen tube stuck up his nose, but it looked like they had reduced his IVs from two bags of fluid to one. *Good.*

Travis just hoped he could get Daddy home soon, because that house and that garage and that piece of property were his life, especially since Momma died. He'd been going to church quite a bit since then, too, and that seemed to give him a lot of comfort, which was fine with Travis. Daddy even managed to get LJ and him to church once in awhile, when he promised to take them to Ryan's afterward for the all-you-can-eat buffet.

It wasn't like Daddy to sleep late, but he was probably still drugged up. Travis stood, took his parka off, and laid it over the chair so Daddy would see it when he awoke. Then he set out to get a paper and some of the vending machine coffee he "loved" so much.

He had the route down pat—out the door, turn right, down the hall, around the nurses' station. He admired nurses and doctors—people who helped people. Maybe they didn't make them like they used to, but most were still compassionate and good at comforting those who were hurting in all kinds of ways.

The cramped sitting room was bordered by red chairs. Only one was occupied, by a middle-aged man with blond hair and a cleft lip that had been surgically repaired, and poorly at that. He wore a black overcoat and sat hunched over, elbows on knees, cell phone glued to ear. Several coffee tables were strewn with newspapers and magazines. A TV in the corner blared *Good Morning America*. The vending machines were in a nook off to one side.

The seated man didn't acknowledge Travis, which he thought was rude. But the man looked like he was in a pretty deep discussion and, who knew, his wife or momma or daddy might be on their deathbed.

Travis put his money in and hit dark roast. It was as weak as the coffee they served at Daddy's church, but he needed some go-joe. He picked up the steaming cup from the machine and turned around, and the blond man was gone. *Good.* He plopped down on the edge of a chair and went through the reading materials.

Wouldn't you know it … smack-dab on top was a recent Sunday edition of the *Trenton City Dispatch*, featuring a huge color picture of Leonard Bendickson III, CEO of Demler-Vargus. And sure enough, it was written by none other than their buddy Jack Crittendon, who had just ridden in Travis's Jeep!

How do you like them apples?

Bendickson's picture had been taken as he stood inside the plant in an expensive-looking suit with a roll of blueprints under one arm, a hard hat and goggles on his head, one shiny shoe perched on the edge of a fancy fiberglass boat. Behind him was a massive puzzle of heavy-duty machinery, tanks, air ducts, conveyor belts, tubes, scaffolding, drums, gauges, and a giant furnace throwing flames and sparks. Travis dropped back in the chair and began to read.

Trenton City's Person of the Year
— Leonard Bendickson III—
Mastermind of the Fiberglass Universe

By Jack Crittendon

As one might guess from his formal name and expensive taste in clothes, Leonard Lee Spalding Bendickson III, known as Lenny B to his yacht club pals, was reared in a wealthy Virginia home, attended Ivy League universities, and never wanted for anything.

And he doesn't plan to.

Since taking the helm as CEO of Demler-Vargus thirteen years ago, Bendickson has steered the Fortune 500 company to unfathomable heights. On its climb, the $7.9 billion corporation has consistently surpassed Wall Street expectations on its way to becoming one of the world's most prolific manufacturers of fiberglass— all kinds of fiberglass.

"When I was asked to take over as CEO, the Demler Corporation mainly produced fiberglass insulation. I knew that was the tip of the iceberg," Bendickson said.

after words

It didn't take him long to make waves. Within eight months of his arrival, the Demler Corporation had acquired Vargus International, a huge player in the fiberglass arena, based in Brussels and with plants around the globe. Over the next five years the companies consolidated nine plants into five. Since then, each has become a perennial powerhouse in the world of fiberglass manufacturing.

Travis let the paper crumple in his lap. He had never met Bendickson, though he'd seen him once at the bank on the square downtown. He wondered what the truth was. Could LJ be right? Were pollutants from Demler-Vargus hurting employees and neighbors? Were they what killed his mother and made his father sick?

The Demler-Vargus plant on Winchester Boulevard on Trenton City's east side is the largest of all, churning out dozens of kinds of fiberglass, which is then shipped to manufacturers worldwide and used to produce boats, car parts, buildings, sporting goods, windmills, insulation, fabric, bulletproof vests, and more.

"We hit our stride when we purchased the old Trenton City refinery and its 225 acres," Bendickson said. "We built the new plant and that was the turning point for Demler-Vargus. We've never looked back. We are always exploring new ideas, techniques, and venues for our products."

Although Demler-Vargus has been the subject of complaints about air pollution from Trenton City neighbors over the years, Bendickson insists the company has worked diligently to comply with the Occupational Safety and Health Administration and the Environmental Protection Agency.

"I love the natural beauty of our land, lakes, rivers, and seas; that's one of the reasons I studied environmental engineering at Rutgers," Bendickson said.

"Being a good environmental steward and a leader in green initiatives is one of my passions. When it comes to educating and properly fitting our employees with the safest, most state-of-the-art equipment and resources, we lead the way. And when it comes to reducing overall hazardous air pollutants in our community, Demler-Vargus is at the cutting edge. You won't find a more conscientious corporation."

Travis couldn't take anymore in one sitting. He glanced at the elevators outside the waiting area and noticed a boy in an Ohio State ski cap pushing his gray grandpa in a wheelchair. If LJ saw the story, he would go directly to the moon, do not pass go, do not collect two hundred dollars. But if Demler-Vargus was dirty, wouldn't OSHA and the EPA have caught on and stopped them? Was Bendickson lying or was he running a clean shop?

Jack was a good writer. Travis wondered if he would really pursue a story about Demler-Vargus. He took the paper and coffee and went back around the nurses' station.

"Good morning." A different nurse was behind the counter now, an attractive brunette.

Travis looked behind him and, seeing no one there, concluded she was speaking to him. "Hello. How is the morning treating you?"

"Very well." Her name tag read Meredith. "Can I help you with anything?"

"Ahh …" Travis wanted to keep the conversation going. "I'm Galen Randall's son, he's in room 411. I was wonderin', is he gonna get to go home today?"

She flipped through pages on a clipboard and paused. "His doctor is supposed to come by this morning and give him a look. He has definitely shown improvement. It shouldn't be too much longer."

"Very good, then." Travis tapped the counter, wishing there was more to talk about. "By the way, my name's Travis—Travis Randall."

Meredith lost her pretty smile for a split second. She shot a glance at another nurse seated behind the counter, who made eye contact and then looked back down at his paperwork. Meredith gave Travis a sealed-mouth smile. "Nice to meet you, Mr. Randall. I hope your father gets to go home soon."

Mr. Randall. See how she immediately shut him down? Slammed the door right in his uneducated, country-bumpkin face.

"Thank you." Travis headed back toward his father's room.

He was forty two. His folks had married in their twenties; they were together over fifty years. They'd had their two sons, built a business, taken care of each other and their neighbors—*that* was living.

Travis was sick and tired of being alone. It frustrated him that his life was half over and he had no one. The problem was, he never had any opportunities to meet nice women. He didn't hang out in the bars. Most of the clients at the garage were men or housewives. Daddy told him he needed to go to the singles' class at church, and he was half tempted to try it. What did he have to lose? But he'd probably only embarrass himself there too.

'Course LJ was in the same boat as Travis, but his brother hung out at the Twisted Tavern and the East End Grill now and again, so he had a bigger pool of ladies to draw from—if you wanted to call them that.

LJ had been married once, to Roxanne. They were the proud parents of Bo. When LJ got a tip Roxanne might be seeing somebody on the sly, he went after the fella in the Big Lots parking lot; tore him limb from limb. But then the man sent a posse after LJ one night, and they carved him up so badly he lost his left eye. After the divorce, LJ got shared custody of Bo.

Rounding the corner and walking back down the long hallway, Travis said hey to the nurse Candace, who was typing something at a workstation in the hallway. *'Course she didn't mention nothing about Daddy's waffles.*

Down the long hallway near his father's room, Travis suddenly saw the man in the black overcoat pop into the hallway. He glanced both ways, held his eyes on Travis for a second, and whipped off in the opposite direction.

That's odd.

The man practically ran out of there.

Travis picked up the pace. He'd take a look into the room the man had come from. He walked faster. Then his heart kicked up a notch.

Wait a minute …

It hit him like a bomb.

The man had not been *near* his father's room—he'd been *in* it!

Travis busted through the heavy door, past the bathroom, hoping to turn the corner to see a nurse doting over Daddy, hoping to see his father awake with his glasses on, eating his waffle, looking out the window, complaining about how much longer he would have to stay.

Travis jammed on the brakes at the foot of the bed.

The room was still. Everything was fine.

Daddy slept.

The breakfast tray had been delivered; it sat on the swinging table next to the bed, but the food hadn't been touched. Nothing was beeping on the monitors. Travis stared at Daddy's chest until he saw movement.

"Phew-wee."

Travis hurried back into the hallway, looking for the man in black, but he was long gone. Could he be sure the man had left this room? Perhaps he was mistaken.

He went back in and plunked into the chair, still holding the crumpled newspaper.

He reached over and lifted the silver lid off the main breakfast plate.

Egg.

"Dang." He dropped back into the chair.

Incompetents.

Travis was worn out already and the day had hardly begun.

He leaned back, folded the newspaper, and found his place.

Bendickson felt so strongly about Demler-Vargus's green initiative that he appointed his son, Devon Bendickson, 28, as the company's environmental liaison. Devon has degrees from Furman and Rutgers and is Bendickson's only child, by his first wife, Patricia.

Enjoying his third marriage, this one to concert pianist Celeste Excelsior, Bendickson resides in a 15,000-square-foot solar-powered mansion in Cool Springs. The glass, metal, and stone architectural award-winning structure has indoor and outdoor pools and spas, tennis and basketball courts, and a professional par-three golf hole designed by golf great and Columbus native Jack Nicklaus.

Although Trenton City residents may see Bendickson cruising around town in a silver Range Rover, his daily vehicle, the fiberglass king also has a collection of automobiles in his seven-car garage, including his prized possession, a 1982 DeLorean. He loves boating, mainly in the Atlantic, on his 32-foot yacht, aptly named *Fiberglass Slipper*, which he docks at the Sea Pines Resort on Hilton Head Island in South Carolina.

Travis wasn't interested in finishing the story. He tossed the paper aside and looked at his father. Why was he sleeping so long? The food had to be cold by now, and Daddy detested cold food.

Travis would have them heat it up when his father awoke. Until then, he decided to turn on the TV, real low.

He scanned the room for the remote.

Wait …

The silver IV stand had been moved.

It had been back toward the wall earlier.

He looked from the wheels up the silver pole to the IV bag.

A pinkish solution floated with the clear liquid in the bag.

With three giant steps, Travis grabbed the pouch and followed the tube leading to Daddy's right arm.

A sudden, violent cough from his father jolted Travis, drawing his attention away from his task. Daddy's face was purple as a bruise. His coughing turned to choking, then to a loud, alarming screeching for air.

"Oh dear Lord." Travis's hands shook violently.

His father gasped and his arms flailed. His hands moved to his throat. His brown eyes searched Travis in despair.

Travis snatched Daddy's wrist and pulled it toward him, fumbling for the IV tube and ripping it away.

His father's body was limp, his head grotesquely twisted to one side, and the color was draining from his face like antifreeze flushing from a radiator.

The monitor next to him pinged and flashed, pinged and flashed.

"No!"

"Mr. Randall?" came a voice from the intercom.

Travis grabbed it with trembling hands and pressed talk. "Hurry! We need a doctor! *Emergency!*"

Going one way, then another, uncertain what to do, Travis straightened his father's torso and shifted his head back to a normal position, trying to make him look right. But the older man's lips were almost as white as his now ashen face.

Travis sprinted into the hallway and yelled as loud as he could toward the nurses' station. "Emergency. Room 411! Get a doctor!"

Seeing they were scrambling, Travis ran back in and took his father's face in his hands. "Come on, Daddy. Hang on. Please … "

Travis put his arms around him and hugged. "Hold on, Daddy. Hold on." As he rocked him, Travis's eyes fell to the dangling IV tube, dripping a steady flow of the liquid that, he was certain, had been tainted by the stranger in black.